The Pirate's Daughter

Also by Robert Girardi

Madeleine's Ghost

THE PIRATE'S DAUGHTER

A Novel of Adventure

Robert Girardi

Delacorte  Press

Published by
Delacorte Press
Bantam Doubleday Dell Publishing Group, Inc.
1540 Broadway
New York, New York 10036

Library of Congress Cataloging in Publication Data
  Girardi, Robert.
    The pirate's daughter : a novel of adventure / by Robert Girardi.
      p.   cm.
    ISBN 0-385-31485-X
    I. Title.
  PS3557.I694P57   1997
  813'.54—dc20   96-17048
                                                                        CIP

Book design by Susan Maksuta

Manufactured in the United States of America

Published simultaneously in Canada

January 1997

10   9   8   7   6   5   4   3   2   1

BVG

. . . and in those for ever exiled waters, I had lost the miserable warping memories of traditions and of towns.

—Herman Melville

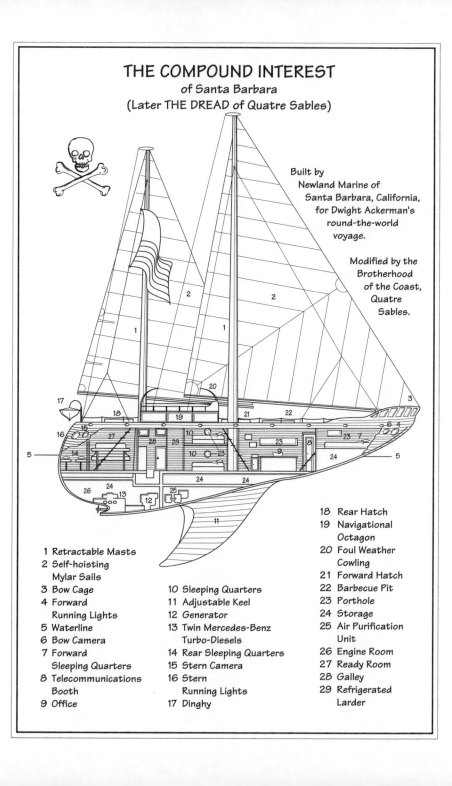

THE COMPOUND INTEREST
of Santa Barbara
(Later THE DREAD of Quatre Sables)

Built by
Newland Marine of
Santa Barbara, California,
for Dwight Ackerman's
round-the-world
voyage.

Modified by the
Brotherhood
of the Coast,
Quatre
Sables.

1 Retractable Masts
2 Self-hoisting
  Mylar Sails
3 Bow Cage
4 Forward
  Running Lights
5 Waterline
6 Bow Camera
7 Forward
  Sleeping Quarters
8 Telecommunications
  Booth
9 Office

10 Sleeping Quarters
11 Adjustable Keel
12 Generator
13 Twin Mercedes-Benz
   Turbo-Diesels
14 Rear Sleeping Quarters
15 Stern Camera
16 Stern
   Running Lights
17 Dinghy

18 Rear Hatch
19 Navigational
   Octagon
20 Foul Weather
   Cowling
21 Forward Hatch
22 Barbecue Pit
23 Porthole
24 Storage
25 Air Purification
   Unit
26 Engine Room
27 Ready Room
28 Galley
29 Refrigerated
   Larder

The
Pirate's
Daughter

PART ONE

THE EMPEROR, THE PAGE OF WANDS

1

COMING HOME FROM WORK one Monday evening in August, Wilson Lander found two tarot cards face up on a side street of the out-of-the-way neighborhood where he lived. They were the Emperor and the Page of Wands. In the peculiar light of that hour, the cards seemed to glow with hidden meaning, two bright rectangles against the dull brick pavement.

Wilson paused, loosened his tie, bent toward them. The empty street ticked like a clock. The Emperor showed a stern white-bearded old man perched on a throne set against an arid mountainous landscape that looked like Africa. The Roman numeral IV floated in the sky over the head of this mysterious potentate. The Page of Wands was a young man wearing a red cloak and holding a wooden quarterstaff from which new leaves were sprouting. In the far distance, the same dry African-looking peaks.

Wilson studied the cards for almost five minutes, a curious prickling at the back of his neck. He was not an irrational man, but a tragic childhood had colored his adult life with a pervasive sense of dread. Dread was a way of life for Wilson Lander. He breathed it in as air, he wore dread as other men wear underpants and socks, and so he took the tarot cards as a sign of terrible events to come. Almost without thinking, he scooped them up and put them in the breast pocket of his blazer.

"This thing could mean good luck," he announced to the blank facades of the warehouses, to the emulsion stink in the air. "Why the hell not? Luck can be good or bad just as easily . . ." But he was a man who did not usually talk to himself, and he did not believe his own bravado. How did the cards get there in the first place? During the day, the streets of the Rubicon District were full of tough, plaid-shirted truck drivers and factory workers in steel-toed boots—not the sort of men to be fooling around with superstitious nonsense. Dread sounded in Wilson's head like a great bell ringing the Angelus.

Later, in his small apartment overlooking the wharves of the Black Star Line in the Harvey Channel, Wilson tried to forget about the tarot cards. He drank a beer, watched the news, made himself a quesadilla and salad for dinner, and got into bed early, in his pajamas. The small bedroom pooled with fading blue light. The sense of dread was so strong now it made his stomach hurt. He lay sleepless for hours beneath the thin sheets, listening to the rattle of the air-conditioning unit in the window, imagining his mortality taking shape just beyond the thin membrane of mundane events. Growing claws, sprouting feathers and scales, a monster on the other side in the eschatological gloom.

2

THE NEXT DAY, WILSON called his girlfriend and told her he would not be coming to work.

"What is it this time?" Andrea said, her voice tight through the crackle of her portable phone. "Another panic attack?"

"Don't ask me to explain," Wilson said, not wanting to tell her about the tarot cards.

"Because, you know, they make pills for anxiety. I read that anxiety comes from a buildup of the wrong kind of chemicals in the brain. You swallow one pill, and it lifts like a cloud."

"That's just not true," Wilson said.

"I'm really worried about you," Andrea said, softening a little. "You should go back to that therapist."

"Don't start," Wilson said.

Andrea believed Wilson's sense of dread was a sickness, like the flu, that could be cured through subtle alterations of brain chemistry with mood-altering drugs. He saw it as something far more spectacular, an epic curse borne through the generations: When Wilson was nine, his father perished in the famous wreck of the four forty-five, an overcrowded express train that derailed and plunged off the Trohog Bridge into the Potswahnamee River; less than a year later his mother was crushed to death in a bizarre accident. And there had been a great-uncle—the details were sketchy—who had gone to seek his fortune in the diamond mines of Peru a half century before and disappeared without a trace.

"Just give me a day," Wilson said. "I'll be fine tomorrow."

A tense silence followed in which Wilson heard the faint computerized rattle of Andrea's office and the traffic coming along Commerce Avenue and her even breath. At last she gave a sigh and a hard "Fine—see you first thing in the morning," and hung up the phone.

Andrea was Wilson's employer as well as his lover. A junior vice-president at the Tea Exchange, a small but respected brokerage firm in the Financial Mile, she dealt in commodities futures on minerals at the bottom of the sea, on herds of cattle in Bolivia, on boatloads full of big blue tiger shrimp from the Marianas Trench, on silos of barley in the Ukraine—everything except tea. She had hired Wilson as her executive assistant the year before when he couldn't find a job, but as everyone knows, professionalism and passion don't mix. Things had been a little cool between them of late. The job was an act of kindness they both had come to regret.

3

WILSON ATE A SOBER bowl of bran cereal for breakfast, dressed in unobtrusive gray clothes, and took the eleven o'clock bus over the bridge into the city.

From Metropolitan Terminal, he walked up twenty blocks to an odd little store tucked away between a new French restaurant and a warehouse full of rubber bands in a dark canyon of a street, in a part of the city that was just becoming trendy. The store was marked only by an orange banner of a silhouetted witch on a broom. Its small display window contained a few ancient tomes with faded gilt bindings, ceramic canisters full of unspecified herbs, and, most remarkably, a dusty stuffed monkey wearing a fez and dressed in a red velvet robe embroidered with pentagrams and half-moons. The monkey bared blackened teeth at the passerby, its eyes were sewn shut, and mange or termites had eaten away half the fur, revealing shiny dark skin hard as asphalt.

Wilson stared at this grisly relic through the grime-streaked glass. A police cruiser inched by along the curb behind him; a step van full of rubber bands bounced over a pothole. A yellow banner showing a bottle of wine and a clove of garlic flapped noisily above the French restaurant next door. New city ordinances enforced banners over any other kind of sign for this district, perhaps seeking to invoke an atmosphere of medieval trade guilds and painstaking handcraftsmanship. Then, Wilson noticed the reflection of his own face in the glass, worried, specter pale.

The store formed a long, triangular cave that narrowed to a point at the back. A fat orange cat eyed Wilson from a pink pillow near the door as he stepped inside. On one wall hung cast iron cauldrons of different sizes, pewter charms in stapled Baggies, bundles of dried roots. Against the other wall, shelves of books with titles like *Rune Casting Made Easy, Orgasming with the Goddess, Witchcraft and Lesbianism, Sorcery in 101 Easy Lessons*. At the counter in the middle, a young woman sat balanced on a stool, painting her toenails. Wilson approached cautiously; he was the only customer. A loud, sonorous chanting vibrated from the sound system.

"Excuse me, I was wondering if I could ask you a favor," Wilson began.

The young woman looked up, and Wilson forgot himself. She was very pretty, with sea green eyes and a tangle of windblown coppery hair. Her skin was tanned except for a raccoon mask of whiteness where sunglasses had been. Her lips were chapped. She wore a pair of white cotton drawstring pants and a hooded sweatshirt that read USS *William Eaton* over the left breast. She didn't look at all like the kind of person you would expect to find working in a place like that. She looked like she belonged on the deck of a ship somewhere off the Cape Verde Islands as a fine salt spray washed over the gunwales and the sky went dark with storm.

"O.K.," the young woman said, frowning, "speak."

"Are you—do you . . . answer questions?" Wilson cast a helpless glance around at the love philters and voodoo dolls hanging from the ceiling.

"Jungle Red," the young woman said, screwing the cap back on the bottle of nail polish and waving it in his direction. "What do you think?" She held up her newly painted toes.

"Nice," Wilson said.

"Don't worry," the woman said. "I can answer any questions you might have."

Wilson took the two tarot cards out of his pocket and laid them on the counter at right angles to each other. "I found them, like that, in the street on my way home."

"The Emperor, the Page of Wands," she said. "Major Arcana, Minor Arcana."

"I don't believe in any of this stuff, of course," Wilson said, "but what the hell. Could mean something, right?"

The young woman stared up at him for a long moment with her raccoon eyes. Wilson squirmed uncomfortably beneath this scrutiny. His intellect knew a couple of cards found on the street couldn't predict the future, but his dread had other ideas.

"O.K. I'll need to find out a few things before I can give you an informed opinion," the young woman said, nodding at the cards. "Your moon sign, your sun sign, your shoe size. Your likes and dislikes, your favorite color, the exact day, hour, and minute of your birth, whether you have any distinguishing marks on your body, whether you came out of the womb with a caul over your face or butt first."

"A caul?"

"Yes. It's a thin membrane of embryonic tissue that in a small percentage of births covers the newborn's face when it emerges from the birth canal. A caul can mean that the child is marked by fate, that it has been signaled out for good luck or bad luck, but in either case certain sensitivities are bound to be inherent."

"A caul . . . I don't know."

"Ask your mother."

"She's dead."

"What about your father?"

"He's dead too," Wilson said.

"What did he do for a living?"

"Is this relevant?" Wilson said.

"Of course," the young woman said. "Everything is relevant."

Wilson hesitated. "Actually, he was a gambler."

"Professional?" She suddenly looked interested. Her eyes flickered with a secret intelligence.

"Yes," Wilson said, slightly embarrassed.

"Was he good?"

Wilson shrugged. "He made money at it."

"How much money?"

"Look . . ."

"Are you a gambler too?"

Wilson shook his head emphatically. "Not me. I work in an office."

"You've never gambled?" She seemed disappointed.

"I've played a few hands of poker."

"Ever lost?"

"Come to think of it, no."

The young woman smiled, and there was something behind the smile that Wilson found uncomfortable and thrilling at once, and there was a knot in his stomach when he looked at her that was not the dread at all.

The woman pushed the cards around the glass counter with the tips of her fingers. Her brow wrinkled in concentration. Wilson could almost hear the gears working. "Let's get on with this," she said. "Can you tell me if you wear boxers or Jockeys?"

"Boxers," Wilson said, before he realized that she was making fun of him. "Thanks for your help," he said, and gathered the cards and went quickly out onto the sidewalk. But then he saw the garlic clove and wine bottle floating in the breeze next door, and he felt his stomach knot up again and he stepped back inside.

"Do you want to go to lunch?" Wilson said from the safe distance of the doorway.

"If it's someplace close," the young woman said.

4

THE WHITE DINING ROOM was empty except for two old men wearing pressed seersucker jackets and striped bow ties. They ate the same pumpkin-colored soup, and might have been brothers except that they sat wrapped in their own silence at tables far removed from each other. The maître d', a tall Frenchman dressed in an expensive gray three-piece, led Wilson and the woman through the dining room onto a back patio set with five small tables and planted with rosebushes. In his suit the waiter looked more like a businessman or a lawyer than someone who worked in a restaurant.

"Usually, we have a dress code here," he said. "That is why I sit you on the patio, O.K.?"

He left them alone with the menus and the wine list. A small fountain plashed quietly from just inside. Robins had built a nest in the ivy up the wall of the tenement building opposite. Directly across from Wilson, one of those terra-cotta sunburst masks from Mexico was cemented into the old brick. It stared at him with hollow Mexican eyes.

The young woman licked her chapped lips and read the menu. The descriptions were in French, and everything was expensive. She belonged here in the sun, it seemed to Wilson, not in the grim dreariness of the store amidst shrunken heads and books about raising the dead and conjuring demons.

"This place isn't cheap," Wilson said.

"Then let's just get something light," the young woman said, closing the menu. "A salad, soup. French bread and cheese."

"Sounds good," Wilson said.

"And a bottle of wine."

"I don't know much about wine," he said.

"Leave it to me."

She glanced at the wine list and closed it with a quick snap. When she ordered, Wilson felt a wicked thrill. He thought of Andrea at the office peering at the small screen of her laptop, going over the previous day's market closings, spending hours on conference calls to the home office in Denver, as around her eyes those imperceptible lines deepened each day, her forehead worried with stress, her mouth tightened into a permanent frown.

The wine waiter brought an '82 Mont Orgeuil Côtes du Rhône; then the first food waiter brought the bread and the second food waiter brought the cheese. It was one of those restaurants where they have a half dozen waiters for every table.

The young woman's name was Cricket.

"Like the bug?" Wilson asked.

"Yes."

"That's your real name?"

"Susan," she said. "But people call me Cricket."

Beneath the mane of hair, Wilson noticed heavy gold pendant earrings, set with pearls and rubies. They looked Spanish and very old and they dangled toward the table as she leaned forward to eat. She was working at the occult store as a favor to a friend and to make a little money, she said.

"Cauldron central, that's not really me. I know a little bit about the stuff, and I guess I keep an open mind. Still, you should see the characters that come in off the street. Look like they crawled out from under a rock."

Wilson felt hot behind the ears.

"No, I don't mean you, honey," Cricket said. "You seem nice and normal, just a guy with a lot of worries."

"How can you tell?"

Cricket shrugged. "In any case, I'm waiting for a ship."

"Are you in the merchant marine?"

"No, I crew on private yachts. I do a little navigating, take care of the charts. I keep the deckhands in line."

"I knew it," Wilson said. "You're a sailor."

"You could say that," Cricket said. "I've circumnavigated the globe, like Magellan."

"Magellan didn't make it," Wilson said. "The natives got him in the Philippines."

"You're gloomy," Cricket said.

"I know."

A third food waiter brought French country salads of endive and bacon with nuggets of goat cheese. They finished the salads quickly, then the wine a few minutes later, and Cricket signaled the wine waiter and ordered another bottle without asking Wilson. It was a '77 Château Maronne, a white Burgundy with an impressive gold-rimmed label, that the wine waiter brought out in a bucket of ice.

"This story will interest you because of your father," Cricket said, filling up Wilson's glass.

"My father?" Wilson said.

"He was a gambler, right?"

Wilson shrugged.

As they drank and nibbled at the last of the bread, Cricket told Wilson about growing up in the Palmetto Keys, a small cluster of egg-shaped islands, mostly sand and shells and a few live oaks, fifty miles southeast of the mouth of the Mississippi in the Gulf of Mexico.

"There's a little town called St. George on Outer Key," she said. "That's where I was born. My father owned a hotel and a charter boat service there, which made him about the only man around with a steady job that didn't have anything to do with gambling. I hear tourism is the thing now. In those days, before they changed the law, it was gambling. The keys are owned half by Florida and half by Alabama. For years, on the Alabama side, high-stakes private poker games were legal. Maybe your father played down there."

"He preferred the horses," Wilson said.

"In any case, you could gamble for millions of dollars as long as you didn't run a casino," Cricket said, "which meant you didn't employ anybody and you did it out of your own house—and about every weekend, gangster types with big wads of cash would come down from places like New Orleans and Miami, and even Chicago or New York, and there would be these big poker games in the fancy private houses along the lagoon on the leeward side. After my parents got divorced, my father spent a lot of time over there with one of the local gamblers called Johnny Mazep, who ran a high-stakes game every Sunday from September to May.

"One night, just before Christmas when I was about seven years old, my father showed up drunk in the middle of the night at my window. He cut the screen out with a pocketknife, and wrapped me in a sweater and put me in his outboard. We took the Palmetto Passage between Outer and Inner Key, and I remember the smell of diesel and my father's cigarette and the sky black as ink, no stars, nothing.

"We tied up at Mazep's dock and went into the place, a garish pink bungalow the size of a parking garage. In the living room there were about twenty-five guys in suits, all with guns drawn. The scene was very tense. In an inflatable kiddie pool on the floor was all this money—about two million dollars in cash, my father told me later—all of it riding on a single cut of the cards between Mazep and some big shot from Chicago. They wanted somebody totally disinterested to cut the cards, and they couldn't find anybody there, so my father went and got me.

"I was scared shitless, shaking like a leaf, but I didn't cry. They opened up a new pack. I can still hear the sound of the cellophane, and I can still smell the beer and body odor and whiskey and their big gangster cigars. I cut the cards. It was the king of hearts. They had bet high-low, Mazep low, the big shot high. Johnny Mazep lost everything. His wife, who was Brazilian and always a little crazy anyway, committed suicide. Two months later, he sold his house and left the Palmettos for good, and his family had been there for two hundred years, first as wreckers and privateers, then smugglers and gamblers. Always something like that.

"The big shot from Chicago gave me four five-hundred-dollar bills for cutting the cards for him. I kept them folded up tight in my hand all the way home in the outboard, the moon up and shining on the dark water. In the morning my mother found the screen cut and the two thousand dollars under my pillow. I told her the tooth fairy came during the night and left the money. 'Mighty expensive tooth,' she said, and she fixed the screen and put the money in a savings account for me and didn't say anything else. As soon as I could, about ten years later, I took that money out of the bank, and I went to sea and I haven't been back to the Palmettos since."

The second bottle of wine was almost empty now. Little bits of cork floated in the inch or so of pale yellow liquid at the bottom. Wilson felt fine. He poured the last few drops into Cricket's glass. When she brought the glass to her lips, he noticed with a start that her hands were rough and broken nailed, work scarred, hard looking. They didn't seem to go with the coppery hair and the green eyes the color of tropic shallows full of fish and coral. Cricket caught Wilson looking at her hands, flushed a little, and hid them quickly under the tablecloth.

"Why have you stayed away from your home for so long?" Wilson said to cover the awkwardness.

Cricket shrugged, her hair glinting in the sunlight. "I prefer the sea," she said. "It's so changeable, one minute stormy, the next flat as a plate. It's supposed to be that way, so you're ready for whatever happens. On land we have this illusion of stability. But that's a big lie; everything can ride on the single turn of a card. At least at sea you know where you stand. I'll tell you what a sailor is, a sailor—"

But she was interrupted by the maître d' in the suit, who stepped up and proffered the bill on a glossy black tray.

"*L'addition,*" he said with the gravity of a cardinal pronouncing a blessing.

"How much is it?" Cricket said.

Wilson waved her away. "On me," he said.

It came to $178.29, not including tax and tip—more than his food budget for the entire month. "Shit, just for soup and salad . . . I guess it's the wine. . . ." He checked the wine list and saw that the first bottle Cricket had ordered was listed at $65, the second at $78.

As he was fumbling with his credit card, she got up quickly. "Thanks for lunch," she said. "Better get back to the store."

Figuring out the tip, Wilson barely heard, and when he looked up, she was gone.

5

TWO DAYS LATER WILSON met Andrea for happy hour at Marina's in the Marina, a large, noisy restaurant-bar popular with the Financial Mile after-work crowd.

Marina's was the kind of place Wilson hated—slick, overpackaged, too many rules: You couldn't drink on the patio without ordering food; you couldn't get a booth between five and eight o'clock in the evening without at least four persons in your party; there was a ten-dollar minimum at the bar, where no checks were accepted in the absence of a driver's license and two credit cards. Muscular crew-cut men in blue shorts and red Marina's in the Marina T-shirts and carrying walkie-talkies, patrolled the roped-off perimeter of the outdoor terrace, looking for patrons who had managed somehow to get drunk off the overpriced watery drinks and those foolish few who had dared seat themselves without applying to the hostess first. Whenever Wilson went to Marina's, he felt like a prisoner in a fascist state for the upwardly mobile.

At the upstairs bar, Andrea looked harried and tired. Her briefcase, fat with memos and spreadsheets and the morning's Exchange Commission reports, stood on the counter beside her. For three days she'd been using a temp to fill Wilson's job, and the temp didn't know where important files were located, was unfamiliar with office routine, had trouble accessing the database from the PC in Wilson's cubicle.

"Thanks to you, things have been just fucking crazy the last couple of days," was the first thing Andrea said as Wilson stepped up to the bar. He was a half hour late. A watery Caipirinha waited on the counter, ice melting in the glass.

"Is this mine?" he said.

"You were supposed to be here at six. I ordered it for you because happy hour prices ended fifteen minutes ago." She glared over at him from her modest glass of house white, her eyes angry. "I gave the temp the ax today."

"Why did you do that?" Wilson said, surprised.

"Because he was a fuckup. He couldn't find the Marti Sugar File, and there it was, sitting on the S drive—"

"Christ," Wilson said, "you didn't give the kid a chance. Probably some college kid."

She ignored him. "—and because you're coming back tomorrow. Enough of this playing-sick shit. You seem fine to me."

Wilson shook his head and looked out the green-tinted window at the white boats passing in and out of the marina and didn't say anything. For the last two days, he'd been at the public library in

City Center reading books on the interpretation of the tarot deck. Depending on whom you read, the Emperor and the Page of Wands when arranged in juxtaposition could mean any number of things, both good and bad. But the meaning was never static; it changed according to their position relative to the other cards in the classic fifteen-card H pattern used for divination. The books didn't say anything about what it could mean to find two cards like that on the sidewalk, at the end of a dusty afternoon, on the way home from work, in the middle of your life.

"You coming back, or do I have to find someone else?" Andrea glowered up at him.

"They make their Caipirinhas with salt here," Wilson said shaking the melting ice cubes in his drink. "Someone should tell the bartender that they're not margaritas; they're Caipirinhas. No salt. No tequila. Just Pitú, limes, and sugar."

"I knew it was a bad idea from the start," Andrea said. "Unprofessional. A woman with my responsibilities just doesn't hire her boyfriend as executive assistant. But you were broke; you needed a job. As usual."

It was an old, familiar argument, and they carried it between them like a sick friend—into the cab on the way to Andrea's apartment in the Pond Park Tower, into the lobby of that bland monolith, and up thirty stories in the high-speed elevator, the attendant grimacing his boredom to the chrome template of buttons to hear them going at it again. Once behind the steel door of number 3017, they let the argument drop briefly, as Andrea checked the eight messages from the office put on her answering machine in the hour and a half since she left work.

Wilson and Andrea had met six years before at Straight and Straight, the bond trading firm that occupies ten floors of the Maas Tower downtown. Wilson had only just recently accepted a leave of absence from the graduate archaeology program at Ashland College for financial reasons and had accepted a job with Straight and Straight as an administrative assistant in the commodities department—a temporary measure, until he earned enough to go back to school. In those days, Andrea had been a bright young M.B.A. account executive just twenty-four years old, on the way up, with two three-hundred-dollar suits and five pairs of imitation Italian pumps in her closet, an intuitive grasp of the municipal bond market, a cute ass, and a nice sense of humor. The dust of the city would not settle on her as it settled on so many. Now, she was an executive vice-president at the Tea Exchange, owned seven six-hundred-dollar suits, twenty-two pairs of genuine Italian pumps, and eight weeks of a vacation condominium on the Mexican Atlantic coast at Sangre de Oro she never had time to use.

For the last two years their arguments had been about Wilson's agenda. Andrea wanted to know why he didn't do anything with his life, why he didn't—for example—go back to Ashland and finish up, or get a career-track job with the state historical society, anything. Wilson couldn't say, really. His reasons were inarticulate, having to do with the dread that afflicted even his best days. He was not an idle man, just a man who was waiting—though he couldn't say for what. And to wait properly, you must be in readiness, free from extraneous attachments. Also, he had decided, there was something horrible about archaeologists. They dug up things that the earth had meant to conceal, put to rest: the bones of the ancient dead buried in sandy graves with the pitiful objects—pots and spoons and combs—that had served them in life; shattered bits of monuments to forgotten, murderous kings; vanished cities of execrable memory marked only by a few postholes filled with rubble and a dark stain in the clay. To Wilson, there was more than a little bit of grave robbing about the discipline.

But it was the teeth that had finally done it for him. In the year before Wilson quit school, he had gone on a dig at Asidonhoppo in Brokopondo State, Suriname. They opened a sacred cave dedicated to Ampuka, the Warrou Indian god of the mouth. Before the dig was over two months later, they had removed nearly 300,000 sacrificial teeth from the dank hole—human molars, incisors, canines—all very interesting indications of the diet and physical condition of the original owners, and so forth, but, from Wilson's point of view, the most dreadful thing he had ever seen. His dreams for years afterward were haunted by the million teeth of some monster mouth, chomping down and masticating whole families, villages, the landscape itself.

The eight messages noted or returned, Andrea shook out of her work clothes on the white rug in the living room in a sort of spasm of suit, silk blouse, pumps, and pearls and, with a wave toward Wilson that meant "wait," padded down the hall to the bathroom for her home-from-the-office shower.

He watched the door close, heard the sound of the water, then skulked around the apartment, hands in his pockets. He couldn't bring himself to sit down on her stylish, uncomfortable furniture, couldn't say just now why he had come over tonight. He squatted for no reason, put his hand palm flat against Andrea's expensive clothes in a smooth heap on the rug. They still held the warmth of her body. Then, he went out onto the granite balcony and stood staring down at the panorama below.

You can see a long way from the thirtieth floor of Pond Park Tower—from the Harvey Channel in the east to the hazy suburban hills of Warinocco County north of the interstate. It was the last long moment before evening. The sky above the city looked swollen with color. The earth curved away to the sea, toward far islands, each concealing its own secret life, its own story: a house on an unknown stretch of beach, over-hung with royal palms and tamarinds, a room with rattan shades drawn against the bright sunset, a white bed draped with mosquito netting, a wooden bowl full of pomegranates on the table. In the garden, the wide leaves of a banana tree nattering in the wind as a beautiful woman emerges from the surf . . . One is filled with such ridiculous longings in that diminishing hour. Wilson, no better than the rest of us, stood helpless as a child before the tragic vastness of the world at dusk.

The city teeming to the bridges, the vague outline of mountains behind, the ocean's monotonous swell, all the faces he would never know.

When the shower went off in the bathroom, Wilson stepped back inside and pulled the heavy sliding glass door shut. Andrea padded into the living room naked, rubbing her dark hair with a blue towel. She paused when she came onto the rug and let the towel drop to her side. Her body looked perfect. Wilson could never see her naked, especially at this time of day, and not want to make love. If the effect was calculated—hundreds of hours at the health club with a personal trainer, on the StairMaster, on the little track around which two hundred laps make up a mile—the end results were still primal and redeeming.

"You look great, honey," Wilson said. "You . . ." He couldn't finish.

"It's about time you noticed that," Andrea said. "I've been losing weight lately. Four and a half pounds since July."

Wilson couldn't see her eyes in the dim light.

"I wanted you to come over the other night," she said in a small-girlish voice. "I almost called you, I almost picked up the phone. Twice."

"Why didn't you?"

"I don't know."

"How long has it been?"

"Eight, no, ten days."

"I'm sorry," Wilson said, moving toward her, "that's too long." Soft yellow lights came up over the leather couch on the automatic timer, and Andrea lay back on the damp towel on the jungle thick pile of the rug, her legs open, her clean shampoo-smelling hair curling damp in Wilson's hands.

Later, in the darkness of the bedroom on the big bed, they kissed and said "I love you" to the hollow echo of the apartment and fell asleep at last, digital clock glowing amber and watchful on the nightstand beside them.

6

ON FRIDAY, WILSON WENT back to work at the Tea Exchange and was immediately up to his ears in the minutiae that runs one year into the next: mailing lists, franking privileges, Xerox machines, lost documents, software and hardware, all the crap—he told himself bitterly—invented by the prosaic to keep the rest of us from asking the reasons for things. You look up, it's years later, the mind is dull, and none of the Great Questions have been attempted.

He finished the day exhausted by the effort of catching up, by nothing, by the routine, by sitting in chairs that he had sat in before, and he boarded the Rubicon bus and loosened his tie and fell asleep against the smudge of grease on the scarred plastic bus window.

Asleep, Wilson's temperature rose; he sweated into the collar of his Brooks Brothers shirt and began to dream.

A bright afternoon in early spring, he is ten years old. His mother, young and pretty, wearing her shiny black hair in a flip and a leopard print pillbox hat and a thin leopard-print coat, holds his hand tightly as they cross the street from Lazar and Martin's department store, where she has bought him a tin ray gun that makes whirring noises when he pulls the trigger. The Maas Tower is under construction, a skeleton of black girders rising up to the sun. As they pass beneath the scaffolding, he is the first to see the long shadow on the sidewalk. He stares up, not understanding for a few seconds; then there is no time to cry out before the deadly rush and the pavement bending like a springboard. He is heaved up and thrown through the air—the secret joy of flying in his heart—over the ranks of slow-moving cars, over the gawkers, over the policeman on the horse. But he does not land with a thump on a bag of concrete mix, as he did in life. Instead he spreads his arms and soars up and over the tops of the buildings, past the snapped crane cable, past the horror-stricken construction workers in their yellow hard hats gaping down at the woman smashed like a bug beneath the girder, past the deco silver needle of the Rubicon Building, and out over the Harvey Channel and Blackpool Island and the gray-blue sea churning with whitecaps and ships heading for the harbor. And at last, all sight of land left behind, he is robbed by the wind of his child's clothes, and in the next second he is a grown man hurtling naked a mile above the earth to meet an approaching darkness that is not a storm or the night coming on, that is the empty space on the horizon from which the future breaks like a thunderhead over the weary hearts of men and women.

7

WILSON GOT OFF THE bus half dazed and stumbled down Overlook Avenue. The industrial streets of the Rubicon District were filled with a melancholy silence that was like the sound of water running over rocks in the wilderness. The dream had left his shirt stuck to his back with sweat; his head would not clear. He unlocked the street door to his apartment, went up the rutted stairs, and undid the double locks on the steel door. Just inside there was another door of leaded glass panes, enclosing a small foyer, barely large enough for an umbrella stand and a broken end table. The tarot cards lay on the end table with a set of spare keys and a half dozen pennies. Wilson stared down at the cards and once again felt the dread gnaw at his insides.

The air in the living room was heavy and stale and smelled like dirty socks, even though the windows always stood open to the Harvey Channel below; only the bedroom was air-conditioned. A fine coating of dust covered Wilson's life as it covered his books stacked to the ceiling against every wall and in the bricked-up fireplace. For the first time, he wished he had a cat to greet him when he came home, but he knew it would be cruel to leave a cat alone in the apartment all day. Suddenly, the next breath, the next second seemed unbearable. He picked up a book, Bernal Díaz's *Conquest of New Spain,* wiped the dust off the cover with his finger, put it down again. The moment passed. He went into the bedroom and changed his clothes, got a beer from the refrigerator, and turned on the TV, as he did every evening during the week.

Halfway through the news, just as Wilson began to doze off, the phone rang. He sat up straight, startled. Andrea was en route to Denver for a weekend management retreat—he couldn't think who it might be; somehow, in the course of life's ordinary disconnections, he had lost touch with all his friends. He waited till the fifth ring to pick up the receiver, his palms asweat with dread.

"Yes?"

"Wilson?" A woman's voice.

Silence.

"Is this Wilson Lander?"

"Yes, who's this?"

"Wilson, it's Susan Page."

"Page?" Wilson said.

"You know, Cricket—don't you remember me? You came into Nancy's shop on Tuesday, and we went to lunch at L'Aille. I ordered all that expensive wine."

"Yes, I remember," Wilson said, and he tried to sound annoyed but found himself picturing her coppery hair in the sunlight.

"Look, I'd like to return the favor."

Wilson hesitated. He felt the tug of his dread somewhere inside. And for a brief second he thought of Andrea on the flight west, spreadsheet across her lap, that business-worried expression on her face as she figured the numbers again on her calculator. Then he put the image completely out of his mind.

8

THE USUAL SATURDAY NIGHT spectacle in the Bend.

Boom boxes boomed from the backs of tricked-out jeeps jammed to a standstill up Cooper Avenue. Along the dirty pavement, immigrants from parts of the world where men wear turbans and women go about with their faces veiled sold cheap sunglasses, bead jewelry, and T-shirts from plywood stalls. At the corner of Morton and Fifth, a man with one withered arm plucked a three-string guitar with his teeth; across the street a woman in a wheelchair sang songs from *Brigadoon* at the top of her lungs, accompanied by a midget on an ocarina carved from a potato. Gypsies told fortunes off fold-up card tables in tiny storefronts. The yellow tang of car exhaust hung in the air.

Wilson pushed his way through this mess, through the crowds up McDermot to the Orion Hotel and went in the back way and found Cricket at the bar beneath the big neon clock.

"Hello," he said. "Where's my wine?"

She turned around and smiled. "Martinis," she said, indicating her drink. "What else would you order at the Orion?" And she leaned over and kissed him on the side of the mouth.

Wilson was a little startled by this gesture, but Cricket didn't seem to notice. "Oops, got some lipstick on your face," she said, and licked her thumb and rubbed his bottom lip.

Wilson ordered a martini with extra olives, and when the drink came, he took a long sip and studied her over the rim of the glass: She had abandoned the unflattering sweatshirt and canvas pants of their first meeting for a tight-fitting striped top and fashionable bell-bottoms of some gauzy material that allowed the curious to glimpse the smooth lines of her hips and legs through the fabric. Her narrow waist was cinched by a wide leather square-buckled belt, and she wore a half dozen silver bracelets and glossy red lipstick, and her coppery mess of hair was tamed and pulled back in a sophisticated bun. Except for her work-scarred hands and the muscles in her arms, Wilson thought, she could have stepped right off the cover of *Vogue,* and he felt a hollow thrill in the pit of his stomach when he considered that she had probably dressed up like this for his sake.

They drank their martinis and watched the place fill up. The Orion Hotel, built in 1915—Calvin Coolidge had once stayed in the Presidential Suite—had been fashionable for about thirty years, but its fortunes declined with the neighborhood, and by the late sixties it had become a skid row flophouse frequented by prostitutes and junkies. Then, in the early eighties, bohemians and homosexuals began to move into the big loft apartments overlooking the Harvey Channel and up Fleet Street. Vegetarian restaurants, health food stores, coffee shops, and used-book stores followed this migration, sprouting up like weeds on every corner. In 1989 a famous French interior designer bought the decrepit hotel, tore out the faded gilt lobby, and redecorated the rooms with steel sinks, trendy wall sconces, and sharkskin furniture. For two million dollars he restored the old bar to original specifications, including the 1928 mural of George and Martha Washington relaxing over mint juleps at Mount Vernon, done in the style of Maxfield Parrish.

Wilson stared up at Martha with her bonnet and prim, capable expression, and he couldn't suppress a flash of Andrea and a stab of guilt. He was having a hard time keeping his eyes off Cricket's breasts beneath the tight striped top. He had never cheated on his girlfriend before. Is that what was happening now?

Conversation lagged. Cricket finished her martini. She ate the three olives from the plastic sword and put her drink on the bar with a decisive click.

"Aren't you going to ask me how I got your phone number?" she said.

"Yeah," Wilson said. "I was wondering about that. I didn't think you had my last name."

Cricket smiled. "I'm very resourceful, which means I'm dangerous," she said. "I might as well warn you right now. After work Tuesday I went next door to L'Aille and told the manager that you were my lover and we had gotten in a fight and I was through with you and as a matter of principle I wanted to pay for the lunch. He pulled the credit card receipt and *voilà*. Your name and phone number."

"Did you pay the bill?" Wilson said.

"No," Cricket said. "That was just an excuse. I let the manager talk me out of it."

They ordered another round of martinis, and Wilson began to loosen up. Bar light glinted off Cricket's silver jewelry. The place was crowded now with attractive, expensively dressed young-society types. Wilson wore an old plaid sports jacket, a comfortably broken-in pair of khakis, a pair of down-at-heel loafers, and a rumpled white shirt with a raveling collar.

"I'm a little underdressed," he said, looking around at the slick Italian-tailored suits and evening dresses.

Cricket waved her hand. "Hell," she said, "you look just like you're supposed to look."

"How's that?" Wilson said.

"Oh"—she thought for a second—"like the young Gregory Peck in *Valley of Decision*. Have you ever seen that?"

"No," Wilson said.

She started to explain the plot; then she shook her head. "Trust me," she said. "It's a ridiculous old movie, but he plays a very earnest young man, and he's very convincing. I'll be the first to confess I always had a big crush on Gregory Peck."

Wilson changed the subject.

For a while they talked about traveling and about the sea. Cricket hadn't always crewed the yachts of the wealthy. In her late teens she had worked a tramp steamer owned by a friend of her father's. Wilson hadn't been many places, and he listened, fascinated, to stories of Rangoon and Maracaibo, of Santiago de Chile and Bangladesh. She had seen knife fights in the barrios of Valparaíso, tribesmen in Borneo who still took the heads of their enemies and lived as humans lived forty thousand years ago, mutiny and yellow fever and beautiful sunsets and strange unnamed fish and devastating storms off the African coast.

"My God! Sounds like you really lead an exciting life," Wilson said.

"I do," Cricket said. "And if I stay in any one place too long, I start getting fat and lazy and bored. I'm looking for a berth right now. Next ship, I'm out of here."

"Oh, well," Wilson said. "You'll have to send me a postcard from Timbuktu."

"Just might," Cricket said.

"I like the *idea* of travel," Wilson said, "but not travel itself. Truth is, I'm a terrible traveler. I can't sleep; I can't shit. I have to come home to go to the bathroom, so trips any longer than three days can be extremely painful."

Cricket laughed.

"Also, there's something else. A while back I spent a few months in Suriname on a dig sponsored by Ashland College and the Deutsche Bank—my one time out of the continental U.S. We had an air-conditioned trailer with all the amenities and even cable TV from a satellite dish, but that didn't take the edge off the foreignness. Each place has its own soul, I think. It's in the water like bacteria. And it takes a lot of time to get used to that soul; you've got to know how the air smells after it rains, watch how the sun hits the trees in the morning every day for years to get a real handle on it. Maybe you've got to bury your people in the ground before you can understand a place. Hell, it could take generations."

"You're a romantic," Cricket said.

"Just sensitive to my environment," Wilson said. He was careful not to mention the dread. "One of the reasons why I gave up archaeology. Traipsing all over the world to dig up other people's bones. I suppose I'd rather read about it in *National Geographic*."

When he looked at his illuminated digital watch a few minutes later, it was ten twenty-two and the bar was very crowded. They were wedged into a corner by a loud party in tuxedos and black dresses, the men rich and obnoxious, the women tanned and drunk. One of the latter began laughing like a hyena, shrieking in Wilson's ear. She laughed so hard some of her drink came out her nose.

"You want to go someplace else?" Wilson said. He put his hand on Cricket's back and leaned close. He felt a kind of electric charge go through his fingertips.

"Yes," Cricket said. "If we hurry, we might just have time to catch the last couple of races."

"Races?" Wilson said.

9

THE DOG TRACK AT Mimosa Park was a broken-down reminder of its days of deco glory. Lime green paint peeled off the streamlined towers; tube lights fritzed off and on around the silhouette of the neon greyhound above the main gate. The big clock had stopped at a quarter after two on some forgotten windblown afternoon thirty years gone. From across the parking lot the track looked like an ocean liner left to rot in dry dock.

Cricket paid for the cab, and they walked up through the gates and along the cement path littered with ticket stubs and cigarette butts. Carbon arc lamps buzzed overhead. The smell of cigarettes and sand and night and the faint uretic reek of dog piss hung in the air. It was the lull between races. The grooms—underdeveloped youths wearing shorts pulled up to their belly buttons, knee socks, and cleated patent leather shoes—led eight mixed greyhounds around the sandy oval to the starting gate. A couple of dozen gamblers lounged against the railing of the promenade, watching this dismal parade. Wilson saw sullen, bony-elbowed old men in short-sleeve shirts and porkpie hats, trailer park women with frosted hair, tough teens armed with sharp sideburns, leather jackets slung over their shoulder. Two dirty children chased garbage across the tarry apron. A Chinaman chewed on a piece of fat, staring into the darkness beyond the sweep of highway.

The few remaining mimosa trees decorating the infield melted in the light wind like cotton candy under a heat lamp. One frail pink blossom alighted in Cricket's coppery hair.

"Ever been here before?" Cricket said.

"No," Wilson said. "I've only seen it from the highway."

"What do you think?"

"Seedy, depressing," Wilson said, looking around. "This must be where the other half goes on Saturday night."

"Stop being so sensitive to your environment," Cricket said. "Or I should say, stop being a snob."

"O.K.," Wilson said, "but what are we doing here?"

Cricket put her hand on Wilson's arm. "I'm going to pay you back for those bottles of wine," she said, and led him toward the glass-fronted grandstand.

A rust-flecked chrome strip ran the length of the inside bar empty except for two whiskey-smelling old men smoking cigars. The dogs were at the starting gate. A closed-circuit TV broadcast the race live for those gamblers who could not get off their stools. Wilson found a table as Cricket angled up to the bar. She came back with a program and two pints of Colonial lager in plastic cups.

"When at the dog track, drink what the dogs drink," she said, and put the cheap beer down on the table.

Wilson took a sip of the stuff and grimaced. It reminded him of high school—drunken rides in jacked-up cars, empty cans rolling around in the backseat.

Cricket pushed the program at him. "The guy behind the bar says we've got two races left and seven minutes to place a bet for the next one," she said. "You pick the dogs, I'll lay the money down. You keep the winnings. Hopefully we'll walk out of here with enough to cover the wine and a little change to spare. Come on, it'll be fun.''

Wilson stared down at the brightly colored boxes on the program. His head still felt a bit thick from the martinis at the Orion, and he had a hard time concentrating on the names of the dogs: Darcy's Lord, Southwind, Bartholomew Roberts, Honeysuckle Rose, Stinky, Mnemosyne, Battle, Crazy Eight.

"Dog racing," he said. "My father is spinning in his grave."

"Don't think about him," Cricket said. "Do your stuff," and she smiled, and her smile was as dangerous and irresistible as anything Wilson had ever seen.

"This is such a random thing," Wilson said, looking back at the program. "With the horses, the most important factor is the jockey. Here it's just the dogs and the track, and from what I hear about the dogs, they're capricious, unpredictable."

"See, you are a gambler," Cricket said.

"Not me," Wilson said, but he ran down the odds and felt something turn inside him, and he picked Darcy's Lord and Mnemosyne for the quinella. Cricket placed the bet just under the wire, and they took the program and the pints of Colonial out to the promenade to watch the dogs come around the track. A damp wind now blew from the direction of the sea. The dogs went into the slots and began barking and yapping and jumping at the gate.

"Here comes Swifty," the announcer called, and a groom loaded the stuffed rabbit on the pulley and a shot went off and the gates sprang up and the dogs went clawing over one another, once around in a blur of haunch and paw and numbers and flying sand.

Wilson's dogs came in second and first. Cricket had placed a two-dollar bet. She came back from the cashier's window smiling and handed Wilson sixty dollars in ten-dollar bills.

"There's one bottle," she said.

"Beginner's luck," Wilson said, trying to sound nonchalant, but he couldn't keep the grin from his face.

The last race on the ticket was the Mimosa Maidens' Cup—once around with a field of eight virgin bitches. Wilson felt a strange, queasy twisting in his stomach that was familiar yet not familiar. His palms began to sweat; he felt the desire to win like a metallic taste in his mouth. Then he was disgusted with himself, and he tossed the program into the nearest wire trash basket. "Let's get out of here," he said. "I'm not in the mood for this."

Cricket stepped around and put a hand against his chest. Her eyes were brilliant green stones in the greenish illumination of the carbon arcs.

"One last race," she said quietly, and there was a serious edge to her voice. "Please, for me."

Flags snapped noisily in the wind. Wilson saw the goose bumps raise themselves across Cricket's bare arms.

He hit the trifecta in disorder, with Mysore, Emma, and Little Flower. The payoff was fifty-to-one on a three-dollar bet.

With the extra money, Cricket rented a limousine for the ride back to town, a 1941 Lincoln Continental, long as a houseboat, with big flared fenders, lots of chrome, and an open section for the driver. The track kept this relic around for high rollers, but no one ever used it, and the interior smelled like dust and mildew. The driver was half shaved; he wore no tie or jacket, just a white shirt rolled up to the elbows and a baseball cap with the Mimosa Park logo on the crown. He seemed slightly irritated at having to drive them back to the city and handed over the complimentary bottle of domestic champagne with a grunt.

As the big machine lumbered out to the highway, canned forties-era swing music came over the speakers from up front. The instruments threw a faint green glow through the privacy window, touching the contours of Cricket's body with the delicacy of a shy lover until she settled back into the padded dimness of the Lincoln. Wilson gulped down three glasses of the champagne before they passed Exit 17 to Palmyra and East Morea. The stuff had a rank, fishy bouquet, but he drank a fourth glass and was suddenly very drunk.

"I told you, it's in your blood." Cricket's voice came disembodied from across the long seat.

"The alcohol?" Wilson slurred.

"The gambling," Cricket said. "Hell, I was raised around enough of them to know. And I can tell you that the knack, luck—whatever you want to call it—is passed down through the generations. Think of the odds against what you just did! You hit the quinella and the Maiden's Cup right in a row! Amazing! You're probably a better gambler than your father was."

"Get this straight, I'm a failed archaeologist," Wilson said, and his lips had trouble forming the words. "Dem bones just got the better of me."

"What?" Cricket said.

"Sorry," Wilson said, "not used to all this drinking. Generally I lead a very quiet life."

"Not for much longer," Cricket said, and when she smiled, all Wilson saw was her teeth like the Cheshire cat smiling from the shadows.

Landscape passed, dark and featureless. Soon the city lit the horizon with an orange haze. Then there were green signs with white lettering, and the Lacey Memorial Bridge and then the Overlook, and somehow Wilson found himself stumbling alone down the empty streets of the Rubicon District, and the next thing he knew it was morning and he woke up with a nasty hangover, fully clothed on the couch in his apartment.

He couldn't remember exactly how he had gotten there, but could remember why he didn't drink much anymore: He was too old for the hangovers, and after five or six drinks he suffered from blackouts. He lay around all day recuperating, swallowing aspirins and Coke, and trying to piece together the final events of the previous evening. Had Cricket said anything, given him a good night kiss, her phone number? There were no scraps of paper, no matchbook covers scrawled with seven digits in his pockets. Had they made plans to go out some other time? He couldn't remember, and at the thought that he might never see her again part of him felt relieved.

But the vague suspicion that he had forgotten something important nagged for the next few days, until Andrea got back from Denver.

10

A WEEK WENT BY. At the end of it, Wilson dragged himself home on the Rubicon bus and got into bed in his pajamas, just after eight o'clock. Then the stars rose and shone so brilliantly out his bedroom window he couldn't sleep, a problem shared with a million other residents of the city that night. The stars seemed to hover just twenty feet above his roof, and there was no moon, and the sky was beautiful with just the stars like porch lights in the blackness.

Wilson had read an article explaining this phenomenon in that morning's edition of the *Times-Chronicle,* but he had not been prepared for something so utterly marvelous. It was caused by a rare atmospheric distortion known as Klett's Mirage, first recorded at the North Pole by the Dutch explorer W. G. Klett on the disastrous polar expedition of 1911. This time Klett's Mirage would be observable up and down the coast, though not below Taneville or above St. Charles, which is to say from forty-two degrees north or south of the meridian, where a distinct line divided the sky between dim and bright, between those inhabitants who dwelt in darkness and those, for the time being, blessed or cursed with an abundance of starlight. According to the article, the science of it was nothing special—gases in the atmosphere and certain types of industrial pollutants acted to magnify starlight in a mundane chemical reaction—

but just now the huge stars out Wilson's bedroom window sent chills up his spine.

Wilson got out of bed, leaned against the air-conditioning unit, and stared up at the sky. He had been restless since his excursion to the dog track; for days the dread had been gnawing with unusual force at the inside of his stomach, mixed with a longing he did not care to examine. Cricket hadn't called; perhaps he had done something to offend her. He couldn't remember. Earlier in the week, he thought about dropping by the magic store; then he thought about not dropping by. Andrea was a fine woman, they were just going through a rocky period, no reason to throw it all away on someone he hardly knew. Of course, once he started thinking about Cricket, sleep was impossible.

The vast night full of stars beckoned.

11

THE RUBICON BUS ACROSS the bridge stopped running after rush hour, so Wilson walked down to Ferry Point and caught the ten o'clock express through the tunnel.

At half past, the sidewalks of the city were still crowded with star-struck pedestrians. The bars along the esplanade were packed. The tunnel bus, full of Salvadoran hotel workers just getting off work, lurched up through the fish markets and the wharves and reached its terminus in the old Alcazar District—once a Portuguese neighborhood, now called Buptown—home to thousands of recent refugees from the war-torn West African nation of Bupanda.

Wilson decided to walk over to the Bend, get a drink at Tony's, then catch the 1:30 bus back through the tunnel. Tonight Buptown was teeming. Bupandan men squatted on small squares of carpet at low tables on the terraces of their open-fronted cafés, little more than holes in the wall. They ate kif with their fingers, scooping the spicy stuff off polished brass trays with the spongy rice bread called panu; they drank tejiyaa or coffee out of oiled leather cups. The sound of their African dialect, their rages and enthusiasms filled the night. At the corner of Reeve and Middleton, a Bupandan tinka band played homemade flutes and five-gallon plastic paint drums and old men danced on the sidewalk under the stars. The Bupandans lived in Buptown much as they did in their distant West African homeland. Their lives were lived in public, in the streets, even the most intimate acts. As Wilson walked down Windermere to Fifth, hands in his pockets, he stepped around families of fifteen sprawled across blankets spread before the stoops of the tenements. They scratched and yawned and quarreled; they dressed and undressed. Young couples made love oblivious in tattered sleeping bags as naked children jumped rope not ten feet away.

Suddenly, Wilson didn't want to be alone. He stopped at the first pay phone on Fifth and called Andrea and got her machine. Was she out or asleep? He called home for his messages on the off chance she had left one, and the machine kicked in after the first ring. There was one message, but not from Andrea.

"Wilson, sorry I'm late. Just got back into town. We had a date, remember?" It was Cricket. The skin on the back of Wilson's neck prickled. "Wake up! We're supposed to go to the fights tonight. They don't start for a while yet. And there's something else I want to talk to you about. Come on, pick up the phone. Wilson?" There was a sigh, and the machine gave three beeps and disconnected. She didn't leave a number.

Wilson replaced the receiver carefully, his hand shaking a little. Just hearing Cricket's voice affected his nerves. The fights? He racked his brain for some memory of their arrangements and came up with nothing. Was Cricket talking about boxing, a restaurant, a club? He tried Information for her name—there were twenty S. Pages, and no Cricket—then he tried Sportsline and found there was no boxing anywhere in town tonight; then he tried Information again and came up with a gym in Reevetown called the Fight Place. That couldn't be it. He felt abandoned. Desire and guilt washed over him in alternating waves like the fever and chills of the flu.

Directly across from the pay phone, a tiny, brightly lit terrace restaurant called the Kifto advertised a full seven-course Bupandan meal for $11.75. On a whim, he crossed the street and sat down at one of the low tables on a square of stained tartan plaid carpet. The patronage here tonight consisted of one large party of young Bupandan men, their skin the rich black of coffee beans shining with sweat in the swaying light of paper lanterns. They were just being served heaping platters of kif and panu by three thin Bupandan women wearing the traditional scarf and headdress of their country. A good two dozen blue glass bottles of tejiyaa stood empty at the center of their table. Wilson sat for a while feeling sorry for himself, watching them talk and laugh and eat. At last, a yellow-eyed old man wearing a Guinea T and a moth-eaten pair of tuxedo pants came over to his table.

"You want to eat?" he said, closing his eyes with the question.

"Yes," Wilson said. "That stuff smells pretty good."

"No, no," the old man said, "kitchen is closed. We have only tejiyaa now."

"A glass of tejiyaa's fine, but you couldn't bring me a little something to go along with it? An appetizer?"

"Impossible," the old man said.

"Nothing?"

The old man gestured to the table where the Bupandans sat devouring mounds of food. "We serve them everything," he said. "Special celebration tonight."

"All right," Wilson said, but he must have looked disappointed because the old man raised a hand.

"Wait, O.K.?" and he turned and went over to the other table. A few quick words were exchanged in Bupandan; then he stepped back again.

"They say you may join them if you wish," he said. "But you must buy your own bottle of tejiyaa."

"Thanks," Wilson said, "but I couldn't impose—"

The old man's yellow eyes came to life for a moment. "You may join them," he insisted. "Bupandan hospitality."

Wilson didn't have much of a choice. A place was made at the crowded table, and he found himself squatting in the midst of a Bupandan birthday party. The sleek youth to his right had just turned twenty-one. He wore a birthday outfit of purple shorts, a black silk shirt printed with yellow soccer balls, and black-and-gold woven sandals. His name, if Wilson could make it out right was Kuji N'fumi. His brother, about ten years older, sat on Wilson's left. He was Tulj Ra'au. The other dozen or so young men introduced themselves one by one, but Wilson didn't catch more than a mouthful of syllables. They seemed a jovial group, laughing and telling jokes in Bupandan, with an occasional lapse into a colorful sort of English for Wilson's benefit, and the blue bottles of tejiyaa came and went, and the kif was eaten and replaced by na'kif and kif'tu—all variations of the same spicy goulash, with chickpeas, beets, and chicken respectively. It was not until halfway through the meal that Wilson noticed the scars.

Each man had them, sinister pinkish lacerations showing distinctly against the dark black skin. They were not tribal markings, but healed-over wounds, as if someone had once attacked this group with a rather long knife. A few lacked the usual number of fingers or toes. On his left hand Tulj Ra'au had only the thumb and little finger, the stub of the third digit decorated grotesquely with a gaudy ring of intricate gold openwork.

"You like my ring?" Tulj saw Wilson looking at it.

"Y-yes," Wilson stuttered unconvincingly.

Tulj took the ring off his stub and handed it over to Wilson, who held it up to the light, nodded politely and handed it back.

"It's very . . . elaborate," Wilson said.

Tulj threw his head back and laughed, showing healthy white

teeth and gold fillings. "No, it is Anda crap," he said. "You are just being polite. The Andas are like savages, children. They are fond of gaudy trinkets, like this ring. I wear it only to remind me of the Anda pig I killed. I cut his throat and took the ring; then I cut off his ears; then I cut off his head, like that!" He brought his mutilated hand down on the table in a karate chop with sudden fury, and the atmosphere of the party changed in that instant. Tulj let loose in Bupandan, shaking the ring at his companions. A few of the young men covered their faces with their hands and began rocking back and forth. N'fumi's eyes filled with tears. Others rose quickly, stalked halfway down the block, and stalked back. It was as if the severed head that Tulj had mentioned had just been flung into the center of the table. After a few minutes of general lamentation, Tulj said something and everyone settled down again.

"Please, you must forgive us poor Bupus," he said to Wilson. "But we are all of us from the village of Lifdawa, and it was upon that place one Saturday, when everyone was at the markets, that the Andas first came down from the mountains with the guns and the machetes and the killing. They killed everyone, men, women, children. They killed all day long till the dry ground was muddy with Bupu blood. All here were wounded and left for dead in the piles of butchered bodies, but at night we crawled away to the jungle. Many months later, we got on the boats to come to America. Your country is good to us, but it is also not too good. In Bupanda I went to the mission school, and before the Time of Killing I was a student at the university in Rigala. I studied engineering. Now"—he gestured with his mutilated hand—"I drive a truck."

Wilson nodded respectfully. The whole world remembered the horrible Bupandan massacres of five years before. The Bupus and the Andas, two tribes that had shared that part of West Africa for a thousand years suddenly rose up and began slaughtering each other, with all the force of a natural disaster. The causes were inscrutable, beyond rational understanding—what is the motivation of a tidal wave or an erupting volcano?—but the effects were immediate. A million dead on both sides, a million refugees already, and more coming.

The last of the food was consumed a little after midnight, and the women came and cleared the table. A last bottle of tejiyaa was poured and drunk. This potent stuff tasted like kerosene. Wilson had a hard time choking it down, but choke it down he did, in the final round of toasts to N'fumi, the birthday boy. The stars glittered brilliantly overhead, the crowds passed along the streets, and there was a warm, comfortable feeling in his chest. These Bupus were all fine fellows. He felt he was among friends. The tragedies they had witnessed did not prevent them from enjoying life. Let that be a lesson to his dread! He looked from the stars into his oiled leather cup, and when he looked up again, he was alone at the table with Tulj and N'fumi.

"Where is everyone?" Wilson said.

Tulj laughed. "They went to the dancing at the Nkifta Discotheque, but us, we do not go to the dancing."

"Where do you go?" Wilson said.

"We go to the fights," Tulj said. "Very big fights tonight."

"You're kidding," Wilson said, excited. "I was supposed to go to the fights, but"—he looked down at his watch—"isn't it a little late?"

"Oh, no, they have not yet started," Tulj said.

"Would you mind if I come along?" Wilson said.

The African leaned back and smiled. "How much money do you have?"

12

TULJ DROVE AN OLD Fiat three-wheel cycle truck with a four-and-a-half-foot open bed and a single wavering headlight. The brothers sat pressed knee to knee in the small cab up front; Wilson took the back and held on as best he could. Through rust holes in the bed, he could see the pavement passing beneath, and when they slowed down, he caught the gassy stink of exhaust. The air and the stars did him good. He leaned back, sobering, against the curve of the cab as they pulled over the Lacey Memorial Bridge onto the interstate.

Tonight, Wilson's dread manifested itself as a dull pulse of pain in his gut like a toothache. He had lived so much of his life by schedules and routine; he took the same bus at the same time, went to the same office, and did mostly the same things. Until recently there had been few surprises. It was through this sad and careful voodoo that he had sought to keep the dread at bay. But since the discovery of the tarot cards his routines had failed him. He knew something terrible was on its way, closing in; a clinching in his gut told him so: Even the blandest of foods, the egg salad sandwich he ate for lunch every day, gave him indigestion. He was deciding all at once, tonight, with the stars up and the wind in his hair, that perhaps it was time to lead a different sort of life.

Tulj and N'fumi were arguing loudly in the cab and passing a bottle of tejiyaa back and forth. The Fiat swerved dangerously when they pulled off the highway at Lazarus onto Route 27 and into the confusion of cross-state traffic. Wilson sat up and watched the lights of the city recede behind the nearest tree line; soon there was little more than a dull glow in the sky. Ten minutes later they veered off 27 onto a fire road and then slowed and turned up a dirt track that bumped away into the pine and frog darkness of the Falling Rock Nature Preserve. Soon the stars were lost in the branches, and

Wilson heard the hoot and scratch of animals in the brush and the slow, long-needled rustling of the firs. About fifteen minutes passed on Wilson's illuminated digital watch before the truck emerged from the trees into a mud clearing full of cars. At the center, a large cinder-block bunkhouse showed a row of small yellow-lit windows just beneath the eaves.

Wilson hopped out of the bed and stood on the loamy ground, hands in his pockets, waiting for the Africans to disengage themselves from the cramped interior. The Fiat was so small, like one of those clown cars at the circus. A dull thrumming, which was the sound of men's voices, came from inside the bunkhouse. Thin, silvery clouds of smoke steamed out of the yellow windows into the clear night air.

"Please, can you lend a hand here?" It was Tulj from the compartment of the Fiat.

Wilson stepped over to the passenger-side window and saw that N'fumi had passed out, mouth open against the dashboard.

"Too much tejiyaa," Tulj said. "He is young yet; he does not know how to handle his liquor."

"What the hell," Wilson said. "Twenty-one. Everyone's allowed to float the boat at twenty-one."

"Yes, but I do not want him floating the boat, as you say, in the front seat of my truck," Tulj said.

They managed to carry N'fumi around to the back. Tulj let down the gate, and they hoisted him up into the bed and covered him to the chin with an old tarp. N'fumi's legs stuck out a good two feet over the end, one of his sandals dangling off his foot. The effect was comic or sinister, Wilson couldn't decide which.

"My foolish brother is best off sleeping here," Tulj said. "Meanwhile, we will proceed to the fights. Have you ever attended such an event in the past?"

Wilson was going to lie, then thought better of it and shook his head.

"It is much fun," the African said, then he laughed. "I wasted my youth in such places, at home in the days before the Time of Killing."

13

THE BUNKHOUSE WAS PACKED to the walls with men of many nationalities. Wilson looked around for Cricket but did not see a single woman in the crowd.

There were Bupandans, Nigerians, Haitians, Salvadorans, Mexicans, Brazilians, Vietnamese, even a few white shack-trash rednecks wearing plaid workshirts and vinyl mesh baseball caps plastered with rebel flags, all gathered around a dirt pit about forty feet across, covered with blood and straw and feathers. The feathers were everywhere, floating on clouds of cigarette smoke in the yellow light. The smell was overpowering. At first, Wilson could hardly breathe. Then, suddenly, he grew used to the stifling, flatulent air.

Tulj managed to push his way up to the railing over the pit, and Wilson took a position beside him. Sugarcane liquor in cloudy vinegar bottles was passed forward from the back of the crowd. Wilson drank and wiped his mouth on his hand as he'd seen someone do in a movie, and he passed it to Tulj, who drank and passed it to someone else. A dangerous, testosterone-charged atmosphere hung about the place, but it was not alien or unfamiliar. Here, Wilson got the sense, men were doing what they did best: drinking, fighting, gambling on violent sport.

After a while two squat Salvadorans climbed into the pit. A roar went up from the crowd. The Salvadorans wore blood-spattered white T-shirts, and each carried a wire cage that contained a big, sleek, blue-feathered rooster. The birds were removed from their cages and held tightly beak to beak against the straw. Vicious-looking steel spurs glinted dully from their legs. They squawked and scratched and tried to get at each other as the betting went down around the pit. A half dozen dark youths of uncertain ethnicity ran through the crowd collecting bets, which they marked with playing cards torn in half. The dirty concrete floor was stuck with the torn cards and pink handbills in five languages. Broken glass crunched under Wilson's shoes.

Wilson was surprised. He had expected men, not birds. He decided that these were probably not the fights that Cricket had been talking about; then he changed his mind. Until the dogs two weeks ago, he hadn't been to a track in all the years since his father's death. This was the second gambling event he had attended in a month. In a way, Cricket was like a voice calling him back to his past.

"In the mission school the Reverend Father told us a story about the fighting cocks," Tulj said now in Wilson's ear.

"Yeah?" Wilson said.

"There was once a great soldier in the country of Ancient Greece called Themistocles. He was in charge of fighting another country neighboring. I forget which—"

"Persia," Wilson said.

"Ah, you know this story?"

"Go ahead."

"You see, the Ancient Greek Themistocles, he was moving his army to the front when he came upon two wild cocks in a field fighting each other to the death. He stopped and showed the brave animals to his troops. 'Watch how they fight to the death,' he said. 'Take heed, my men!' The next day the army, though badly outnumbered, won the battle, a great battle. This is how we may draw inspiration from animals. . . ." Tulj went on to explain what to look for when betting on cocks: clear eyes, good stance, size, and, most important, whether the bird evacuated its bowels just before the match.

"If he does his business, it is very good luck indeed," Tulj said. "Makes him lighter, faster, ready to fight. . . ."

Tulj signaled a boy, who rushed over to take their bets. The boy was dark-skinned, big-eyed, Guatemalan or Mexican. He looked like Dondi, the Italian orphan, from Sunday comics of Wilson's youth.

"Señor," he said to Wilson.

Wilson turned to Tulj, who shrugged and pulled out his pockets.

"All spent on tejiyaa and kif and panu," Tulj said, putting his mutilated hand on Wilson's shoulder. "The honor of my brother's name day is with you, my new friend."

Wilson took out his wallet. He had a hundred dollars and some change, his walking money till the fifteenth.

"*¿Cuánto, señor?*" the boy said, impatient. "*Ándale.*"

Wilson looked into the pit, and in that moment the smaller of the two birds dropped two perfectly round chicken turds.

"That one," Wilson said, and on an impulse handed the boy everything he had. The boy made a quick notation on the back of a playing card, tore it in half, gave half to Wilson, then ran off into the crowd. Wilson looked at the torn card in his hand. The king of diamonds. "Here goes nothing," he said to Tulj.

The African smiled.

A moment later, the handlers released their birds, jumped back, and the fight was on. Wilson saw little more than the quick flash of steel, flying feathers, and the spurting blood. The whole thing was over in less than a minute. The victorious bird, one wing hanging limp, reared back, flapped his good wing, and made an appalling crowing sound. Then he began to peck at the corpse of his opponent. Wilson won six hundred dollars, the odds on this bird, the long shot at six-to-one. In the next match he bet everything again and won again at seven-to-one. Then he won at three-to-one and five-to-one. There was money stuffed in the pockets of his jacket, in his khakis. He was dazed, his face was hot, he couldn't seem to breathe right, he hardly knew what he was doing, but he wanted to win—this was the feeling that had come over him at the dog track.

He felt the same metallic taste in his mouth, the same sweaty palms. It couldn't be real, but the money kept on coming.

An hour later, in a lull between fights, his head cleared a little, and he stepped back from the pit to see that a space had cleared around him. He stood alone in a circle of rough, dangerous-looking men. From across the room other men watched him, knives gleaming from their belts. Tulj was nowhere in sight. Wilson figured quickly that he had something like eight thousand dollars in his pocket. Directly on the other side of the pit a man in a white linen suit tapped long fingernails against the railing. Wilson looked up. The man's sand-colored skin gleamed like oiled wood. His hair was jet black; his eyes a weird shade of dark blue. His suit held the shimmer of summer nights in a place that no one could afford.

"So, you like to bet against my birds?" the man said in a voice that was little more than a whisper.

"Huh?" Wilson said.

"Who sent you?" the man said.

"You're kidding," Wilson said.

The man nodded as if he knew something that Wilson didn't know. Then he waved a hand through the air and whispered, "Good luck," in a way that made Wilson shudder.

When the boy came up to take the bets for the next fight, Wilson palmed off a fifty-dollar bill.

"The guy across the way in the white suit," Wilson said. "Know anything?"

The boy glanced quickly over his shoulder, and his mouth drooped. "El Señor Hidalgo," he said, and shook his head. *"Muy peligroso.* You better lose this time, I think."

Wilson felt a tightening in his upper bowels and resolved to follow the boy's advice. The match was between a scrawny bird with half a comb and a large, glossy specimen that looked like the bellicose rooster pictured on French stamps as the symbol of the French Republic. For some reason the odds were only two-to-one in favor of the larger bird. Wilson bet everything to lose on the scrawny bird and won sixteen thousand dollars. An angry hiss went up from the crowd. The man in the white suit across the way dug his long nails into the soft wood of the railing. One of them broke off, a small snapping sound, before he turned away. Wilson's heart sank as the boy came over, dragging a mound of cash in a torn cardboard box. With or without the sixteen grand, he knew he wouldn't get out of this place alive. The world hates nothing so much as a lucky man. He looked around, and suddenly Tulj was at his elbow.

"If you were planning to win so bloody much money, you should have brought an army," the African said angrily, "like the Ancient Greek Themistocles."

"Christ, let's get out of here," Wilson said, but the African backed away, making an X with his forearms.

"I did not live through the Time of Killing in Bupanda to die for a box full of paper in a country I do not love," he said. "I am sorry." Then he turned and hurried away through the crowd.

Wilson lingered desperately at the rail. He counted the crumpled money in the box, made neat stacks, and folded all of it into the pockets of his jacket. He was vaguely aware of the man in the white suit talking intensely to a group of thugs at the door. Two of them wore cowboy hats and shirts with the sleeves torn off. Another one, his face covered with strange hairy growths, sported the kind of gangsterish borsalino once known as a Little Caesar. Wilson's dread had taken palpable form at last. A crowd of strangers, a man in an expensive white suit, a half dozen cheap hoodlums, sixteen thousand dollars in cash. He almost laughed out loud. It was like the fable about the appointment in Samarra: A rich man, told that Death is near, goes to the next town, Samarra, to escape his fate. There, of course, Death is waiting for him in the marketplace.

Wilson held on awhile longer, till the place cleared out. Then he turned heavily toward the door. But before he rounded the pit, the Guatemalan boy who had taken the bets was at his side.

"*Señor, por favor,*" the boy said.

"What's that?" Wilson said.

"The beck door," the boy said. "Trees, dark, *vámosnos.*" And he made a whistling noise through his teeth.

Wilson followed him without thinking. They went behind a curtain into a small utility room where two Guatemalan men sat at a picnic table counting the house take. Taped to the wall behind them, an airbrushed beaver shot from *Hustler* and a Catholic prayer card showing the Virgin of Guadalupe balanced delicately on her sliver of moon. The men grunted when Wilson went past; they didn't say anything. The rusty back door swung out onto the parking lot. The night burned beautiful with stars. The trees loomed, a dark refuge, twenty-five yards away across the dull backs of the cars. Wilson hesitated on the threshold.

"*Vámosnos,* trees, dark," the boy said, and tried to push Wilson into the night.

"Take it easy," Wilson said. He didn't want to be rushed into this, his last sky full of stars, his last breath. When he stepped down into the parking lot, the door slammed behind him, and he knew it was a trap. Still, he took it slow and easy between the cars. Though he did not smoke much, he wished he had a cigarette; it is better to meet such moments with a cigarette in hand. Two groups of men, about a dozen in all, stepped out from either side of the bunkhouse. They fanned out, flanking him, intending to catch him in the last stretch before the trees. Their boots made squelchy noises on the soft ground. Wilson heard the sound of their breath and from somewhere, like hope departing, the distant howl of a freight train. They were close now, wolves loping alongside. Wilson reached a small open space between the cars. There, two men blocked the way, arms crossed, huge, just ahead. It came down to this last second, this silence, the woods waiting.

Then, the sound of shattering glass, gunshots, and an uproar from the front side of the bunkhouse. A high, unnatural screaming was followed by more screams, coming closer. Wilson swung toward this sound; the men following Wilson swung toward this sound. In the next second, a black man wearing one sandal came running wildly around the corner, pursued by fifteen others. Wilson saw the yellow soccer balls on the man's shirt and the purple shorts and knew it to be N'fumi. Ten more dragged Tulj along at a distance. The side of his face was bloody, his clothing torn.

The men tackled N'fumi in the mud just beyond the last row of cars. Three of them grabbed him by the legs; two others took his arms. Wilson could see that they were Africans, heard them speak what sounded like Bupandan. One of the men drew out a long knife with a serrated edge and held it against N'fumi's throat. The poor boy's eyes rolled with fear in the starlight. In an instant there was a crowd. A hundred men watched from between the cars, their faces bright with the prospect of more blood. Tulj was dragged up, made to kneel beside his brother. Wilson didn't need to be told what was going on. There was a large Anda community in nearby Parkerville. Like the Bupus, they had fled the hatred and tragedy of their unfortunate nation, only to bring all of it along in their bellies, in their dark hearts.

Someone switched on the headlights of a car, and the scene was illuminated in a harsh white light. The Anda holding the knife to N'fumi's throat shouted a last obscenity and made ready to draw its serrated edge across the boy's jugular. A man across the way—it didn't matter who—licked his lips in anticipation. In that instant, an unnamed righteousness welled up inside Wilson's breast. Without thinking, he put his foot on the bumper of the nearest car, a battered sixties-era Mercury, jumped onto the hood of a Chevy Impala of similar vintage, and in another short hop stood directly overlooking the action.

"Stop!" Wilson cried, and something in his voice made the Anda hesitate. "You heard me! Put down that knife!" This sounded foolish to Wilson's ears, but he didn't know what else to say.

The Anda kept the knife at N'fumi's throat and looked up lazily. "What you want here, mistah?" he said. "You got your cash won, now go home. Sure, if you can get home." Then he snickered, an evil rattling sound at the back of his throat.

"Let me ask you something," Wilson said, the same tone of authority in his voice. "How much is a man's life worth to you?"

The Anda blinked, his eyes bloodshot from drink and cigarettes, his lids wrinkly as old Morocco leather.

"I asked you a question," Wilson persisted. "How much?"

The Anda shrugged. "This is a pig," he said, slapping N'fumi's neck with the flat side of the knife. "A pig and the son of a pig. A stinking Bupu. In my country we hunt them down and cut their throats like pigs."

"This is my country," Wilson said. "And in my country a man's life is still worth something. How much for this one?"

The Anda blinked again, slow as an owl.

"A thousand dollars, two thousand dollars, six thousand dollars?" Wilson said, and began to take the bills out of his pocket and throw them at the Anda's feet. When there was quite a pile of money down there, Wilson paused dramatically and said, "Is that enough?"

The Anda prodded the bills with his toe and smiled genially. "No," he said.

"All right," Wilson said, "I'll tell you what . . ." He reached into his pockets and drew out two fistfuls of cash. "I've got about sixteen thousand dollars here," he said. "I'll give you all of it for both of them." He nodded toward N'fumi and Tulj. The latter stared up at him, a blank expression in his eyes.

The Anda thought for a moment, then he nodded slowly. "You have a deal, mistah," he said.

"You'll let them go?" Wilson said.

The Anda drew up straight. "When an Anda gives his word," he said.

Wilson opened his fists and let the money drop. It fluttered in the headlights. The Anda threw N'fumi facefirst into the mud and gave him a hard kick in the ass. A shout of laughter went up from the crowd. The tension broke. Tulj was released and stood helpless, rubbing his wrist with his good hand.

"Go!" the Anda yelled at them in English. "Go!"

In a moment the brothers were gone, scrambling on hands and knees for the woods.

Wilson watched from the hood of the Impala till they were lost in the darkness, then he stepped down. The crowd parted respectfully. Hands in his pockets, he walked across the soft ground to the front parking lot, wondering how he would get back home. The thugs in the cowboy hats faded off into the night to the sound of car engines and the smell of carbon monoxide. He didn't matter to them now that the money was gone. A match flared from nearby. Wilson looked up. The man in the white linen suit leaned gracefully against the body of a late-model silver Mercedes limousine. He lit a thin cigarillo and shook the match out slowly as Wilson passed.

"A gesture," he said. "So—"

Wilson stopped and turned to face him.

"—so pretty." Then he smiled a weary, knowing smile and nodded. "Very pretty. Passing out men's lives like a king, eh? No! Like an emperor!" He poked the cigarillo at Wilson's chest for emphasis.

"An emperor," Wilson said, turning the word over in his mind.

The man nodded. "That's the thing about gamblers," he said. "Sometimes they get to play emperor for a night. But the next morning, what are they?" He turned his hands empty, palm up.

"I'm no gambler," Wilson said. "I'm just an average guy."

The man drew on his cigarillo and blew smoke toward the bright stars. "I lost seventy-five thousand dollars betting against you tonight," he said. "You are a gambler, my friend."

Wilson was about to turn away, but instead he stepped forward and put out his hand. "My name is Wilson Lander," he said.

Surprised, the man in the white suit hesitated, but at last he shook Wilson's hand.

"Don Luis Gabriel Hidalgo de la Vaca," he said.

"Luis, I wonder if you could do me a favor," Wilson said.

14

WILSON RODE UP FRONT with the chauffeur all the way back to the city. The chauffeur, an enormous Filipino man with an acne-pitted face, had once been a professional wrestler called the Killa from Manila, though he actually hailed from a small rice-growing community in the foothills of Mindanao and many years before had gone to the seminary to study for the priesthood. Wilson remembered the man's face from Sunday morning wrestling extravaganzas on TV when he was a kid, and his story from wrestling magazines of the era. He tried to start up a conversation, but the Killa wouldn't talk.

"Do you mind if I put the radio on?" Wilson said, still restless from the turmoil of the evening.

The chauffeur shook his massive head. "Can't do it," he said. "Boss doesn't like music." Wilson glanced over his shoulder and could just barely make out the shadowy outline of Luis de la Vaca through the one-way glass.

Wilson got out of the car at the far side of the bridge. The stars above the great Gothic pilings were going pale, a purplish light rising in the east. He stepped around and knocked on the back window. After a moment the glass hummed down with a faint musical note. Luis de la Vaca's face appeared, half in shadow, half in light.

"Hey, thanks for the ride," Wilson said. "I'll take it from here." He waved in the direction of the bridge.

The gambler was silent, then he said, "You cannot find a peril so great that the hope of reward will not be greater."

Wilson nodded, digesting this.

"Prince Henry the Navigator told that to one of my ancestors five hundred years ago. His name was Gil Eannes; he was the first white man to sail around the hip of Africa, which was thought impossible. And I extend the same advice to you."

"Thanks," Wilson said.

"But the next time, you may be sure, the peril will be much greater, Mr. Lander." And the window hummed up again, and the car pulled a U-turn and bumped over the cobbles into the brightening city.

Wilson followed the fading stars across the bridge and through the bare industrial streets of the Rubicon District. A few of the warehouses showed activity; the delivery trucks along Overlook Avenue were warming their engines. When he reached his apartment, the clock on the mantel read 5:20 A.M. He had to be at work in little under three hours. He took off his jacket and shoes and emptied his pockets of comb and wallet and house keys, the torn half of a playing card—the jack of hearts—and something else, two crumpled five-hundred-dollar bills. It was more than he took home in two weeks of work at the Tea Exchange.

When he got out of the shower a half hour later, the phone rang. He stood dripping on the bathroom tiles and let it ring until his machine picked up.

"Wilson, I know you're there," Cricket's voice called through the speaker. "Answer the phone."

He wrapped a towel around his gut and went out into the living room. "Do you always call at six in the morning?" he said when he picked up the receiver.

"No, but this is important," Cricket said. "I wanted to tell you last night, but you blew me off."

"I didn't blow you off, I—"

"Hush," she interrupted, "I've got a ship. A fancy experimental sailing yacht called the *Compound Interest,* out of Santa Barbara, California. This incredibly rich investment type is in the middle of sailing around the world. Put in yesterday for supplies, and a couple of the crew deserted to get married. So they need a navigator's mate and an assistant cook, and I thought—"

"Cricket, wait a minute."

"What?"

"I don't know the first thing about sailing, and I don't travel well. I told you that."

The phone crackled with morning static.

"Hello?" Wilson said.

"Wilson," she whispered at last, "do you know what a sailor is? I was going to tell you the day we had lunch, but I didn't get the chance. Do you know what a sailor is?"

"Someone who sails," Wilson said.

"Wrong," Cricket said. "A sailor is a guy looking for a way out."

Wilson didn't say anything.

"The hypos are upon you, Wilson," Cricket said. "I can smell them on your clothes. Something's eating at your guts. I count it high time you get yourself to sea."

"That's ridiculous," Wilson said, but his voice wavered a little.

"Do you have thirteen hundred dollars on hand?"

"No," Wilson said.

"Then I can loan you the money. You're going to need it for some gear and for your assistant cook's license. There's actually some sort of exam, but we can waive all that. I've got connections at the union. Can you peel potatoes, fry an egg? That's all you need to know."

"Cricket—"

"Meet me at the Mariners' Union Hall downtown today at noon. I'll take care of the paperwork, but you'll need to sign everything and hand over the money in person."

Wilson looked over at the two crumpled five-hundred-dollar bills lying with his keys and comb on the foyer table. The tarot cards were there still, propped against a vase full of withered flowers that had been fresh when Andrea gave them to him a month before. He closed his eyes for a second and saw Cricket's hair in the moonlight, glowing against the dark nights of strange and doubtful seas, the smell of jungle islands in the air, the salt tang of faraway lagoons,

Southern Cross rising on the horizon. Dread tugged him back to reality.

"No, Cricket," he said at last. "I can't go with you."

"Why not?" She sounded disappointed.

"I just can't."

"Look, are you happy where you are? With your life? Because it doesn't seem to me—"

"There's too much holding me here."

"Like what?"

"I'm not going to explain myself to you at six in the morning."

"Come on, Wilson—"

"No."

When he hung up the phone, he went into the kitchen and ate his breakfast, a bowl of bran cereal, which he munched slowly and carefully. Then, he went into the bedroom, put on a fresh blue button-down, a pair of dress khakis, a flowered tie, and a pair of tasseled loafers, which he spit-polished with a paper towel, and he thought about the day ahead. Offices have an unforgettable stale smell; they smell of beige plastic and fluorescent lights and powdery dust no one can see.

Soon it was 7:00 A.M. In a half hour, Wilson would walk six blocks down to the roundabout and catch the bus into the city. But now, he went into his bedroom with a screwdriver from the box under the kitchen sink, and took the air-conditioning unit out of the bedroom window and pulled open the casement. The bright stars were gone now, given way to the haze of another morning—who could say when the stars would come like that again?—and the city steamed banal in the ordinary light.

Wilson sat in the window for a long time, legs dangling against the side of the building, a warm wind on his face, missing buses and watching the big tankers of the Black Star Line, long as city blocks, rise off their moorings in the channel below.

PART TWO

ABOARD
THE
COMPOUND
INTEREST

1

THE *COMPOUND INTEREST* SAT low and gleaming in the water at the Presidential Slip of the Harvey Marina.

" '. . . eighty-five feet from stem to stern, her radical new carrot-shaped hull has been wind tunnel–tested in California by NASA scientists,' " Cricket read aloud from a xeroxed copy of an article out of July's *Yachting News*. " 'An onboard computer gauges the currents, satellite uplinks give precise coordinates,' blah, blah, blah, 'the experimental conical sails of tough, weather-resistant Mylar fibers raise and lower themselves as if hoisted by a crew of ghosts—' Disgusting, don't you think?" Cricket folded the article into the pocket of her jeans. "And you should see what goes on belowdecks. It's like a goddamned hotel down there. Staterooms, offices, showers. On a sailboat. There's even a walk-in refrigerator full of all kinds of food. Apparently the owner is a real heavy eater, a big gourmet. That's where you come in."

They stood on the concrete pier just below Marina's in the Marina, its chartered terraces now filling up with the lunchtime crowd. The morning haze had burned off to blue sky, and the sun shone high and bright directly above the Harvey Channel. The *Compound Interest*'s strange conical sails stood out against this brightness like two huge folded white beach umbrellas.

"All that stuff sounds good to me," Wilson said. "The more comfortable the better."

"You don't get it," Cricket said, but she didn't try to explain.

They went up to Marina's for lunch on the terrace because it was only a few steps away. Wilson always seemed to end up there, perhaps because he hated the place so much. He ordered the lunch special of crab cakes and asparagus spears wrapped in ham, and Cricket ordered a glass of wine and the guacamole-shrimp salad. Waiting for the food, they sat enveloped in an awkward silence. They were still strangers, really, on unfamiliar ground. He watched the professional lunchers from the Financial Mile, half afraid he'd see Andrea coming through the crowd. What could he say to her?

Cricket's rope-scarred hands looked out of place against the creased white tablecloth. She put them in her lap and nodded at the sleek vessel moored below.

"I'll tell you what," she said, "that ugly tub should be called the Ignoble Experiment. I don't like the way she sits in the water. Too low. Like a submarine."

"O.K.," Wilson said, relief in his voice. "So you're not shipping out."

Cricket turned quickly, a strand of her coppery hair loose and snaky along her neck. "I may not like her looks, but she's safer than an aircraft carrier. You read the article. Cost something like a hundred million dollars to develop and build. Got everything, all the latest equipment. Can't sink."

"That's what they said about the *Titanic*."

Cricket frowned into her dark sunglasses and shook her head. "There's too much negativity in your life," she said. "You need a change of air, a new perspective."

Maybe you're right, Wilson thought, but he didn't say anything.

A few minutes later the waiter, a fey mustachioed youth, wearing a white dress shirt and bib overalls, brought the food. Wilson munched hopelessly on his crab cakes and asparagus, and when he looked up again, Cricket had already finished her salad and was staring right at him, sunglasses off, green eyes shining with an uncomfortable light.

"You've heard of Dwight Ackerman?" she said.

Wilson blinked. "You mean the Wall Street guy?"

"Yeah, the one they call the Attila the Hun of Mergers and Acquisitions." Cricket leaned close at this and lowered her voice. "It's his ship. They don't tell you in the article, but I've got the inside scoop. He plans to sail it across the Atlantic, around the horn of Africa, and up into the Indian Ocean. That should take something like nine months. When we reach Rangoon at the beginning of next fall, twenty-five thousand dollars will be deposited in your account over here. If you go the rest of the way, another twenty-five thousand dollars is yours when we make San Francisco. Fifty thousand dollars for eighteen months' work, all expenses paid. That's fifty Gs in the bank when you get home. Not fucking bad for an ordinary seaman. So, what do you think of that?''

Wilson stopped munching on his crab cakes and thought about it for a moment. The most ridiculous of schemes can be seen in a new light when there's a lot of money involved.

''I guess that sounds all right,'' he said at last, and was prepared to feel good about the whole thing, but suddenly a buoy in the channel sounded its bell three times and then went abruptly silent. A distant tolling that seemed to reverberate ominously in the too-bright sky of noon.

2

THE REST OF THE day passed in a blur. None of it seemed real to Wilson. He was dreaming a dream about a man who was about to leave an ordinary, settled existence of bus rides, fax machines, and canned soup for the unknown perils of the sea. This man didn't seem to resemble the Wilson he knew, the ordinary fellow plagued by uncertainty and dread that he woke up with every morning. Soon, he would snap out of it, find himself back at the office at his computer terminal, Andrea hovering tense in the background.

But for now, Wilson let the dream continue and took Cricket out to his apartment on the Rubicon bus. There, he changed out of his work clothes and packed the few items in his possession that might be suitable for a long voyage. Cricket lounged on the couch watching a game show on Wilson's small black-and-white TV. She had no interest in the books, mostly ancient classics and archaeological texts, that completed the backdrop of his life.

"You should thank God that you can't take any of that shit with you," Cricket said when they went down the narrow stairs into the street.

"What shit?" Wilson said.

"All those books," she said. "Sophocles, Aeschylus, all the rest of those dead white bastards. Books are bad for the soul. Took me awhile to learn that. They make you forget about real life."

"So what's real life supposed to be like as far as you're concerned?" Wilson said.

"Full of action," Cricket said. "What else?"

They took the bus back across the river. As they bounced over the potholes of Buptown, windows rattling, Wilson told Cricket about his experience at the cockfight. He had been reluctant to say anything, reluctant to confirm the odd opinion she had of him—he was an ordinary guy, not a gambler or an adventurer—but it had been one of the most extraordinary evenings of his life so far.

Cricket listened quietly, her face reflected as a sunny blur in the gravel-scratched glass. "Yes, I know all about that," she said when he finished. "You were great. A real hero."

"You were there?" Wilson said, surprised. "I didn't see you or any other woman in the crowd."

She shook her head. "I got there really late, with some friends. Just in time to see you throw your money away on those two miserable Bupus. Then you jumped down from that car, and I lost you in the crowd. A few minutes later, someone said you had left in a limousine. So how much did you win?"

Wilson hesitated. Suddenly he felt ashamed of himself. "Sixteen thousand," he mumbled.

Cricket grinned and squeezed his arm. Her grip was like iron. "Ha!" she said. "The man who doesn't gamble."

"I'm not a gambler," Wilson insisted. "I don't want you to get the wrong idea."

"Is gambling against your religion or something?"

Wilson shrugged. "Gambling caused a lot of friction between my parents. My mom always wanted my dad to settle down, get a real job. He kept really strange hours and was never around when you needed him, that's what I remember most. And we were either rich or poor; there was no in between, no stability. Don't get me wrong, Dad was not a compulsive type. Gambling was a business to him. He always played the smart odds, and he never lost real money. But I remember arguments through closed doors, my mother crying. It wasn't great."

They rode along a few stops in silence. Bupandan women, their heads wrapped in colorful scarves, got off and on, dragging three or four children behind.

"I guess it can be tough if you're like them," Cricket said, "if you have kids. Do you have any kids?"

"None that I know of," Wilson said.

They got off the bus at the corner of Lowry and Cantor and walked over into the Bend to the army-navy surplus place on Allen Street. There, Wilson picked out a compass and jackknife, a dual-lens flashlight, a large canvas duffel bag, a rain poncho, deck shoes, several sweaters permeated with a waxy, waterproof substance, cans of insect repellent, and, at Cricket's insistence, a pair of army-issue night-vision goggles.

These odd binoculars reminded Wilson of an old-fashioned stereopticon, the Victorian visual toy that made images of famous places and people look three-dimensional, and he recalled the stereopticon and box of slides he had found at the bottom of a mildewed trunk in the attic of his great-aunt's house in Warwick years ago. He had stayed at the old woman's house on forlorn holidays away from the Catholic orphanage-school where she had sent him after his mother's death. And now, as he fitted the night-vision goggles across the bridge of his nose, he half expected to see some of those old sepia slides again: Queen Victoria, President Taft, Fatty Arbuckle, the Cathedral at Chartres, the Sphinx in Egypt, the lobby of the Empire Hotel in Parkerville, complete with spittoons, overstuffed sofas, and potted palms.

But the night-vision goggles showed only a few vague shapes outlined in hazy static.

"These are no good," Wilson said.

Cricket took them off his face, made a few adjustments, peered through the eyepieces at the cash register overhung by the canopy of a World War II–era silk parachute. "They're fine," she said. "It just has to be dark for them to work properly."

"One hundred seventy-five bucks!" Wilson fingered the price tag.

"You never know when someone will come at you in the dark," Cricket said, and threw them into the basket.

Outside again, along Allen Street, Wilson paused at a secondhand bookstall and picked out a few of the longest volumes he could find: An old Modern Library version of *Don Quixote,* Gibbon's *Decline and Fall of the Roman Empire,* Caulaincourt's *With Napoleon in Russia,* Steadman's *History of World War One,* and a lurid fifties-era paperback edition of *Manon Lescaut*—described in hysterical jacket copy as a novel of "betrayal and obsessive love"—by the eighteenth-century French priest, the Abbé Prévost.

Cricket stood by, her arms crossed in disgust. "Dead weight," she said when Wilson stepped over with his bag of books.

"I'm not going on an eighteen-month voyage without anything to read," Wilson said.

"You think you're going to have time to read?" Cricket said. "Minute I catch you reading, we stick a mop in your hand."

"You're anti-intellectual," Wilson said.

"No," Cricket said. "I'm just anti that shit, whatever it is that's turned you inside out."

3

I<small>T WASN'T UNTIL THEY</small> reached the worn stone steps of the Mariners' Union that the reality of the situation hit him. Wilson felt his chest contract, and he sank to the bottom step, short of breath. Annoyed and concerned at once, Cricket stared down at him.

"What's wrong now?" she said.

Wilson's white face was reflected in the darkness of her sunglasses. He made an inarticulate gesture. The stained Beaux Arts–era Mariners' Union Hall rose up behind like the ruins of an ancient fortress. From bathtub-shaped niches in the facade, greening bronze statues of the great mariners stared out, their empty eyes full of the sea. There was Columbus holding the terrestrial globe, Magellan with astrolabe and sword, Sir Francis Drake cradling a model of the *Golden Hind,* Captain Cook peering through a telescope that had long since rusted from his hands.

Cricket sighed, unshouldered her bag, and sat on the steps beside him. "Everything's arranged," she said. "All you have to do is go inside and sign your name on the dotted line—Lander, Wilson, ordinary seaman. Vessel, *Compound Interest,* bound for Rangoon and points east—and tomorrow at this time all the crap will be behind you."

She meant the city and its streets thick with people, the world full of complications, and roads leading to and fro across undulations of landscape—the entirety of Wilson's life on solid ground.

"I can't go," he said in a hoarse whisper. "I don't know what I was thinking. I'm sorry."

"What about all the stuff you just bought?" Cricket said.

"You can have it."

"Don't do this," Cricket said.

"Tell me one thing," Wilson said. "Why me?"

Cricket looked at him through her sunglasses, then she looked away. "These long voyages can be really lonely," she said at last. "No one to talk to, no one to . . . Well, let's just say that I liked your face the day you came into Nancy's store with those ridiculous tarot cards. You seemed lost. Right then, I decided to take you away with me. And there's something else. A practical reason."

"What?"

"Guess."

"No."

"I need a good gambler in my life."

"Why?"

She gave an ambiguous shrug. "I'll tell you later about that," she said. "When I know you better. Call it the story of my life."

"Cricket, I'm not—"

"I know what you're going to say," she cut him short. "It was beginner's luck. O.K., maybe you could say that about the dogs last week, but not about the cockfights last night. My God, you were brilliant."

"Almost got myself killed."

"But you didn't. You were brave."

"I was scared shitless."

"That's what being brave is all about."

Wilson put his head on his knees and was silent for a while. The grime of the city filled the cracks in the old stone. Across the street a construction site pounded away, sunlight on the red-brown musty earth dug up by a backhoe. Such places always made him shudder. He closed his eyes and saw a black girder falling through the sky. Then Cricket put her hand on his shoulder, and the girder vanished before it hit pavement, and Wilson opened his eyes and looked up. She was standing above him, sun behind her coppery hair like a halo, one thick hand extended.

"Come on," she said.

"You don't really know anything about me," he said.

"Don't worry, we've got plenty of time ahead of us for that."

Wilson stood up and took Cricket's hand, and she pulled him over to the bronze mermaids that guard the portals of the Mariners' Union, their bronze breasts worn to a dull metallic sheen by generations of sailors copping a feel.

"Go ahead," Cricket said. "Kiss her tit. This one's Stormy; that one's Windy. You get your choice."

"You're kidding," Wilson said.

"No," Cricket said. "You've got to kiss it. Been a tradition for all first timers for years. Brings good luck on the voyage."

Wilson felt stupid about it, but he did what she said. He kissed the bare metal nipple of the nearest mermaid to a faint acrid, brassy taste. Cricket laughed and took his hand again, and they crossed the threshold together into the echoing shadows of the union hall.

4

IN THE EVENING, THE wind blew high and steady from the southeast. The sky was touched with green and gold below the dark layer of night. Waves beat against the seawall. The moon pulled the tides of the world. All roads seemed to lead away from home. Duffel bag over his shoulder, Wilson felt the dread curled inside him like a sleeping animal, but he also felt calm and resolved. He walked with Cricket along the boardwalk on Blackpool Island. Black rocks, some large as boulders, led down to the dark water. Aluminum fishing skiffs rocked violently on the waves at their moorings below the pier. Wilson saw the faint silhouette of a departing tanker on the horizon.

They went to Bazzano's at the far end of the Blackpool Amusement Pier. Cricket chose a table on the bricks beneath the lights of the loggia, which is open to the sea. A few hipsters slumped at the old tin-topped bar inside, drinking espresso and smoking French cigarettes. The waiter was a squat Peruvian man with a face the color of a beet. He seemed distraught when they both ordered steaks; no one orders steak at Bazzano's which was famous for its Italian-style seafood. The restaurant was an institution in the city: Open continually since 1908, its walls were decorated with scenes of the simple life in a Sicilian fishing village, painted in bright, fanciful colors that had faded with the century. After a decade or so of decline and a diminishing tourist trade, Bazzano's had caught on with the young, artsy set that lived in the garrets and lofts of the Bend. The Terminal Street Ferry made the round trip four times a night, bringing Bend bohemians shambling up from the foot of the pier with their sideburns, their ancient thrift store suits, their vague hopes, their beautiful tattooed women fleeing the possibility of life in the suburbs. Bazzano's, Wilson had read recently in the Life section of the *Dispatch,* was one of the last unvarnished relics of the city our grandparents knew, a metropolis full of gangsters and so-cialites, bootleg gin, cigarettes, lipstick, and love affairs. Not exactly true, Wilson thought, but modern life was so relentlessly unroman-tic, and Bazzano's had somehow managed to maintain a certain atmosphere.

The steaks were a long time coming. The Peruvian waiter sent a Peruvian boy, perhaps his son, who explained that the steaks had been fetched up from the basement freezer, were hard as rocks, and needed to thaw a bit more before cooking.

"Don't you people have a microwave?" Cricket said. "Stick the steaks in and switch on the defrost setting."

"No microwave," the boy said.

"Maybe we should change our order to scallops," Wilson said.

Cricket shook her head. "No way," she said. "How much steak do you think we'll get in eighteen months at sea?"

"I thought Friday night was steak night on every self-respecting sailboat," Wilson said.

"Funny," Cricket said.

They didn't speak for a while. The dark deepened, but there was still a glow behind the skyline in the west. Wilson felt shy and didn't know what to say. The animal in his gut woke a little and began gnawing at his resolve. Then the steaks came, and they were a little charred but not bad, and there was the house red wine in a carafe and a side order of thick spaghetti.

"I'm really doing this," Wilson said almost to himself.

"Look in your wallet," Cricket said.

Wilson looked through his card carrier and pulled out the new laminated seaman's identification card. The terrible photograph made him look like a murderer or someone who had just gotten out of bed.

Cricket held the picture to the light and smiled. "There you are," she said.

"O.K.," Wilson said, "but what about my apartment, all my possessions—"

"Nancy will take care of the place for you," Cricket said. "She's going over Saturday to put your personal stuff in boxes. She's always got someone from her coven blowing into town, some sorcerer's apprentice. The place will be rented within the week."

Wilson finished his steak; then he cleared his throat. "Cricket, there's something else," he said.

Cricket narrowed her eyes. "You're not married? You don't strike me as a married man, unless that messy bachelor apartment of yours is some kind of scam."

"That's not quite it," Wilson said.

"A girlfriend?"

"Five years."

"Shit."

"But it hasn't been going too well lately."

"You better call her. I'll wait."

5

WILSON WENT INSIDE TO use the phone booth in the breezeway between the kitchen and the bathroom. A cook in a stained white jacket smoked a cigarette at the back door open to the night and the sea. More kids playing beatnik had filled up the stools at the bar. A young woman with blue hair did a strange writhing dance while two body-pierced men clapped their hands. In the dining room a blond German tourist couple sat eating the house specialty of scallops steamed in garlic and wine. Wilson's face felt hot, though the night was cool for September.

The phone rang in Andrea's apartment five times, six times. He was about to hang up, maybe send a telegram from some fly-infested, dusty city on the African coast, when Andrea picked up the receiver, out of breath.

"Hello?"

"Andrea . . ."

"Wilson, sorry, I just got in with some groceries. Hold on a minute."

He waited, his palms sweating.

When she picked up again, she said quickly, "Listen, I want you to know I'm not mad at you for not showing up at work today. You probably needed a break. I think I'm too hard on you sometimes, O.K.?"

One of the would-be beatniks at the bar took up a harmonica and the blue-haired young woman began singing in a high-pitched crazy voice.

"Where are you?" Andrea said.

"Bazzano's."

"What are you doing all the way out there?"

Wilson didn't know how to begin, then he blurted out, "Andrea, I'm going away."

Silence.

"Andrea, did you hear what I said?"

"I heard you," Andrea said. "It just took a minute to sink in." Her voice was calm and flat.

"Things haven't been good with us, not for a long time. We both know that," Wilson said. "There's nothing in my life right now that makes me happy. We fight, we make up, we fight, we make up. It's always the same. I get on the same bus; the same files are sitting on my computer at work. I feel like I can't breathe. I need a change."

"So where are you going?"

"Does it matter?"

"No, I guess not. How long?"

Wilson hesitated. "A year, two. Maybe longer."

There was a sudden crash, then the staticky sound of fumbling for the receiver. "You call me to tell me you're leaving for two years?" Andrea's voice came back angry a moment later. "After all the crap we've been through together, you tell me you're leaving me *over the phone?*"

"I'm sorry it worked out this way," Wilson said. "But I just don't have time to hash things out in person. I'm leaving in a couple of hours."

All at once, Andrea began to sob in great, broken gasps. Wilson listened, his stomach twisting in knots.

"Andrea, please," he said at last. "I'm really sorry. I feel like hell about this."

"You feel like hell? It's always about you, isn't it? You bastard, you—" But she couldn't finish. The sobbing went on for another few minutes, then subsided. "Wilson, I love you," she said, her voice calmer. "I know we don't talk about things. We need to talk more. I always thought we'd get married. I was sure of it. I've just been waiting for you to find out what you want to do with your life. That's all. I thought you'd decide to go back to school, something like that. That's what's making you miserable! Not me, not us! You don't know what to do with yourself. Running away isn't going to help.''

''It's all I've got right now, Andrea,'' Wilson said.

''Let's talk about this in person, O.K.? Maybe we could go to couples counseling. Things will get better, I know they will.''

''It's too late,'' Wilson said.

''Is there someone else? Are you there with someone else?''

''No,'' Wilson lied.

''You're lying,'' she said, and started to sob again. The sound was like a knife turning in his gut. When the conversation ended a half hour later, he found his face was wet with tears. He could still hear Andrea's last, frightened whisper.

''You're not coming back to me; you're never coming back to me. I thought after all these years—I thought you—''

But Wilson did not catch the rest because the line went dead. Whether she hung up on him or there was a problem with the connection, he never knew. He leaned into the fetid booth and squeezed his eyes shut and tried to hold in his tears with the palm of his hand. He had not expected this pain, these tears, but he couldn't say whether leaving Andrea or change itself had caused the reaction. He realized now that he hated change more than anything else in the world; change meant death and sadness. He hated change as much as he was drawn to it. Suddenly he remembered a vacation trip to Maine he and Andrea had taken three years before, when things had been good between them: On the way up they had pulled over somewhere in rural New England and spent the night in the car. They woke at dawn and walked out into a dew-wet field of waist-high wildflowers and made love there, surrounded by red and purple blooms, the sky bright as hope above. He could still remember the feel of her body beneath his, her breath close in his ear. No. It was best not to think of those things. He dried his face on his sleeve and went back out onto the loggia.

One arm hooked over the back of her chair, Cricket smoked a harsh foreign cigarette that she had bummed from someone at the bar. Another bottle of red wine sat half empty on the table. She looked up as Wilson approached, a long, appraising look, with something dangerous hidden in the depths.

"So, it's done?" she said when he sat down.

Wilson nodded miserably. He felt so rotten he could hardly speak.

"Hey, Wilson," Cricket said. She took his wrist tightly in her hand callused as any farmer's, pulled him over, and kissed him hard on the lips. Wilson's first impulse was to pull away; then he felt her breasts through the striped top, and he didn't pull away. She drew her lips off his after a minute or so, panting a little, but stayed close enough for Wilson to smell the cigarette and the wine on her breath.

"O.K.," she said. "That's all you get for a while."

"What do you mean?" Wilson said.

"Two reasons," Cricket said. "First, you're not ready yet. You're going to be thinking about your girlfriend for a while, I can tell. Second—and this is important—we have to pretend we're brother and sister. That's what your papers say, and that's what I told the captain of the *Compound Interest*. He's a tough old bastard named Amundsen, and if he finds out any different, he'll put us ashore the first chance he gets."

"You're crazy," Wilson said.

"No. It's because the last couple they had aboard jumped ship to get married. I told you, remember? He doesn't want that happening again. We've got to keep up appearances at least until we make the Azores. O.K.? That's only a few weeks away."

"Why the Azores?" Wilson said, but Cricket wouldn't answer. She kissed him one more time and leaned back and took up the bottle of wine. She pulled Wilson's glass across the tablecloth, filled it, pushed it back again. "Drink up," she said. "We've got to be aboard the *Compound Interest* for the midnight tide."

They finished the wine quickly, then stood and shouldered their bags and walked up the pier, in and out of the lamplight, quiet as two conspirators, the sea murmuring its furtive promises to the night at their backs.

6

PALE LIGHTS ALONG THE dark river. The jungle infested with silence. Small men in the underbrush hold flashlights beneath their chins like children at a Halloween party. Then, a screaming wells up out of nowhere, and the full moon above beats red against a black sky, and the river begins to froth and boil, something ancient rising to the surface, something terrible—

Wilson snapped awake in an unfamiliar gloom, unable to breathe, his T-shirt drenched with sweat. He couldn't see a thing. From all around came a deep, monotonous hush, familiar and alien at once, and the unmistakable surge of forward motion. The place where he lay was stuffy and windowless, and there was the sound of someone else breathing in the blackness nearby. If he didn't get a lung full of fresh air soon, Wilson knew he would suffocate.

In a panic he threw himself to the floor and stumbled off blindly. Instinct led him down a narrow corridor and up a ladder and at last out into the salt wind and the hazy dark of a warm night at sea. Here his lungs opened, and he fell back gasping against the bulkhead, and the events of the last twenty-four hours came flooding back. He was aboard the *Compound Interest,* making south-southeast across the At-lantic for the Azores. He had shipped out at midnight, chasing a beautiful woman and because life onshore had become intolerable to him—and for other reasons that were still not clear in his mind. He was sure the rightness of his decision would assert itself once this momentary panic subsided. After all, wasn't the possibility of drowning in a storm at sea better than drowning slowly in the day-to-dayness of life?

When Wilson could breathe again, he looked up and found himself facing the stern of the vessel, its white, frothy wake vanishing in the ocean black like a road disappearing in a snowstorm. But the night and the ocean and the ship's running lights could not obscure the vast bulk of the continent they were leaving behind. Just there, beyond the rim of darkness, a darker shape where the sky still held the light of cities. Wilson thought of baseball diamonds lit for night games, cocktail hour in a crowded bar, highways bumper to bumper with taillights at rush hour, and he thought of Andrea sleeping alone tonight, and he felt the terrible weight of the things he was leaving behind.

"Hey there! Why aren't you below with the rest?"

Wilson swung around to face a short barrel of a man standing just the other side of the hatchway. The man's wind-weathered face was covered with a bush of gray hair that seemed to grow in every direction. He wore a captain's hat, a garish yellow plastic rain slicker, and blue shorts. Thick, hairy legs ended abruptly in a pair of worn leather boat shoes. Wilson didn't need to be told that this was Captain Amundsen.

"I asked you a question, mister!" The captain took an aggressive step forward. "You're on my watch. Ship's rules, no extraneous crew members taking their leisure topside during the night."

Wilson stuttered out a response. He had needed some fresh air, he said. He was sorry. Hard to breathe below.

The captain stepped down to get a closer look. Wilson was suddenly aware of his own state of undress: a pair of green boxers printed with pink rabbits that had been a present from Andrea one Easter, a ratty old Ashland College T-shirt, faded and full of holes. His bare feet felt cold against the scrubbed wood of the deck.

"Come aboard tonight with Cricket Page?"

"Yes, sir," Wilson said.

"You're the brother."

"Yes, sir."

The captain scratched his beard. "That girl's one of the best damn natural sailors I've ever seen," he said. "And I've seen a few. I hope it runs in the family."

"I hope so too, sir," Wilson said.

"Of course, her navigational skills could use a little improving."

"Yes, sir."

The captain scratched his beard again. "Well, what can it hurt?" he said. "I was just about to light a cigar."

They went up the deck to the navigational octagon, a sunken area at the center of the ship between the two masts, protected on seven sides by a thick Plexiglas cowling. The Mylar beach umbrella sails folded and unfolded above, and the vessel stayed an even course in the prevailing light winds. A foul-weather top lay open to the sky bleary with indistinct stars. The ship's wheel, no larger than steering wheels found in ordinary sedans, was surrounded by a bewildering array of glowing radar screens and monitors showing crisp and colorful digital readouts. Gone the rope and wood, gone the brass instrumentation of former days. A computer terminal glowed quietly to one side, its clear plastic keys lit from within.

They settled on waterproof flotation pillows on a polished aluminum bench that made up one angle of the octagon. The captain crossed his short legs with some difficulty, reached into the pocket of his windbreaker, and withdrew a small wooden box. Inside lay a half dozen fragrant finger-size cigars, wrapped in gold foil.

"Cubans," he said. "Got 'em in Havana." He took a cigar out of the box, unwrapped it carefully, bit off the end, and lit up with the cigarette lighter from the console. Then he handed one to Wilson. For a while, the two of them sat back and drew on the cigars and watched clouds of pungent smoke blow off into the night.

"There's nothing like a good cigar," the captain said at last. "Everything else will fail you or grow wearisome, including women. But a good cigar, hell, that's a thing a man will never tire of."

Wilson smiled. A cool breeze from the west touched his face with gentle curiosity. Cigars reminded Wilson of his father. Years after his father's death in the wreck of the four forty-five, Wilson inherited an old cardboard suitcase of the man's possessions from his great-aunt's estate. The suitcase had contained rubber-banded piles of yellowed racing forms, six small notebooks heavy with mathematical formulas for placing bets at certain tracks, stock certificates issued by companies long since bankrupt—but there had also been a handful of silver foreign coins and a fancy box of imported cigars. These had been the extent of his patrimony, fifty hand-rolled Coronado Supremos, each sealed with wax in airtight glass tubes. He had smoked them slowly over the years, always lighting up at four forty-five exactly in honor of his father, at one of the outdoor cafés in Buptown or the Bend. Now just one cigar remained, nestled in its tube with his spare socks at the bottom of the closet in his apartment back home.

Wilson told the captain about the inherited Coronados with the theatrical gesticulations that cigars often seem to inspire in the amateur smoker. "When I get home again, and who knows how long that will be," Wilson said, waving his cigar in a rueful arc, "I'll buy a glass of the sixty-five-dollar Armagnac on the patio at the Cat and Cradle, and I'll smoke that last cigar very, very slowly."

The captain's cigar showed a steady glowing coal in the darkness. "At least you got something from your father," he said. "I never got anything from mine but a kick in the ass. My old man was a bishop of the Reformed Lutheran Danish Church. You weren't arguing with him, you know; you were arguing with God. When I was twelve, I ran off to Copenhagen and took ship for Africa. The sea receives all kinds of orphans, mister."

The captain was from a small fishing village on the bleak Frisian coast of Denmark, where it rains most of the year. When the sun comes out, the people weep, get drunk, make love to their neighbors' wives, dance naked in the streets. The beauty of sunny days is too much for them; they go slightly mad until the rain comes back again. The captain had served on American vessels for thirty years;

his English was perfect, bore no trace of the gray, rockbound coasts of his youth.

"Amundsen," Wilson said. "Any relation to the man who beat Scott to the pole?"

"None," the captain said. "A bunch of pasty-faced churchmen in my family for generations. I'm the first in a hundred fifty years to get some wind in my hair."

The sky above the sails brightened. A dull purple grew on the horizon, and the running lights began to dim. A button on the navigational console blinked on and off three times. Captain Amundsen threw up his hands.

"These damn computers," he said. "They tell me dawn is coming as if I couldn't see it for myself." He stood, made some quick adjustments, and turned to Wilson. "You'd better get below. Get some sleep. It'll start soon enough."

Just as Wilson reached the hatchway, the wind picked up and the sails spread themselves above like wings, and in that breathy silence peculiar to wind and sail, the vessel heeled in a straight run toward morning.

7

THE *COMPOUND INTEREST* WAS temporary home to four human beings and a rumor, Dwight Ackerman. Wilson spent hours every morning toiling beneath the iron thumb of a diminutive Vietnamese cook named Nguyen, but the man they cooked for didn't seem to exist outside the prodigious appetite that made Wilson's presence on the ship necessary.

They fed their invisible master like a wild animal in the zoo. Once a day, a little after noon, Nguyen delivered a massive tray of food into the mouth of Ackerman's cave—the forward suite of stateroom and office from which the billionaire never emerged. The plates came back an hour later, licked clean. Wilson pictured a freak the size of a house stuffed into the bow of the ship, a behemoth wearing a polo shirt big as a tent, arms like joints of ham. Or nothing, a devouring void.

The routine was always the same. Wilson rose bleary-eyed at 5:00 A.M. and stumbled through the gloom to the galley. Still half asleep, he attempted to decipher instructions written in yellow chalk in the cook's barely legible scrawl on a chalkboard fixed to the bulkhead. The next two hours were filled with any number of menial tasks in preparation for the onslaught to come. Wilson lit pilot lights, sharpened knives, chopped onions and a dozen other vegetables, beat eggs, gutted fish, shelled shrimp, deboned chicken, tenderized cuts of pork and beef with a leather mallet, and threw all the scraps out to sea for the sharks following in the vessel's wake.

At 7:00 A.M. exactly, Nguyen appeared, wearing a spotless white double-breasted chef's jacket and improbably tall chef's hat, and the real work began on the *menu du jour,* usually Vietnamese in character: On a typical morning, they made spring rolls, lemon chicken, shrimp curry, barbecued spareribs, cinnamon beef, Saigon fish soup, scallion pancakes, boiled dumplings, twice-cooked pork—these just a sampling of the complicated dishes that could easily exhaust the entire repertoire of a good-sized Vietnamese restaurant back home. Ackerman had become addicted to the subtle cuisine of Indo-China while serving in the Quartermaster Corps during the War.

Wilson's job was more like battle than cooking. The little cook barked orders and darted around as if he were under artillery fire at Khe Sanh. The galley was a tight, airless corridor squeezed between the ready room and the forward hold. Stainless steel gas burners, a convection oven, and a refrigerator filled half the narrow space; small as he was, Nguyen managed to fill the other half with the force of his personality. He looked about thirty-eight but was probably closer to sixty, his skin brown and thick as an animal hide, after the manner of men who have spent too much time out of doors. A long, ragged scar bisected his left eyebrow; the back of his right hand showed a faded tattoo of the Legion's five-pointed bomb insignia, surmounted by the regimental motto *Marche ou Crève*.

To the natural peevishness of the chef, Nguyen added the career soldier's love of discipline. He had learned his trade from the French in the days before Dien-Bien-Phu, had cooked for a Foreign Legion regimental mess, then for the American Army before Ackerman found him in a restaurant in Saigon. His chef's whites didn't seem to suit him. Wilson saw the man squatting in the jungle in camouflage and khaki, Sten gun slung over one shoulder.

Of course Wilson could do nothing right. He diced and deboned too slow, couldn't sauté an onion, didn't even know how to scrub pots properly.

"I think you raised by a family of stupids, joe!" Nguyen screamed at Wilson on his first day as cook's assistant. "How you get cook license? You listen too much Buffalo Springfield, I think! And Mr. Jimi Hendrix! I think you smoke Mary Jane before work and you hear rock and roll banging around your head when you supposed to concentrate on food! Purple Haze in your brain right now, yes?"

The cook had received the impression during the Vietnam War that Americans spent most of their time doing drugs and listening to loud music. Not only had these vices lost the U.S. a sure victory, Nguyen insisted, but they continued to foul up the lives of Americans everywhere.

"In States you all a bunch of drugged-out stupids wearing head-phones," the cook said. "It's amazing you can still take a piss without messing your pants!" Wilson tried to argue with him, but soon learned to keep his mouth shut. These theories, based on firsthand experience, circa 1967, were now set in stone. No amount of rational argument could break them down. Besides, there was just enough truth in what the cook said to dull Wilson's enthusiasm. He remembered all too well the bright eccentric kids in high school who blew their minds out on bong-hits and Thai stick, and ended up dumb and impotent or dead or worse—sorting packages on the line for the postal service for the rest of their lives.

After cleanup, at about two every afternoon, Wilson went topside and assumed the role of ordinary seaman. His hours on deck beneath the spreading Mylar and the bright sky more than made up for the heated torment of the galley. The ocean was a great field of poppies whose colors changed with the changing light: ultramarine at three, iris blue at five, lavender at sunset, then black with the darkness that dropped down above the masts like velvet cloth over a parrot cage. There seemed no end to the water and sky, the horizon a pale demarcation at the farthest distance.

Wilson was speechless in the face of this severe beauty, dazzled by wind and sun and stars, by the immense, lovely emptiness of the waves. When on watch in the bow cage, his rapt attention to the simplicity of his new environment achieved something like the intensity of meditation, and it seemed that the old fearful, dread-haunted Wilson was emptying out at last, filling up with someone new. An untested person forming like a golem out of ocean air and the common mulch of experience and dreams.

Ten days passed like this. The *Compound Interest* cut like an arrow through the brightness, sails folding and unfolding in the wind, meal following meal in the cramped galley below. Wilson and Cricket rarely exchanged a single word. He had her promise that things would change after the Azores and didn't worry. She bunked in separate quarters, kept up a sisterly demeanor. But there wasn't much time to think about the situation—always something to do on board ship.

The good sailing held, the following winds and fast seas. Wilson slept the deep sleep of sailors that comes from weary limbs and sea air. The ocean lulled and unwound itself on all sides. Beneath the keel, the sand and shells of the continental shelf gave way to the dark, pure water, unimaginably deep.

8

ON THE ELEVENTH DAY out, in the morning, the *Compound Interest* crossed the twenty-seventh parallel at forty degrees west and passed from high winds and bright skies into the morass of seaweed and current-borne garbage known as the Sargasso Sea. The vessel sat becalmed, in the long hours after ten o'clock, awaiting the slightest wind. The beach umbrella sails flexed, found nothing, and settled back again with a mechanical sigh.

"I've never known the dirty stuff to come this far north," Captain Amundsen said. His charts showed good winds at this latitude, clear sailing. Wilson looked up from the brightwork, laid chamois and saddle soap aside for a few minutes, and came into the navigational octagon for a cigar. The captain did not like to smoke alone. The sea makes some men quiet, others garrulous; the captain was one of the latter.

"In my lifetime, I've seen the ocean's currents changing, the Sargasso getting nastier." He poked his Cuban in Wilson's direction. "Used to be just weeds. Now it's full of junk. Petrochemical waste floating along in rusty fifty-gallon drums—you name it. Look at this shit. It's the ocean's toilet."

Wilson shielded his eyes against the flat yellow sky. Gulls hung motionless above the masts. A powerful stench of dead fish filled his nostrils; clumps of tangled seaweed floated along like giant turds. The black water was foul with crumpled cans and plastic jugs, six-pack holders, and other bits of trash. A broken dining room chair floated by upright, its legs tangled in a clump of seaweed big as a traffic island.

"How does all this stuff get here?" Wilson said. "We're in the middle of the ocean."

"I've seen a busted piano, even the burnt-out hulk of a Volkswagen floating on the weeds," the captain said, studying the distance for a gust of wind. "Once saw three sealed wooden coffins bobbing along like corks. The currents bring it in. Your garbage scows come out of the major cities and dump illegally, just beyond the twelve-mile limit. The stuff has to end up somewhere. Here it is."

"Did you retrieve the coffins?" Wilson said, but didn't wait for a reply. A whiff of something indescribably foul from the port side tied a knot in his stomach. "Jesus, Captain, you've got two good engines ready to go. Can't we motor out of here?"

The captain shook his head. "Ackerman says no. He has some cockeyed notion about sailing round the world. And that means we sail; we don't use the engines except in emergencies."

"What's this?" Wilson said.

"This is waiting," the captain said, and went back to his charts.

9

THREE MORE DAYS PASSED in motionless torpor. The sun rose high and yellow through the haze, and the clouds burned off, and the becalmed *Compound Interest* roasted in the dead heat. A few limp clouds sagged in the blazing white sky.

Just aft of the foremast was an open-air gas grill, covered by an aluminum cap when not in use. On the evening of the third day, at the invitation of the owner, the ship's company assembled around this piece of hardware for an ocean barbecue. As the sun set over the Sargasso, Nguyen removed the cap, struck a match, and set ten sirloin steaks to sear in the yellow and blue gas fire. He brushed each steak carefully with marinade, turned the red meat into the flame with a professional flourish. Soon, the rancid air filled with the familiar backyard smell of grilling meat. This was a special occasion. The crew survived mostly on sea rations; real food was reserved for the billionaire.

Dwight Ackerman emerged blinking from the forward hatch, his nose in the air. The Sargasso, almost tolerable at this twilight hour, smelled like a big dog on a hot afternoon.

"Glad you folks could make it," he called, then he stopped and blinked out at the endless expanse of muck and water, as if for a moment surprised to find himself at sea. He was a lean, timid fellow of about forty-five with a washed-out complexion and thick glasses that made his eyes big as the eyes of a bug in a cartoon. He wore a Lakers T-shirt and droopy Levi's rolled halfway up his white shins. The fading sun cast rose half-moon shadows through the glasses on his cheeks. Wilson was deeply disappointed. The man seemed relentlessly normal. He did not look like the mysterious devourer of fifteen-course meals, nor did he bear any resemblance to the famous shark of the financial pages, the corporate raider worth one and a quarter billion dollars.

"I sure am hungry," Ackerman said, and settled with a sheepish grin to the left of Nguyen. He crossed his legs, showing smooth, womanish ankles protruding from a pair of squeaky-clean baby-blue Converse low-tops. "Make yourselves comfortable." He gestured at the food. "Enjoy."

In addition to the meat, there was a watercress-walnut salad and rice pilaf and eggplant moussaka and garlic bread and a bottle of decent Chilean red. Wilson had helped with the preparations in the usual sweat and hysteria of the galley. But now he forgot about his unpleasant labors and thought of the last steak dinner at Bazzano's. He tried to catch Cricket's attention across the grill. Her face was shadowed, turned to the darkness on the eastern horizon.

Ackerman ate four of the ten steaks and nearly half the side dishes. He ate methodically, turning the plate around and sweeping the food before him like the hands of a clock. Wilson, amazed, watched him eat. It was probably some kind of accelerated metabolism problem. The shit that must come out of the man! No conversation interrupted this serious business of eating; there was only the scrape of silverware on china and the slop of seaweed against the hull. At last the billionaire belched and put his plate aside. He pushed his glasses up the bridge of his nose, blinked around at the assembled company, and raised his glass of wine in a toast.

"Well, crew! Let's say, to, uh . . . the Azores. How about that? Our next destination, right, Captain? If we ever get any wind, that is."

Captain Amundsen nodded imperceptibly.

"And I would like to point out that we have two new crewpersons with us. Welcome aboard! Would you like to tell us something about yourselves? I always like to know a few things about my employees." He turned to Cricket first.

Cricket put down her wine and looked up, her eyes blank and innocent. "Nothing to tell, sir," she said. "I'm a professional sailor. Always have been."

"Well, where are you from? Tell us that."

She shrugged. "The sea more than anyplace else."

"I see." He frowned and turned to Wilson. "Are you a professional sailor too?"

"Actually, before this voyage I worked in brokerage houses in the city," Wilson said. "Straight and Straight, the Tea Exchange—"

Ackerman's eyes widened behind his bug glasses. "You were a broker?" he said.

Wilson shook his head. "No, sir. I did support work in commodities."

"That's exactly what I'm doing right now, commodities," Ackerman said, excited. "Sort of a change of pace for me. Spent the week trading corn futures over the wire. Been a great week for corn, let me tell you."

"Yes, sir."

"You come down to the office sometime—heck, why not tomorrow afternoon? I've got a personal telecommunications satellite following along about two miles up. I'm hooked up to every commodi-

ties market in the world! We'll have a real nice chat." He seemed
sincere; the grin on his face made him look like a boy who had just
found a new friend. "Really, I mean it. Heck, here's an idea, why
don't you bring in my lunch from now on? I'm sure Nguyen's got
better things to do with his time. Wouldn't be bad to have company.
We could chat while I eat!"

"Yes, sir," Wilson said.

They lingered around the grill for another half hour over the last
of the wine. Ackerman and Nguyen discussed tomorrow's menu;
Captain Amundsen nursed his own thoughts in silence. The sudden
blackness of the night, and the vastness of the sea lent itself to
whispers. After a while Wilson felt Cricket beside him. She sat to
his right and a little behind, half in shadow. He glanced over and saw
the side of her face lit blue in the light of the grill. She wore a denim
work shirt and a pair of ragged white shorts. Wilson had never seen
her bare legs up close before; they were firm and muscular and sleek
as the flank of a dolphin. The back of his neck began to prickle.

"Wilson"—Cricket's voice came to him in a low hush—"I
don't want you to think I'm ignoring you."

"That's O.K., I've been busy." When he turned to her, she
shook her head.

"Don't talk, just listen."

Wilson turned back to the grill.

"Like I said, I want to play it safe at least till the Azores. Amundsen's been showing me the ropes. This tub's as complicated as the
goddamned space shuttle, but . . ." Cricket paused for effect. "I
have been thinking about you."

"Swell," Wilson said.

"But we've got to be patient. There's nothing I can do about the
situation right now. You bunk in the hold with the cook. I'm in a
hammock in a utility closet within spitting distance of the captain's
cabin. It's just too dangerous." She was silent for a beat. Wilson felt
her breath warm on his ear.

"Give me your hand," she whispered.

Wilson leaned away from the light and reached back. She took his hand, ran it up the side of her leg, and closed it between her thighs. After a moment, he began to feel a warm dampness against his palm.

"Just be patient," Cricket whispered. She squeezed him hard with her thigh muscles and let him go. Then she was back on the other side of the grill, her eyes unreadable in the darkness, a glass of black wine at her lips.

A little after midnight, a fresh wind swept the haze off the water and the stars looked like white points of frost in the empyrean. The beach umbrella sails filled with wind. The *Compound Interest* crossed the fortieth parallel at sixty degrees north on a dead run for the Azores.

Tossing in his narrow berth in the hold an hour later, Wilson felt a familiar ache for which there is only one remedy. He didn't get to sleep till dawn showed its first light over the bow.

10

ACKERMAN'S OFFICE OCCUPIED A large cabin that took up most of the forward hold. Except for the fact that all furniture stood bolted to the deck, the office would have looked at home in any corporate tower in any city in the world. There was a large glossy desk with a computer and printer, two fax machines and a telex, file cabinets, a video tele-conferencing setup, and a twenty-two-inch television monitor built in along the starboard bulkhead. Bookshelves held leather-bound ledgers and several hundred videotapes. Diplomas and photographs in cleverly curved frames hung from the port bulkhead above Ackerman's desk. A large square porthole let in the sea light, but this didn't make much difference: The moment Wilson stepped through the hatchway with Ackerman's daily mound of food in hand, he recognized it immediately—the plastic closeness, the pale, powdery smell of offices.

Over the next few days, Wilson spent an hour each afternoon in there watching Ackerman stuff his face. Afterward, they talked about basketball and the commodities market and played games of tick-tack-toe or hangman on scraps of paper. Except for the occasional startling financial insight, it was exactly like visiting with a kid in the third grade. Behind the desk strewn with spreadsheets and faxes, Ackerman seemed truly himself, at ease as he was not on the deck of the ship. He liked to arm-wrestle, indulged in boyish bathroom humor, told moronic stories, crumpled paper balls, and shot them for the trash can. "Two points!" he would shout when he made a basket, and Wilson would cringe.

But despite the jokes and the horseplay, Wilson sensed something pathetic about the man, something desperate. And at the beginning of the fifth day of lunch duty he came forward into the office with his tray to find Ackerman slumped over the desk, head down on his arm. Wilson stood unnoticed for a few seconds, then cleared his throat.

"Sir? Are you hungry today?"

Ackerman raised his head slowly. "Not really, but I better eat something." His eyes were puffy and bloodshot. He had been crying.

Wilson set the tray on the desk blotter and turned to the hatchway.

"No, it's O.K.," Ackerman sniffed miserably. "Sit down."

Wilson sat in the stenographer's chair beside the desk and watched while Ackerman ate. Today, for a rare change of pace, the meal was French. Nguyen had prepared a coq au vin, coquilles St. Jacques, boeuf bourguignon, escargots in garlic butter, a salade aux écrevisses, and duck à l'orange, followed by cheese and fruit and accompanied by a bottle of 'Neuf-du-Pape. Ackerman managed to down barely half this feast. Then he let out a long groan that was caught between a sigh and a belch and put down his spoon.

"You can have the rest if you want," he said. It was the first time he had offered any of his lunch. Wilson was tempted—sea rations generally tasted like cardboard—but as a matter of principle, he refused. Ackerman groaned again and leaned back in his desk chair. His face was the color of ash.

"Is something bothering you, sir?" Wilson said at last.

Ackerman gave Wilson a puffy-faced glare. "Given the hierarchical nature of our relationship," he said stiffly, "you being the employee and I the employer, I feel it is inappropriate to discuss deeply personal matters."

"No problem," Wilson said.

"But damn it!" Ackerman's voice cracked suddenly. "I've got no one else to talk to on this boat!" He pushed away from the desk, stepped over to the porthole, and leaned his head against the thick glass. "You know I've made a bundle these last couple of weeks," he said. "Twenty million dollars. And on the commodities market! I'm a fucking investment banker; I don't know anything about the commodities market! And the other day I calculated that I've netted something like four and a half billion dollars in my lifetime. Sure, for tax purposes, I'm worth just over a billion, but there's two billion more sitting in an unnumbered Swiss account that the IRS doesn't know about—" Then he swung around crazily. "Go ahead, tell the bastards. Try and collect your ten percent! I don't care anymore. Because I've finally realized the truth! Money can't buy . . . it can't buy—" He shook his head; he couldn't finish. Tears drained down his cheeks, and he slumped back into the chair behind the desk.

"—happiness?" Wilson suggested.

The billionaire rubbed his knuckles into his eyes and nodded. "Claire married me for my money. I guess that's obvious," he said, sniffling. "At the time I thought she loved me. I guess I was wrong."

"Claire?"

"My ex-wife. She's the French actress, Claire Denoyer." Ackerman brightened for a moment. "Maybe you've seen her movies— *Elena's Passion, Elena and the Bachelors*—there's a whole series of them."

"No, I don't think so," Wilson said.

"Oh. Well, you probably wonder why I bought this boat, why I took this voyage in the first place. Around the world? I hate the sea! Did you notice I hardly ever come up on deck? But it seemed like the only way to forget about the woman. Sometimes, when the market is jumping, I can go through a whole day without thinking of her. But not today. Today I've got it bad."

"What happened?" Wilson said gently.

Ackerman took a remote out of his desk. "This happened!"

The video monitor across the cabin flashed on, and Wilson almost fell out of his chair: On the screen a high-resolution, full-color image of a two naked people—a black man and a white woman— paused in mid fuck. They were doing it doggie style, the woman bent over the back of a flowered sofa, her face contorted in open-mouthed slobbery ecstasy, the man looming above her, one eye closed, a snarl on his lips, both hands pressed flat against her tanned ass cheeks, which were as perfectly formed as the halves of a pear.

"Pretty picture, eh?" Ackerman said. He pressed play, and the lovers rocked into motion, with the usual grunts and moans and sweat of the primal act.

"O.K.," Wilson said. "I get the point—"

But the billionaire didn't seem to hear. "That's Claire and her personal trainer. He was a washed-up pro football player who went by the name of Ironhead Jackson. I set up surveillance cameras all over our house in Santa Barbara and videotaped them for months. I also caught her on tape with two other men and with the maid, a seventeen-year-old girl from Venezuela—that's a pretty hot scene, let me tell you.''

Ackerman clicked up the volume, and the sounds of videotaped lovemaking filled the cabin, and his eyes grew round and crazy as he watched his wife rise to orgasm on the television screen, screeching like a banshee. This din proved too much for Ironhead. He gave a loud grunt and pulled out, spattering across Claire's backside. Then the two collapsed in a sticky, panting heap across the sofa.

Wilson was speechless.

Ackerman gave an odd smile and touched the remote. The screen went blank.

''I know,'' he said. ''It's just like a cheap porn movie. Lord knows, she made enough of those! All you need is that cheesy seventies music in the background. And the coitus interruptus! Classic! It was the man's preferred mode of birth control. I've got about three hundred tapes.'' He gestured dolefully at the bookcase. ''They did it about three times a day for six months. And during the whole time she was sleeping with me two or three times a week. We'd fuck—not perhaps as vigorously as that—but it wasn't bad either. I don't need to tell you the divorce was an open-and-shut case. Cut her off without a penny, and that's not easy to do in California. I hear she's a junkie now, living with some pimp in a cheap hotel on Sunset Boulevard in L.A.'' Ackerman leaned back and put a hand over his eyes.

Wilson was quiet for a while, thinking.

''If you ask me, Mr. Ackerman, the video camera is an evil invention,'' he said at last. ''Memory is a soft, forgiving thing. The Greeks made memory a goddess and gave her a name, Mnemosyne. She blunts the worst of it over time, softens the painful edges for us. But video is unforgiving. On video it's always there, the same sins over and over again. You can relive your most horrible moments frame by frame forever. Let me give you some free advice, sir. Get rid of the damn things. Let memory, as the Greeks might say, apply the healing balm of time. Cut your wife loose; drop every last tape into the drink!''

Ackerman blinked back new tears. ''I can't,'' he said. ''I still love her. These tapes are all I have left.'' Then he put his head on the desk and wouldn't look up.

After a while, Wilson exited quietly and mounted topside into the bright sunlight. He went forward to the bow cage and sat with the salt spray washing over him, the clean air filling his lungs. Up here in the wind, it was a bright Atlantic afternoon, sun falling back across the continent toward the western ocean, Africa somewhere up ahead, just off the starboard. But in the office below, in the powdery dimness, time stood still. There were no bright Atlantic afternoons, no stormy ocean midnights. Down there, as corn futures telexed in from around the world, it would always be the same raw half second before Ackerman's wife, taken by another man, reached orgasm.

11

THEY SIGHTED CORVO IN the Azores on October 17. It rose from the gray sea, a gray, attenuated shape shrouded in clouds. After nearly three weeks out of sight of land, it was hard to believe in the existence of such a thing: solid, immovable rock. The *Compound Interest* sailed around Corvo in four hours—it is a tiny island, not five miles across—and the captain pointed out Rosario in the misty distance.

''That's a town?'' Wilson said. He studied Rosario through the captain's powerful binoculars. He saw a half dozen white box houses strung in a line up the cliff of volcanic rock, a few fishing boats riding at anchor in the tiny harbor.

''Yes, it's a town,'' Captain Amundsen said. ''And a very old one. Awhile back a storm blew over a great old oak in the square. In the roots they found a pot of Phoenician coins. Amazing when you think about it, what fearless sailors the ancients were. Coming all the way out here from the coast of North Africa in square-rigged galleys, nothing but big rowboats, really. Hell, Africa is more than a thousand miles away. Those poor bastards probably thought they were going to sail right off the edge of the earth.''

In the evening they rounded the cape toward the inner islands, Flores lost in the night and the fog to the south. It took two more days of cold weather sailing to reach Gomez Point on Graciosa, and there, because the prevailing winds were against them from the west, the captain changed course for a straight run to Fayal. At dawn, Wilson saw signs of habitation on the headlands—the lights of towns, radio antennas blinking red from the interior—and the realization came over him in a rush of sadness: What a lonely life was to be had upon the sea! Always sailing along foreign coasts, making for elsewhere; elsewhere achieved just to turn around and sail back again across the dark and unknowable ocean. The sailor, Wilson understood now, was a wandering soul, never truly at home.

The Azores are a forbidding, volcanic archipelago where it rains much of the year; its towns are small and poor. But when the *Compound Interest* entered the harbor of Angra do Heroismo on Terceira at eight the next evening, Wilson thought he had never seen such a beautiful city: The whitewashed houses rose from the waterfront up a steep slope of cobbled streets and narrow stairways to a baroque cathedral, its spire decorated with colored lights. Along the quay, cafés and restaurants were full of patrons, and from somewhere on the wind came the sound of a woman singing a Spanish song. Wilson saw the cranes and derricks of industrial wharves off the starboard, the trawlers and tankers moored in the roads, the familiar black and green smokestack of Black Star Line cargo ships, the gray-mottled bulk of Portuguese Navy destroyers.

They tied up in the marina beside a large yacht flying the blue and yellow ensign of the king of Sweden. The crew was given four days' leave. Wilson packed his duffel and headed for Portuguese customs, a large nineteenth-century building of pink stucco at the end of a cobblestone wharf. Inside, it was like a bus station, the dirty marble floor littered with scraps of paper, long lines of crewmen from various vessels waiting to see the official for release to the outside. Captain Amundsen saved a place in line for Wilson.

"Atlantic traffic is picking up these days," the captain said when Wilson stepped up, unshouldering his duffel bag. "Just in the last couple of years. It's a very strange thing."

Wilson looked around at the sailors in line. He saw dark faces and light, men of all continents and nations. Many were dressed in cheap suits, hair slicked back, like tough guys in a gangster movie. A tall sailor behind played the harmonica, a soft tune quickening into a familiar Irish jig.

" 'Rocky Road to Dublin,' " Wilson said, tapping his foot. "Do you know that one?" He was a little giddy; the sensation of being on land was disconcerting. The rocking of the ship persisted in his legs, in his bones.

The captain frowned. He seemed disturbed by all the activity.

"Come on, it's shore leave, Captain," Wilson said, and put a convivial hand on the man's shoulder.

"I'm as glad to go ashore as the next fellow," the captain said. "But there's something unnatural about all of this."

"How do you mean?" Wilson said.

"I've been shipping through the Azores for thirty years, and I've never seen the kind of traffic that's come in and out of here in the last few years. Either the world economy's gone wild and someone forgot to tell me or there's something else going on."

"Like what?" Wilson was barely paying attention.

"Like some illegal trade," the captain said. "Drugs, contraband, who can say? Something sinister. Something out of Africa, it's always something out of Africa. And it's not just the Azores; it's the Cape Verde Islands and the Canaries. Riberia Grande, that used to be a dismal port, forgotten by the world, now it's like a damned boom-town. Same thing here. It's damned peculiar."

Wilson shrugged. His mind was elsewhere.

12

WILSON PARTED FROM THE captain an hour later, on a corner in the Baxia District. The captain got in a cab for the Hotel Cristobal, a modern high-rise at the edge of town. Wilson walked along the cobbles, lost for a few minutes. The streets were full. The air held the fragrance of old stones and earth. After a while, he stepped back into a doorway and watched the crowds pass. It was the beginning of the Festival of São Xoxsa, a Portuguese martyr who had been thrown to the sharks by Barbary pirates in the fifteenth century. Thickset peasants from the countryside went by barefoot, sacred relics around their necks, drinking grappa from inflated sharkskins. Dark women wheeled barrels full of yellow calla flowers.

The scrawled map in Wilson's pocket led him to a café called the Arquipleago. It was a small, dirty place, open to the street, with smoke-blackened beams and a gaudy, incongruous American pinball machine in one corner. Wilson took a table outside. Half a block down the dark leaves and flowering palms of the Parque Citadino. Young *ilhéu* couples strolled its sandy lanes in the dark, their voices reaching Wilson as a soft murmur. The waiter came, a young man slim as a bullfighter, with sideburns shaved to a point.

"*Senhor?*"

Wilson hesitated, then pointed to a poster in the window showing a raven-haired, buxom woman in a bathing suit posing beside an enlarged and distinctly phallic bottle of something alcoholic.

"*Uma botelha de aguardente?*" the waiter said.

Wilson nodded, helpless. The waiter brought a whole bottle of yellowish liquid and one small glass. Wilson tasted the stuff. It was a sort of brandy made from white grapes, strong and sour. He did a quick shot, and it burned the back of his throat.

"So you found the place?" Cricket sat down at the table a few minutes later, smelling of perfume. Wilson stared.

"You look great," he said.

She smiled shyly at him, then turned to call for another glass in Portuguese. "I'll join you," she said.

Tonight Cricket wore her hair pulled back in a French braid, a little dark eye shadow, and bright red lipstick. She had put aside her shipboard jeans and sweatshirt in favor of a bolero jacket of dark wool and a short, tight silky dress printed with blue and black flowers. A dozen thick bracelets jangled together on her left wrist. They were studded with stones and seemed made of a white metal that was far brighter and more lustrous than silver—platinum? Where would a common sailor get such jewelry? Wilson wondered. Then he put the question out of his head. She looked beautiful tonight. Right now, nothing else mattered.

When the glass came, she poured a shot of the yellow liquid and raised it in the light of the street. "We made it this far in that ship of fools," she said. "Here's to the next leg of the journey."

"Sure," Wilson said, and they both drank.

When they had finished half the bottle of aguardente, Cricket went inside to pay the waiter and came out again. Wilson tried to give her some of the crisp new Portuguese money he'd exchanged his dollars for at the customs house, but she waved him away.

"It's on me," she said. "Let's go."

"What about the rest of the bottle?"

"Bring it along."

They walked side by side without touching up the cobbled streets, past stone-fronted houses, shuttered against the night, turned up a narrow alley into a plaza where a bronze horseman sat on his horse pointing out to the sea, and went past him up two flights of stairs. Now, they were out of the lower town on quiet, residential streets.

Some of the houses here were painted powder blue with white trim, others pale yellow with blue trim. Across the terra-cotta back of the town Wilson caught a glimpse of the harbor below. Clouds ran across the moon. A black cat crossed in front of them, stopped and hissed, then disappeared into a cul-de-sac.

"Bad luck," Wilson said, shivering.

Cricket put her arms around him and pushed him against the side of a blue house. She kissed him; then she kissed him again.

"O.K.," Wilson said.

At the end of the cul-de-sac there was a small pension of two stories, its flat facade lit by three large plastic lanterns in the shape of owls. The lobby was a narrow hallway with one overstuffed easy chair and a bunch of calla flowers in a brass pot. The concierge, an old woman wearing an old woman's black dress and a dirty white cardigan, sat in the chair, dozing over a copy of the *Courier Ilheú*. On the cover Wilson recognized a picture of Michael Jackson. The concierge woke up when Cricket closed the door, and a brief exchange followed in Portuguese. They gestured at Wilson several times and spoke quickly in raised voices. After ten more minutes of bargaining, the concierge produced a key from her sweater, and Cricket took it and led Wilson up the stairs.

The room was large with a double bed on a raised platform and a window that opened on a straight view down the cul-de-sac, between the houses to the harbor and the sea.

"This is the only room in the place worth a damn," Cricket said. "The other ones look out on plaster walls or have an illuminated owl hanging in the window. Also, it's the only room with a big enough bed."

Wilson nodded. He felt unaccountably nervous. He set his duffel on a cane-bottom chair, put his hands in his pocket, and walked around the room. Bare wood floors except for a small oval throw rug; on the walls, a colored chalk drawing of the terraced fields of São Miguel and a fifties-era framed photograph of the queen of England in the scarlet uniform of the Horse Guards. In the bathroom, a deep marble tub with claw-and-ball feet. When he walked back into the bedroom, Cricket was already out of her jacket and dress, and she stood barefoot beside the bed, her arms elbow-twisted behind her back to undo the clasp of her black bra.

Wilson gaped from across the room, hands still in his pocket, the back of his neck sweating.

"Hey, you going to help me with this?" Cricket turned a coy shoulder.

Wilson crossed over and fumbled with the clasp, his hands trembling. The side of Cricket's face was lit a pale ivory by the reflected light of a plastic owl just beyond the window. Her back was smooth and muscular, the vertebrae like knobs of coral beneath a surface of shallow water. The bra fell loose, and Wilson reached around to take Cricket's breasts in his hands. He stood there quietly for a moment, his heart beating, feeling her nipples harden against his palms. Then he leaned forward and bit into the soft web of skin just above her collarbone. Cricket shuddered and pulled him down, and in another moment, Wilson couldn't quite say how, he was out of his clothes, and Cricket's legs fell open and they were rolling across the bedspread of the double bed in a room of an obscure pension on a distant island, girded at every point of the compass by the deep and somber Atlantic night.

13

THEY STAYED IN BED for two days, making love and telling each other stories of their lives. The sun came and went over Fayal and Pico, over São Miguel and Corvo, over all the islands of the Azores and over the dark and burgeoning continents hidden like flaws in the gem of the world. But they did not heed the changing light and lay oblivious in each other's arms, one inside the other, part of the vast, infamous compromise that allows one generation to pass to the next.

Wilson was delighted with Cricket's body. There seemed twice as much of her as there was of Andrea, and she was hard and soft in different places. The muscles in her back and arms were from honest work, not exercise—which is another form of indolence—and when he climbed on top of her, Wilson felt like he was climbing on top of something very solid indeed. It was only her hands that he found disturbing, though he did not tell her so. It was hard to get used to such hands on a woman. They were wider and thicker than his own and a good deal harder. They had held things his would never hold; a whole history of work and hardship was written upon them.

Perhaps Cricket could sense Wilson's reaction. She used her tongue more than her fingers when they made love, and lying together afterward, she would tuck her hands away beneath the sheets. He felt a little guilty because of this, though he also found her shyness a charming inconsistency. Each of us, he thought, has our own secret places, our cherished weaknesses. Then, on the morning of the third day, Wilson took Cricket's hands between his own and tried to kiss her palms.

Startled, she pulled away.

"Come on," Wilson said. "Give me your hands." A steady drizzle fell on Terceira now, and the light was no brighter than it is at eight in the evening in other latitudes.

"No, they're gross. I hate them."

"Come on, how can you hate a part of your own body?"

"That's easy," Cricket said, and turned her head away and the shadows of the rain from the window beaded across her face.

"Let me see them," Wilson insisted.

Cricket turned back to him slow and sullen, withdrew a hand and placed it on the sheet between them like a dead thing. Her eyes were dark; her hair matted and brown-looking across the pillow.

"It's not so bad," Wilson said. But it was bad, scarred and hard as a rock. Gently, he pressed his thumb into her Mons Venus, her Mons Jupiter, where the palmists say lie our desires and our fortunes. These bumps, usually soft and fleshy, were scuffed as the bottom of a shoe.

"Satisfied?" Cricket said, and she took her hand back and rolled away on her hip.

"So what?" Wilson said. "You've worked with your hands. Your life's been different from mine. That's all."

"Different? My life's been hell." It was a statement of fact, not self-pity. Wilson reached out to touch her, but she shrugged him off.

"What about the sea? I thought you loved the sea," Wilson said because he didn't know what else to say.

"Don't be an idiot," Cricket said, then she flopped over suddenly and laid her head on his chest. "I'm sorry," she said, and she put her hands on his shoulders, where they felt like the pads of a nervous animal. "I'm trying to become a different person. I've been too tough for my own good, and I've been very lonely. And I've done a few things that make me lose sleep at night."

"Like what?" Wilson said. The back of his neck prickled.

Cricket shrugged. "Later," she said. "When you know me better."

"What are we talking about here? Weird sex? Did you sleep with the crew of a tramp steamer? Did you kill someone?"

"Not sex. Who cares about that? We're not a couple of virgins here. Right?"

Wilson had to agree.

"Sure, I've probably had sex with too many people. But the worst part is I've never been in love. You asked me before we left why I wanted you along on this voyage. O.K., here's another reason: I need to trust somebody right now or I'll dry up inside. And there was a sadness about you that I thought I could trust with my own sadness."

Wilson nodded. "It's the dread," he said. He had noticed this in women. The very neurosis that made his life so difficult attracted members of the opposite sex. Some women went for the dread the way bees went for honey.

"The what?" Cricket said.

"The feeling I have that something bad is going to happen next, that disaster is always waiting just around the corner."

"I know that feeling," she said, and it sounded like she understood. "At any moment you're prepared to lose everything. That's why you're such a good gambler."

Wilson thought for a minute. "That's one way of looking at it," he said.

14

THAT AFTERNOON, THEY DRESSED and for the first time in two days went downstairs starving, to look for something to eat.

The concierge, drowsing over the same copy of the *Courier Ilheú,* looked up scowling and pointed to a hand-lettered sign over her easy chair.

"We missed breakfast," Cricket said. "We missed lunch too. Dinner isn't for another four hours. No eating between meals, those are the house rules."

"Oh, my God," Wilson said with alarm. "Four hours. I don't think I can wait that long."

Cricket nodded and narrowed her eyes and turned to the old woman. There was another exchange in Portuguese, this one rising to an argument, but Cricket was persistent. At last the woman threw up her hands, heaved out of the easy chair, which bore the permanent indentation of her bony rear end, and slammed off into the kitchen through a heavy door to the right. Cricket and Wilson followed.

"What did you say to her?" Wilson whispered into Cricket's ear.
"I told her if she didn't feed us, I'd break her face," Cricket said.

The kitchen was a large, pleasant, well-lit room with a fireplace, a white ceramic gas stove, and a large old-fashioned wooden sideboard along one wall. Pots bubbled on the stove and filled the room with the rich, delicious smell of food. A glass door opened onto a beautiful little moss garden at the center of which stood a crumbling plaster nymph, glistening in the rain.

"She looks cold out there," Wilson said.

Cricket didn't say anything.

They sat at a tile-topped table. The concierge ladled some of the food from the pots into pottery bowls, slammed them down on the table, and left. Cricket brought over plates and cutlery, a bottle of wine, and bread from the sideboard. They had sopa de Peixes, a delicious soup of fish and squid and shellfish; chicarrones, which are hot Portuguese sausages; and saffron rice. The wine was a red Verdelhoa, which, according to the label on the bottle, once graced the table of the tsars.

"This is great," Wilson said with his mouth full.

Cricket was too busy eating to respond.

When the rice and soup and sausages were gone, they sat sated, finishing the wine. Wilson already knew Cricket well enough to know that good food and wine put her in a confessional mood.

"Tell me more," he said, and filled her glass.

"About what?" she said.

"About you."

She took a quick gulp of the wine and lowered her eyes. "You really want to know?" Her voice sounded small and uncertain.

"Yes."

"I was a lot of trouble in the old days," she said after a pause. "I fell in with a pretty bad crowd my first year at Palmetto High. You know the type, beer-swilling shit-kicking dudes with bad-ass cars; only because it was an island, the thing there was cigarette boats with huge engines. I ran away a couple of times—once to New

Orleans, once to Miami—was in and out of juvie for the usual vandalism and drunkenness. Guess you could say I grew up pretty fast. In any case, my parents couldn't control me, so my dad thought I'd be better off at sea.

"When I was fifteen, he found me a berth as ordinary seaman on the *Jesus of Lubeck,* a rusty hulk of a cargo ship registered out of Rigala in Bupanda. Dad was good friends with the owner, a man we all called the Portugee, a pretty slick gambler who used to play a lot of high-stakes poker at Mazep's. The Portugee was on a losing streak that year, so he came on as captain to get himself away from the cards. That first berth was tough. Real back-breaking work. It was the one that ruined my hands. The Portugee worked me really hard, topside in all sorts of weather. And he was an unpredictable bastard because he smoked a lot of opium—black, sticky stuff he got in jars from Thailand. I was indentured to him for the next four years, supposedly under his protection. What a strange character! Too smart for life at sea, spoke sixteen languages. When he wasn't high, he was bored, and one day he decided to improve my education, as he put it. See, I had pretty much skipped school after the eighth grade.

"His cabin was full of books. He had everything, all the classics, in English, French, Portuguese, Spanish—you name it. We studied four and a half hours a day, starting just before dawn, every day for three years. Maybe that's why I hate all that crap to this day. Greek at four A.M. after barely two hours' sleep, followed by a day of full watches, then more of the same. Still, when I shipped out on that tub, I could hardly read the newspaper. Four years later I was reading Aristotle and Plato, Dante, Shakespeare, Byron. He was a big fan of Byron. I hate Byron.

"Then, one day, the Portugee decided he couldn't teach me anything more on his own and said it was time I go to a real school. He wanted me to go to college. I couldn't believe it. I was a sailor; that's all I ever wanted to be, I told him. But later, on the return crossing from Africa, he put in a course north-northeast, and we sailed into the harbor at New York City, and we tied up at old Pier 26, that used to belong to the old Flying Cloud Line, and we got into a cab and drove up the West Side Highway to St. Mary of the Flowers College, and he put me out on the sidewalk with my bag.''

Cricket slugged back the wine left in her glass and stared out at the moss and the wet in the garden. The moss was the richest green imaginable and looked softer than any bed.

''Go ahead . . .'' Wilson finally had to prompt her.

''So I was stuck at St. Mary's for two years, with the Portugee paying all the bills. It was horrible, worse than anything I had experienced at sea. I was ostracized, humiliated. The place wasn't much of a college. It was really a finishing school for rich, stupid New York chicks, who knew how to make a girl from the outside feel lower than shit. I wasn't like them at all. I had just come from the deck of a gypsy cargo ship, for Christ's sake! And before that, from the most obscure and backward islands in the Gulf of Mexico.

''The rich, I think, are the cruelest people alive; that's how they get their money. It didn't take the girls long to start in on me. My hands gave me away, like a servant trying to pass as an aristocrat in an eighteenth-century novel. I tried to get them massaged, manicured, but it was no use. I'm a big, tough girl, and I'm pretty touchy. If I heard one thing I didn't like, one peep out of one of those bowheads, I'd stick my fist in her face. 'You see this fist?' I'd say; then I'd let her have it. It got to the point where no one would speak to me, not a word—the silent treatment.

''Finally, I couldn't stand any more, and I robbed the poor box in the chapel right before Christmas, when it was stuffed full of donations from their fat-cat parents, and I ran off. I put my name up on the board at the New York Yacht Club and holed up in a cheap motel in Newark until I found a berth on a yacht bound for Valparaíso. And it was only six months later, back at sea in the middle of a storm, that I started to feel safe again. The wind was howling, and the ship was falling into the waves, and there I was, laughing my head off. The crew thought I was nuts. But I'm telling you, anything, even drowning, was better than the girls at St. Mary of the Flowers.''

15

WHEN THE WINE WAS gone, Wilson and Cricket went out to walk the streets of the town. Angra seemed like a dream in the misty light, its pastel buildings dulled by the fog and the rain. They walked down the wet steps into the lower town and along the commercial thoroughfares.

Here the street lamps were lit though it was barely four in the afternoon. Smoked sausages and duck carcasses hung in the windows of restaurants. Fishermen stood at the tin counters of cafés, wearing thick, oily turtleneck sweaters. They stared through the plate glass at the heavy sky, their eyes dark as a winter sea. Cricket pulled close to Wilson; the weather had turned cold with the rain. He pressed her hard palm into his soft one. The world was a cruel place; everyone knew that.

They stopped at a bar marked with the sign of the mermaid, filled with fishermen and drunken farmers from the interior. The floors of the place were old and warped, the white walls gray with years of cigarette smoke. They found a dark corner where the bar jutted out at an angle. Wilson bought two *digestifs*—Doulm, a liquor made from the figs that grow wild on the island. It was bitter and strong as grain alcohol.

''Wow,'' Wilson said, pounding his chest.

Cricket downed hers quickly without comment and put her glass on the scratched tin counter of the bar.

''Turn around,'' she said.

''What?''

"I don't want you looking at me when I say what I'm going to say."

Puzzled, Wilson turned to face the wall. Cricket stepped close behind, her mouth an inch from his ear. She spoke quickly, and there was a seriousness in her voice that struck a grim, hollow note inside him.

"Whatever happens on the rest of this voyage, you've got to stick by me," she said. "You've got to stick by me and do exactly what I tell you to do."

Wilson tried to turn and face her, but she put her rough hands on his shoulders and kept him facing the wall.

"What are you talking about? What's going to happen?" Wilson said, a note of panic in his voice.

"Sh! No questions! By saying anything to you now, I am violating a confidence that could mean my life. If you're not up to a little trouble, if your heart is weak, if you can walk away and not look back, now's your chance to do it."

Wilson stood rigid, unmoving. His hands felt clammy, his mouth dry. His dread told him to run. But what if the dread was playing a trick on him and he was running right back into its arms?

"Cricket—"

Her grip tightened on his shoulder. "No questions," she said, then she continued in a softer voice. "If you want to leave now, it's O.K. We had a great couple of days; a lot of people never even get that. You can go back to the pension and pack your things and fly out of here back to the States in the morning. If you don't have enough money, I'll give you some. But if you want to come with me, just turn around and kiss me and don't say a word about this conversation now or ever. Take a minute to breathe quietly, and when you're finished breathing quietly, decide. I know it's not fair, but it's the best I can do."

Wilson's shoulders sagged. Despite himself, his breath came in short gasps. Suddenly he heard the raucous din of the bar, the men talking and laughing, the accordionist in the corner playing "Lady of

Spain''; then just as suddenly, all of it was reduced to a faint buzzing in his ears. He closed his eyes and tried to look into the darkness of what would come ahead, but his intellect could not penetrate the cloud of unknowing. From somewhere near at hand came the shattering of a glass. Without thinking, he turned and took Cricket in his arms and kissed her on the lips.

PART THREE

THE
PIRATE'S
DAUGHTER

1

TWELVE HOURS OUT OF Angra do Heroismo's white harbor, just past the barren rock of Formigas, at sunset, the sky turned the color of dried blood, and the sea went brown and mottled as the shell of a turtle.

Wilson had never seen sea and sky such colors—a whole palette of warning.

"Thirty years of sailing, you realize the sky is hardly ever blue," the captain said, a grim tone in his voice. "When it gets like this, you know there's trouble on the way. Going to be one for the record books. A real killer."

The *Compound Interest* pitched and rolled in the swells. Its beach umbrella sails stuttered nervously in the wind. All of a sudden, the shortwave was full of faraway distress signals, anguished voices calling out in the naked, unintelligible language of men in fear for their lives. A wild front of rain, hail, and hurricane-force wind was blowing off the Serengeti and across the Atlantic to form a solid gray barrier of terrible weather one thousand miles wide and two thousand miles long. The captain bent an ear to the receiver as a crazy riff of Morse code came across the wire, then he shook his head and switched off the set.

"There's nothing to do now but plow right through it," he said. "It's heading right for us, coming fast. If we turn back, it will catch us from behind. Let's put up the bubble and see what this tub can do."

They took down the canvas foul-weather cowling, retracted the beach umbrella sails, and switched over to the turbo-diesels. Then the captain and Wilson and Cricket went into the hold and brought up the eight Plexiglas sections and bolted them into place over the octagon. The *Compound Interest* was now watertight as a submarine. The air-purifying system cranked on with a comforting whirring sound. Sealed hatches divided the vessel into three airtight sections, each section equipped with its own supply of drinking water, freeze-dried food, and emergency locator beacon. If the vessel broke apart in heavy seas, the three compartments would float free, beacons pulsing distress through the airwaves to a five-hundred-mile radius.

The navigational octagon, sealed by a hatch from below, could turn into a sort of self-contained microvessel. It came equipped with a compressed gas–hydrofoil propulsion system—no larger than a suitcase, but with a range of three hundred miles—manufactured by Newland Marine of Santa Barbara. In the event of structural collapse the octagon could separate from the foundering wreck and scoot off to Africa under its own power, a tiny plastic bubble of high-tech engineering on the trackless sea.

2

FLUORESCENT TUBES GLARED DOWN with a green and poisonous light. The unpaneled bulkhead lay bare of decor, except for an Italian pinup calendar that nobody had bothered to change since July. The ready room was a stuffy, narrow closet furnished with a chipped Formica-topped table and a padded bench covered in green baize fabric.

Wilson was confined to this green purgatory as the storm lashed the ship, with nothing to do but ride it out. He took a book from his duffel bag, strapped himself into the bench, and began to read: It was Gibbon's *Decline and Fall of the Roman Empire,* the tattered single-volume edition from the used-book stall in the Bend. His eyes grew weary of the small text after a while, but that didn't matter; the weeks of relentless motion had left him thirsty for the nonphysical, for the study and contemplation of his former, half-dreaming life.

Beyond the thick polymer ribbing of the hull, the waves came down like mountains. At times the ship was inundated, completely underwater, its bow descending into the colorless valleys of the troughs. Meanwhile, Wilson's head was full of emperors, assassinations, aqueducts, barbarians, roads that led to Rome, cruel twists of fate, the deeds of centurions, courtesans, and slaves, an endless procession of the great and the mediocre, the depraved and the forgotten. For twenty-two hundred pages and mile after mile of heavy seas, the famous city held out against the chaos of history till there was nothing palpable left of Rome at all, nothing except a few broken ruins and its essential component, the idea of order.

Wilson looked up from his reading fourteen hours later. He had barely moved from his place in the ready room. Sometime during that interval Nguyen had taken a seat at the other end of the table. The Vietnamese cook seemed to possess an equilibrium all his own. Without benefit of safety harness, he sat upright on the bench, playing solitaire and smoking unfiltered Gauloises bleus from a crumpled pack, ash dropping a good inch off the end of his cigarette. As the vessel rolled, Nguyen swayed in that direction, like a gyroscope on a string. He laid the cards in meticulous rows; through some miracle of static electricity they stayed exactly where he put them.

"So, how're you doing?" Wilson said when he was able to focus on something other than print. He saw squiggles at the corner of his eyes from lack of sleep. "Got all the pots and pans battened down?" It was a stupid question, but he didn't know what else to say. They had never exchanged a single word of conversation outside the galley.

The cook barely raised an eyebrow.

"You beating the odds there?" Wilson gave it his best smile.

"No talk," Nguyen said. He wouldn't look up from the game.

"Why not?"

The cook sighed and folded the cards into the bottom of the deck and began to deal himself again. "All you joes," he said. "The big, stupid joe who is captain, the joe who eats like a pig, and you, the joe who reads too much. After the *français* leave Cochin China, I see many American joes come to my country, joes like flies on shit. The joes come and bring helicopters and drop poison powder on the trees, and everybody dies. When joe comes to your house saying, 'I want to be your friend,' good advice run very fast in opposite direction.''

''What does that mean?'' Wilson said.

''That mean I do not want to talk,'' Nguyen said.

''Why not have a conversation?'' Wilson persisted. He was restless and a little dazed after so many hours of breathing the dust of history. ''Here we are, stuck on a boat in the middle of a storm in the middle of the ocean with nothing to do except talk, and you won't say a word.''

The Vietnamese cook turned his face into the fluorescent glare. Thoughts registered behind his eyes like dark birds coming home to roost. ''Listen up, joe,'' he said. ''I do not wish to make any friends with you. Because on this boat, who knows what happens and because later on I do not wish to be sorry for you.''

Wilson tried to get Nguyen to explain himself, but the man would not say another word.

3

THE STORM LESSENED A bit the next afternoon. Wilson unbolted the deck hatch and went up into the navigational octagon. From this vantage the onslaught of weather was thrilling and terrifying. It seemed to him another world boiled out there in ferment, a landscape unseen since the beginning of time, when—so the story goes—God raised the seas in their fury upon the lifeless rock of the earth.

Captain Amundsen and Cricket were perched over charts and instruments beneath the bubble, like turret gunners in a Flying Fortress. Waves pounded across the Plexiglas, reducing the illumination in the octagon to a dull, watery twilight.

"State your business, mister," the captain said as Wilson rebolted the hatch.

"Permission to remain topside, sir," Wilson said. "Going a little stir-crazy down there."

The captain nodded. "Take a look at this."

Wilson stepped over to the opalescent radar screen. The storm appeared as a writhing, ugly green stain the size of a continent, superimposed on the Atlantic's familiar contours.

"According to our satellite fix, we've been knocked off course by about four hundred nautical miles," the captain said, squinting down at the screen. "We're at two and a half degrees east of the twenty-second parallel, thirty-two degrees south of Greenwich. Making south-southeast for the Mauritanian coast of Africa at an approximate speed of seventeen knots."

"How much time to get back to where we're supposed to be?"

The captain squinted out at the murky turmoil beyond the bubble. "Never can tell. A few days, a week, two. The sea's a mighty queer place. Anything can happen. I've seen tidal waves swallow whole cities and black skies at noon and volcanoes rising out of the dark water all bubbling and spitting up chunks of hot earth like blood, and I've seen worse yet." The captain paused as a quick riff of static came over the shortwave. Wilson could almost make out the rise and fall of human speech before it faded out altogether.

"Once did two years as skipper of an English oceanographic vessel; this is twenty-odd years ago," the captain continued, and a distant haunted look came to his eye. "She was the HMS *Ozymandias,* an old Royal Navy cutter refurbished for scientific work that some joker had renamed the *Sandra Dee,* after that blond girl who was in all those American beach movies."

"Sandra Dee played Gidget," Wilson interrupted, "the original Gidget before the TV show," but at a sharp glance from Cricket, he felt foolish and shut up.

"The Brits outfitted the ship with all the latest technology." The captain flicked a hard fingernail against the sonar screen. "Computers, sonar, radar, and a robot sub built by British Leyland and equipped with video cameras and attached by a two-mile-long umbilical cord. We were doing research on squids. Damned elusive creatures, the giant ones, I mean. But there's been stories about them for centuries—how they can rise from the ocean floor and seize ships in their huge tentacles, how they've been known to do battle with whales. All apocryphal, of course, and ridiculed by marine biologists until some fisherman off the Douglas Reef in the South Pacific pulled up a sizable hunk of squid cartilage in the nets that fixed the whole creature at four hundred and sixty feet long. So everyone got excited, and we sailed out of Bristol in January to take a look down south.

"It was pretty rough going for a while, bad weather and engine trouble, and we ended up spending a month or so in the anchorage at Rorotan till the weather cleared. Then we were out after them. For a while we found nothing remarkable, no squids bigger than the kind they fry up with garlic in Italian restaurants. But one night, I was on watch around midnight and the sonar went crazy, a whole pattern of blips about two fathoms off our port bow. I woke up one of the marine biologists, a Frenchwoman named Adrienne something, and we unleashed the robot, and it went down with its spotlights and video cameras into the blackness. After a few minutes it started sending back pictures. We couldn't believe what we saw: a squid the size of a tractor trailer, its one monster eye about as big around as the aboveground swimming pools you see in humbler suburban neighborhoods in the States.

"The French biologist went white and started to shake. It wasn't the squid so much as what the squid had its tentacles around, a massive unknown thing like a gigantic worm, thrashing in the black water, its long, tubular body disappearing into the depths of the sea. This looked to be some kind of fight—squids are like cats, you know, very territorial—but the squid, huge as it was, didn't have a chance. The other creature was the largest living thing I have ever seen, and I have seen blue whales in the waters off Newfoundland long as two football fields.

"We watched astonished, afraid to breathe. The bit of the creature's flank we could make out was covered with a thick mess of barnacles and plant life, as if it had been resting somewhere on the bottom for centuries. Then the squid let out a massive cloud of black ink, and when the cloud cleared, there was nothing. Just empty water. We could only assume that the unknown thing, giant squid stuck to its back, had sunk forever into the depths."

"Wow," Wilson said, impressed. "What was it?"

The captain took a cigar out of his pocket and put it between his teeth unlit. "The Kraken," he said quietly.

"The what?" Wilson said.

"The primeval worm that lives at the bottom of the sea. When it finally rises to the surface, they say the world will come to an end. And God knows, we've seen enough signs of that lately."

"You're kidding," Wilson said.

At that moment Cricket turned from the navigational computer with a sarcastic grin on her face. "Of course he's kidding," she said. "It's a fish story, the best damn fish story I've ever heard."

Wilson looked from Cricket to the captain, not sure what to believe.

"One thing you need to learn about sailors, Wilson," Cricket said, "is they always tell tall tales. Makes the time pass."

"Captain?" Wilson said.

The captain scratched his shaggy beard and shrugged. "You don't have to believe me," he said, "either of you. But I'm here to tell you now there are more things in the sea and on it than you've ever thought possible. Just look around . . ."

He gestured vaguely toward the ocean's bleak expanse, the horizon black with storm, the waves tall as three-story buildings—then he fixed Wilson with a look of unknown significance.

4

THEY UNBOLTED THE PLEXIGLAS bubble and replaced the foul-weather cowling. The turbo-diesels were switched off. The beach umbrella sails caught a gentle following wind and spread benevolently above the drying deck. The storm had blown itself out in the small hours of the night.

For the first time in six days the airtight hatches were opened and the ship's company emerged dazzled into the sunlight of early afternoon. They strolled the deck like tourists, staring out at the flat blue sea and harmless white clouds on the horizon. The designers had done their job well; a security cable snapped off the forward mast was the only damage to the *Compound Interest* from the worst Atlantic storm since 1935.

The captain managed to get the BBC over the shortwave.

"Reports say the west coast of Africa was hit pretty damn hard," he repeated to Wilson. "From Morocco to the Cameroons. Between fifteen and twenty vessels lost, including a container ship from one of the Scandinavian lines. Three fishing villages in Gambia were washed out to sea. Electrical power went off in the nation of Guinea-Bissau, and in Liberia they were obliged to stop the civil war for a few days. All in all, it looks like casualties might add up to something around five thousand human beings. And we came through the worst of it unscathed. I take back everything I ever said about this tub."

It was one of the unremarkable natural disasters that each year cull millions of lives from the world's multitudes each year, worth no more than a couple of minutes on the evening news in the States. Wilson knew he should be thankful for surviving the watery holocaust. Instead, he was angry and a little nauseated by the utter randomness of the thing. In a world where a gust of wind could blow away thousands, was there sense in taking another breath?

Human beings were no better than ants, Wilson thought, but at least ants could go about their business without the curse of intellect. Then he changed his mind. No, human beings were not like ants; they resembled a different sort of insect altogether. They were like bees in a glass hive, busy at work making honey, full of energy and plans. All it took was one stone.

5

PORPOISES RAN ALONGSIDE THE ship. Rising to the surface, they made a gentle blowing sound as they filled their lungs with air, a light splash as they sank again into the murk. A smell like cinnamon and earth and rotting fruit drifted in on the easterlies. The captain had gone below and left Wilson at the helm for the second watch of the night. But Wilson didn't need the man to tell him what that rich smell meant: Africa was near.

After an hour of wind and porpoises, Wilson felt a hand on his shoulder. It was Cricket, her face indistinct in the sea darkness, her copper hair a black tangle. Her voice, when it came, had a hollow, faraway sound.

"I need to see you tonight," Cricket said.

"O.K.," Wilson said.

"After the third watch. And be careful."

When the captain returned topside, Wilson went below and lay in his berth till his illuminated digital watch read 3:17 A.M., then he crept forward and opened the hatch to the utility closet. Cricket waited, suspended in her hammock like a spider. A little starlight reflected from the sea through the porthole. He could barely make out her pale face, her lips like a black wound. Wilson stepped inside and closed the hatch carefully.

"What's going on?" Wilson said in a whisper. "I think you should tell me now."

For a long time, Cricket was silent. "You ever fuck in a hammock?" she said at last.

"No," Wilson said.

"It's not easy," Cricket said, "but it can be done."

Wilson got out of his T-shirt and shorts and managed to pull himself up beside her. The nylon ropes creaked from steel eyelets anchored into the bulkhead. The canvas bowed dangerously beneath their weight, but the contraption held. Cricket was naked, her skin cool to the touch. From the porthole a damp breeze blew down Wilson's back. This time, it wasn't a question of thrust and counterthrust. Wrapped up in the hammock like a cocoon, the usual movements were useless. It was like making love without the restraining hand of gravity. They moved against each other, and Wilson felt himself locked inside her. Again he heard the faint sound of porpoises clearing their blowholes from the nearby water. The beasts had been following the ship for hours, good luck or bad luck, depending on which sailor you talked to.

When it was over, they lay suspended together, stuck with sweat, part of the same body, bent to the same inscrutable end.

"The hard part is getting down," Cricket said in Wilson's ear.

It took them nearly five minutes to disentangle themselves from the hammock. When they stood barefoot and naked, face-to-face on the cold planking, they were exactly the same height. Wilson reached forward absently and put his hands on her breasts. Cricket rested her elbows on his shoulders.

"This next part's going to hurt," she said quietly. "I've got to mark you, and the mark has to be permanent."

Wilson didn't quite understand, but he heard in her tone that she was serious.

"It has to be done, or else," she said.

"Or else what?" Wilson said.

"Don't ask," she said, and he felt her shudder. "Remember, you promised to do exactly what I told you to do, and no questions. Remember?''

"Yes,'' Wilson said reluctantly.

They crept aft into the galley and closed the hatch behind them. Cricket pulled Wilson over to the gas burners, lit one of them with a kitchen match, and took a thick-bladed table knife from the cutlery rack.

"This might work,'' she said, and held it up. The blue glow of the gas flame shimmered along the dull blade.

"Wait a minute!'' Wilson said in a loud voice.

"Sh!'' Cricket caught the back of his neck with one of her hard hands. "This is crucial! If you don't do exactly what I tell you to do, we could both end up dead.''

"Will you tell me what's going on?''

"No. I can't explain right now. Will you honor your word to me, or not—and jeopardize both our lives?''

She took an oven mitt from the wall and held the table knife, blade first, over the burner in the blue heart of the flame. After a few minutes, the blade glowed a bright red, with blue sparks frizzing off the edges.

Wilson began to sweat and tremble. Suddenly he regretted the empty streets of his out-of-the-way neighborhood, the faces on the Rubicon bus, quiet evenings at home with Andrea, the dusty, nondescript life he had left behind for the sea. But a small voice in the back of his head still said: *Then you were asleep; now you are alive.*

"We're just about ready.'' Cricket turned the knife in the flame. "Do you guys have something like butter or lard in here?''

Wilson found a can of Crisco in the cabinet.

"Open it.''

He opened the can and peeled back the aluminum top. The round surface of congealed fat looked white as a field of untouched snow.

"Now, your shirt.''

He pulled his T-shirt over his head, and Cricket saw that he was afraid.

"Steady," she said in a softer voice. "You've got to hold still for this, and you can't make a sound." She took a wooden spoon from the cutlery rack and put it in Wilson's mouth. "Go ahead, bite down."

Wilson bit down; the dry, splintery taste of the spoon gave him goose bumps. Cricket brought the knife blade out of the flame and set the thick edge into the flesh of Wilson's shoulder. He felt a searing pain, and the galley was full of the rancid odor of seared meat. After a moment, the burning sensation was cooled by a handful of the lard. Cricket took a bandage out of the first-aid kit beneath the grill and bandaged him in an efficient, nurselike manner, and she helped him get his T-shirt back on. The sensation of lifting his arm brought tears to his eyes. She replaced the knife and turned the burner off, and they were in total darkness.

"I'm sorry I had to hurt you," she said, in a voice that seemed to come out of nowhere. "You hide that mark until I tell you different." She set a quick, soft kiss on his lips.

"Cricket . . ." Wilson said, but when he felt for her, she was gone.

6

THE *COMPOUND INTEREST* DREW closer to the vast bulk of Africa. Her bow cut the greening waves. Light as feathers, land birds sailed on the morning breeze.

The captain spotted it first. "My eyes are a little weak these days," he said, and handed over the electronic binoculars.

Wilson peered and fiddled. For a moment he couldn't make out anything but water and sky. Then, all at once, there it was, the vaguest speck on the horizon. From time to time it disappeared among the swells, then appeared again, a shadow at the far limits of vision. They watched it closely for the next hour.

"O.K.," the captain said at last, "I think she's within range of our sensors," and he sat down at the navigational computer and tapped for a few minutes on the keyboard. "She's following a parallel course, making good speed, maybe twenty-five knots." He tapped out another command, and the bow cameras swung to the starboard with an electronic whirring sound. In an instant, a fuzzy video image of something that might be a ship appeared on the screen. It didn't look like much to Wilson, but the captain seemed very tense.

"What is it, sir?" Wilson said.

"Hard to say just yet. No markings. She's obviously a military vessel of some kind. Maybe a coast guard cutter out of the Ivory Coast; they've got two or three rusty old destroyers and a couple of other odds and ends. And look here!"

Wilson leaned closer. He felt a sudden queasiness of the stomach; the burn on his shoulder began to ache again. The screen showed an indistinct grayish blob protruding from the front of another indistinct grayish blob.

"She's pretty heavily armed," the captain said. "I make that out to be a potent piece of ordnance. A big Krupp marine cannon. Fires incendiary shells. Good range, great for shore bombardments. And this"—the captain indicated a slight silvery flash—"a rocket launcher. Most likely Davoust antiship missiles. French-made and murderous."

The captain took the *Compound Interest* off autopilot and for the first time gave Wilson a live wheel. Wilson felt it buck and pull in his hands as the vessel beat against the waves and knew why sailors think of ships as living things. The captain checked his charts, made a few quick calculations.

"We're still about two days out of Conakry," he said. "That's the nearest port. We're going to make a run for it." He retracted the beach umbrella sails, and for a moment there was total silence.

The *Compound Interest* faltered in the water. A wave hit the gunwales amidships with a violent slap.

"I don't understand. The diesels should turn over automatically." Now Wilson heard something in the captain's voice he had not heard before. A single drop of sweat formed on the end of the man's nose and fell into his beard.

The captain went to the manual control board, switched a red-handled switch, and pulled a red knob marked "CHOKE." For a moment the twin diesels began a harmonious rumbling; then they coughed and stuttered out all at once. He turned a baleful eye to Wilson.

"I'm going below," he said. "The ship's in your hands."

7

FOR THE NEXT FIFTEEN minutes, Wilson watched the horizon with an increasing sense of dread. The shadowy vessel had altered its course and was cutting through the waves straight for the *Compound Interest*.

When it was close enough to make out details through the binoculars, Wilson lashed the wheel and took a copy of *Jane's Fighting Ships* from the chart drawer and went through the illustrations till he found a match. It looked like a U.S.-built minesweeper of Korean War vintage that had long ago seen better days. But the vessel's old naval markings had been painted out, and her sides were black with grime and rust-streaked. Two long, foreign-looking skiffs hung loose in the hawsers, and the decking was strewn with debris. Fierce eyes had been painted on either side of the bow—like the eyes that had decorated the warships of the Greeks when they set sail for the sack of Troy. Only the big naval gun on the forward deck, and the missile launcher aft, gleamed bright and new-oiled in the sun.

A few minutes later, the captain emerged from below, pushing the Vietnamese cook before him. There had been a struggle. The captain's face was bruised; the left side of Nguyen's jaw was swollen, his forehead cut. Engine grease and dried blood were scrawled across his chef's whites. His wrists were bound behind his back with a bit of electrical wire.

"Sabotage," the captain said. "I caught this little bastard having a go at the engines. He already smashed the distributor and was in the process of mixing sugar with the oil. I checked, all the spares are gone."

"You can shoot the mechanic," Nguyen said with a yellow-toothed grin, "but engines still broke."

The captain turned and hit the cook across the face with the heel of his hand. Nguyen went sprawling against the taffrail but somehow managed to stay on his feet.

The captain glanced out to sea. He didn't need binoculars to see the vessel bearing down. "I think I know what's happening, and it's a damn shame," he muttered, half to himself. Then he sighed and squared his shoulders. "And me just two years away from retirement."

He fished a small key from his pocket and handed it over to Wilson. "Mr. Wilson, the small arms closet."

Wilson went over to open a wooden chest stowed beneath the port bench in the octagon. The chest contained two Mauser carbines, an over-and-under shotgun, a 30/30 Marlin with a lever-action Winchester stock, three semiautomatic handguns, a few thousand rounds of ammunition, a flare gun and case of flares, a dozen pairs of plastic handcuffs, and a Stentorian Model E police bullhorn.

The captain took a pair of plastic cuffs and one of the Mausers from the small arms closet, loaded it with a 90-round banana clip, then turned to Nguyen and cuffed him to the taffrail. The Vietnamese cook seemed totally unconcerned. He leaned back, licking blood off his lip.

"I gave your sister a pistol and told her to lock herself into the larder," the captain said to Wilson. "She might have a better chance that way. I'm sorry."

Then he went below and emerged a quick moment later wearing his gold-braided hat and dress uniform jacket. Gold captain's stripes and gold hash marks denoting more than thirty-five years' professional experience glinted from the sleeves. He stepped over to the communications console, smashed a small glass panel with his fist, and activated the yellow switch inside. A yellow light began to wink on the console. It was the emergency locator beacon that would go out on all channels to all ships and installations for five hundred miles. Then he went to the small arms closet and took out the flare gun and the case of sausage-shaped flares.

Wilson watched as the captain fired them off the starboard, one by one. Silver streaks of exhaust arched into the blue sky and exploded in powdery stars at the apex of trajectory. In another minute the octagon was full of sulfurous clouds of propellant. Wilson coughed, his mouth dry. He turned to the port side for a breath of air. Just above, the beach umbrella sails filled with wind, useless as a child's balloon. The captain handed him the over-and-under.

"I don't know what to do with this, sir," Wilson said. The shotgun felt thick and ugly in his grasp.

"It's a shotgun," the captain said. "You point in the general direction and shoot."

Nothing in Wilson's life had prepared him for the shock of what he saw when he turned back starboard. The approaching vessel had raised its colors, a black flag bearing a white skull and crossbones, flanked on one side by a horned demon drinking a bottle of rum and on the other by a bare-breasted mermaid holding a dagger in her hand.

"Ha! There's all the answers you need," the captain said. "That black flag means no quarter. We're all dead men."

"They're kidding," Wilson said, his voice wavering. "That sort of thing is out of fashion these days, right?"

"Last year there were one thousand and thirteen acts of piracy on the high seas, my friend," the captain said grimly. "Call Lloyd's of London; it's a matter of public record. But someone here's got a sense of humor or at least a sense of history. I've seen that flag before in old books. It was the ensign of an infamous pirate clan from the golden age of piracy. Captain Elzevir Montague was the worst of them. He sacked Portobello with Morgan. They passed the dirty trade down from father to son for more than two hundred years. Did a little bit of slaving, you know, a little wrecking. But killing innocent people on the high seas was their favorite occupation. Terrorized the shipping lanes from the Spanish Main to Madagascar until the British Navy finally put a stop to the whole bloody crew in 1805. Wiped out their home base, a group of obscure islands in the Gulf of Mexico not too far from the mouth of the Mississippi."

Wilson felt a cold hand on his heart. The pirate ship was not more than a hundred yards off now. He could see the rusty eyes, the cannon gleaming, the murderous black flag flying in the wind.

These last moments were strangely calm.

"Do you remember the name of the islands?" Wilson heard himself say.

The captain thought for a moment. "Yes," he said. "The Palmetto Keys."

8

SOON THE PIRATE SHIP was alongside. The rusty black hull rose up like the side of a cliff. But it seemed deserted, a ghost ship. Not a single face showed above the rail. The captain took the bullhorn from the small arms closet.

"I've got your man here," he shouted through the speaker. "The cook. Make a move and I blow his head off!"

In the wake of this crackling announcement, silence.

The captain dropped the bullhorn, picked up the Mauser carbine, and raked the side with gunfire. The sharp metallic explosions rang nastily inside Wilson's head. He dropped to the deck and put his fingers in his ears. It was a natural reaction that did not feel cowardly. Then, the firing stopped abruptly, and he looked up.

Cricket stood holding a nickel-plated .38 revolver to the captain's left occipital bone.

The captain tensed his finger on the trigger of the carbine. For a moment, it was not possible to say what would happen next. Then, his shoulders sagged, and he dropped the gun clattering to the deck.

Cricket shifted on her haunches. "Get some handcuffs," she called to Wilson.

All Wilson could do was stare.

"Get some fucking handcuffs!"

Wilson took a pair of plastic handcuffs from the small arms closet. Then he shook his head and dropped them back inside.

"This just isn't right," he said.

Cricket's jaw tightened. Her forehead seemed to bulge. "If you don't cuff the man," she hissed, "I'll have to kill him."

"You wouldn't do that," Wilson said. He felt the sweat rolling down his face; he blinked sweat from his eyes.

"Captain?" Cricket said, and cocked the hammer.

"You heard the lady, mister," the captain said.

Wilson took up the cuffs again and locked them around the captain's wrists.

"I'm sorry, sir," he said.

"You traitorous little bitch," the captain said to Cricket.

"Shut up, old man," Cricket said.

Wilson stood back and held up his hands. "Whatever you've got going here, it's not for me."

Cricket swung around, her eyes blank and steely. "Too late for remorse now," she said.

9

THE PIRATES TOOK CONTROL of the *Compound Interest* in less than two minutes. Wilson watched, helpless, as thirty brown men swung over the side. A few actually had knives between their teeth. Most were Africans, their faces marked with tribal scars, but Wilson saw a few red-turbaned Malays, a handful of South American types, and an Asian or two.

Ackerman was hauled out of his office and tied with nylon cord to the forward mast. "I was in the middle of a very important conference call," he said, "corn prices—" but they bashed the thick glasses off his face with the butt of a rifle before he could finish.

A moment later two Africans came up behind Wilson and knocked him down. They pushed his face into the deck, snapped plastic bands tight around his wrists. He had been seduced away from his quiet life in the city for this final moment of irony. What would Andrea say if she could see him now? It was a ridiculous thought. Didn't these people kill everyone so as to leave no witnesses? The dread took a knowing bite out of the inside of his stomach.

The leader of the boarding party was a tall, narrow-faced African wearing an oil-smeared pair of gabardine dress slacks cut off at the knees. His bare chest was crisscrossed with a complicated pattern of raised scars, and he carried a leather quirt wrapped with silver wire that seemed to be a badge of office. His men in place, he approached Cricket with a respectful gesture and said a few words in a language that Wilson could not understand.

"O.K., Mustapha. Good job," Cricket said in English when the man was done. "It's good to see you again." Then she picked up the bullhorn. "Ahoy aboard the *Storm Car,*" she called. "This is the all clear. Prepare to come aboard."

A chain ladder lowered over the side with a loud rattling noise.

Two men descended. The first was a youngish fellow with a helmet of Germanic blond hair, wearing an expensive-looking plaid blazer, creased khakis, and new leather boat shoes. A notebook computer in a clear waterproof carrying case hung from one shoulder. Wilson heard the man's shoes squeak as they touched the deck. He was tall and nicely proportioned, with the earnest Aryan type face that appeared on Nazi propaganda posters of the thirties. He blinked his pale blue eyes at the glare for a moment, then stood aside for his companion.

The second man was of a different type entirely: a short, bow-legged, scruffy gnome in a gaudy Hawaiian shirt. He wore his thong sandals with white socks, Japanese style. His pockets bulged with bits of rope and other odds and ends. A rectangle of duct tape crept halfway up one leg of his baggy shorts. His shirt lay open, revealing a half dozen barbaric gold chains hidden like snakes in grizzled chest hair.

This man's face looked familiar to Wilson: the strong jaw, the Roman nose, the lines of determination around the mouth. A wind-blown tangle of thinning coppery hair sat atop his head like a coon-skin cap. A black eye patch covered one eye. The other eye, large and malevolent, studied the three prisoners slumped together now beneath the mast. When he had seen what he wanted to see, he smiled the smile of the Devil surveying the sorrows of mankind. Wilson felt a chill to the bone and looked away.

For a moment the deck was quiet. He could hear the sound of the wind, and porpoises gamboling oblivious off the bow, and the grating of the two hulls scraping together. And a loud thumping sound that was the beating of his own heart.

Cricket stuck the .38 in the waistband of her jeans and went over to embrace the little man. The top of his head barely reached her breasts. "Dad," she said.

"How's my big girl?" the man said, and patted her on the ass.

"I'm fine," she said. "But it was a little touch and go there for a minute. The old bastard caught Noog doing his thing to the engines."

"When this is over, we'll go on vacation, honey," the man said soothingly. "Where do you want to go?"

Cricket thought for a minute, raised an eyebrow to the blue sky, insouciant as a coed. "Oh, Paris, I guess," she said. "I could do a little shopping."

"That's a date," he said, then he rubbed his hands together. "Now, where's our prize turkey?"

Wilson shot a glance at Ackerman. The billionaire trembled violently in the hot sun, his face white with fear. The shadow of the mast fell like a great weight across his shoulder. Tears slid down his cheeks into the collar of the foolish pink shirt he wore.

The pirate who was Cricket's father approached and stood, hands on his hips, staring down. Ackerman fixed his myopic eyes on the polished planking of the deck and would not look up. At last the pirate prodded him with one white stockinged toe.

"You Ackerman?"

The billionaire blinked painfully, the side of his face sore and bruised. "No," he said in a small, miserable voice. "Could I have my glasses back?"

"I wanted to congratulate you on that Caltech Industries takeover three years ago," the pirate said. "Fastest, meanest leveraged buyout I ever saw. Damned elegant. Stockholders never knew what hit them."

"You heard about that?" Ackerman said, surprised.

"It was in all the financial papers. The *Wall Street Journal,* the *Financial Times of London.* Both had good in-depth articles on your maneuverings."

"Who are you?" Ackerman said.

"I'm Captain Page, in command of the good ship you see yonder," the man said, and nodded over his shoulder at the rusty vessel looming behind. "Member in good standing of the Brotherhood of the Coast. That's all you need to know."

"You're a p-pirate?" Ackerman stuttered.

The pirate shrugged. "You see the eye patch, don't you?"

"Is it real?" Ackerman said.

"Lost the eye in a household accident," the pirate said. "A drill bit snapped and went right through my cornea. Then the thing got a nasty infection and had to come out. Could have gotten a glass one, but what the hell. Guess you could say I'm a traditionalist as far as my work is concerned."

"You're a goddamned murderous thief," Captain Amundsen spit out suddenly, "a robber who kills innocent people. Tell him what that black flag means. Tell him what you plan to do with us when you've got what you want."

"What are you going to do?" Ackerman cried out, hysteria in his voice. "I've got money, I'll pay you. Please . . ." His words disappeared into a whine.

"We know you have money, Ackerman," the pirate said quietly. "It's just a question of how much."

"That's not fair," Ackerman said, petulant as a child.

"What's fair, Schlüber?" the pirate called over his shoulder.

The young man in the blazer approached, unshouldered his notebook computer, and snapped it out of the clear plastic case. Then he sat cross-legged on the deck, and Wilson heard the tiny click and whine of the computer's hard drive coming up to speed.

"Give me a second, sir," he said. "Got to call up the database." He spoke the correct, faintly accented English common to most educated Germans. He peered at the screen with his pale blue eyes for a few seconds. The keys made demure clicking noises beneath his fingertips.

"Here he is," he said at last. "Filed under rich bastards. Ackerman, Dwight A. Born San Luis Obispo, California, April seventeenth, 1946. Paid federal income tax last year on income and assets totaling just over one and a half billion. Means he ought to be worth at least two billion more, sir. These bastards always have substantial amounts tucked away in banks in Switzerland or the Bahamas."

Ackerman licked his lips. "That's just not true," he began, but Captain Page made an impatient gesture, and Mustapha came forward and clubbed Ackerman on the back of the neck with the quirt. It made a sharp snapping sound, and the billionaire slumped forward into the nylon rope.

Wilson turned his eyes to the white sky and tried not to see or hear any more. The pirate boarding party loitered in the background, smoking cigarettes and laughing like construction workers on a lunch break. The shadow of the forward mast inched across the deck.

10

WILSON WAS TAKEN TO the pirate ship and locked in a small, airless cabin on a deck below the waterline.

After a few minutes, the overhead bulb blew out, and he spent his time in stale blackness, curled up in the berth on a bare mattress that smelled like urine. A vent in the bulkhead admitted a faint grid of light. Small scuttling noises across the floor announced the presence of rats. Once someone brought him water and a candy bar; the door opened for a second, then closed again. According to his illuminated digital watch, one whole day passed, each hour, each minute, each second heavy as lead. He watched the tiny green screen as if it were a television set.

For a few of these dead hours, Wilson thought of his father. Most people associated gamblers with gangsters and thugs. Wilson's father had been a quiet, kind man, the antithesis of the flashy racetrack tough guy. He still had a clear picture of his father's face, and he could remember the harsh jangle of the phone the night of the wreck of the four forty-five and the sound of his mother's anguished sobbing through the bedroom wall.

The cover of the next morning's *Dispatch* had shown the crumpled passenger cars sticking out of the black, frozen waters of the Potswahnamee like the fingers of a skeletal hand. There had been a second photograph, in the Sunday edition of the *Telegraph-Journal*. This one was later awarded some sort of photojournalism prize that year, and Wilson had seen it since, reproduced in books: The corpses both burnt and frozen lined the riverbank stiff as firewood. Police and coastguardmen stood casually in the foreground in black coats wet with rain, talking about sports. From the toes of the dead, white tags fluttered in the wind like prayers.

Just a week before the disaster Wilson's father had taken him out to Ardmore Downs on the old trolley. Now Wilson closed his eyes and saw the wide green oval, the bland suburbs stretching away beyond the fence. A few cold flamingos, their wings clipped, wandered the infield like lost dogs. It was a steeplechase—the horses went over the jumps, brush and log, and a few jockeys went down each race, tumbling across the turf beneath the hooves of the stragglers. He caught the smell of freshly cut grass and manure and pipe smoke. He saw the big flanks of the horses, the sour expressions on the faces of the gamblers when they lost, the big sedate homburg and fresh tweed jacket his father wore.

During the seventh race his father put a hand on Wilson's shoulder and knelt down. A father-son outing must necessarily be accompanied by a father-son talk, and the man pushed his hat back with a sigh and gave it his best shot.

"I know you've heard your mother and me fight about money sometimes," he said, then he paused and looked up as the horses thumped by in a cloud of sod, their bright silks flashing against the green. "She's a fine woman and very smart, but sometimes she gets things mixed up. Your mother thinks people need money more than anything else, but that's not exactly true. They need love, of course, but what they really need is dignity. Everybody needs dignity, and there's not enough of the stuff to go around. And let me tell you a secret—dignity has no price. No man alive is rich enough to buy it.''

He went on to explain that the only dignity he found in life was in being a gambler, that there was beauty in the work because it was always just him and the odds. ''Even when the numbers aren't going my way, I don't have to take crap from anybody,'' he said. ''Think of all the nine-to-fivers marching down into the subway like rats. They're miserable. If someone says jump, they jump. They traded their dignity for better odds. Don't ever do that, son. Promise me.''

Wilson promised solemnly, though he didn't know at the time what he was promising, and a week later his father got on the four forty-five express to another racetrack and his odds gave out and the train went down into the black water and ice of the Potswahnamee.

Now, curled up on a reeking mattress in the bowels of a pirate ship bound for points unknown, Wilson thought about the things his father had said, and he wondered how he would meet his end. Who could say what his father had felt in the last few seconds of life as the baggage flew loose and the passenger cars screamed off the trestle into oblivion? Is it possible to hold on to dignity in such a situation? Most likely the accident had happened too fast for him to feel anything but panic.

But this time, Wilson had time to prepare himself, a day in the dark to construct the artifice that he was not afraid, that life didn't matter so much as how you left it.

11

THE PIRATE SAT AT an old wooden table on the quarterdeck of the *Storm Car,* finishing a breakfast of eggs, bacon, sausages, and toast. A bottle of vodka stood half empty at his right hand. A black youth in a clean white jacket, napkin over one arm, hovered just behind with a glass pitcher of orange juice. The orange juice glowed an intolerable yellow in the bright, hot light of noon. The pirate wore a tattered red bathrobe hanging open over his chest, a pair of green boxer shorts, and green fuzzy slippers.

After the blackness of his prison in the hold, all this color and light gave Wilson a terrible headache.

Wilson and Captain Amundsen sprawled side by side handcuffed on the deck in the sun, waiting for the pirate to finish eating. Crates of ordnance packed in straw and lashed with canvas strapping made black tombstone-shaped shadows on the deck. The pirate ate slowly, reading a copy of the *Financial Times,* folding and refolding the on-ionskin pages carefully between each bite. Mustapha stood guarding the prisoners, leather quirt in hand, an automatic rifle slung over his scarred black shoulder.

During the day and a half since the attack, the *Storm Car,* with the *Compound Interest* in tow, had sailed to a different patch of sea. Now close off the port bow lay a jungle island. Its green tangle of vegetation straggled down to a rim of white beach, and Wilson could just make out parrots in the trees. In the distance, more islands, the channels between them clogged with reeds and saw grass. The humid air was thick with insects and the rank malarial smell of the tropics.

Then the pirate finished eating and the dishes were cleared away and Cricket and Schlüber came down the companionway and folding chairs were brought up and they joined him at the table. Today, Schlüber wore a pin-striped suit with a red paisley power tie and polished tassel loafers. He flipped open the notebook computer, which made a few noncommittal beeps, and set about fiddling with the thing with the self-important air common to computer people. Cricket seemed clean and rested; her skin showed a healthy glow. She wore a pair of stiff white sailor pants and a short blue naval jacket with gilt epaulets and braiding. Two rows of gold buttons rose over her breasts. She looked like a fresh-faced midshipman just out of the Naval Academy.

The pirate kissed her cheek as she settled beside him. "Morning, honey," he said.

"You need a shave, Dad," Cricket said, frowning. "And it's not morning; it's afternoon. And you should have put on some decent clothes. The Articles insist on the solemn nature of the occasion."

"On my ship I am the Articles," the pirate growled, rolling his one malevolent eye. But he pulled his bathrobe closed and sat forward. "Listen-up, shipmate," he said to Captain Amundsen. "Any questions before we begin?"

"Yes, what have you done with Ackerman?" the captain said, his voice a parched croak. "As skipper of the *Compound Interest,* the man was my responsibility. Did you filthy bastards kill him?"

The pirate gave a wan smile. "Don't worry," he said. "Mr. Ackerman is worth quite a bit of money to us. He's quite comfortable right now. More comfortable than you, in fact. For your information, the black flag is a gesture to tradition, as is the plank you see yonder." He waved in the direction of two Malay crewmen just now coming down the companionway. They carried a long wooden plank like a diving board, which they fixed into a slot in the starboard gunwale with a chain and iron pegs. Wilson shuddered when he saw this thing. It was painted an uneasy shade of turquoise and extended a good twenty feet off the side of the ship, quivering over the water as the *Storm Car* hawed at anchor in the swells.

"Killing everyone we capture is a waste of good human resources," the pirate said. "The Brotherhood needs men, especially qualified ones! Mr. Schlüber, let's hear the captain's biography."

" 'Amundsen, Lars Olaf,' " Schlüber read quickly from the screen. "Born Esbjerg, Denmark, 1945. Naturalized United States citizen. Thirty-six years' active service, Merchant Marine. Fifteen different vessels listed here, including a couple of the big old liners of the United States Line. Second mate USS *Constitution,* 1967; first mate USS *Independence,* '72. Five official commendations for meticulous attention to duty. Navigator's license, Double Star class. Excellent record. We've got a first-rate skipper here."

The pirate seemed impressed. He put his fingers together and thought for a moment. Then he ordered Captain Amundsen released from his handcuffs. The captain stood, rubbing his wrists. The pirate offered a glass of orange juice. The captain refused, even though he was half dead with thirst.

"Then I'll come to the point," the pirate said. "The Brotherhood needs good skippers like you. As you can imagine, half our men don't know the difference between a scupper and a sextant, and the other half are bloody drunken savages from some of the worst places on earth. Last year, we nabbed a smallish trawler about two hundred miles off the coast of Patagonia, and I came across one of my men eating the heart of a captured sailor. It was disgusting. Of course, once you're in our service, you're in for life, but I can promise you riches beyond your wildest dreams. Sooner or later, the wealth of the whole world comes through our hands."

He gave the captain five minutes to decide. When the five minutes ended, Captain Amundsen drew himself up straight and spoke out in a clear voice.

"Satan made a similar offer to Jesus in the desert," he said. "He was promised the kingdoms of the earth in exchange for his immortal soul. I spit on you as Our Lord spit on Satan," and with this he cleared his throat and expectorated a wad of green phlegm on the deck.

The pirate sighed. "Mustapha," he said.

But as Mustapha leveled the automatic rifle, Captain Amundsen raised a hand. "Wait. I'm a man of the sea and, like you, something of a traditionalist. I ask for the plank."

"Suit yourself," the pirate shrugged.

The captain buttoned his dress jacket, now soiled and tattered, and turned smartly toward the starboard. When he reached the side, he hesitated a moment, squinting out to sea. Mustapha came up behind and pushed the barrel of his automatic rifle between the captain's shoulder blades.

"That's not necessary," the captain said in a quiet voice. He stepped up on the gunwale and out onto the length of turquoise wood. Halfway down, he turned for a moment. The sea sparkled bright at his back; the sun stood at two o'clock. The horizon looked blue as a dream.

"Mr. Wilson," he called.

Wilson looked up.

"My father still lives in Esbjerg. He's ninety-six. Bishop Ingmar Amundsen. If you survive this nightmare, tell him I died a Christian, and tell him I'm sorry for running away."

Then the captain turned back and was gone. He simply disappeared into the bright day. This time Wilson didn't even hear the splash. Mustapha stepped quickly over to the railing. Shots were fired, a few quick popping sounds, then silence. Wilson hung his head and said a prayer to the unknown God who permitted such atrocities, a prayer for the soul of a brave man who had just left the world.

At last it was Wilson's turn. The sun was in his eyes. His mouth tasted like ashes. His wrists were cut and bleeding from the plastic handcuffs. His nose was burnt, the sunblock he'd put on days before had long since worn off. He hadn't once looked at Cricket during this ordeal. But now he couldn't help himself, and he raised his eyes from the tombstone shadows of the deck. She stared down at him, her face impassive, her stone green eyes hidden behind black sunglasses.

A perplexed tapping came from Schlüber's fingers as he worked the keys of the notebook computer. "I can't find any record on this fellow," he said. "Must have signed on after Santa Barbara."

"Is that true, honey?" the pirate said to Cricket.

"Yes," Cricket said in a flat voice.

"What's your name, mister?" the pirate said to Wilson.

Wilson rose slowly, pushing off the deck with the knuckles of his cuffed hands, his knees creaking. "Wilson Lander," he heard himself say. "Seventy-Seven Overlook Avenue, top-floor apartment. You take the Rubicon bus across the river, walk a few blocks down

Grace Street and take a right on Rubicon. . . .'' His voice trailed off.

"What's that?'' the pirate said.

"There's nothing in the database,'' Schlüber said. "He's not in the Merchant Marine listings. Checking the American Yachting Association . . .'' Wilson heard the machine beep a negative. "Nothing. As far as my records go, he's not official. Not licensed by any authority in the U.S.''

The pirate considered for a moment, frowning. "What are you?'' he said to Wilson, "Interpol? CIA?''

"I'm a human being like you,'' Wilson said, and he was surprised to find that his voice did not waver. "I was born like you, and will die like you. The world's a mighty strange place. That's all I have to say.'' When he had finished speaking, he looked over at Cricket. Her coppery hair wisped in the ocean breeze, and Wilson got a sudden flash of their days in bed in the Azores. Even surrounded by these horrors and with her black heart revealed and ugly as a sore, she looked beautiful.

"Any skills, shipmate?'' It was Schlüber's voice, sounding helpful. "Anything the Brotherhood might find useful?''

Wilson shrugged. "I have an undergraduate degree in comparative literature with a minor in ancient anthropology from Ashland College in Beaufort. And most of a master's in archaeology of the Americas from the same institution. I know a good book when I read one. I've been told I'm good with children. And I can date a pre-Columbian potsherd to within a couple of hundred years.''

"Enough,'' the pirate said, cutting him short. "We've heard all we need to hear.''

Out of the corner of his eye, Wilson saw the shimmer of the gun barrel, the scarred ridges on Mustapha's dark skin sheening with sweat. He turned his head toward the sea and tried to think about dignity, but fear turned the horizon red, and he felt like he was going to faint.

"Wilson!" It was Cricket's voice, followed by the clattering sound of a chair falling over.

Wilson looked back. Cricket stood at the table, chair collapsed on the deck behind her. She towered over her father like a goddess over a gargoyle. He scratched his head and squinted up at her. "Honey?" he said, surprised.

"This man is my property," she said. "I'm claiming him now."

The pirate shot Wilson a dark, furious look; then he reached up and took his daughter harshly by the arm. "Don't go sentimental on me, girl," he hissed. "Sentiment is dangerous for our kind. And it's against the Articles! A membership in the Brotherhood is not to be granted for personal reasons. We've got no choice but to throw this one to the sharks."

Cricket pulled her arm away. "No," she said. "He bears my mark. He is mine. I call your attention to Paragraph twenty-one, Section seven, of the Articles of Brotherhood." She came quickly around to Wilson and tore open his shirt. "Here is my mark," she said, and gestured to his shoulder.

There, the brand from the knife, a scraggly pink *C,* showed raw with new skin.

"Schlüber?" the pirate said between his teeth.

The German fiddled with the computer for a long minute. "Got to change databases, sir," he said. "Wait, here it is. The subsection on spoils, Clause 6 A: 'Any prize aboard a captured vessel designated or otherwise set aside by a member of the Brotherhood with special mark or signature, prior to capture of said vessel—' "

"Well?" The pirate hit the table with his fist.

"I'm afraid so, Captain," Schlüber said. He looked up for a curious beat, registering Wilson for the first time. "Your daughter knows the Articles. This one belongs to her."

12

CRICKET'S SPARSE CABIN ABOARD the *Storm Car* contained a narrow bunk, a steel sink, a scrap of Aubusson carpet on the floor, and a fan-backed club chair upholstered in red Morocco leather. Wilson sank into this incongruous piece of furniture like a man giving up the ghost. Hot afternoon sun shone a bright oval through the single porthole in the bulkhead.

"Go ahead, judge me," Cricket said when she had closed the hatch behind them. "But you can never know what my life has been like. The choices I've been forced to make!"

Wilson felt numb. Dumb happiness at being alive.

"Water . . ." He managed a parched whisper.

For a moment, Cricket looked crestfallen. Her lower lip trembled. "I'm sorry," she said. "I'm being inconsiderate. The thought that you probably consider me a monster made me crazy for a few minutes." She took a coffee cup from somewhere and filled it with brown water from the sink. It tasted rusty, but Wilson didn't care.

"Don't open the hatch for anyone except me," Cricket said. "Lock it after I'm gone. I'm going to the galley to get you something to eat."

The thought of moving an inch from the club chair set his head spinning. He closed his eyes and listened to the slow rumble of the ship, felt it in his bones. When he opened them again, Cricket was kneeling before him, her hand on his knee. She had changed her midshipman's outfit for a T-shirt and jeans. Concern showed like flecks of gold in her green eyes. "Do you feel like eating?"

Wilson nodded yes and sat forward with an effort. She placed a blue plastic tray on his lap. There was a grilled cheese sandwich, a large deli pickle, a pile of barbecued potato chips, and a tall glass of lemonade sweating in the heat.

"That's made from real African lemons," Cricket said. "Good stuff. Drink it slowly."

Wilson took small sips of the lemonade and ate half the sandwich. The cheese had an odd sharp taste, not altogether bad.

"Goat cheese," Cricket said. "All we've got on the island is goats. A few sheep. No cows. Goats will eat garbage, and there's plenty of that."

"The island?" Wilson said.

"I'll tell you all about it when we get there." She handed him a little pillbox full of aspirin.

He swallowed three of them and a few minutes later felt better.

"How do you feel now?"

"Not bad, considering I've just had a near-death experience."

"I know you're exhausted," Cricket said, "and probably still in shock, but I don't want . . ." Her voice trailed off. She went over to the porthole, then came back and sat cross-legged on the bunk. "Like I said, I'm not a monster."

"So you're not a monster," Wilson said. "But you're not a hell of a lot better. You're a pirate."

"Barely." Cricket blinked at him. "I'm just a woman who's had to make some unfortunate decisions. I'm trapped in this life. It's all I've ever known."

"What about Captain Amundsen?" Wilson said. "Was that one of your unfortunate decisions?"

Cricket bit her lip and looked away. "I went to him last night," she said in a small voice. "They had him down in the hold, tied to a steam pipe so he couldn't sit or lie down. I untied him, I gave him something to eat. 'Just go along with us for a little while,' I said. 'When Dad asks you to work for the Brotherhood, say you will. You play along now, and later, after a couple of years, when they stop watching you so closely, you'll have a chance to escape.' Do you know what he did?"

"I have an idea," Wilson said.

"He spit the food back in my face. Black bean soup. Got in my hair, all over. The captain practically threw himself off that plank, Wilson! Maybe he wanted to prove something; maybe he was tired of life and wanted to go out a martyr. But he did have a choice!"

"He's dead now," Wilson said.

"Yes." Cricket's voice trembled. "And I regret that more than I can say. I really liked the old guy. What makes it worse is this whole operation was about kidnapping Ackerman, not about the captain at all."

Wilson was silent. Cricket stared at the oval patch of sunlight as it moved up the bulkhead to three in the afternoon. Finally, she looked over at him, her green eyes dark and fathomless. Then her lip began to tremble again, and she leaned forward, and tears made dark splotches on her jeans.

"Wilson, don't hate me," she said. "I'm so lonely. You can help me out of this nightmare."

Wilson shook his head. "How?" he said at last.

Cricket shrugged miserably. "You're good. I need your goodness. Sometimes I can't say what's right or wrong. My father tells me to do something, and I do it because that's the way it's been since I was a kid. It's always been the family and the Brotherhood against the rest of the world. What's right for the family has often been wrong for someone else. You're different. You know what's right and wrong for everyone."

"You're asking me to be your conscience?" Wilson raised an eyebrow.

"Something like that," Cricket said.

"You don't need a degree in moral philosophy to figure out making an innocent person walk the plank is not a good thing," Wilson said. "If you don't know that, I can't help you."

"But you can help me in another way that's very important." Cricket looked up at him, suddenly dry-eyed. "You can gamble."

"Why the hell does gambling matter so much to you?"

"Let's not talk anymore. You need some rest right now."

Cricket stood and helped Wilson over to the bunk. They lay together side by side but not touching as dusk fell, a scarlet dome over green islands and Africa in the distance, and the night came on, full of piteous stars.

PART FOUR

QUATRE SABLES

1

SMALL ISLANDS LAY CLOSE off either bow, half hidden in malarial haze. The reedy channels were full of crocodiles and kingfishers. Knobby-rooted trees, home to birds of every description, grew down to the black water. By 10:00 A.M. the sky burned white with heat, so bright it became impossible to look out the porthole.

Wilson had never experienced such oppressive weather. Trying to breathe here was like trying to breathe underwater. The *Storm Car*'s ancient diesels droned loud and soft in maddening, irregular pulses. For hours the two of them lay naked and sweating in the bunk, caught in a sort of erotic torpor. They reached for each other, sweated together for a while, then lay apart and sweated into the moist sheets.

Cricket rose at dusk, wet a rag in the rusty water of the sink, and sponged Wilson's flesh. This cooled him for the barest second, till the water evaporated, rising like steam in the moist air.

"These goddamned islands," Cricket said, her eyes purple-lidded from the heat. "The climate's terrible where we're going, but nothing's as terrible as this."

"Where are we?"

"The Mojango Archipelago."

"It's not Africa?"

"Close enough," Cricket said. "We're about sixty miles off the Bupandan coast. Dad comes through the Mojangos whenever he's towing a prize. It's very private. The islands were declared a wildlife sanctuary by the United Nations about twenty years ago. There's a no-fly zone overhead because of all the birds, and there's only one channel through this muck, which is off limits to international shipping. Come here."

Wilson got up with some effort and went over to the porthole. Hummocks overgrown with salt grass slid by in the channel below. Tall birds with red and yellow feathers stood on one leg in the muddy shallows, watching the vessel pass with lusterless, uncurious eyes. Blue-tailed African thrushes sat preening themselves on the rusty railing of the companionway, dropping splotches of guano to the deck. Clouds of scarlet wrens swirled through the thick air overhead.

Wilson watched for a while and the world seemed alive with feathery movement. "There are a hell of a lot of birds out there," he said.

"As of last count three hundred and seventy-five separate species, and half of them exist nowhere else in the world," Cricket said.

"Why here, particularly?" Wilson said.

"Actually it's because of the bugs," Cricket said. "The birds eat the bugs. The bugs are here because the reeds and the tide pools make an ideal habitat. The reeds and the tide pools are here because—" She shrugged. "You get the idea."

"What kind of bugs?" Wilson said.

"Locusts, flying cockroaches, termites, Java beetles, bottle flies, mosquitoes, giant gnats, winged African earwigs, you name it. Go ahead, listen," Cricket said. "You've got to concentrate to hear them."

Wilson steadied himself against the bulkhead and listened. After a few seconds another sound became clear beneath the monotonous rumble of the diesel, a small pervasive chattering that was everywhere and nowhere. Then his eyes adjusted, and he saw them against the hazy, descending sun. Millions of black specks, the air thick and grainy with them.

"My God!" he said.

"Yeah," Cricket said. "You can't open your mouth topside without something flying in. The crew wears these mesh beekeeper's hats when they go topside. Except for Dad. He just bats them away like they're nothing. But I can't stand the goddamn things, they give me the creeps. That's why we're down here for the duration of the voyage."

"That the only reason?" Wilson said.

Cricket smiled, her breasts faintly translucent in the diminishing light.

Later that night, it was too hot to sleep. They lay in the hot darkness not touching because of the heat. Wilson listened to the chug of the engines and the dull drone of the insects and wondered what the future would hold. How would he find his way home again? Where would he wake up tomorrow or a week from tomorrow? What did his dread have in store for him next?

"My father will kill you if he can find a way," Cricket said suddenly.

Wilson was startled; it seemed she could read his mind.

"So why doesn't he just come down now and get it over with?" Wilson said.

"He wouldn't dare with me around," Cricket said. "He knows I'd report him to the Thirty Captains. Even we pirates live by rules, you know. You're mine by authority of the Articles, and the Articles are law with us. There's nothing more sacred to a pirate than property rights. But Dad is an unscrupulous bastard. There will be plenty of quiet opportunities ashore. We're going to have to be very careful until he gets used to the idea of you being around."

Cricket turned on her side. Then she turned back and put a hand on his thigh. "I love you," she said in a voice that Wilson had to strain to hear. "You don't have to say anything, not a word, if you don't want to."

Wilson didn't say anything.

"You don't believe me."

"O.K., you love me," Wilson said with some bitterness. "Is that why you dragged me into this mess against my will? I'm not a pirate, I'm not a murderer," she pulled away at this "and I'm telling you now, the first chance I get, I'm clearing out."

"Impossible," Cricket said quietly. "Where would you go?"

"Home," Wilson said.

"Your home's here with me now. Remember that mark on your shoulder?"

Before he could reply, Wilson felt her slide down the damp mattress and he felt her breasts against his leg, and he stiffened and her mouth was on him there.

Grassy hummocks covered with sleeping birds fell away into tropical gloom beyond the porthole. The shallow black water swarmed with insects. Slowly evolving creatures, unnamed and sinewy, half fish, half something else, swam up toward the fading light.

2

ALONG THE CROWDED CEMENT wharves, cranes hoisted pallets full of dark cargo into dilapidated freighters that showed no flag or registry. The dockyard was a mess of crates and livestock and rusty scrap metal. Native dockworkers labored bare to the waist, their purple-black skin shining in the sun. Beyond a fifteen-foot barbed-wire fence, a shanty city lay strewn up the slope. Paths of red mud straggled and intersected in a crazy web through a maze of plywood shacks, lean-tos made from brush, and cardboard box huts tied together with vine. *No, city was the wrong word for this ugly sprawl,* Wilson thought. *More like a garbage dump, teeming with humanity.*

"Where are we?" He stood naked with a pair of binoculars at the porthole. It was only an hour or two after dawn but already hot enough to fry an egg on deck.

Cricket yawned and stuck her nose in the air. "From the putrid stench, I'd say it's Quatre Sables," she said. "No plumbing, no sewers, no nothing."

"So this is Africa," Wilson said, and there was an unexpected thrill at the thought. "Which country?"

"Sorry, it's not quite Africa," Cricket said. She sat up, scratching her head. "We're still twenty-five miles or so off the Bupandan coast. You're looking at the island of Quatre Sables, just south of the Mojangos. And it's no country at all. Used to belong to Portugal, I guess; now it belongs to us. It's a pirate republic."

"What does that mean exactly?"

Cricket shrugged. "We claim no flag except the skull and crossbones. We govern ourselves by the Confederation of Thirty Captains under the Articles of Brotherhood. Everyone's got their place in the chain of command."

She came up and pressed into him from behind and put her arms around him and put her hands over his shoulders. "Look up there. Do you see the big places on the ridge?"

Wilson pointed the binoculars: high up the slope, a semicircle of fine white houses separated by a wall from the cardboard slums below. He caught a glimpse of green lawns and palm trees, thought he saw the sun glint off the windshield of a car.

"We live up there," Cricket said.

"Who's we?" Wilson said.

"The Thirty Captains. My father's one of them. I called Quatre Sables a republic. That's the wrong word. Oligarchy is better, I suppose. We own the ships; we plan the missions; we make the money; we make the rules."

"What about all of them?" Wilson lowered the binoculars and gestured toward the trash city on the slope.

"Refugees, mostly. From the civil war in Bupanda. They're not part of the Brotherhood."

"What are they, then?"

Cricket shrugged, a cruel glint in her eye. "Cannon fodder."

3

WILSON STOOD BEWILDERED ON the quay, his skin alive with prickly heat as the light faded lavender over the back of the island to the west. He felt light-headed after two days in Cricket's cabin aboard the *Storm Car*. His jaw popped every time he swallowed; his knees ached. The gangs of dockworkers and the disembarking pirate crews passed in a blur of sweat and muscle.

"You look a little green," Cricket said.

"I'm fine," Wilson said, but there was a faint buzzing in his inner ear.

"I've got to take care of a couple of things, shouldn't be longer than fifteen," Cricket said. "Here . . . ." She reached into her duffel bag and pulled out her nickel-plated .38 and pushed it into the waistband of Wilson's jeans. "If anyone bothers you, shoot them." Then she was gone.

Wilson sat on a splintered crate and watched the crowds go by. He tried to concentrate and was taken with the grim realization that he would most likely never find his way home from this godforsaken place. Then nausea passed over him in a wave, and he closed his eyes and fought it down. When he opened his eyes again, he saw a column of about a hundred African men and women coming along the quay in a peculiar shuffling manner. As they drew closer, he heard the rattle and clink of metal and saw that they were shackled each to each; steel chains led from steel collars to manacles around their wrists and ankles. Guards armed with machine guns and cattle prods herded the column along toward a large cinder-block hangar at the far perimeter. Over the next half hour, ten such columns passed. On the faces of the captives Wilson saw the same despair, the same hunted look, and it did not take long for him to realize the truth: These human beings were caught in the claws of an ancient evil.

When Cricket returned after an hour, Wilson rose off the crate and stood unsteadily before her. The .38 fell out of his jeans and clattered across the pavement.

"Hey!" Cricket said. "Be careful with that. You could shoot somebody in the foot." But when she caught sight of his eyes, she crossed her arms and looked away. The silver pistol glinted on the stained cement between them.

"Slaves," Wilson said, his voice a bare croak.

"I thought you knew," Cricket said, and she would not meet his eyes.

"Where do they come from?" Wilson said.

"Africa." Cricket shrugged. "Bupanda mostly."

"Where are they taking them?"

"For now, the barracoon over there." She pointed out the concrete hangars. "It's where they hold the auctions."

"My God," Wilson said, and a shiver ran up his back.

"It's the way things are here," Cricket said gently. When she looked back at him, her eyes were lost in shadow. "I don't like it either, but there's nothing I can do right now. You can't make good money from piracy alone. It's too hard these days, too many risks involved. We only do the occasional special job, like the one we just pulled on Ackerman's boat—well planned in advance, with an inside man, the works. Mostly it's slaving raids to the Bupandan coast, then back here to the barracoon, where we unload the merchandise for sale."

Now the sky bloomed black as dried blood against the dim bulk of the hill.

"How do you sleep at night?" Wilson managed.

"I don't. That's why I need you," Cricket said, and she put her hard hands on the back of his neck and kissed him. "There's a way out of this life. I want you to show me the way."

Wilson let himself be led up the quay and through a gap in the barbed-wire fence to a waiting car. It was a battered Volkswagen Thing, bumpers and windshield missing, still painted the original purple, with the factory flower power decal kit popular in the late sixties. Mustapha sat in the passenger seat, shotgun on his lap, scars written across his skin like a threatening message. He watched with wary yellow eyes as Wilson climbed into the backseat.

"Hi," Wilson said for no reason at all.

The man tapped the butt of his shotgun with two fingers. "Next time," he said under his breath.

Cricket came around and got into the driver's seat and put the Thing in gear, and they lurched over a rutted path and after a while turned left up a wider road that ascended the slope. The trash dwellings loomed in a primitive darkness unrelieved by electric lights. Wilson thought of the crazy cubist city in *The Cabinet of Dr. Caligari,* and his head hurt with the thought. Unfamiliar constellations wheeled above. Starved faces passed before the wavering headlights, the faces of people of whom it could rightly be said were poor as dirt. Big-headed, ribby children lay in the mud around fires of scrap wood and dung. Shallow ditches were piled high with offal and the picked-over carcasses of dead animals. The stench was unbearable.

"They float across the straits in rafts made from old tires and oil drums," Cricket said over the sputter of the engine. "We cull the strongest for sale in the barracoon, but even so, they keep on coming. Even this squalor is better for them than the massacres still going on in Bupanda."

Wilson felt hot and cold at the same time, and the pain in his knees became so intense he stopped breathing for a few seconds. Cricket's words faded in and out like a bad radio station. When he sank unconscious against the torn backseat, it was as if he were drowning in a sea of dirty water the color of human misery.

4

THE MONKEY TITTERED LIKE A bird on the windowsill, just the other side of the mosquito netting. About the size of a squirrel, with silky orange fur, a black tail, and a black tuft sticking straight up from its head like a Mohawk, it ate a mango in quick, nervous bites, turning the green fruit over between its paws as Wilson had seen humans turning an ear of buttered corn. He watched in silence for as long as he could; then he couldn't stand the pain any longer and let out a short gasp. The monkey dropped the fruit, its face twisted up in surprise for half a second; then it began to howl. The sound was ear-shattering, loud, spiraling whoops like a siren, a sound ten times as big as the creature itself.

"Goddamned howler monkeys!" Wilson heard a man's voice from the next room. He tried to turn toward the voice, but he could not move because of the pain in his joints. When he looked back at the windowsill, the monkey was gone.

A few minutes later a tall, stoop-shouldered man in a dingy white doctor's coat entered the room. He was about forty, with a long red European face, scraggly brown hair that hung lank over his forehead and a nose with pores wide enough to drive a truck through. When the man sat beside the bed, Wilson caught the strong stench of alcohol. He put a limp hand on Wilson's forehead, examined Wilson's eyes, thumped on his chest.

"Are you a doctor?" Wilson said, and was surprised that his voice sounded so weak and uncertain.

"Evidently," the doctor said, alcohol wafting out with the word.

"You're drunk," Wilson said.

The doctor shrugged. "Not drunk, exactly. Just a little—you know," he wagged his hand back and forth. "It's the only way to bear life in this pirate hell."

"What am I doing here?" Wilson said, but his voice was already growing faint, and when he spoke, his knees hurt. The doctor put a hand on Wilson's arm, a gesture that was neither friendly nor un-friendly.

"Tomorrow," he said. "Rest now." Then he took a needle out of somewhere and gave Wilson an injection in his thigh and went away.

After that, Wilson fell into a drugged sleep in which he dreamed he was chained to a palm tree on a beach made of different-colored sand, all twisted up like chocolate-vanilla swirl ice cream. In the dream, a man who resembled the doctor came along carrying a large scalpel in one hand and a strange animal in a wooden cage in the other. The animal was a sort of cross between a monkey and a wolf, with webbed claws and a mane of coppery hair and large, wet, innocent eyes. It was the eyes that made the animal dangerous. The doctor cut a square hole in Wilson's stomach with the scalpel, took the animal out of the cage, put it in the hole, and sewed the hole back up. Wilson waited a minute or so, then he felt the animal scratching, and he felt the small, pointed teeth, and he knew the thing wouldn't take long to eat its way out again.

5

IN THE MORNING, THE sun shone saffron yellow through the big windows. Wilson lay on a square white bed under a canopy of mosquito netting in a room that gave out onto a tile patio with a view of the shanty city below. Rattan shades rattled at the window in a hot breeze. The walls of the room were painted terra-cotta red except for a creamy border around the ceiling, and there was an antique dresser and a large vanity and a table of inlaid wood upon which rested a bowl of pomegranates. Next to the door hung a very good reproduction of a nineteenth-century French painting, Léon

Gérôme's *Le Bain aux Harem,* which depicts an African slave girl bathing a white concubine in a blue-tiled pool. The room had a feminine feel that Wilson found pleasant and familiar. He lay in the sunlight and stretched and realized that his joints did not ache so much this morning.

When the light changed a little, a large black woman came through the door with a tray of spicy soup, bread, and sharp-tasting milk that probably came from a goat. Awhile later, the doctor called, still smelling of alcohol. He examined Wilson's eyes, took his pulse, and listened to his lungs again.

"You're eating today," the doctor said, a vein in his nose pulsing gently. "Good. And you look much better."

"Thanks," Wilson said. "What's wrong with me?"

"If we're going to have a little talk, do you mind if I make myself a drink?" the doctor said. Before Wilson could speak, the doctor was gone. He returned a few minutes later with a glass full of pink gin and ice.

"I'd offer you one," he said, "but in your condition . . ." Then he took a long, greedy drink of the gin and wiped his mouth on the back of his hand. "That's why I like working up here on the ridge," he said. "Great booze. Hard to get the good stuff down there."

"O.K., Doctor," Wilson said.

The doctor nodded, finished off the glass, and set it on the inlaid table. "You are recovering from a case of dengue fever, of a particularly virulent type common to equatorial regions of Africa. The natives call it *ka-dinge pwepe,* literally the stiff knees, because the fever attacks your knees, and for a while afterward you walk around like a mechanical man. This type of dengue—which I call Dengue Boursaly, after myself—seems to be unique to this miserable island, in that unlike continental types of the disease, which is caused by bacteria, this type appears to be viral. And it can act on the nervous system in the latter stages if not checked with the proper combination of diuretics and antibiotics, which is also very unusual. I would write a paper for the medical journals on the subject but''—the doctor gave a Gallic shrug—''I am a prisoner here, and they do not allow me to publish.''

Wilson focused on the ceiling, taking this in. ''How long have I been out?'' he said at last.

''About three and a half weeks,'' Dr. Boursaly said. ''You were absolutely raving when they first brought you up. Now you're as good as on your feet again, thank God. Otherwise, it would have meant my head.''

Wilson started to smile; then he realized the doctor wasn't kidding.

''Not really . . .'' Wilson said.

Dr. Boursaly picked up the empty glass, stared at the melting ice cubes for a second, and put it down again with a sigh. ''Your Mistress Page was very clear about the matter. She went off on a raid with her father—last chance before the rainy season, you know—and she left you in my care. If you are not well by the time she returns, she told me, ouf ''—he drew his hand across his neck— ''it's my head on a stick. And that's no bloody joke. Old Dr. Raimee misdiagnosed a malignant tumor; you know what they did to him?''

''No,'' Wilson said.

''They buried the poor bastard up to his neck, covered his face with honey, and dumped out a jar of red ants.''

''Ouch,'' Wilson said.

''He lived, but he never looked the same. So don't worry, I'll be stopping by every day just to make sure you don't step on a splinter or wet the bed and catch cold.''

When the doctor was gone, Wilson lay gazing up at the ceiling, his mind unpleasantly jumbled. A large flat cockroach scuttled across it upside down, hit a sweaty patch, and fell with a solid thunk to the vanity, where it waved its legs in the air for a moment before it went still. After a while, Wilson dozed off and dreamed that the orange monkey came back and stared at him from the other side of the mosquito netting, its silky orange fur stirring slightly in a breeze from the sea.

6

THE HOUSE WAS BUILT against the slope on two levels, with plaster walls painted in earthy red or mustard pastel and low ceilings that reminded Wilson of the hold of a ship. On the upper floor, a living room furnished with eighteenth-century antiques, a bathroom with a skylight and sunken marble tub that looked big enough for two people, and a walk-in closet full of Cricket's clothes. The bedroom and kitchen and dining room occupied the lower floor, open to the tile patio, which was sheltered by a green-and-white-striped awning and set with wrought-iron deck furniture. A low wall topped with terra-cotta urns full of huge tropical flowers framed the bay, blue and brown and green in the near distance.

Lying beneath the awning, stiff-kneed in one of the patio chairs, Wilson was shielded from view of the heaving shanty city below. He could only see the flowers and the water, and when the wind blew from the Atlantic, he could not smell the horrible stench of the place. Then, for a few moments, it was possible to believe some picturesque hamlet of the French Riviera lay down there, not an ugly warren of hovels and misery on an obscure island off the coast of Africa. Except for the black woman who came twice a day to cook, Wilson was alone in the house, and he looked forward to Dr. Boursaly's daily visits. The doctor usually stopped by in the morn-ing, an hour or two before the heat of noon, and joined Wilson with a drink on the patio.

Today Dr. Boursaly drank three pink gins in quick succession and was very drunk by 11:00 A.M. He reeled around the patio, bumping into the wrought-iron furniture, and almost knocked one of the terra-cotta urns off the wall onto the tiles. Wilson began to grow alarmed. The doctor waved his fourth drink toward the town, ice and gin sloshing out of the glass for emphasis.

"From this distance you might find that panorama quite romantic," he said.

"Actually no," Wilson said.

"Poverty is always romantic from a distance," the doctor said, ignoring him. "Next time you're down in the middle of that *merde,* take a microscope and watch where you step, because it's a filthy swamp full of bacteria, full of the nastiness Africa is famous for. Africa, Mother of diseases, my friend! In my six years of captivity here I have seen them all—elephantitis, hepatitis, dysentery, malaria, meningitis, scarlet fever, yellow fever, typhus, beri-beri, cafard, scurvy, tuberculosis, cholera, bubonic plague, pneumonic plague, ten different mutations of AIDS, dengue, even Ebola and Blarh's syndrome, not to mention flus, ordinary fevers, rickets, and madness—all increasingly immune to commonly prescribed anything. A virologists' paradise, you might say. Well, I'm not a virologist, I'm a cardiologist."

The doctor's story was an unfortunate one. He was Swiss by birth, educated at the University of Lausanne and at the University of Michigan's medical school. After fifteen years of lucrative practice in London and Geneva, he had burned out on rich people with bad hearts and decided to do a year of charity work at the Nursing Sisters of the Cross hospital in Tananarive on the island of Madagascar. The Malagasy people, with a diet heavy in salted beef, coconut oil, and macassar nuts, have one of the highest incidents of heart disease in the world.

"Understand, I'm used to tidy Swiss cantons where everybody's in bed by nine"—Dr. Boursaly continued—"pine forests where the underbrush has been carefully swept out of sight. In Geneva, as you may have heard, they distribute needles to our few dozen heroin addicts in a certain park. These people are not just addicts, mind you, but Swiss addicts. The addicts shoot up there in the park around eight in the evening and hang out till midnight. But when children walk through to school in the morning, the park is spotless. Needles and spoons and so forth have been picked up and thrown away, not by city sanitation workers but by the addicts themselves. This is Switzerland. Do you understand?''

Wilson said he did.

''In the end, all this tidiness began to grate on me, so I decided on Madagascar, which sounded like a place of marvelous strangeness. In that country every October the natives dig up their ancestors, who have been mummified, wrapped in tar-soaked mats, and buried. They take these tarry, rotting corpses to dinner, out dancing, get into cabs, sleep with them. I had to see this for myself, so I went to Madagascar, and I made many friends there and had a very interesting time. But I'll say this—Madagascar is not an easy place, and after two years, I needed an extended vacation. So a few of my friends and I rented an Arab dhow and attempted to sail across the straits to Zanzibar. Halfway there our dhow was attacked and taken by pirates off the *Storm Car*. I was saved because the Brotherhood needed a doctor. My friends were tied to the railings and the dhow was scuttled and I heard them screaming for help as it went down, and there was nothing I could do.''

The doctor lowered his eyes. The gin flush in his cheeks faded. Suddenly he seemed sober, and he poured the remainder of his gin into the nearest urn full of flowers and stood for a full minute, hands in the pockets of his doctor's smock, staring into the distance. Then he turned around, and his face looked pale and masklike. ''A prison doesn't need to have four walls and bars to be a prison,'' he said. ''You'll soon discover that. And you too will begin to drink like me, like everyone else in this paradise of monsters.''

Something, a heat shimmer in the sky, a dark cloud obscuring the horizon, told Wilson this was true.

7

THE STIFFNESS IN WILSON'S knees gradually disappeared. After a few weeks, he was able to go about the shanty city with Dr. Boursaly. At first his eyes could not grow accustomed to the misery he saw there, then one morning, all at once, he became inured to the sufferings of others. A hot African wind blew the stench hard against the island, the tropical sun hung like a yellow grapefruit in the relentless blue sky, and as the doctor had predicted, Wilson began to drink.

Hard against the fence of the barracoon stood Quatre Sables's business district. Here an alley of rusty tin-sided rumshops intersected with a wider street of brothels and other commercial concerns. There were money changers' tents, stalls that sold vegetables, pawnshops, a booth in which a sort of Punch and Judy show with shadow puppets ran continuously. Twice a week, old men spread blankets full of ruta—giant African turnips, the dietary staple of the island—along the muddy banks that passed for a sidewalk. The accepted medium of exchange was the cowrie shell, American cigarettes, and any type of money—given value by the locals according to size and color rather than denomination. Large bright bills from Italy and France would fetch more ruta than U.S. greenbacks worth ten times their value.

Wilson and the doctor spent several hours of each day at the Black Spot, a tin-sided, open-front rumshop run by a Jamaican ex-pirate who called himself Ben Gunn after the old pirate in *Treasure Island*. A warped piece of plywood set on rusty fifty-gallon oil drums served for the bar; packing crates and empty five-gallon paint tubs, for chairs and tables. The drink of choice at this establishment was rumfustian, a noxious mixture of native beer, gin, and a sort of sherry made from wild berries. A half pound of cowrie shells would buy a dirty plastic milk jug full of the stuff. Wilson drank his rumfustian out of a chipped, handleless coffee mug. The doctor did not bother with such niceties, swilling the stuff straight from the jug. A Bupandan tinka band played on a platform of tires and cardboard boxes across the way. The pleasant lilting music rose with the heat into the hot blue sky.

Today, Wilson listened to the music and watched the crowds pass along the street. At that hour of the afternoon, the place was empty except for a couple of drunks passed out facedown on the muddy floor. Ben Gunn sat propped on a three-legged stool behind the bar, big marijuana spliff smoldering between his teeth, his eyes red with the stuff. His hair hung down in gnarled dreadlocks, tied at the end with bedraggled bits of ribbon; his skin showed the unhealthy color of burnt coffee. Roaches the size of Wilson's hand ran out of the rusty barrels and over the plywood counter. Ben Gunn ignored them.

Dr. Boursaly assured Wilson that dengue fever did not affect the liver permanently and ordered another milk jug of rumfustian. He carried about ten pounds of cowrie shells and assorted Italian bills in a worn black medical bag held together with duct tape, which he kept nestled safely between his knees.

"I told you there's nothing to do on this island but drink," Dr. Boursaly said to Wilson when Ben Gunn straggled over with the fresh jug.

"Maybe for you," Wilson said. "But I'm getting out of here as soon as Cricket comes back."

Dr. Boursaly shook his head. "Except for the Thirty Captains not one of us gets off this island for good. It's too much of an international secret. Can you see the headlines in the *New York Times?* 'Pirate Paradise Discovered off African Coast—Slave Trade Alive and Well'? The decadent nations of the West would have to do something. And that wouldn't please certain people in certain circles in Europe and America and Japan who make quite a bit of money off this place."

"I still can't believe it," Wilson said with a loose gesture indicating the activity of the waterfront. "Pirates! Thousands of them. And

the Thirty Captains sound like something out of Gilbert and Sulli-
van. Who are they? Where do they come from?''

"They are the ruined men of all nations," Dr. Boursaly said.
"The hunted refugees of all vanquished parties, everyone that is
wretched and daring. And where is there not misery and vice in this
unhappy age? . . . I'm quoting, but you get the idea. It's nothing
new, of course; these rat's nests spring up like weeds at the edge of
the world. Think of the great pirate republic of Port Royal, Jamaica,
in the seventeenth century; think of New Providence and Tortuga in
the eighteenth, of Campeche and Key West in the nineteenth. In any
case, pirates below the rank of captain who decide to retire from the
bloody trade can only do so here at Quatre Sables. There's a sort of
retirement community on the other side of the island, a little village
with a sulfur spring, full of aging buccaneers. Pegleg Bay they call it.
If the men refuse the honor of living there, the only other option is a
watery grave.''

"The mon's right," Ben Gunn called over from the bar.
"There's no land for us Brothers of the Coast but right here at
Quatre Sables. An' when we die, there's still a watery grave to rest
our bones. It's in the Articles, mon. Dead shipmates are always
buried at sea.''

"But you are a different case, Wilson." Dr. Boursaly leaned
across the jug of rumfustian and lowered his tone. "So terribly
different. I'm worried that you might not make it to retirement.''

Wilson felt the back of his neck prickle. "Oh, Christ . . ." he
murmured.

"Of course it's none of my business, but I understand your Mistress Page is already spoken for.''

"Aye, mon, she's the Portugee's woman," Ben called from the
bar. "The Portugee's no one to fuck with.''

"Shut up, Ben," the doctor said.

"Who is this Portugee?" Wilson said.

"He's chairman of the Council of Thirty Captains, he—''

"No." Wilson made a quick chopping motion. "I don't want to know. Whatever comes."

The doctor shrugged.

"It's a wise mon that don't worry about the sky gonna fall," Ben Gunn said from behind the bar. " 'Cause no hat's gonna save his po' head from the big pieces."

8

THREE NIGHTS LATER, DR. Boursaly barged into the bathroom of the house on the ridge as Wilson took a cool bath in the big marble tub. The doctor's eyes were wild and excited, his clothes in disarray. As usual he reeked of alcohol.

"Don't you knock?" Wilson said.

"I couldn't," Dr. Boursaly said. "There are no doors in this place. Dry off and put on your clothes. Something I want you to see."

"We're going out?"

"Yes."

Wilson had never been through the shanty city on foot after dark, had in fact been warned against it by the doctor himself. "Isn't it a little dangerous?" he said.

The doctor waved a dismissive hand. "With all the infectious microbes floating in the air here, even breathing is dangerous."

They walked down through the rustling, shadowy streets to the barracoon. When they came through the barbed wire into the compound, Wilson saw an unusual sort of activity around the concrete hangars where the slaves were kept. Men in business suits milled about the entrance or stood talking in subdued groups of three or four. The great wooden doors were open, harsh white light spilling from within. Floods lit the bare cinder blocks. Wilson heard the sputter and burp of generators and caught the sharp reek of gasoline in the air.

"What's going on?" he said.

"It's the night of the big dance," Dr. Boursaly said. "I'm the doctor on call in case anyone breaks an ankle."

Inside the hangar spotlights shone down from the rafters, and the air smelled of sweat and wax and disinfectant, very much like a high school gym. Bleachers rose up one wall over a polished wooden platform about half the size of a basketball court. Wilson and the doctor took a seat at the corner of the bleachers in the front row and waited. Soon an evil odor, half submerged beneath the disinfectant, announced itself to Wilson's nose.

"They're moving up from the pens," the doctor said. "You can smell them coming. Clean the place from top to bottom, spray it with heavy chemicals, still won't get that stench out. If I believed in God, I'd say the whole island stinks to high heaven."

After a few minutes, the bleachers began to fill. Wilson turned and looked back at the crowd and saw clean-shaven white faces hanging like half-moons above crisp white shirts and power ties; Japanese executives hunched over calculators; Arab merchants dressed in Savile Row elegance, diamond rings flashing from their fingers. And he heard the hushed, self-important mutter of the universal language in which business is done.

Soon, the first lot came up for sale: ten young Bupu men chained together from the neck and ankles, stainless steel links gleaming like coins in the white light. Sitting barely thirty feet away, Wilson could see the despair in the eyes of these young Africans, could smell the raw fear lift off their skin in waves. The second one from the end dropped to his knees suddenly and began to call on his God in a loud, hysterical shrieking but was whipped to his feet again. The bidding proceeded in English, in American dollars, and was simultaneously translated into a dozen languages through portable headsets. The auctioneer, a stout Englishman wearing a tuxedo, spoke with an educated accent, but his was the brutish cant of auctioneers everywhere.

"A coffle of ten strong black bucks for the field," he announced, "what am I bid? All healthy, certified by our company doctors and guaranteed for six months of hard labor, barring accidents. Good Bupu stock, straight from the bush. Do I hear a hundred thousand dollars?"

The businessmen in the stands raised discreet pencils, and the bidding spiraled upward. The first lot of ten men went for just over seventy-five thousand. The second lot, seven large Andas from a mountain clan known for their endurance, went for half as much more. Over the next few hours more than eight hundred African men, women, and children were sold to sober-suited representatives of the great industrialized nations of the East and West.

When Wilson could speak, he turned to Dr. Boursaly in horror. "How could this go on?" he said under his breath, his voice trembling. "How could—" He choked on his words.

Dr. Boursaly shrugged. "You're looking at the global economy at work, my friend," he said. "The world's multinational corporations—I am talking about manufacturers of everything from computer components to blue jeans—need cheap labor to keep the overhead low. What's cheaper than a slave? No need to pay benefits, health insurance, vacations, all the rest of it. Makes perfect economic sense, really."

"But where do they go?" Wilson managed. "Where are the factories, the fields?"

The doctor leaned close. "There are certain factory islands in the South Pacific," he said in a whisper. "And off the coast of Africa and Central America and in the Java Sea. Anywhere the local government is corrupt and easily bribed to look the other way. How, you might ask, has all this been kept a big secret from the community of civilized nations? No one likely to talk gets off Quatre Sables, true, but there are always leaks. Look at it this way—maybe it's not such a big secret. Maybe the community of civilized nations just doesn't want to know. It is perhaps a commonplace to say so, but as long as everyone has their television sets and automobiles and all the rest, who cares what happens to a few hundred thousand poor wretches out of Africa? Speaking for myself, I don't particularly want to know about much more than the next drink.''

9

AFTER THE AUCTION MEN in white jackets and bow ties set up a catered party along the quay. Long draped tables were quickly covered with silver platters of lobster and caviar, pheasant under glass, suckling pig, great slabs of roast beef. Ice sculpture swans dripped in the equatorial heat. The bar showed a full array of fine wines and liquor. Champagne streamed out of a plastic fountain. Colored lights decorating the prows of corporate yachts glimmered in the dark water. Wilson saw the *Compound Interest* moored among them, listing a little to the starboard.

''When was the last time you had caviar on this damned island?'' Dr. Boursaly said, and plunged into the crowd of businessmen.

Wilson felt sick to his stomach and sick at heart. He downed a shot of straight bourbon to steady his nerves and looked out across the bright cluster of white yachts and across the shimmering water toward Africa and saw a familiar darkness blooming there, a darkness that would soon cover the earth: Civilizations lasted barely a moment in the long day of history; the lives of men and women were as good as wasted on behalf of order. Chaos lurked always, a beast in the shadows just beyond the campfire, biding its time. One day there was regular mail service, the churches were full, with the flip of a switch pleasant light illuminated a room—the next day great cities lay in ruins, and the cry of the wolf was heard again upon the moor. Musing upon such melancholy thoughts, Wilson hardly noticed when a man in a business suit came to stand at his elbow. He took in the jacket of fine navy blue silk, the red paisley tie, the gold Rolex before he recognized the face.

"Feeling better, Wilson?" the man said. "I heard you were sick." It was Ackerman.

"Didn't recognize you without your glasses," Wilson said when he regained his composure. It was a ridiculous statement, but he could think of nothing else to say.

"I've got my contact lenses in," Ackerman said, smiling. "Never wear my glasses when I'm doing business." He looked fit; his cheeks showed a healthy, ruddy color. He put a paternalistic hand on Wilson's shoulder. "How are they treating you?"

"Fine," Wilson said, "you?"

"Actually, I'm pretty good," Ackerman said. "This guy Captain Page is really quite an entrepreneur. That billion he wanted for my ransom, I convinced him to put it to work for the both of us." Then he began talking quickly, a monied gleam in his eye. "The trade the Brotherhood's got going here is fantastic, a stroke of genius, good for everyone. We get rich and relieve population pressures in Africa at the same time. Beautiful, pure unadulterated capitalism at work. If you ask me—"

"Do you know what happened to Captain Amundsen?" Wilson interrupted.

Ackerman's smile faded. He looked into his drink and blinked at the *Compound Interest* moored down the quay. "I heard. He was a good man. It's really too bad he wouldn't join us."

When Ackerman looked back, he saw something in Wilson's face and began to back away.

"Murderer!" Wilson cried. "Slaver! They're human beings, not units of merchandise!" At this a few businessmen stopped eating and looked in Wilson's direction.

"S-slavery is a value-laden term," Ackerman stuttered, "and it's not entirely accurate. We prefer uncompensated labor or coerced manpower, or—"

Wilson didn't wait for Ackerman to finish. He lunged forward and closed his hands around the billionaire's throat and squeezed as hard as he could. Ackerman's eyes registered shock, then they began to bulge slightly, and one contact came rolling out like a large round tear. In the next second two of the bartenders pulled Wilson away. Gasping for breath, Ackerman fell back against a table full of suckling pig and slid to the pavement. Wilson heard the man's silk trousers rip.

Dr. Boursaly hurried over and put an arm around Wilson's shoulder. "Come with me, quickly," he said into Wilson's ear, and led him through the crowd and up the hill through the darkness of the shanty city. When they were halfway up, Wilson stopped and squatted in the mud and dug his knuckles in his eyes and wept soundlessly. Dr. Boursaly squatted beside him and lit a cigarette.

"I'm going to do something about that," Wilson said when he stopped weeping, and he actually shook his fist in the direction of the barracoon. "One way or another I'm going to stop that shit, I swear it."

"That's what I thought when I first came here," Dr. Boursaly said glumly. "But what can any one of us do against their machine? It's all we can do to stay alive. Sorry I brought you along with me tonight. Didn't know it would inspire such a *crise de conscience.*" He fell silent; there was nothing more to say.

The black hemisphere of the bay was pricked out with the running lights of freighters awaiting a cargo of human flesh.

10

THE RAINY SEASON STARTED with an odd greenish glow in the sky. Heavy purple clouds gathered against the green like disapproving deities in a Greek play, but for days there was no rain at all, just an oppressive humidity so thick the air felt like quicksand. Heat lightning flashed obscure messages on the horizon, and from somewhere far away came the beating of tribal drums. Then, all at once, in the middle of the night it began to rain. The sky opened up, and buckets of the stuff poured down. Wilson woke to the thunderous noise of the water and lay sweating in the big bed beneath the mosquito netting, listening to a chorus of screaming from the shanty city.

At dawn, he rose to the window to see that half the slope had been washed down into the bay, its black water stained red by a tide of mud and garbage.

"Happens every year like this," Dr. Boursaly said when he came up for his breakfast gin at ten. "Between five and ten thousand will die from exposure in the next few months. In May they'll rebuild again, and there will be more brown babies born on garbage heaps, and thousands more of the wretched floating over from Africa, and the whole bloody miserable cycle continues."

They sat at the polished oak table in the dining room. Rain had torn ragged holes in the striped awning of the patio; large water stains spread across the kitchen ceiling; water dripped into aluminum pots set on the tile floor. The doctor finished his first gin, gave out a melancholy sigh, and poured another—no different from any other morning. But Wilson felt a sudden rush of revulsion and realized he could no longer abide the man.

"Doctor, have you ever tried to get off the island?" Wilson said, an irritated edge in his voice.

Dr. Boursaly registered the accusation and sighed again. "You mean, escape? How could I?'' he said. ''We're sealed up tighter than a fortress here,'' but when he took his next drink, his hand shook.

''There's got to be a way,'' Wilson said. ''It's a goddamned island. If all those poor bastards can float over from Africa, it seems to me, someone could float in the opposite direction, maybe tell the authorities about this place.''

The doctor said nothing; his red eyes looked out wearily from thick red-rimmed lids that made Wilson think of a turtle in its shell. The vein in the doctor's nose pulsed out a gentle rhythm of despair.

Wilson felt sorry for the man, but there was something in the air, a curious pressure, and he couldn't stop himself.

''Here's what I think, Doctor,'' Wilson said. ''I think you've been a drunk for years. I think that's why you left Switzerland, and that's why you've never tried to get off the island. You belong here. Who's going to notice a drunken doctor in the midst of all this squalor?'' Wilson knew this for the truth as soon as he said it. He regretted the statement, but it was too late.

Dr. Boursaly rose unsteadily, with as much dignity as he could muster, and ran a hand through his thinning brown hair.

''I understand,'' he said. ''The rainy season. There have been studies. The unusually dense atmosphere puts hydraulic pressure on certain chemicals in the brain. I get that way myself, snappish, irritable, everyone a nuisance. I'll see you in three months when the weather clears.''

Then he finished his drink in a quick gulp and went through the kitchen and out into the rain.

11

OVER THE NEXT FEW weeks it rained every day from dawn to dusk and on into the night, and Wilson read *Don Quixote,* Caulaincourt's *With Napoleon in Russia,* and *Manon Lescaut*—the last of the books he had brought with him from his old life. The only book of any interest he found in the house was a copy of Rimbaud's poems that contained a short biography of the poet: After a wild youth of madness and excess Rimbaud had exiled himself to Africa, entered the slave trade, married an Abyssinian woman. Somehow the most egotistical of men from a nation known for its egotism had forgotten all about himself under the hot African sun. Twenty dusty years later, when he lay dying from a cancerous leg in Marseilles and was already famous in Paris, he could hardly remember that he had ever written a single poem.

Africa has that effect on the urban temperament, Wilson decided. A sort of deadening lethargy descends, you perfect the art of staring at the wall, and one day blurs into the next. So it was not possible for him to say how many more weeks passed before Cricket came home again from the sea. One morning, purple sky full of rain over the island, the muddy streets impassible and awash with garbage, Wilson awoke to hear noises coming from the big bathroom. He put on a robe and went to investigate and found Cricket taking a bath in the tub beneath the skylight. The rain light made green shadows in the room, and the water in the tub was strewn with delicate pink and yellow rose petals.

"Hello, Wilson, sweet," Cricket said when he came up. She smiled a lazy smile and made small splashing noises with her fingers. "I told that drunk if you weren't well when I got back, there would be hell to pay. Are you well?"

Wilson said nothing and looked at her body through the water. The rose petals obscured his view.

"Where did you find roses on this island?" he said finally.

"They come out of a package, from France," Cricket said, adjusting herself in the tub. "They're freeze-dried, look like little turds. Put them in the water and poof—rose petals. But is that all you have to say? It's been three months. Aren't you even happy to see me?"

"Yes, it's good to see you," Wilson said, but he didn't move out of the doorway.

"Sorry it took so long, honey," Cricket said. "We had some trouble in Bupanda. There's a war going on, you know. Can be a little hard to do business. And I'm sorry for a lot of other things too. . . ." She held out her arms, and the green rain light shimmered along them like static electricity. "During all the nastiness over there," she whispered, "all I thought about was getting back to you. I thought about how sad I would be if you died."

Wilson dropped his robe and stepped into the tub. The water was warm on his thighs, and Cricket lay back, floating among the petals like Ophelia, and she closed her eyes and didn't make a sound. For Wilson, it was like guilt. Making love to her had the sweet, dreadful savor of sleeping with another man's wife. She was part of this pirate hell; she was implicated. Now, by accepting her body, he was implicated too. His brain and his heart knew this, but he couldn't stop himself, and the razor of his conscience lent the undeniable thrill of pain to the act. Afterward they lay half submerged in the tepid water, rose petals stuck to their skin.

"Cricket, we need to talk," Wilson said.

"Not now, sweet," Cricket said sleepily. "It's so nice just floating here with you. Listen to the rain on the roof."

"Now," Wilson said.

12

THEY FOLLOWED THE SHELL drive that made up the single road of the ridge settlement, past the homes of the Thirty Captains set back among the tamarinds. Wilson had never seen anyone pass along here, and with a few exceptions the white houses were shuttered and closed.

"They're all in London or Miami or somewhere this time of year," Cricket said. "It's only hardworking old Dad who pulls a raid going into the rainy season."

The rain poured buckets and then let up for a bit. A few cars stood under canvas covers along the drive; Wilson recognized the familiar silhouette of a Mercedes-Benz. A big tabby cat crouched underneath it, just behind the front wheels. Cricket made a plaintive mewing sound; the cat mewed back but would not venture out across the wet shell gravel.

"That's Petey," Cricket said. "Used to be the ship's cat aboard the *Esperance,* Evan Matthews's tub. He's another Palmetto scrub like Dad. Matthews ran into an Argentine coast guard cutter off the Maldives awhile back. The cutter went down after a pretty hairy fight, but so did the *Esperance.* Captain Matthews and Petey for breakfast and two other sailors—all that was left of the crew—floated around in a rubber raft for a week, and were just about to eat poor Petey before they were picked up. When they got back here, Captain Matthews retired him, but you know, I think that cat misses the life of a pirate."

Cricket and Wilson walked on in silence, and the shell drive became a rutted trail that wound up the ridge through a thicket of scrub and brush grass and into a patch of jungle that was like going into a long green tunnel. They folded their umbrellas. The heavy-leaved trees protected them from the rain. Small orange monkeys scuttled about in the green dimness; black-scaled lizards ran up the rough bark. A quarter mile further on, the trail passed out into an open space along the ridge, a rocky outcropping that faced the interior of the island.

Wilson had never been this far up, and he was surprised by what he saw below. The ridge sloped down to a jungle-covered valley that gave way to open, cultivated land about three miles off. There were rice paddies and orchards full of mangoes and banana trees, rich black squares of fallow earth, carefully tended stone walls. A straight road led to a massive-looking country house of ancient stone. Wilson's fix on architecture was vague, but he put the building at fifteenth- or sixteenth-century Spanish or Portuguese, probably the fortified residence of some long-gone colonial governor. Nicely tended green lawns led down to a reflecting pool and the clipped hedge cones of a classical garden. Wilson did not need to be told who owned this estate, but Cricket squeezed his hand and told him anyway.

"That's the Portugee's place," she said, "Villa Real. His people have lived down there for over four hundred years. At one time, they supplied nearly all the slaves for plantations in the New World. The king of Portugal gave this island as a gift to one of his ancestors, the first white man to sail around the bulge of Africa and live to tell the tale—"

"Yes, Gil Eannes was his name," Wilson said.

"That's right," Cricket said, surprised. "How did you know that?"

"I'm not sure," Wilson said uneasily, and at that moment he didn't.

"In any case, the Portugee is one of our problems," Cricket said. "My father is another one of our problems."

They went back up the trail into the trees. Then Cricket turned to the left and led Wilson through the underbrush. About twenty yards off the trail a large banyan tree spread its leaves down to the ground, forming a sort of waterproof cave. On the ground beneath the leaves, someone had spread one of the oriental rugs from the house and set a silver tray with two crystal glasses and a bottle of champagne on ice not yet completely melted.

"Very slick," Wilson said. "I think I've been set up."

Cricket grinned and kissed him. They sat down on the rug and took off their rain ponchos, and there was the heavy root smell of jungle earth and the sad rustling of the monkeys in the trees. Cricket opened the bottle of champagne. The cork popped off and shot into the leaves, an incongruously civilized sound in the wet hushing of the jungle. She filled a glass, handed it to Wilson. "Champagne?" she said.

Wilson knew less about champagne than he knew about architecture, but after one sip he took a shot and put the stuff at five hundred dollars a bottle.

"Should we have a toast?" Cricket said.

"I suppose so," Wilson said.

Cricket hesitated. Then her smile faded, and she drank down her glass in one nervous swallow. "Look at me, Wilson." Her voice was serious.

Wilson looked up. Her eyes matched the green of the jungle, but with some darker shade roiling in the surface.

"This is my way of proposing," she said. "If you want to stay alive, you'll have to marry me."

Wilson didn't know what to say. An orange monkey peered down at him through the leaves. Its wizened face looked like the face of an old man. This was one of the strangest moments in his life.

"Marriage is the only way out, sweet," Cricket said softly, "otherwise they will kill you." She reached for his hand and pressed it to her face and addressed the rest of her speech to his knuckles. "Under the Articles, you are my slave, a piece of property. A slave has no rights here. If someone kills your slave, you've got to be compensated, of course, but it's only a question of money. Now a husband, that's very different. That means you're part of the family, one of the Company of the Thirty Captains. Protected by the full authority of the Articles, do you see?"

Wilson pulled away and folded his arms across his chest. "Not really," he said quietly. "Why don't you tell me the whole story this time?"

Four glasses of champagne later Cricket took a deep breath and was ready to begin.

"I'm going to give you a little bit of background first," she said. "When I was a kid, the economy of the Palmettos was based entirely on gambling, and everyone did pretty well by it. Then organized crime got involved, and there were a couple of very public murders on Outer Key, and in '76 the Alabama legislature outlawed our high-stakes poker games for good. About three thousand people were put out of work just like that and needed to find another way to make a living. For hundreds of years before gambling got big in the 1920s, Palmetto Scrubs like Dad had always looked to the sea— we live on a bunch of islands, right? Hell, the place was first settled by buccaneers under the famous Elzevir Montague, who is a direct ancestor of mine. So, back to the sea we went.

"Dad had enough in his savings to buy the *Storm Car* off the Costa Rican Navy, and he started going after expensive yachts in the Caribbean and tramps full of dope coming out of South America. Other guys did the same thing. They formed a loose confederation, just like in the bad old pirate days, and called it the Brotherhood of the Coast. Over the next five years, the Brotherhood disappeared about two hundred boats. Blame it on the Bermuda Triangle—that was the big joke then, and it was even funnier that a lot of people in the news media actually did blame it on stuff like magnetic whirlpools and UFOs.

"Meanwhile, right around this time, the civil war in Bupanda was just starting to heat up. A few enterprising Lebanese ship owners were buying Bupu POWs off the Andas and Anda POWs off the Bupus and selling them to the Arabs along the Red Sea. Dad was one of the first on our side of the pond to figure the real potential there. He set up a barracoon at Grand Terre, which is a flyspeck of an island just northwest of the Palmetto Passage, recruited thirty captains out of the Brotherhood, and headed out for Africa.

"Everyone started making a ton of money almost immediately. Second year of operation, Dad sold two hundred Bupus to Dominion Sugar to work their cane fields in Guyana for something like a quarter of a million bucks. But one night, during a hurricane, six of the Bupus got loose. One who could speak English eventually made it to Jamaica, and rumors trickled back to the States. Then the coast guard started to sniff around, and all of a sudden the Palmetto setup just wasn't going to work anymore, so Dad started to look for another home base for the Bupanda trade. That's when the Portugee came over and proposed a little private high-stakes card game just between him and Dad. If Dad won, he could bring the slave trade to Quatre Sables and turn it into a big-time operation and run the show, with no percentage off the top. If the Portugee won, Dad could still come out to Quatre Sables, but the Portugee would run the show with a twenty-five percent straight cut off the top, and one other little thing. Call it an added bonus—"

Cricket paused to swig a mouthful of champagne straight out of the bottle. She topped up Wilson's glass, spilling some over the side. When she drank again, Wilson heard the bottle chatter against her teeth. She wiped her mouth on her sleeve and went on in a shaky voice.

"The Portugee is a real gambler; he's addicted to gambling in the way that other people are addicted to drugs or booze. I told you a few things about him before, but not the whole truth. I've known the man since I was a little girl. He used to play in Johnny Mazep's poker games in the old days and stayed with us off and on in the big house in St. George, and I guess I used to flirt with him in the way that little girls do. He seemed so fine with his perfect white suits and his swishy European manners. Then, one day, when I was about eleven, he drove me out to Capstan Head for a picnic—he had this white Mercedes limousine with a chauffeur that he always brought over from Miami on the ferry—and on the way back he pulled down my sundress and put his hands all over my chest and between my legs and took his dick out and his face got all red, and he started jerking off. I screamed, but the chauffeur didn't even turn around. When he was done, he cleaned me up and told me to stop crying and acted as if nothing had happened. I didn't say anything about the incident to my mom, because I was terrified and I felt guilty and I didn't know if I had done something to cause the Portugee to act that way. I put the whole thing in the back of my mind where you put the bad stuff, and I tried to forget about it.

"Five years later, the night the Portugee played his private card game with Dad, I had just come back from a dance at Palmetto High, where I had gotten stoned and fucked some greaser in the backseat of his car. It was about three in the morning, I was listening to Foghat on my headphones and getting undressed, and I didn't hear the Portugee come into my bedroom. He pushed me down on the bed, put a pillow over my face, and raped me. Then, he took the pillow off my face and told me not to be scared, and he raped me again. I wasn't a virgin, but it was horrible. At one point I looked up and saw Dad standing in the doorway, watching and taking hits off a bottle of bourbon.

"The Portugee raped me one more time in the morning before he left. About ten A.M. Dad heard me crying and came in and told me that he had lost me to the Portugee in a poker game, that I was no longer his daughter, that I belonged to the Portugee now just like a slave and that I had no choice in the matter. I cried and cried, but my mother was dead by then, and there was nothing I could do. I didn't fight it. How could I? I couldn't run away again. Every time I ran away I just ended up fucking somebody for a place to stay, for a decent meal. You know what happens to naive young girls on the streets. What was the point? So a week later, I shipped out on the Portugee's ship, the *Jesus of Lubeck*. I told you about that. The only part I left out was that he fucked me from noon till night the whole time, used me like a convict. I've been his woman ever since then. The man is obsessed with me. Whenever I try to leave him, he finds me, brings me back. He's done that twice. The only life I know is the sea, I don't know how to do anything else, and he's got connections in shipping companies all over the world.

"There's just one way to escape the Portugee for good. I need a good gambler. You're sweet and smart, and you're a good gambler, right, Wilson? The minute you walked into Nancy's shop, I knew there was something about you. I was attracted to you right away, and when you told me that your father had been a professional gambler, the wheels started turning. Right then and there I dreamed up the whole scheme to take you away with me."

"Cricket—"

"No, let me finish. Every time I come home to Quatre Sables, I go stay at Villa Real for a few days and the Portugee fucks me. It's not great, but I'm used to it. I was even sort of content with my life until you came along. It wasn't so bad. Plenty of action on board one ship or the next, and I'm on my own most of the year, so if I have a fling in some distant corner of the world, who will know? But now the Portugee's on this kick where he wants to marry me. I've been able to put him off for the past two years, but he doesn't want to wait any longer, and he's serious. Says he's getting old, says he wants to settle down, have kids to take over that damned pile of old stones in the valley. Listen, Wilson, this Ackerman thing is my first real operation as a full partner. I have a legitimate share in the profits under the Articles. Until now, it's been pocket change—ten thousand here, twenty there. But when that rich bastard finally coughs up, we're talking about millions! Enough money to get away and live for the rest of our lives! I mean anywhere, Europe, South America, you name it. We can live like normal people! We can have a house together and who knows, and we—"

Cricket's voice cracked. She leaned forward and put her face in her hands and began to sob in loud, jerky spasms. Wilson felt embarrassed, didn't know what to do. He wanted to tell her that he didn't trust her, that he couldn't live off the earnings of piracy and murder and slavery, that you could never base your own happiness

on the sufferings of others. In the end, he finished by doing what
men of feeling have always done when faced with a desperate woman
in tears. He took her in his arms and held her close and offered what
comfort he could.

13

THE BIG BLUE LAGONDA pulled onto the main road of the
shanty city from an alley halfway down the slope. Making his way to
the Black Spot through the rain and the sodden crowds, Wilson
stepped beneath an overhang to let the elegant vehicle pass. It was a
fifties-era Rapide, royal blue, with a lovely Tickford body and
chrome wire wheels. He had only seen pictures of cars like that in
books. Rain beaded the surface of its glossy waxed hood; the engine
purred along, no louder than a clock. When it came past Wilson's
overhang, the car stopped and idled there for a moment, water
hissing against the big radiator. Then two men got out of the front
and stepped over to him, and Wilson recognized Mustapha and
Schlüber, Captain Page's lieutenants.

"Don't make a fuss," the German said. "Just get in the car."

For emphasis, Mustapha pulled open his raincoat and showed
Wilson the butt end of an old U.S. Army issue Colt .45. Wilson
shrugged and slid into the back of the Lagonda, the door closing
behind with a solid chunking sound. The seats were of fragrant,
worn leather; the trim along the doors burled mahogany with silver
accents. Front and back were separated by a privacy screen of thick
glass. The mahogany dash, set with pearl-faced gauges and a steering
wheel of solid crystal, reminded Wilson of a dining room table laid
out for Christmas dinner. Mustapha came around to the right-hand
side and got in behind the wheel, Schlüber got in from the other

side, and the car eased into gear and bumped down the muddy slope.

When Wilson's eyes adjusted to the dull rain light of the interior, he realized he was not alone in the backseat; the pirate captain slumped against the door in the far corner. Today, he wore a rumpled brown suit and a stained yellow tie. His eye patch was askew. A half pint bottle of vodka stuck out of his breast pocket.

"You going to kill me this time, Captain?" Wilson said.

The pirate would not reply. He grunted, mumbled something to himself, and took the bottle of vodka out of his pocket and knocked back a healthy slug.

They reached the docks and veered up to the left of the barracoon. The windshield wipers made a soft thumping sound on the glass. The road curved around the ragged outskirts of the city, then widened out and entered thick jungle a half mile beyond the last shanty. After a minute, Wilson felt the tires cross a bumpy surface. He pressed his nose to the window to see a pavement of ancient cobbles passing below. Along both sides of the road here, crumbling neoclassical statues were set at intervals of every hundred-odd feet: nymphs and goddesses, satyrs and heroes, all vine-covered, half eaten by jungle.

At last, the pirate held out his bottle of vodka. "Have a drink, citizen," he said, but would not look in Wilson's direction.

"That's all anyone seems to do on this island," Wilson said. He took a small sip from the bottle and handed it back.

"I hear you want to marry my daughter," the pirate said, and he swung around suddenly and fixed Wilson with his one watery eye.

"Not exactly," Wilson said.

"Good, because she's not mine to give away," the pirate said. "I lost her to the Portugee years ago in a poker game. I suppose she didn't tell you that."

"She did," Wilson said. "And as far as I'm concerned, she doesn't belong to anyone but herself. She's got the right to do whatever she wants with her own life."

The pirate gave a grin that showed a mouthful of yellow teeth. "Very funny," he said. "Tell that joke to the Portugee. This isn't the States, kid. My daughter's not some average middle-class bimbo from Bumfuck, Illinois. There are no rights in Quatre Sables except property rights. Everybody belongs to somebody else."

"That's not why I'm hesitating about this," Wilson said.

"Huh?"

"First of all, you've got to admit, the circumstances are very weird. Second, even under normal conditions, I just don't think I'm ready for marriage right now."

"You're kidding," the pirate said.

"No," Wilson said. "And there's more. To make a successful marriage, two people should have certain interests in common. They should at least share a similar temperament. Cricket's a fascinating, beautiful woman, but my tolerance for murder, slavery, and piracy is very low."

"You're killing me, citizen!" The Pirate started to laugh, and he tipped his head back and his laughter came out in a long, drunken howl.

"One last thing," Wilson said. "The in-laws."

The pirate stopped laughing, and his eye narrowed.

"Unsavory," Wilson said. "That's the best I can say. In truth, this whole business gives me the hives. I've never asked God for anything in my life, but when I saw those poor miserable Africans down there in chains, I asked Him to give me a chance for revenge on all of you."

"Let me tell you something," the pirate said in a calm voice. "You may not like slavery, but it's the wave of the future. They've got just one thing in Africa, and it's a thing they don't need—more people. There's just too fucking many of them, look at Bupanda now. Three million dead in the last ten years from starvation and butchery and civil war didn't even make a dent in their population problem. I've seen Bupu tribesmen with ten wives and seventy-three kids, living on garbage heaps. Did you know that Bupanda is the most densely populated country in Africa? Every little nigger slut over there has an average of ten kids, we're talking average. The Western press never reported that, did they? I remember Rigala before the war; you had to crawl over your neighbor just to take a shit. The country was beautiful once, rolling hills, forests—reminded me of Ireland. Now, except for a few clicks of heavy jungle in the highlands, the forests are practically gone, the hills are covered with decomposing bodies. Two hundred years ago, Malthus said the only way to control population was through misery or vice. The Bupandans, they've got the misery part down pat. We're the vice part."

The pirate chuckled to himself and sloshed more vodka into his mouth. Wilson stared out the Lagonda's rain-wet window and considered what the pirate had said. The jungle slid by, a tangle of underbrush and moral complexity.

"I've seen a lot of terrible things these last few months," Wilson said when he was ready to speak. "And I've decided that I'm going to live in the world as if it is a better place. Call this the romantic approach to life, a simple solution to a difficult problem. In any case it's the only way I can figure to keep my moral balance and my sanity. My gut tells me slavery is a great evil, and I'm going to live by what my gut tells me—that's another way of saying I'm going to live by my principles. But I'm afraid it may be too late for Cricket. She's been wallowing in your mire for most of her life. She desperately wants to come clean, but it may be too late to get the dirt off."

The pirate sat up and capped the bottle of vodka and shoved it back into the pocket of his rumpled brown suit.

"I could cut your throat right now," he growled. "Cut you ear to fucking ear and drop your body in the jungle for your guts to be eaten out by animals." Then he rapped a sharp knuckle on the partition, and the glass slid down and Schlüber turned around.

"What is it, Captain?" the German said.

"Show this little bastard your knife."

The German grinned and reached into his coat and pulled out a bone-handled knife, its long blade curved like a sardonic smile.

"I wouldn't," Wilson said. "The Portugee is a friend of mine."

"Bullshit," the pirate said, and made a throat-cutting gesture. "Cut him, Schlüber."

"What about the car, Captain?" Schlüber's grin faded. "What would the Portugee say if we got blood all over his Wilton carpets?"

"You heard me," the pirate said. "Cut him!"

Wilson tried to stay calm. Sweat broke out on his forehead. He looked from the pirate to Schlüber and leaned back slowly into the door. The jungle was only a few yards away. But the German's face went white, and he turned without another word and put the screen back up. Wilson let out an inaudible sigh of relief.

"Look at this, you bastard," the pirate said to Wilson.

Wilson looked down.

The pirate held out a knobby hand, and Wilson saw it was trembling with rage.

"That's how close you came," the pirate said. "If I had real men working for me instead of goddamned M.B.A.'s, you would already be dead. Now keep your fucking mouth shut."

Wilson turned again to the window. Out in the rain in the jungle underbrush, he saw a statue of the virgin huntress Diana, a headless deer at her feet, on a pedestal of marble taken by creepers. Her bow hand was gone, and with it half her arm; the other hand plucked at raindrops. Moss grew in the empty marble sockets of her eyes.

14

SHEEP GRAZED PLACIDLY ON grass at the bottom of the disused moat. A great wrought-iron gate perhaps thirty feet high led into a cobbled courtyard where a fountain modeled after the Trevi in

Rome splashed quiet water into a basin full of lily pads. The Lagonda pulled into the courtyard and stopped before the main entrance of the house, a baroque portico alive with saints and angels and arabesques carved in a pinkish stone that looked softer than sand.

"I hope you come back in chunks, you insufferable little fuck," the pirate said as Wilson stepped out of the dark interior.

"We'll see about that," Wilson said, and was going to say more, but the pirate slammed the door, and the Lagonda lurched over the cobbles and out the mouth of the wrought-iron gate.

Wilson stood in the rain looking up at the house till the shoulders of his jacket were soaked through. He found a handkerchief in his pocket and blew his nose. A second later, the front door opened. A diminutive woman wearing a housedress and flowered apron peered out and said something in a rapid language he did not understand.

Wilson shook his head. "English," he said. "A little French."

"You get wet," the woman said. "Come inside."

Wilson went up the wide marble steps and, after wiping his feet carefully on a mat that read "Bienvenudo," stepped inside. The Villa Real had been extensively remodeled sometime during the last hundred years. The walls were covered with dark Victorian wainscoting and hung with paintings in ornate gilt frames of the same era. Wilson noticed an uncatalogued Madonna by Murillo and two Goya bullfighting canvases he had never seen before.

The woman showed him to the library, a vast room with Gothic arched ceilings and bookshelves two stories high. Diamond-pane windows overlooked the formal gardens. The Portugee was on a ladder selecting a book when Wilson entered. Wilson remembered the man immediately. Don Luis Hidalgo de la Vaca looked the same as he had the night of the cockfight, except he had traded his white linen suit for a red silk smoking jacket and quilted Moroccan slippers of yellow suede. His chauffeur, the Killa from Manila, sat quietly in a Tudor armchair by the window reading a biography of Bismarck. He closed the book and followed Wilson's progress across the room with heavy-lidded eyes.

"Patron," the wrestler called.

Don Luis gave a quick look over his shoulder. "Do you know the poet Byron, Mr. Lander?" he said.

"Not personally," Wilson said. "I read him in college."

Don Luis pulled a heavy volume off the shelf and descended carefully, one rung at a time. "Byron was such a passionate writer, don't you think?"

"That's what they say," Wilson said. "Supposedly he slept with every man, woman, and child in Europe below the age of fifty."

Don Luis frowned. "That's not what I mean," he said. "I'm talking about the poems." He crossed to a library table strewn with books, pulled up a wing-backed easy chair, and sat down, volume of Byron in his lap like a cat.

Wilson shrugged. *"Childe Harold's Pilgrimage* was dull," he said. "They made us read it in college. *Don Juan* was a little better. I prefer Keats."

"Keats was sentimental and weak," Don Luis said. "Think of all those whining letters to Fanny Brown," then he pointed to a stool at his feet. "Sit down."

Wilson shook his head. "I'll stand," he said.

Don Luis fingered his small mustache and looked up at Wilson through weary eyes. It was impossible to know what was going on behind that aristocratic poker face. Not knowing made Wilson uneasy.

"Say what you will about Byron." Don Luis tapped the volume with his thin, elegant fingers. "But his life lived up to his poems. He was heroic, a man of action in the best sense. An aristocrat. His poetry reflects his life, and so it's better suited to our times than the paler work of more contemplative poets."

Wilson made an ambivalent gesture that Don Luis interpreted as skepticism. He sat forward in the chair, eyes bright at the prospect of an argument.

"Look around, Mr. Lander, we are entering a new era in the history of the world," he said, assuming a lecturing tone. "Men have grown tired of the rule of law. The seas are alive again with pirates. At last we are leaving behind the petty, the bourgeois, the comfortable. Leaving the age of corporate man and entering an age of wolves. Physical heroism and brute force will become the virtues of the future. Personal honor, and I mean the honor of the warrior, will replace all the lies of international commercial culture. Look at your own country! The dominant classes are morally bankrupt, too self-absorbed even to reproduce themselves. They value luxury more than power, safety more than their own souls. What have they wrought in the absence of honor? Suburbia! A place without texture in which all originalities of character are suppressed by tranquilizing drugs, where blandness is deemed the greatest good, where a man's highest aspiration is to become a lawyer or a marketing consultant. You Americans have become a soft nasty people, a people who want neither terror nor virtue. Thank God all that is changing now. Your decaying cities are breeding a new race of assassins whose hands will never tire of reaching for the sword. One day soon they will rise up and slit your throats while you sleep. Well then . . ."

"Wait a minute, Luis," Wilson interrupted. "Forget the philosophizing and the Romantic poets. You intend to kill me, right?" and he slumped down on the stool, exhausted suddenly, and put his elbows on the table. "How are you going to do it?"

"I'll probably have Alfonso snap your neck," Don Luis said after a moment's consideration. "It's really the quickest way, with the least fuss and mess. Relax and it's over in seconds."

Wilson shot a glance at the massive wrestler, once again engrossed in his biography of Bismarck, and already felt the man's meaty fingers crushing his windpipe. Wilson went dizzy suddenly and leaned his forehead against the library table. For a whole minute, he stared down at the worn marble of the floor, at the Portugee's quilted yellow slippers. When he lifted his head back up again, Don Luis was waiting, fingertips pressed together.

"Before you kill me," Wilson said in a voice as calm as he could make it, "let me tell you a story about my father."

Don Luis smiled patiently. He had all the time in the world.

"During World War Two, my father served with the U.S. Army Air Corps stationed out of Lancaster Field in England," Wilson said. "They ran bombing runs to France and Germany in those big planes, you know, B-17's, the Flying Fortresses. My father was the radio operator, but many of the missions he flew went out under radio silence, so most of the time he just sat there in the belly of the plane, waiting for the flak to rip open the fuselage. They went up four and five times a week, the odds were terrible, something like ninety percent of the airmen were hit. In the last six months of 1943 the Allies lost more than ten thousand men in the sky over Europe. The more you went up, the worse your odds of surviving. But if you survived twenty-five missions, they would rotate you out. That was the magic number.

"My father survived his twenty-five missions without a scratch, but he didn't want to be rotated out. Instead he asked for a transfer to a new plane for twenty-five more missions. They never had enough experienced men on hand, so he got the twenty-five missions he asked for, and the next twenty-five. He ended up flying more missions than any other radio operator in the Army Air Corps during World War Two. Everybody thought he was crazy. He wasn't crazy; he was a gambler who knew he was better than the odds.

"Before the war he had been a law student at Ashland College, someone who had never gambled in his whole life, never touched a pack of cards. He became a gambler after his very first mission in the air over Europe. It was a famous air disaster; it's in the history books. A whole squadron went up without support to bomb a munitions factory and ran into a nest of German fighters. Out of fifty-seven planes, only one came back—his. Wasn't even touched, not a single bullet hole. After that they changed the plane's name from something stupid and patriotic, like the *Winged Victory,* to the *Lucky Linda* and painted a big happy naked girl on the side. Father figured he had already cheated the worst odds of all on his very first mission, so why couldn't he do it again and again? He loved cheating the odds. He told me once that cheating the odds was the only thing that makes us human beings. There was no real skill, no art involved, he said—it was all style.

"So when he was discharged in 1945, he became a professional gambler. He loved the horses most of all, but he would play roulette, poker, shoot craps, anything but the dogs. He figured the odds were always against him, they always were, and he always won. And you know what, Luis? I'm the same way. I spent half my life denying it, trying to live very cautiously, trying to build up a wall of probability between myself and the unknown. Now I know the truth. Like my father, I'm a gambler and a damned good one. Like my father, I can't be beat at any game of chance where the odds are against me. Not by anyone alive."

Don Luis was silent after Wilson finished speaking. Then he rose and went over to the window and looked out at the garden and the rain.

"The stakes," he said at last. "What do you have to offer besides your life?"

"It's Cricket," Wilson said. "If you win, she'll marry you next week, no questions asked."

"If I lose?"

Wilson shrugged. "She says she loves me."

"Do you believe her?"

"I don't know. But killing me right now won't do any good. She won't marry you with my blood on your hands. She wanted me to tell you that."

Don Luis did not turn from the window.

Wilson waited an interminable minute. He opened the volume of Byron and saw this line from *Manfred*: "Accursed! What have I to do with days? They are too long already . . ." Then he closed it again.

15

THEY HAD HIGH TEA at five in the afternoon. The house-keeper brought out focaccia bread and finger sandwiches and a pot of spiced hot tisane, followed by a tray of sweets. When she cleared this away a half hour later, the Killa from Manila took all the books from the library table and brought out two chairs and a strongbox. He opened the lid, and Wilson couldn't help a gasp. It was full of gold Krugerrands. Alive with their own light, they looked like every picture of pirate treasure he had ever seen.

Don Luis drew out a handful and scattered them across the table. Wilson took one between his fingertips. The obverse showed a bust of F. W. Botha, Champion of Apartheid; the reverse showed an innocent springbok gamboling on the veldt.

"Rather gaudy, don't you think?" Don Luis said. "But they're handy to gamble with. So much more impressive than poker chips."

They divided the Krugerrands into equal piles of one thousand and began with stud poker, nothing wild. Every few hands Don Luis would open a fresh pack, which he removed from a Renaissance cabinet across the room. Later in the evening the housekeeper brought a platter of cold meats and cheeses, followed by cigars and shots of mango liqueur made from fruit grown on the estate. After that, they smoked and played and spoke little. There were no stars out the diamond-pane windows, just rain and jungle black. At the end of six hours, Wilson was five hundred Krugerrands up. Two hours later he was fifty down. But he was never worried. The odds sang to him, and he felt the truth quite simply: Don Luis was a man he could beat.

As dawn showed the first stroke in the sky, Wilson took the Portugee's last coin. They were piled up at Wilson's elbow's now, like gold in a fairy tale. At any moment he expected them to turn into lumps of coal.

Don Luis leaned back, a distant wisdom in his gaze. Wilson stretched; he heard the bones of his vertebrae crackle like popcorn.

"Now I have to decide whether to kill you or to let you get away with my woman," Don Luis said.

Wilson shrugged. His eyes hurt from lack of sleep, but he didn't feel tired. "You are a gentleman," he said. "I assume your word is worth something."

"Unfortunately it is," Don Luis said.

They got up from the table and went downstairs to the kitchen, a large room with rough stone walls and slit windows. Huge impractical copper pots hung on pegs beside a fireplace big enough to roast a horse. Above the mantel, a dusty leather shield showed a falcon and two stars on a yellow ground.

"This is the oldest part of the house," Don Luis said. "Built around 1500. Look at the hand-hewn beams in the ceiling."

Wilson glanced up at the beams, which seemed unremarkable. He took a stool along the counter to the left of the sink and waited as Don Luis rummaged in the pantry.

"I must confess a liking for the hearty American breakfast," Don Luis called. "But I don't come down here very often. It will take me a moment to find the right ingredients." He emerged a few minutes later with the eggs, coffee, bread, a half wheel of Gruyère, and a slab of country bacon.

"Need any help?" Wilson said. "I was assistant cook aboard the *Compound Interest*."

"You were a galley scullion, Mr. Lander?" the Portugee said, and raised an eyebrow.

"Assistant cook," Wilson said.

"Good. I will leave it to you."

Wilson boiled the coffee African style and sliced the cheese and bacon and beat the eggs for the omelets and set them to fry in olive oil on the big steel range.

When the food was ready, they sat at the counter to eat. The bread was fresh and the country bacon had a sharp, smoky taste and the coffee was fine and strong. Wilson thought he had never eaten a better meal. They finished in silence and sat brooding over their coffee afterward. From somewhere in the villa came the sound of a vacuum cleaner.

"The story about your father and World War Two, was it true?" Don Luis said after a while.

"No," Wilson said.

"You were right, Mr. Lander," Don Luis said. "You are a good gambler."

"So are you," Wilson said.

The Portugee waved a hand. "But I hope you know what you're getting yourself into."

"You mean with Cricket?"

"None other. I was a married man once, with three beautiful children, two boys and a girl. I have not seen them in years. They live in Paris with their mother, where they are good little leftists, studying at the Sorbonne. I don't mind telling you that I am now of an age where the comforts of family life begin to seem very appealing. But their mother has taught my children to hate me. She has enough money of her own and wants nothing to do with me. All this land, all this tradition—and the Hidalgos de la Vaca can be traced back more than a thousand years—will end when I die. I threw the future away for Susan Page."

"How did you do that?" Wilson said.

"In the usual way." Don Luis shrugged. "Many years ago I went every spring to the Palmettos to play cards and stayed often at the home of Susan's mother. Susan was a beautiful young child in those days, very mature for her age. I remember the first incident quite well. One night after the gambling, she came into my bedroom and lifted up her nightdress to show me her new breasts. My God, she was probably no more than twelve years old, and her skin was pure white. That time I resisted her, it was easy, she was so young—but it was not so easy the next time. She was fifteen, a flower in bloom, a beauty, and she was waiting naked in my bed. I should have sent her packing, but"—Don Luis shook his head sadly—"such forbear-ance would take a better man than myself. In a few moments, everything—my children, my wife, my honor—turned to dust. I have wasted many years of my life on Susan Page. I won her from her father with a pair of treys, took her to sea. I educated her. I taught her everything I know—about the sea, about life, about books. I even sent her to university. It was all a terrible mistake. She has grown tired of me, and all she wants to do now is get away. I am half glad you are removing her from my life for good."

Wilson put down his coffee cup, a large European-style breakfast bowl without handles. The last of it tasted sharp and bitter on his tongue. "That's not how Cricket tells the story," Wilson said qui-etly. "Her version is exactly the opposite. She said that you raped her, then forced her into a kind of sexual slavery."

"Of course," Don Luis said, "perfect!" and he started to say something else, but he covered his eyes with his hand and began to laugh.

Wilson was unnerved by the sound of it, a weird metallic ringing in the empty kitchen.

16

CRICKET LAY IN THE rain on the patio, naked except for a pair of socks and very high on something that smelled like burnt oranges. Her hair scrawled wet snakes to her shoulders; her socks hung from her feet like sodden rags. Wilson knelt and took her hand, cold and wet in his own. Her pupils were dilated; she didn't seem to recognize him. He had a hard time keeping his eyes off the coppery hair between her legs, and his ears burned at the thought of it.

"Let's go inside," he said. "We'll get you dry and into bed."

Cricket made an incoherent gurgling noise and had to be hefted into her bedroom like a bagful of dirty laundry.

An hour later she had come down enough to speak in quick, gasping sentences.

"You're alive," she seemed incredulous. "You beat the odds. You beat the Portugee."

"I did," Wilson said, and he couldn't suppress a little smile. Then he held up a jar of sticky, orange-smelling black paste that he had found on the dining room table.

"What is this shit?"

Cricket lay damp and feeble in the bed, sheet tucked up to her chin. Wilson had to repeat his question.

"Opium," she said at last.

"Where's the pipe?" Wilson said.

Cricket shook her head. "No pipe," she said. "Ate it. On crackers."

"You ate it?" Wilson said, and in response she rolled over and vomited off the other side of the bed. He went to the bathroom to get the wastebasket and a wet facecloth. When he came back, he gently washed Cricket's face and put the wastebasket by the bed and pulled up a chair. He was afraid to leave her alone in this condition.

"Said they got you," Cricket said in a gasp. "Dad . . . he said—"

"Don't worry about me," Wilson said. "Here I am, in the flesh."

"—you were dead," she said, not hearing. "That the Portugee cut your head off, like they did to my poor Webster. Poor, poor old Webster. Cut his head off and stuck it up on a pole in the middle of town."

"Who's Webster?" Wilson said. His rain-damp shirt felt like a cold hand on his back.

Cricket made a wobbly movement on the pillow with her head. "Webster—he was my last lover. I really dug Webster. Handsome dude. Muscles like an ox. But stupid. Not like you. Thought he could beat them at their game. They cut off his head. He was hard to love without a head—''

"That's enough," Wilson said.

"I think I'm going to be sick," Cricket said, and she leaned over the wastebasket with Wilson's help and vomited up a mouthful of evil-smelling black goop.

"Shit," Wilson said when she came up, gasping. "You're a mess."

"It's the opium," Cricket said. "I ate too much of it. I think I'll be O.K. now."

Wilson wiped her face, and she leaned back against the pillow. She appeared to sleep for a few minutes; then her eyes snapped open with a suddenness that he found startling. She sounded quite sober when she spoke; only her crazy eyes gave her away.

". . . understand how lonely I am without you," she said as if resuming a conversation that had been going on in her head. "Not like Webster. He was funny, and I liked him in bed, but afterward there was this cold wind blowing over our bodies. Dad and the Portugee, they always taught me to be hard—a regular pirate's daughter. With you, Wilson, I forget about that, become a human being. See, your life has got to be a part of mine. Got to. We just jump over the broom, that's all. Pirate marriage, just jump over the broom like the slaves."

Wilson looked down at her face, puffy and greenish against the white pillow. Her eyes were red-rimmed and muddied by the opium, her cheeks pricked out with tiny purple spots from the effort of the vomiting. Still, he felt an odd tug at his heart.

"There's still too much I don't know about you," he said gently. "You haven't been straight with me. Every time we talk it's a different story. The truth is always somewhere off the port bow, floundering in deep water, so to speak. We set our sails for it but never quite get there, do we?"

Cricket managed a weak smile. "Spoken like a true sailor," she said. "I got you out of your library. Give me credit for that." She reached up suddenly and caught his arm in a grip so tight it hurt. Her fingers dug into his flesh. "You want the truth? I love you! I've never said that to anyone. I love you, but it doesn't matter. You've got to marry me! If you value your life, you have no choice!"

Wilson pulled away. Small purple bruises already showed on his skin where her fingers had been. "So I marry you to save my ass," he said, rubbing his arm. "It will be a marriage in name only, I want you to know that. Just until the first opportunity to escape from this filthy hole comes along. Do you understand, Cricket? Can you live with that?"

But in the next instant she was gone again.

Wilson waited a few minutes, then he sighed and drew a canvas poncho over his clothes and wandered outside into the drizzle and down the shell drive through the trees to the ridge. There, he stared down at the Portugee's villa in the valley below, his thoughts rising like steam from the jungle. It began to rain heavily. Soon all he could see of the landscape was the rain coming across in great blinding sheets. As he was about to turn back, a loud cry like a child's voice came from behind. He tensed and spun around just in time to catch a dozen howler monkeys, their orange fur matted and wet, calling to him from the branches of a monstrous teak. He blinked, and they vanished, the jungle reverberating with the sound of screaming in their wake.

PART FIVE

THE
DARK
CONTINENT

1

IN JUNE, THE RAINS stopped.

Trade winds blew the stench of Quatre Sables out toward Africa.
The blue sky above the jungle filled with mating birds. The morning
of the ceremony was clear and bright, with the barest flush of heat
rising in the eastern sky.

Wilson waited alone and slightly bewildered at the center of the
topiary maze of English boxwood in the Portugee's garden. He had
been led blindfolded to this spot—a perfect green oval of grass
completely surrounded by high hedge. A red velvet canopy billowed
and snapped over his head like a sail in the warm breeze. A broom
tied with a black bow lay at his feet. Off to the side in two fragile
reed cages, yellow African swallows twittered pleasantly in the sun.
It was all part of a tradition he didn't quite understand. From over
the hedge came the sound of laughter and voices and the light
metallic harmonies of a Bupandan Tinka band. His borrowed suit of
white linen pinched in the crotch and sagged under the arms. He
waited fifteen minutes more and began to sweat. Then, at a light
rustling of leaves, he turned to see Cricket emerge from the green
wall, eyes down, shy as a virgin. He held his breath. She was barefoot; her toes made little indentations in the springy grass.

Her dress was cut out of a bolt of iridescent Javanese silk once
intended for the wives of the Marahaja of Puj, taken from a mer-
chantman captured off the Malabar Coast—a fantastic fabric whose
absolute whiteness was not white at all, rather a silken blue static,
like the color of light reflected on water. Several layers of the stuff
arranged in petticoats made up the flowing skirt; a short vest left her
midriff and arms bare. A black pearl on a silver hoop pierced her
navel. She wore her hair caught up in a net of silver thread studded
with seed pearls, and carried a bouquet of African coral lilies.

Wilson couldn't keep a stunned smile from his face, though as
always uncertainty and dread gnawed at his heart around the edges,
and he knew the world beyond this moment of silk and green grass

and blue sky was full of grief and violence which had them both caught like something helpless in a spider web.

"O.K., how do we do this?" he said when Cricket stepped up to the other side of the broom. She hid her face in the lilies and didn't answer. Wilson's ears felt hot, his palms sweaty, and the back of his neck prickled, though for a moment he couldn't say why. It seemed ridiculous to think of himself as a groom. The canopy billowed with a sharp snapping sound.

"So where's the witnesses, the priest?" Wilson said. His voice came out thin and nervous.

Cricket looked up, her eyes jade green. "It's just us and whatever we believe in," she said.

"What do you believe in?" Wilson said.

Cricket shrugged. "Right now, you," she said.

"Is that enough?"

"I wish my mother were here. That would have been nice."

"Where is she?"

"Dead, remember? Like yours."

"Oh . . ."

Cricket lowered her flowers and took a deep breath. "Ready?" she said, but she waited another second before she came around the broom and took Wilson by the arm. "O.K., it's simple enough. We step over together, at the same time."

"Wait," Wilson said. He shook his head and put a hand on her cheek. "You look beautiful right now."

"Just like any other bride." Cricket smiled, and she leaned up and kissed him, and as she kissed him, almost without knowing it, they stepped over the broom.

Wilson didn't feel any different when they were on the other side. He thought for a moment of the Catholic icons that had hung in his great-aunt's house—Jesus of the Bleeding Heart, the Madonna poised on a silver cloud surrounded by cherubim—and he remembered the high mass wedding of a friend in college, the incense and chanting and readings from the Gospel, how it was all meant to invoke the presence of God, the celebration of a sacrament. And for a moment, on the other side of the broom, Cricket on his arm, he felt lost.

"I know," Cricket's voice in his ear sounded far away. "Seems like there should be more to it."

"Maybe," Wilson said.

"That's why I got the birds. My own little touch."

She took his hand and led him over to the reed cages full of birds. From each of them came a slightly different sweet-shrill note.

"These are the males, and these are the females," she said. "The only way to tell is by the sound they make. The higher-pitched ones are—"

"The females?" Wilson said.

"The males," Cricket said. "So the rains are gone, which means it's mating season now, and they're itching to fly off to the trees and do what birds do in mating season."

"Not to mention bees," Wilson said.

"It's cruel to keep them apart any longer," Cricket said. "Here goes."

The ribbons that held the cages together at the top came undone with a single pull; the ribs fell apart. Wilson and Cricket shielded their eyes against the sun as the birds ascended in a yellow cloud into the bright blue sky.

2

THE TINKA BAND PLAYED sentimental tunes that sounded like the music of a calliope. Awkward couples danced across the grass. A drunk fat lady in a pink dress waltzed alone, flinging her arms out as she spun around. After the dancing there was champagne and caviar, followed by a luncheon of roast chicken and smoked ham, asparagus, new potatoes, salad, cheese, fruit. During dessert, three brown children in child-size suits and bow ties chased a little white dog into the hedge maze. They got lost in there and had to be rescued by an Indian woman in a sari with a baby in one hand and a glass of champagne in the other. A few paunchy middle-aged men stuck close to the punch bowl, drinking one cup of rum punch after another and talking about the *Nikkei* index.

These were people Wilson did not know.

"Who the hell do you think they are?" Cricket whispered as the two of them stood in the receiving line after lunch. "You're looking at the Thirty Captains, plus wives and families. The Portugee told them to come, so here they are."

"You're kidding!" Wilson said.

"All of them except Dad," Cricket said. "He's off sulking somewhere. Thinks you're a bad choice for a son-in-law."

"Long as he doesn't make me walk the plank."

The Thirty Captains proved to be a disappointingly mundane lot. They patted Wilson on the back in a fatherly way, offered grave, polite congratulations as if this were any other middle-class wedding. Wilson had expected eyes full of cruel fire, earrings, parrots, velvet pantaloons; instead he got middle management in slightly dated Pierre Cardin suits. Ordinary fellows whose lives at sea as slavers and pirates made no mark that showed in their faces.

"That's the thing about evil," Dr. Boursaly said later, the red smear of evening blooming over the jungle behind him. "It doesn't exist in the end. Not only is it possible to murder a hundred people and sit down to tea and toast undisturbed by conscience an hour later—I have seen it happen!"

"You're wrong there, Doctor," Wilson said. "Evil exists, especially here. All you have to do is walk down the slope of Quatre Sables any day of the week."

"That's what I like about you," the doctor said. "You haven't let the heat sap your moral certainties . . ." then he looked right and left and leaned close, spilling half a cup of the pink punch across his shoes. The Tinka band started on a tinny rendition of something by the Beatles. "It's too late for me," the doctor whispered. "But I have been thinking about what you said when the rains started. You've still got some fire in your gut, Wilson. Here's a piece of well-considered advice—Do something. Bide your time and wait for the right moment or until you can't stand it anymore. Then hit them as hard as you can."

Red and yellow stars exploded in the darkness above the garden; the baroque facade of the Villa Real was lit by brilliant flashes of color and light. Don Luis had hovered in the background all day, a sad ghost haunting his own house. Wilson found him now at midnight, and shook his hand. The man looked tired, older than Wilson remembered.

"I want to thank you," Wilson said. "You've been very gracious about this. Thanks for the party and thanks for the use of the suit."

Don Luis made an inexpressible gesture, halfway between exhaustion and resignation. His mustache drooped sadly in the half-light of the torches.

"It was the wedding I had always planned for Susan and myself," he said after a beat. "I have been saving the fireworks and the silk for Susan's dress for several years now. Why let them go to waste?"

"Still, you stuck to your word—"

"No." Don Luis interrupted. "I am an aristocrat! The only thing that separates me from"—he hesitated—"you and the rest of the rabble is my word—that is to say, my sense of personal honor. This has been so for a thousand years in my family. It is my misfortune that I was born into a world that has no use for honor of any kind."

The sound of breaking glass drew Wilson's attention away for a moment, and when he turned back, the Portugee was gone, faded off into the baroque shadows of his garden.

A few seconds later, Cricket rustled up in her silks, her hair loosed from its silver net, her face flushed with wedding punch.

"I've been looking for you," she said, and Wilson saw that she was drunk.

"Here I am," Wilson said.

"Do you love me?" Cricket said.

For a beat, Wilson did not know how to respond. His passion for her was undeniable—but love? Wilson figured he didn't understand the emotion. This marriage was an expedient. Better married to Cricket than strangled and chopped up into little pieces. Alive, he could figure a way to get out, and maybe he could take her with him. Maybe in some other part of the world, far from the moral uncertainties of Quatre Sables, he would come to love her in the way he had loved Andrea before things went sour and the dread locked him away from the world more completely than any prison.

Cricket seemed to read his thoughts. She bit her lip and looked down. "O.K. I shouldn't have asked. So the situation isn't real great just now, sort of a shotgun wedding. But we'll get off this island one day, and we'll go to another island—I mean the Ile St.-Louis in the middle of the Seine in the middle of Paris, and we'll buy a big old gloomy town house with high ceilings and dusty chandeliers and we'll be happy and you'll fall completely in love with me there because we'll be free and you won't be able to help yourself."

"Yes," Wilson said, and just then he wanted to believe that what she said was true.

The sharp tang of the fireworks still hung in the air at three in the morning. Cricket took Wilson by the hand and led him across the littered acre of grass, over the stone bridge spanning the moat where the sheep lay sleeping at this uncertain hour, and into the courtyard of the villa. The ancient house stood lifeless, its windows staring down like empty eyes. The fountain plashed quietly in the cobbled darkness. The entrance hall smelled of mold and the wax of candles long gone. Cricket felt her way up the stairs, along shadowy corridors, through dim portrait-lined galleries at whose dimensions Wilson could only guess. They came to a set of double doors and passed through them into a large chamber, empty except for a big white bed hung with mosquito netting, and a single straight-backed wooden chair. Casement windows stood open onto the garden below, and a few mosquitoes droned lightly in the cool night air.

"You forgot to carry me over the threshold," Cricket said. In a single gesture she stepped out of her skirts, and the silk gleamed like a pool of water on the floor around her ankles.

Wilson took off his borrowed suit, folded it carefully over the back of the chair. Then, he lifted her in his arms and the mosquito netting parted for them like smoke, and they were in bed and their hands were upon each other. When he was inside her, Wilson heard a strange cat cry from the jungle. Afterward, he thought of the equator, passing across land and sea not a hundred miles beyond their window, an invisible line circling the earth.

3

A WEEK LATER, WILSON and Cricket left the room with the single chair and the big bed, and got into her Volkswagen Thing and took the road that led through the Portugee's orchards and fields, through the jungle into town. The heat had returned with full ferocity in the previous day or two, and the island felt like a blast furnace. The vinyl of the driver's seat burned Wilson's legs through his shorts. Cricket wore a floppy straw hat with a brim as wide as a bicycle tire, a tank top and shorts, and Swiss-made sunglasses with special black lenses that rendered even the maddening glare of tropical noon into a murky green twilight.

"These glasses are great," Cricket said, "but I can't see for shit. I hope you don't mind driving."

"That's fine," Wilson said.

"This is the worst season here," she said. "The beginning of summer. Good time to get out of Dodge. How do you feel about a little trip?''

"Where are we going?" Wilson said.

"You could call it a working honeymoon," Cricket said, and was about to say more when they passed into the jungle and the steam heat beneath the leaves hit them like a wall, and all of a sudden it was too hot to speak. The shanty city was little better. Garbage lay rotting in the middle of the street in large fetid piles. Human femurs stuck out of the rubbish, common as chicken bones.

At Cricket's direction Wilson pulled the Thing into the water-front complex, drove around the barracoon and down an alley flanked by cinder-block walls topped with broken glass set in cement. He stopped before a steel gate covered with corrugated sheeting. Cricket leaned across his lap and beeped the horn, two long, one short. The idling engine made a beating sound as they waited. At last Wilson heard the grating of steel on steel, and the gate swung open to reveal a working boatyard. Mustapha waved them in. Wilson parked alongside a dilapidated air-conditioned trailer of the kind he had seen in low-rent trailer parks back home.

The *Compound Interest* sat in dry dock at the far end of the boatyard. A structure of unpainted wooden ribs supported the vessel above the concrete ramp that led down to the black water of the harbor. A crew of workmen labored on her deck in the hot sun. Wilson saw with a pang that the splendid white experiment of the Atlantic crossing was no more. The retractable Mylar beach umbrella sails were gone, the barbecue pit, the polished brightwork. The hull showed a new blue-green camouflage pattern, and aft of the bow cage a marine cannon of indeterminate specifications had been bolted to the deck. The navigational octagon was now protected by steel plating with slits just wide enough to admit the barrels of automatic weapons. Suspended from the stern, a workman struggled to remove the walnut nameplate with a dull screwdriver.

"What are they doing to her?" Wilson asked when he got out of the car. Cricket heard some distress in the question and came around to put a hand on his shoulder.

"It's Dad's idea," she said. "They're going to turn her into a pirate ship."

"Come on," Wilson said. "Isn't she a little too fancy for that kind of work?"

Cricket shook her head. "You should see what they did below-decks. Ripped everything out. All the furniture, the fixtures, the antiques, the carpets. Everything except the galley and the ready room."

"That's terrible."

"I know, but Dad's got something very special in mind."

The pirate stood at a long worktable in the trailer, bent over a topographical map of Bupanda. Schlüber stood to one side, nodding his head like a mechanical dog. The artificial cool of the air conditioning felt weird to Wilson's developing equatorial sensibilities. Almost a year had passed since he had experienced the frigid atmosphere of air-conditioned places, and he was immediately taken with a chill that announced itself in goose bumps across his skin. He rubbed his arms and looked around. The trailer was half office, half living quarters, all mess. On a pressboard wall above the cluttered desk hung a collection of antique edged weapons—two heavy-looking naval cutlasses, a rapier, and a short sword with a thick, stubby blade like a Bowie knife. Beyond the partition, an unmade sofa-bed and a plaid easy chair were arranged before a dirty plate glass window overlooking the harbor.

Cricket approached the worktable with tentative steps. Wilson hung behind.

"Uh, Dad?" Cricket said.

The pirate jerked up, caught sight of Wilson, and scowled. Cricket motioned for Wilson to come forward and took him by the hand and the pirate's scowl turned to rage. His eyes went black, and his face flushed beet red from the ears forward.

"You bring that miserable son of a bitch into my home?" It came out as a sort of howl.

"Wilson is my husband now," Cricket said with a slight tremor in her voice. "Your son-in-law."

The pirate brought his fist down on the table in a violent blow that sent pencils flying. Cricket flinched. At that moment she was more like a disobedient teenager expecting a beating than a grown woman. Schlüber gathered a few papers and backed quietly into the living area. The pirate took a menacing step in Wilson's direction.

Wilson gently let go of Cricket's hand and stepped up to meet him. "Sorry you missed the wedding, Dad," he said. "It was a very nice—" Before he had time to finish, the pirate sprung forward quick as a baboon, fists clenched. Wilson wasn't surprised; he had half expected something like this. He ducked out of the way just before the pirate swung up with a solid left hook. The pirate's fist connected with the pressboard over the desk. The impact knocked the short-bladed sword from its hook, and the little man scooped up the weapon and lunged. He slashed at the air, his mouth working unintelligible obscenities.

Wilson jumped around the desk to get out of the way, but in that second, an ancient instinct cut loose inside him, like cargo broken free of restraints in heavy seas. He reached over and pulled down one of the cutlasses and swung out wildly. The cutlass was heavier than he thought; it carried him along with a momentum of its own. His body followed through the swing, and the tip caught the pocket of the pirate's Hawaiian shirt and there was a dull tearing sound. The pirate fell back with a gasp and went sprawling. Wilson stepped around quickly and brought the point to the pirate's throat.

Cricket let out a small cry and raised a trembling hand. "Wilson—" she began, then stopped. Her face had a white, pinched look. The trailer was still. Wilson heard his own heavy breathing and the calls of the men gutting the *Compound Interest* outside in the heat. He looked down the length of the heavy blade and saw an expression of pure hatred in the pirate's eyes.

"Listen to me, Cricket," Wilson said when he caught his breath. "You tell this evil worm that I'm sick of being bullied and threatened. You tell him if he touches me again, even so much as spits in my direction, I will kill him." Then he threw the cutlass to the floor and went out of the trailer and got into the driver seat of the Thing. He rested his elbows on the wheel and sat there for a long time in the sun, calming himself and listening to voices raised in anger from inside the trailer. He watched the workmen turning the *Compound Interest* from a luxury yacht to a vessel of war, and suddenly he longed to get to sea, to leave this precarious life on land behind, to reduce existence to its fundamentals—wind, sea, sky, and stars.

A half hour later Cricket came out and climbed into the passenger seat. "I'm sorry," she said. She put a hand like ice from the air-conditioning on his knee. "I didn't think Dad's reaction . . ." Her voice trailed off.

"Does the man try to kill all your boyfriends?" Wilson said. "Or just me and Webster, whoever he was, that poor bastard."

"You're not my boyfriend. You're my husband, remember?" Cricket said.

"Oh, yeah," Wilson said.

"I just spent the last hour trying to explain the fact of our wedding to Dad. I told him that I loved you, that if he hurt you, he would be hurting me. And I also reminded him that as my husband you are now protected under the Articles of Brotherhood . . . and well, I got him to agree to a truce. O.K.?"

Wilson shrugged toward the horizon.

"O.K.?"

"Fine," Wilson said, and Cricket went in and got her father. She lingered in the shade on the steps of the trailer as the pirate approached. His shirt hung in tatters. The thick gold chains gleamed from the grizzled hair of his chest.

"You ruined my shirt," the pirate said.

Wilson looked down at the man's balding scalp and didn't say anything.

The pirate blinked and looked away. "I'm told I have to get used to this thing," he said. "We've had citizens in the family before, like Cricket's mother, that law-abiding bitch. It doesn't usually work out too well."

"Citizens?" Wilson said.

"Anyone who's not a pirate, we call them citizens," the pirate said. "And you don't strike me as much of a pirate. Too much conscience. It's written all over you. But I guess we'll see about that. There's not much room for conscience where we're going."

"Where's that?" Wilson said.

The pirate gave a wolfish grin. "The Dark Continent," he said and waved in the direction of Africa.

Just then, another workman climbed the scaffold to the stern with a pot of black paint. The walnut nameplate was gone now, and the spot had been sanded and primered. "What you want I should call her, Captain?" he called down.

The pirate turned to Wilson. "Go ahead, citizen. You're part of the family now. You give her a name."

The workman waited, brush poised.

"The *Dread,*" Wilson said without hesitation. "Call her the *Dread.*"

4

THE SKYLINE OF RIGALA rose like a mouthful of broken teeth off the starboard bow. The *Dread* pitched in the swells a half mile out. Even from this distance Wilson could make out the pulverized facades of modern office towers, their shattered windows catching the afternoon sun, and he could see the white puffs of exploding shells coming from the slopes of Mount Mtungu, direct hits somewhere in the center city.

"They used to call it the Paris of Central West Africa," Cricket said. She came up behind Wilson at the taffrail and draped a tanned arm over his shoulder. "I remember shopping there as a kid. They had a Bon Marché, an Au Printemps; those are big French department stores. I bought a hat with flowers on it and a skimpy French bathing suit. There was already trouble then, but I remember a lot of music in the streets, and the people seemed happy."

"Shows you didn't know crap, daughter." Captain Page grunted from his place behind the wheel in the navigational octagon. "The Bupandans have always been a bloodthirsty lot. That was right around the time of the Oluzu District massacre. A whole ghetto neighborhood full of Andas hacked to pieces by government troops—men, women, children. I remember the screaming. Went on all night. You were asleep in the hotel room."

"That hotel was beautiful," Cricket said, ignoring him. "It had a beautiful name, the Star of Africa. There was an old panoramic photograph from the colonial era in the lobby, the staff in white jackets posing on the front steps."

The pirate snorted from the octagon. "Those days are long gone," he said, and he came around and shoved a pair of electronic binoculars into Wilson's hand. "Have at it with these, citizen."

Wilson scanned the ruined skyline. The waterfront looked in sad shape. The docks were a mass of rubble. The stacks and towers of sunken vessels protruded from the black water of the harbor. Dark smoke from oil fires smudged the horizon like a greasy fingerprint.

"The main body of Anda rebels holds the countryside to the west," the pirate said with a sweep of his hand. "That includes Mount Mtungu, but not Mount Nbuni, which is in Bupu control. You're looking at a very fucked situation that gets more fucked each day. It's turned into a clan thing now, so you've got Andas fighting against Bupus siding with Andas and vice versa. As of last count there were six major factions fighting for control of the capital: the Bupu Patriotic Front Militia, which contains elements of the old Bupandan National Guard; the Anda National Militia, which controls all the highland areas; the Bupu People's party—they're the hard-line Marxists; they control the old university town of Seme and surrounding countryside—the Anda People's party, who were supported by the Cubans before the end of the Cold War; and the conservative Bupu National Congressional Militia, who control the northeast industrial corridor from Cangulu to Nevrongo. And a couple of other clan groups of either tribe who have no real political agenda and exist just to kill each other. And of course in the jungle you've got the Iwo people. Let's not forget about them."

"Who are they?" Wilson said.

"They are not so much a people as a delicacy, like fancy mushrooms or caviar. They exist to be eaten up by everyone else."

"What the hell does that mean?"

The pirate shrugged. "They're bushmen. Pygmies, about so high. The women are prized as sex objects by both the Andas and Bupus. They say it's like fucking a ten-year-old girl with fully developed breasts. Something of a turn-on, I hear. The men are either killed or taken to Cangulu to work in the copper mines, and the infants are raised as house slaves. But the real market is with the Arabs. They will pay fifty thousand dollars for a single Iwo maiden. There are brothels in Qatar stocked entirely with Iwo women. In any case, until now we've had to deal with Bupu or Anda traders if we wanted to get our hands on them. That's a nut we're going to crack."

Wilson was silent for a moment, scanning the ruins of the skyline for something, a flag, a Red Cross tent, any sign of hope or order. He lowered the binoculars and turned toward the pirate, grinning like death at his elbow.

"So what's the point?" Wilson said. "Why do they keep killing each other year after year?"

The pirate let out a short laugh like a bark. "Why?" he said. "Don't be ridiculous. People kill each other because they enjoy it, because that's what they do best. Been that way since the first ape-man hit the second ape-man over the head with a bone. Gives them something to wake up to every morning."

5

WITH SUNSET THE SEA calmed. The *Dread* idled beneath a pink sky on the gently heaving main. The ship's company assembled in the octagon in the dying light for their last meal before Africa. There was the pirate, Cricket and Wilson, Schlüber, Mustapha, and Nguyen. Wilson hadn't seen the Vietnamese cook since the seizure of the *Compound Interest,* nearly six months before. Now, that traumatic afternoon seemed like a sepia-toned illustration from another life.

They ate cold lentil soup and bread and cheese and passed three bottles of thick red wine back and forth. Mysterious clouds drifted over the new moon, transparent against the pale pinkish sky. From the shortwave came a muted, plaintive music full of clarinets and saxophones, broadcast from an unimaginable ballroom, perhaps as far away as Cape Town. Wilson felt the deck of the ship beneath him, and the soft swell of the waves, and smelled the fresh air, and was glad to be at sea again, on his way between somewhere and somewhere, the place that is travel, where conclusions are suspended for the duration of the journey.

Nguyen's teeth looked blue from the wine. Wilson watched his blue teeth absently, and was almost surprised when the little man spoke.

"You are one lucky bastard, joe," he said. "Marry the captain's daughter. Some people say smart bastard who save his ass. But what if captain's daughter decide not to marry you? I say lucky bastard."

Wilson managed a weak smile. "I get the feeling that my luck could change in a second," he said.

"Not your luck," the Vietnamese cook said. "Your luck is like the wind. Sometimes blow, sometimes not blow, but it never goes away. Your luck stronger than ours, I think. Captain crazy to take you aboard."

"Keep your mouth shut, Noog," the pirate grunted.

"Call it luck if you want." Schlüber spoke from his cushion on the bench. "I say life is all statistics, probabilities and improbabilities. Wilson marrying Cricket wasn't luck. It was just an improbability. There are mathematical equations to figure out the likelihood. And look at me. I answered an advertisement in the *Frankfurter Allgemeine*—high wages, exciting work, travel, M.B.A. required, it said—and I ended up a pirate. There's an improbability for you."

"You're not a pirate," the pirate said. "You're a goddamned accountant."

At this Mustapha put his head back and laughed, the day's last shadows caught beneath the scarred ridges on his face.

They lapsed into silence for the next hour. Cricket leaned into Wilson's arm, put her head on his shoulder. He could still not get used to the idea that she was his wife. When the light disappeared in the west, the sky was a black smear. The lights of Rigala showed in the distance as two or three wavering points. It would be hours before they could motor any closer to the harbor. In the absence of laws and customs regulations, going ashore required the right man on the right dock, the right amount of money changing hands. Their man wasn't due till midnight. Wilson could not see Cricket's hand upon his own in the sea darkness.

"I never liked these waters," the pirate said. It was a disembodied statement out of the gloom.

"Seems pretty calm," Wilson said in something like his own reasonable voice. "What's wrong with them?" He felt freer to speak now that he could not see the man.

"You were talking about luck," the pirate said. "It's bad luck for pirates along these coasts. There's many a pirate's whitened bones at the bottom of this miserable patch of sea."

Despite himself, a chill went up Wilson's spine.

"Not far from here, about thirty degrees north, they got the greatest pirate of them all, Bartholomew Roberts," the pirate said. "The man was a piratical genius. In just three years he captured over four hundred prizes. Not even my ancestor the great Elzevir Monta-gue could beat that. But it was success that got Roberts in the end. The king sent a squadron of the British Navy, commanded by Cap-tain Ogle in the HMS *Swallow*. Roberts had just captured a Spanish merchant vessel full of Madeira, and they were celebrating when the *Swallow* caught up with the *Royal Venture*—that was Roberts's ship. Roberts himself didn't drink, but the crew was dead drunk to a man. He couldn't get them to their stations in time, and they were outmaneuvered. The poor bastard got it in the first volley of grape-shot. The crew was stunned. There lay the great Captain Roberts, just another corpse in his high hat and feathers, his famous red coat, his hip boots. The fight barely lasted another hour after that. With Roberts dead, the crew lost its gumption. Ogle hanged all of them and would have hanged Roberts's dead body if it hadn't been dumped over the side as he requested. The world has never seen a better pirate or a braver man.''

When the moon brightened, Wilson and Cricket took a sleeping bag forward and lay on the deck beneath the steel wings of the marine cannon. They lay close, and Wilson could feel her breath on his cheek.

''Why is your father like that?'' Wilson said.

''Like what?'' Cricket said.

''Absolutely immoral. I would say amoral, but he's an intelligent man. He knows the difference between right and wrong. How does he justify his life of murder and slavery to himself? For that matter, how do you?''

''Don't go all serious on me,'' Cricket said.

''Tell me,'' Wilson said. ''This is your conscience talking to you, remember?''

''It's in our blood,'' she said, ''just like gambling is in yours. We're pirates. Been pirates since the 1600s. You can't fight blood.''

''You're going to have to give me more than that.''

Cricket thought for a minute. ''It's the social contract,'' she said.

"We Pages have never believed in it. The idea that you go about treating your neighbor like you want to be treated is a crock of shit to us. We don't believe it because we look around and see that the world is the kind of place where your neighbor would stab you in the back for a spare fig. Sure, for a couple of years here and there— during the Pax Romana, say, or the 1950s—the world seemed like a safe place ruled by law and reason. That was an illusion. Maybe the trains ran on time, and there was a proliferation of lawyers, but all of it was just a smokescreen over the chaos."

"You sound like Don Luis," Wilson said, and felt Cricket stiffen.

"O.K., try walking down the street alone at night in certain neighborhoods in your city," she said. "What happens to your social contract then? Out the window."

"Let's admit for a minute that the world is an evil place," Wilson said, "which I deny. It still doesn't give you the right to be part of the evil. We've got to keep fighting for the good, Cricket. Or at the very least not do any harm. That's your first lesson in moral philosophy."

Cricket was silent, taking this in. "My life has been too hard to believe in goodness for its own sake," she said. "All I've seen is big fish eating little fish. Scratch the surface, and you'll find that people have the worst motives for what they do. But stick around. I'm still hoping some of your faith in mankind will rub off before too long. What do you think?"

"It's not me sticking around," Wilson said. "It's me getting you away from them."

"Patience," Cricket whispered. "We're going to need money, and we've got to pick the right moment."

"When will that be?"

"Shut up," Cricket said, and put her arms around Wilson, and as they kissed, the clouds drifted over the moon again, and the sky went black.

6

UNDER THE SAME BLACK sky at midnight the *Dread* crossed at low throttle into Rigala Harbor. Blasted derricks stood above the docks, twisted and skeletal in the flash of a distant bombardment. Half-sunken hulks leaked trails of iridescent oil across the dirty water. A searchlight trailed over low-lying clouds like a blindman's finger reading braille, then winked out.

The pirate took the wheel and guided the *Dread* to the far end of the commercial basin. A thin line of lightbulbs dangling from a bare power cable marked the length of the southernmost slip, padded with used tires. Cricket jumped onto the slip and tied the bowline to a rusty iron plug in the concrete, and the rest of the crew followed. A few minutes later the pirate solemnly distributed weapons from a heavy canvas bag that looked like it had once contained a set of golf clubs. Schlüber and Nguyen shouldered Chinese-made Kalashnikovs. Mustapha took an over-and-under and a machete in a wooden scabbard. Cricket took a MAC-10 machine pistol, a hunting knife, and a vinyl bag of extra clips. The captain took a 12-gauge semiautomatic shotgun and a 9 mm Beretta.

Wilson hesitated. He didn't like the look of the situation.

"Why do we need these?" he said at last.

The pirate frowned. "Because this country is a fucking snake pit," he said. "Full of banditos and the like. Don't be such a citizen. Choose your weapon."

Wilson peered into the bag. He saw an assault rifle, a few pistols, bayonets in greening scabbards. He took one of the bayonets, fixed it to his belt, and selected an ancient revolver in a leather holster. A torn bit of leather strapping dangled from a ring at the base of the grip.

The pirate chuckled, took the revolver from Wilson's hand, broke open the chamber, spun it around.

"It figures," he said. "An old eight-shot Webley-Vickers, World War One vintage. Check the holster."

Wilson turned the holster over. Scraped into the leather on the back was a short inscription: "Ubi Bene, Ibi Patria. Lt. J. F. Hooks, 12th Rgt. 2nd. Btln. Royal Welsh Fusiliers. Flanders, 1917."

Wilson read it out loud.

The pirate nodded. "The dumbshit officers in those days used to go over the top with nothing more than that pistol and a whistle. For God and country and such shit. They got blown to bits. Perfect for you."

He handed it back and fished out a leather pouch of extra ammunition; then, armed and ready, the landing party marched up the slip toward a concrete blockhouse at the far end.

A dozen or so soldiers of the Bupu militia dressed in ragged fatigues squatted around a fire in front of the blockhouse. Well-oiled assault rifles hung off their backs. Their mouths were stuffed with something that looked like dried tobacco, torn from a pile of greenish black leaves in a tattered cardboard shoe box being passed around. They stared into the fire and chewed and spit black juice at the burning scrap wood. As the landing party approached, one of the soldiers stood and leveled his weapon. The others didn't bother to turn around. Captain Page gave his shotgun to Cricket and stepped into the light of the fire. After a brief exchange in Bupu and sign language, the pirate was led into the blockhouse. The rest of the landing party stood waiting uneasily in the shadows.

Wilson heard a faint booming that was the artillery bombardment on the outskirts and the sput-sput sound of the men spitting.

"What if our friend didn't show up tonight?" Schlüber whispered.

"Then they kill us," Nguyen said out loud, "and our problems over."

Mustapha grinned at this in the darkness.

"Comforting thought," Schlüber said.

"So what is that shit?" Wilson said.

"What shit?" Cricket said.

"The soldiers," Wilson said. "What are they chewing?"

"Like a bunch of bloody cows having a go at their cuds, if you ask me," Schlüber said.

"Kaf," Mustapha said. "Makes you talk to God."

"That shit's one of the reasons why things are so fucked up here," Cricket said. "It's a narcotic weed, wouldn't be so dangerous in tea. I've had kaf tea, actually—a mild stimulant, something like an espresso with a shot of brandy. But these characters have been chewing kaf since about noon with nothing in their stomachs except maybe a bottle of tejiyaa. After about six hours of chewing you start to hallucinate. Most of the fighting here goes on at night, when everyone is totally out of their heads and seeing ghosts and demons coming at them out of the dark. At that point no one knows who they are shooting at, and no one cares."

Captain Page came out of the blockhouse fifteen minutes later with a young militia officer in a clean khaki uniform. The officer shook the captain's hand and stepped over to say a few inaudible words to his men. A grumble went up, and there was more spitting. The officer reached down, snatched up the cardboard shoe box of kaf, held it over the fire, and screamed an order in a high, sharp voice. One of the soldiers rose with a heavy sigh and adjusted his assault rifle. Four others followed his lead, and this motley escort led the landing party up the slip through an opening in a wall of sandbags and into the dark night of Rigala.

7

WILSON SAW VAGUE STREETS full of craters, burned-out buses and cars, sidewalks clotted with rubble. A bunch of decomposing corpses were piled against a tumbledown wall, frozen in macabre-comic poses by the effects of rigor mortis. Rats scuttled everywhere. Telephone poles and streetlights had been knocked over to barricade the intersections.

From what Wilson could tell in the darkness, this part of the city dated from the colonial era. It was a district that had once been full of wrought-iron balconies and pastel colonnades and terrace restaurants, like the kind he remembered from Buptown back home. Now the buildings were abandoned and broken. The city held the quiet of the tomb. Cats watched from the empty doorways, their yellow eyes glowing with detached curiosity. The soldiers did not speak. They loped alongside like wolves, the straps of their rifles making a faint leather-creaking noise.

"This used to be such a beautiful city," Cricket said in a low voice. "Now it's mostly depopulated. Everyone is dead or living in the bush or gone across to wallow like pigs at Quatre Sables."

The soldiers led them along a narrow alley between the remains of two large buildings piled up like a mess of Legos, across a vacant lot, and up a hill into the residential sector. Here they followed a broad avenue through a park in which all the palm trees had been burned to black sticks. In the middle of the park on a bullet-scarred pedestal stood an impressively large statue of an African man wearing a 1960s-era three-button suit. In one hand he held an open book; in another, a native ashtzisi, the staff of carved wood and buffalo horn that was the badge of a Bupu chief. He was probably sixty feet high and twenty feet broad at the shoulders. A small chunk of his nose was missing, and bullet holes pocked his jacket, but otherwise he seemed intact.

"That's President Sequhue," the pirate said over his shoulder, his voice ringing hollow in the empty city. At the name one of the soldiers shot over a hostile look, but the pirate continued. "In 1960 Sequhue worked out the terms of independence with the U.K. They called him the Bupandan Gandhi. He was a short little guy, wrote poetry, studied at Cambridge in the thirties. From about 1961 to '75, they had a sort of golden age here in Bupanda, mostly because of Sequhue's progressive policies. In those days it was a prosperous country, very Western in outlook.

"Then Sequhue got sick with spinal meningitis and experienced some sort of mystical revelation and decided all at once the Western influence had to go He outlawed capitalism and due process, beer, the wearing of pants and shirts, the use of zippers—people were shot for using zippers—he kicked out all foreign nationals, gained about two hundred pounds, and took a harem of something like a thousand wives. Then he outlawed Christianity and tried to revive the old animistic religions. They say there were human sacrifices right here in the medina. The civil war started up soon after that. Unfortunately all those bad old Western ideas about the rights of the individual were the only thing keeping the Bupus and Andas from each other's throats. Soon they reverted to the same old crap, the slaughter and slavery they'd practiced for a millennium before the British came in the 1870s.

"Sequhue wasn't mad, understand? Just an idealist. They're the worst kind. He decided the Western model promoted selfish materialism and personal corruption and at the same time didn't make people happy. 'Look at New York, look at London,' he said in a famous speech. 'Go there and find me one good, happy man!' Hell, I guess the old bastard had a point. But it was just the thing this country didn't need. Millions died in the civil war, and there's still no end in sight. I'm not complaining. It's great for business."

"Where's Sequhue now?" Wilson said, and was surprised at the reedy echo of his voice in the empty park.

"He was murdered during an orgy at the presidential palace

about fifteen years ago,'' the pirate said. "She was an Anda prostitute, and he was doing something unspeakable to her when it happened, but both sides still look up to Sequhue as some kind of martyred saint. Just goes to show, objective reality has no bearing on what people believe in the end.''

The landing party crossed the park at a trot and turned left onto another broad street, once lined with date palms and grand old houses with verandas and rose gardens. The date palms looked sick and stunted; the grand old houses and their gardens lay in ruins. Halfway down the second block from the park, a battered white mansion showed signs of life. Slashes of yellow light shone from busted-out windows closed off with sandbags. Barbed wire and guard posts encircled a dusty acre that had once sprouted roses and tulips and daffodils.

They were led past the main guard post and up wide front steps crowded with sleeping soldiers and into the house. Wilson caught the rap of automatic weapons fire in the distance. They came through rooms heaped with broken furniture and strewn with soiled, discarded documents and entered a large ballroom, lit with parlor lamps missing shades. Broken couches and a few dozen chairs sat at odd angles to one another. In one corner a smashed grand piano rested on its two front legs like a dog sitting. Militia officers lounged about chewing kaf and drinking tejiyaa. A few lay passed out on the floor in puddles of urine. The rise and fall of male voices filled the room.

An African the size of Frankenstein's monster sprawled across a yellow velvet couch at the back. He was bare to the waist, his chest covered with soot-black hair. The collar of his khaki uniform jacket draped across a nearby chair showed a star and staff insignia. A neat silver nametag above the right pocket read "Col. Bwultuzu, Bupu Patriotic Front" in thin black letters. A gallon bottle of tejiyaa balanced on one knee. On either side of him sat two naked young girls. They looked no older than ten, each grasping her own gallon bottle of tejiyaa improbably large in her small hands. But as he approached with the others, Wilson saw the girls were not girls at all. They were diminutive young women, about four feet tall, their skin a lustrous purple-black, their breasts perfectly formed, capped with nipples like small black beetles.

Colonel Bwultuzu sprang up and enveloped Captain Page in a massive bear hug. Together the huge African, the Napoleon-size pirate, and the two minuscule naked women looked like the members of a perverse circus act.

"My friend!" the colonel said in a booming voice. He smiled, revealing teeth like square postage stamps. "Good to see you so soon after your last visit!"

"Didn't think I'd be back till September, Colonel," the pirate said, stepping out of reach of the big man's hands. "Something came up. I have a proposition I'd like to discuss."

"You are all business, *comme d'habitude.*" Colonel Bwultuzu wagged his big head in mock disappointment. "But you must know that my soldiers have not yet captured enough of the enemy from the countryside to fill the hold of your ship. The summer campaign is still two weeks away. This time we attack Seme itself. In three months' time I can promise you many strong young men from the hills. Anda traitors, of course. Still, their blood is red, and they will work many months in the sun before they die."

"This is not business as usual," the pirate said. "My proposal will take a bit of explanation."

"Then we drink tejiyaa, we talk awhile, and when we are done talking . . ." The colonel smiled again with his postage stamp teeth and made an operatic gesture toward the two small women on the couch. "Which one do you choose?"

"Iwo women, eh?" The pirate gave a sharp grin and looked down at them. "Never been with an Iwo before."

The small women looked up at him with the sad, imploring eyes of trapped animals.

Colonel Bwultuzu clapped his hands and laughed. "We will make a good Bupu out of you yet, Captain," he said.

The pirate leaned over to the nearest woman and ran a hand across her breasts. She shivered, seemed to hesitate for a moment, then bit his arm with a quick, hard snap. He pulled away and hit her across the mouth. Cricket drew a sharp breath and turned her face into Wilson's shoulder.

"I think I'll take this one," the pirate said. "Teach her a thing or two."

"I warn you, my friend," Colonel Bwultuzu said, smiling. "Once you've had an Iwo woman, you'll never go back to full size."

"That's a risk I'll take," the pirate said.

"I bow to the connoisseur," the colonel said. "You are a man of excellent appetites," and he gave an elegant bow.

The pirate took a few steps back, rubbing his arm where he had been bitten. "My people, Colonel . . ." He indicated the rest of them for the first time.

"Of course." Colonel Bwultuzu bowed again. "I shall make their comfort a question of paramount importance for my staff."

8

WILSON AND CRICKET WERE shown to a large room on the second floor. Charred books and bits of paper lay scattered over the torn carpet. There was an overstuffed easy chair in good condition, a double bed with dirty sheets, and an old armoire that still contained two pairs of neatly folded socks and a yellowing packet of unused handkerchiefs. A bare lightbulb shone from an old table lamp. It cast a garish white light against the sandbags over the window.

As Cricket took off her clothes, Wilson kicked around the junk on the floor, hands in his pockets. The charred books were in

Swedish and French. He saw Eugène Sue's *Mystères de Paris,* Flaubert's *Education Sentimentale,* and a few volumes with unpronounceable names by Pär Lagerqvist. Behind the dresser on the floor he found a photograph of a stout middle-aged Frenchman in a tricolor sash, on his arm a slim blond woman half his age in a white dress. They were at a cocktail party, or perhaps a wedding, glasses of champagne in hand. Wilson knelt and picked the photograph from its broken-out frame. A date along one edge read "3 Fev.67."

"Here's a theory," he said. "This must have been the French ambassador's house once. The master bedroom. And judging from the books and this picture, I'd say he married the youngest daughter of the Swedish ambassador. Figures. Just like a Frenchman."

He turned around to show Cricket the photograph, but she wasn't listening. She sat naked, cross-legged on the bed, working at her toenails with a toenail clipper. The expression on her face registered somewhere between disgust and scorn. Wilson guessed she was thinking of her father and the Iwo woman downstairs. How long had she endured such perversities? He hesitated and studied her in this unlovely demeanor, in the harsh white light, thinking that she looked hard and ugly just now. Then he caught sight of her sex between her legs, and a lewd little spark ran down from the lizard cortex of his brain, and he was filled with a desire that made his knees go weak.

"Cricket," he said softly.

She looked up, scowling.

"Are you all right?"

"Fine," she said, and pressed her lips together and stared back down at her toes. "Actually I'm feeling like I want to be alone right now. Why don't you take a walk, find the bathroom or something?"

"Do you want to talk about what's bothering you?"

"No," she said.

Wilson went out into the dark hallway and closed the door behind him. Halfway down, two militia soldiers were throwing dice against a scuffed patch of baseboard. Shards of a broken vase and bits of plaster lay across a hall table to their left. Plasterwork from the ceiling had fallen in; live electrical wires hung down like live snakes. The soldiers looked up as Wilson approached. One of them chewed a fist-size wad of kaf. The black leaves hung from his mouth, black juices drooling down his chin.

"I'm looking for the bathroom," Wilson said to both of them.

The one with a mouthful of kaf simply blinked and turned away. The other shook his head. Their assault rifles sat propped against the wall, mundane as dust mops.

"*Zum clo,*" Wilson said. "*Le toilet,* WC." Then he made a pissing gesture.

"Ah!" The one without the mouthful of kaf sprang up, took Wilson by the arm, and pulled him down the dark corridor. They turned left, then right, and entered a large European-style bathroom with a ceramic tub and a bidet. The stench here was incredible. The toilet was backed up; urine and fecal matter spread across the floor. The soldier led Wilson past this slop and out a pair of French doors that opened onto a wide balcony. He pushed Wilson up to the railing, pointed over the edge, and made a pissing noise between his teeth.

"O.K.," Wilson said. He unzipped and stared down at the black ruin of Rigala below. The broken towers of downtown showed in uneven silhouette against flashes of artillery from the foot of Mount Mtungu. The faint trill of a woman screaming came from somewhere not far away, and there was the continual background sputter of automatic weapons fire. The soldier stood close behind, breathing heavily. Wilson tried to pee but couldn't. This was embarrassing, happened to him in bus stations and airports. Why didn't the man just go away? Wilson tried to concentrate, cleared his throat, shifted his weight from one foot to the other, and thought about dripping trees after a rainstorm, and running water, but it was no good. Then, he cleared his throat again.

"Ah, forgive me, you will want your privacy," the soldier said after a beat. He spoke good English with an American accent. "I'll just smoke a cigarette. Take your time." He moved down to the far end of the balcony. Wilson heard the snap of a match, stared down into the blackness of the yard below, counted to ten, and watched his urine arc off into the night like a prayer. A slight drumming sound came from below a half second later and he imagined the stuff splattering over the roof of a car. It wasn't till Wilson turned around and zipped up his pants that he realized there was something familiar about the soldier's voice.

The soldier stood in shadow at the far end against the house. All Wilson could make out of his face was the orange tip of his cigarette.

"Cigarette?" the familiar voice said, and a dark hand held a pack of Egyptian cigarettes into the yellow square of light from a nearby window.

Wilson came down the length of the balcony, his mind working. At that moment a big military truck rumbled up the avenue and stopped at the curb in front of the mansion, brakes squealing. Thirty or so soldiers climbed down off the back and ambled up the front steps.

"Changing of the guards," the soldier said. "I'm off duty now for the evening."

Wilson took a cigarette as if he didn't know what to do with it. The soldier held up a match, and in the brief flare Wilson recognized the face but couldn't say where he knew it from. The Egyptian cigarette tasted harsh and bitter as seaweed, and he drew it into his lungs.

"I have been waiting for an opportunity to speak to you," the soldier said. "I was with those who took you up from the Nikongi Jetty."

"I thought you looked familiar," Wilson said.

"You do not remember me from before tonight?" the soldier said.

"Before tonight?" Wilson said, and felt the prickling sensation at the back of his neck. "What do you mean?"

"You do not remember me," the soldier said. "That is very funny," and he laughed and Wilson remembered the laugh but still did not know the man.

"I give up," Wilson said.

The soldier raised his left hand suddenly, and Wilson saw its outline against the dull red illumination of Rigala under fire. The three middle fingers were missing, the stub of the third digit decorated with a gaudy ring of gold openwork. Wilson's memory came on like a slow-moving train. It was an astonishing encounter, but he had come to think of the world as a place in which astonishing things happened every day. Now he remembered the man from the night of the cockfight and the bright stars.

"Your name is Tulj," he said in a calm voice. "Am I right?"

"And your name is Wilson, and you saved my life!" Tulj reached out and took Wilson by the shoulder, excited. "You did more than that. You gave my life back to me, and you saved my brother's life! I didn't have time to thank you then. I was a coward. This has been my one great shame. Later I looked for you, and I could not find you, to my despair. Now God has given you back to me, and I rejoice! But you are in the company of very evil men, men who make slaves of my people. I have been told evil men can do good things, but I do not believe it. Are you an evil man?"

"I don't think so," Wilson said.

"Then we must talk."

"O.K."

Tulj took Wilson by the arm again and led him down through the house. Soldiers milled about in the entrance hall, chewing kaf, drinking tejiyaa. Others replaced the ones who had been asleep on the stairs. The sentry did not seem to notice as the two of them went out the gate to the cab of the truck.

"Get in, Mr. Wilson," Tulj said.

"Just plain Wilson," Wilson said. "It's my first name."

They got in the truck, and Tulj said a few quick words to the driver and handed him four cigarettes. The driver shrugged and nodded, and a few minutes later the truck filled up again with soldiers and they lurched off down the avenue into the night.

"They go to the fighting in the Seventh District," Tulj said, jerking his thumb toward the soldiers through the little mesh window in the back. "Lugluwanougu Street, that's the front these days. I used to buy tires for my bicycle there when I was a student at the University. Last week the front was the garden of what used to be the Sequhue National Library. Seventy-five men died in the fighting between the stone benches."

"Who are you serving with?" Wilson said.

"The BPF," Tulj said.

"Which one's that?" Wilson said.

"The Bupu Patriotic Front," Tulj said. "But it doesn't really matter. Could just as easily be the ANM or the BPP or the APP or the BNCM. It's all a load of manure; they're all a bunch of murderous bastards, just out to grab what they can take, and the country be damned."

The truck bumped over shell craters down the hill into the city center. Fighting here had been quite recent. Wilson saw abandoned ordnance, streets blockaded with fresh barbed wire. Stripped corpses lay in the middle of the road dead ahead. The driver didn't bother to turn out of the way, and Wilson felt a bump and a sick, cracking sound that sent the bile rising in his throat.

"Where the hell are we going?" Wilson said.

"Don't worry. The best bar in town," Tulj said. "I think I owe you a drink."

The truck jounced around a rutted square with a smashed fountain and swung wide down a rather grand street divided by a median strip piled with rubble. Tulj tapped the driver on the shoulder, the truck stopped, and Wilson and Tulj got out. They stood in the cloud of blue exhaust, staring at each other as the truck pulled away. Tulj could not keep a smile from his face. Wilson didn't know what to say.

"This is my lucky day," Tulj said, "my very lucky day."

Wilson considered a moment. "You don't find it strange . . ." His voice trailed off.

"You've heard of Carew and Rawlinson?" Tulj said.

"I've heard of Carew," Wilson said, "the famous explorer."

"Yes, they were both English explorers who came to tell us poor Africans how to find lakes and rivers we already knew how to find, but that is beside the point. In 1824 they journeyed to Bupanda quite unknown to each other and for entirely different purposes. In March of that year they met quite by accident on the road to Bongola. They were the only two Europeans in equatorial Africa at that time. The philosopher Jung called it synchronicity, but we studied Jung at the university, and in my opinion, the man was a quack. Let's go get a drink."

He put his hand on Wilson's shoulder, and they went off across the square.

9

THERE WASN'T MUCH LEFT of the Star of Africa, once the most elegant hotel between Cape Town and Fez. King Edward VII had stayed there in the days before Victoria's death when he was still the Prince of Wales, as had Stanley after his trek to find Livingstone, and more recently Elizabeth Taylor and Richard Burton during the making of *Cleopatra*. The upper floors, shelled during the early days of the civil war, stared out blank and empty on the Avenue of July 16, 1960. The famous veranda sagged under the weight of sandbags and heavy spools of barbed wire, its wooden columns half eaten away by termites.

But by some miracle of war, the Colonial Room Bar had survived intact. Wilson almost gasped when he passed through a heavy velvet curtain from the rubble of the lobby into the plush dimness of the

bar. Waiters in white jackets and bow ties carried trays of drinks between glossy tables and leather booths to the light hum of polite conversation and the rattle of ice in glasses. Broad-bladed ceiling fans turned the hot air overhead with a lazy shooping sound. The bar itself was a magnificent fantasy of rosewood and mahogany, carved natives and crocodiles and snakes with inlaid silver eyes. A full-length portrait of Queen Victoria in her regalia as Empress of India hung on a dusty gold rope over the impressive array of bottles. European businessmen in light-colored suits mixed with party officials and dark soldiers in dress uniforms. Cigar smoke rose to the pressed tin ceiling in a suffocating cloud.

"We will have to get a jacket and tie from the maître d'," Tulj said. "Those are the rules. A jacket and tie must be worn at all times."

A few minutes later, dressed in blue wool blazers and stained, oversize striped ties from the seventies, they were shown to a booth near the bar.

"This is quite a place," Wilson said. "Like having a drink in a time capsule."

"Yes," Tulj said. "Makes you forget about the war for a few minutes. It's practically the only shred of civilization left in our poor country. My father was a waiter here before independence, when no blacks were allowed. President-for-Life Sequhue staged a sit-in at the bar in 1954. In the sixties he used to come here in black tie and white evening jacket for his gin and bitters every Wednesday night at eight o'clock exactly, and continued to do so even after he had outlawed Western ways. It is out of respect for that great man that the bar has been preserved as you see it."

Tulj motioned to one of the waiters, who came over and shook his hand. "This is my brother-in-law Ranji," he said.

Ranji shook Wilson's hand. He was a Bupu with a reddish complexion and bald patches in his hair.

"I recommend a gin and bitters," Tulj said.

"Is that what you're going to have?" Wilson said.

"Always," Tulj said.

"Sounds good to me," Wilson said.

Ranji went off toward the bar. Tulj watched him go, then pointed at the portrait of Victoria, barely visible through the cigar smoke haze.

"Out in the bush they believe the old queen is still alive," he said. "They call her *nu Wan-lazi*—that is the Great Mother—and they say she watches over childbirth and the hearth, along with the goddess Buzu, who is the patroness of birth pains in the old religion. I am an educated man, as you know, so I reject all such superstitions, but I will say this—Victoria presided over a great era in our history. The Mpwanza Canal was built, linking Lake Bupu to the sea. Many roads were carved through the jungle, as was the railroad, which we still use today, and also many hospitals and schools were constructed. The best of us were educated at government expense at mission schools, then sent to Cambridge University in England, and trained to be good administrators. My grandfather was one of these. Yes, the land was exploited, diamonds were taken, timber, tin, copper, but we were given a great gift in return. We were given the gift of law, which brought the blessings of peace. All that is gone now. Now we Bupandans drown each other in our own blood."

Ranji brought the gin and bitters on a battered silver tray, and Tulj and Wilson drank for a while in silence. Wilson watched the crowd at the bar, drinking and talking beneath the steady gaze of Victoria as if beneath the scrutiny of Civilization itself—and for a moment, it was almost possible to believe that certainty still existed, that order was more than the illusion that Cricket claimed it to be.

Tulj sighed and leaned forward. There was a great weariness in his eyes. "I will tell you what has happened to me since the cockfights in your country," he said.

"O.K.," Wilson said.

"After you saved us from the mob, my brother and I escaped through the trees, and walked back to the city along the interstate highway. The journey took several hours beneath the unusual stars

of that evening, and during those hours my fear quieted, and I began to think seriously for the first time in many years. I realized that I was not safe anywhere in the world—not even in America locked in my own bedroom in my own house—as long as the civil war continued and a single Anda was left alive. The country people here have a saying—In the year of the lion the safest place to be is with the lions. So I resolved to return and join my fellow Bupus in the patriotic struggle.

"I sold my possessions and took a plane to Bujumbola and crossed the border on foot and joined up with the BPF, who were then fighting in the jungle east of Seme. I fought with them for five months and saw much senseless killing. Once—and my heart shrinks from the memory—we came upon an Anda village full of women and children. We took the children for slaves and raped the women and killed them. I shall never be able to forget that a few of my comrades cut the heart from a sixteen-year-old girl while she was still alive, divided it between them, ate it, and then fornicated with her dead and bleeding body. Perhaps I have become soft living in America, but this is one tribal custom which I feel should be dispensed with. I was so struck with horror at this act that I made another resolution on the spot. This time I vowed to find a middle way between Bupu and Anda, but before I tell you any more, Mr. Wilson, I must have the answer to a few important questions."

"O.K.," Wilson said.

Tulj paused and reached into his pocket and extracted his pack of Egyptian cigarettes. There were two left. He offered one to Wilson, who shook his head. Then he lit up and put the match out in a ceramic ashtray marked "Star of Africa" in gold letters around the side. When he looked up again, his eyes were hard.

"First, why are you in the company of these evil men?" he said.

"I'm not with the evil men, not really," Wilson said. "It's the woman, the one with the red hair. I followed her across the Atlantic in a boat. It's a long story. Now, she's my wife."

"Ah, a woman," Tulj said as if he understood.

"In a word," Wilson said.

Tulj thought for a second. "Are you a party to slaving operations in my country, Mr. Wilson?"

"Not by choice," Wilson said.

"But you have the confidence of men who are?"

"More or less."

"You are not with them, you are certain—"

"I'll try to be very clear," Wilson said. "I suppose I always knew the world could be a pretty bad place, but until recently I lived a careful, selfish existence and turned away from the badness and pretended it didn't exist. I still do not believe that vice is the natural condition of the world's multitudes, but perhaps I am a foolish optimist. The pirate Page and his murderous band of cutthroats are making things worse for everyone. If I can do anything to stop them, I will. Even if it costs me my life." He felt self-conscious saying it this way, but he meant what he said, and meaning it gave him a slight tingly sensation in his toes.

Tulj nodded, satisfied. "Very good," he said. "Then it is not blind chance but divine Providence that has set us on each other's paths again. Certain friends of mine have a theory. They say it is now very profitable for Bupu and Anda to fight each other, so each side may take slaves to sell to businessmen from industrialized countries. They believe if we stop the slave trade, we stop the war. I agree with them."

"Who are your friends?" Wilson said.

Tulj shook his head. "First, will you help us?"

Wilson glanced at Queen Victoria over the bar and squared his shoulders. "Do you have a cigarette?"

10

THE MWTUTSI FLOWED DARK as dried blood through the green twilight of the jungle. Extravagantly plumed birds and monkeys with fluffy white tails watched from the tangled branches along the banks. Wilson could not hear a single sound over the thrumming of the engines; even the mosquitoes were silent. This was the quietest jungle he had yet experienced, like a strange green cathedral, though to which god it was consecrated he could not say: an unknown deity of absurd fecundity and sudden death. Corpses of soldiers, half eaten by crocodiles, floated past the *Dread*'s camouflaged hull, bobbing gently in the water on their way to the sea two hundred miles away.

Twenty miles past the old logging station at Ulundi, the river fanned out into a swamp of muddy islands and lily-clogged channels. They made slow progress through this morass. The *Dread*'s deep-sea sonar system was fouled by the closeness of the jungle, and the pirate was forced to resort to an old-fashioned lead plumb on a nylon line to gauge the depths of the channels through the mud. Wilson went forward with this primitive device and spent two days perched in the bow cage lowering and raising the nylon line. He didn't mind this duty; it allowed him to stay away from the others and gave him time to think. For most of the journey a black-winged tree shrike with a long plumed tail followed in their wake, alighting from time to time on taffrail or stern rail, but like the other birds that Wilson saw in the trees, it didn't seem to make a sound.

"If I were an African, I'd say that bird meant no good for us, some kind of evil spirit or something." Schlüber had come forward to smoke a cigarette, his sand-colored hair ruffling in the tepid breeze, pale blue eyes reflecting the green of the jungle. He leaned over the bow cage and watched the shrike circle the ship once and fly off into the trees. "Have you noticed that bloody thing's been following us since Ulundi?"

"Yes," Wilson said. "But you guys should be pretty much immune to bad luck by this time."

"What do you mean?" Schlüber said.

"How many slaving raids have you been on?" Wilson said. He lowered the plumb line into the black water and drew it up. "Seventeen and a half feet," he called aft.

"Aye, aye," Cricket called from the octagon, and the *Dread*'s twin diesels thrummed up an octave, and the vessel inched forward through the muck.

"Been at it six years now," Schlüber said. "About three jobs a year, so we're looking at eighteen, twenty jobs, I guess."

"O.K.," Wilson said. "I would think if bad luck or fate or justice—whatever you want to call it—were going to catch up with you, it would have caught up with you after number three or four. Way I figure it, after fifteen, you're home free till Judgment Day."

"You don't get it," Schlüber said. "This one's different. We've never gone into the interior before, and frankly I'm quaking in my boots. The old *Storm Car*'s too big for river travel; this tub's just shallow enough; she'll make it all the way up to Lake Tsuwanga, which is as godforsaken as it gets. Before this, we'd go to Kemal or Brass or any one of a half dozen trading stations along the coast above Rigala and pick up the cargo from native wholesalers. Safe enough, so of course the markup is outrageous, sometimes two hundred and ten percent per unit. Now Captain Page has decided to eliminate the middleman entirely. We're headed to the source, my friend. Risky, if you ask me, but the profit is potentially huge."

Wilson let the plumb drop a few feet, the lead weight thumping against the side of the boat. The black shrike flew across the bow.

"We're going to take slaves onto the *Dread*?" he asked quietly.

"That's the idea," Schlüber said. The smoke of his cigarette hung in the heavy air.

"How many human beings can you fit in the hold?" Wilson said, straining to keep an even tone. "Twenty, thirty? Seems hardly worth the effort."

Schlüber flicked his cigarette into the black water. "We're not talking about full-scale human beings here," he said. "The Iwos are more like some strange species of animal. Little bastards don't even speak. Make these weird clicking noises like chipmunks or something."

Wilson remembered the wild, blank eyes of the Iwo women in Rigala and shuddered. "So how many of them can you cram in below?" he heard himself say. The muddy water of the Mwtutsi made a slight hushing sound against the hull.

Schlüber shrugged. "Eighty-five to a hundred, we figure," he said.

Wilson snapped toward the German. "You lousy sons of bitches!" he said between his teeth.

Schlüber took a step back, shook his head. "I know what you're thinking," he said. "It doesn't work that way for me. Anything's better than what I had before."

"What's worse than the slave trade?" Wilson said.

"Remind me to tell you my life story sometime," Schlüber said. "For now let's just say I had a good job with a top accounting firm in Frankfurt and a pretty girlfriend and a nice new Porsche 911 and a nice apartment, and I played soccer on the weekends with my friends and ate good German food in nice restaurants and drank good beer and smoked a little hash now and then, and I didn't care about any of it. I was dead. That's all civilized society does for you, my friend, makes you dead. There's nothing at stake. At least here"—he pushed his chin toward the tangle of the jungle—"I can feel my heart beating."

Wilson turned to the water and raised the plumb line. His stiff back spoke a volume of scorn. Schlüber hesitated, cursed once, and headed off toward the navigational octagon. But in truth Wilson understood the man all too well. He had experienced the same ennui. It had ripped through his life like a whirlwind, driven him from the solace of Andrea's willing arms, from the comfortable, shabby apartment where he had lived unmolested for eight years, on a strange journey across the sea and into the heart of Africa with the worst sorts of companions available anywhere in the world.

A few seconds later, the flat surface of the Mwtutsi bulged off the starboard, and Wilson caught a dull flash of primordial eye and leathery flank, nubbled as an ear of corn, and a crocodile rose to the surface for a moment before the black river washed over it and the ominous stillness of the jungle descended again.

11

MORNING SUN REVEALED A blighted landscape. The jungle and swamps of the Ulundi country had faded into the night. Now the river flowed past a charred terrain, scattered with burnt-out military equipment. Black, lifeless soil reached into the smudgy distance. Even the water smelled strongly of burned rubber.

"The Andas did this," the pirate said. "About five years ago they torched a swath through the jungle thirty miles wide with surplus Vietnam War–era defoliants. Stopped the Bupu advance on Seme, cold. General Ature with the APP masterminded the whole thing. He was one smart motherfucker. In war, he told me once, the only object is to win. Who cares what you're left with when it's over?"

Wilson peered over the hot armor plating of the navigational octagon. The banks were a tangle of burnt tree roots and rusting black metal. Bones punctuated the ground like question marks.

"How long will it take the trees to grow back?"

"Grow back?" The pirate gave a wolfish laugh. "When the Romans took Carthage, they sowed the ground with salt so nothing would grow there again. You've got a similar situation here. Going to look good and burnt for the next thousand years at least."

At noon they passed an abandoned Bupu village that marked the edge of the devastation and were once again among the trees. Here the river narrowed to no more than twenty yards across. Vegetation grew so thick overhead the sky was hidden from view.

"Watch the jungle along here," the pirate said. It sounded like an order. Wilson went to the small arms closet for the binoculars.

"Don't worry about them." The pirate waved him away. "This is for your own amusement."

Wilson stared foolishly at the far bank for a half hour before he began to see pale beams of light flickering from the darkness between the trees.

"It's the Iwos," the pirate said to Wilson's question. "The primitive little bastards worship light."

"You mean the sun?" Wilson said.

"No. They worship light. Flashlights, actually. Who knows why? Probably because it's so goddamned dark in the deep jungle where they live. They'll sell their own grandmother for a couple of flashlights. Know what we've got in the hold?"

"No," Wilson said.

"Ten crates of cheap plastic flashlights from Taiwan. The batteries wear out in a couple of weeks. It's like an addictive drug to the Iwos; they always need more."

An hour before dark the *Dread* passed close by an Iwo warrior paddling along in a dugout no bigger than a kitchen sink. Long black feathers trailed from his hair, matted down with mud. His chest and arms were streaked with white paint; white circles scrawled around his eyes. A red plastic flashlight hung on a length of twine from his neck. As he came even with them, he stopped paddling, raised his flashlight to his chin, and clicked it on. The faint beam caught the white paint and lit his face like a skull in the green gloom of the jungle. The Iwo remained motionless, flashlight under his chin, as the current of the river bore him out of sight.

12

Lake Tsuwanga glowed a liquid gold in the afternoon sun. A cool breeze blew from the direction of Mount Mosumbawa, which showed its blue peak beyond the nearest foothills. From the bow cage of the *Dread,* Wilson filled his lungs with fresh mountain air and watched the cattails bend in the wind and the scarlet swirl of birds over the lake. A slight dappling of the surface meant the flying fish were running; when they hit the air, it was like a handful of silver coins thrown out of the water toward the sky. He saw the pelicans and cormorants dive to meet them, squabbling gracefully above the tips of the waves. In the hazy distance the yellow sail of a Bupu fishing skiff filled with wind and swelled toward shore.

The lake was famous as much for its scenic quality as for the fact that few white men had seen it and lived—perhaps no more than a few dozen in the 150-year history of African exploration by Europeans. Wilson remembered reading an article in *National Geographic* that told of the lake's discovery in 1830 by Sir Alwyn Carew, who had been looking for the source of the Niger, then one of the great mysteries of geography. After a year and a half in the interior Carew foundered starving and nearly naked onto Tsuwanga's bright shores. This experience, he later wrote, was like emerging into a dream of light from the dark horrors of the jungle.

Carew was right, Wilson thought; the light here was clear and beautiful. But after an hour, Wilson became aware of something else, a disturbing quality he couldn't put his finger on. A disquieting shade lurked in the blue shadows the sun made upon the deck. Here was beauty that did not need human contemplation. The whole lake hummed with its own apartness. Staring out at the blue water, Wilson almost understood what had happened to Carew—in the end the perfect light had driven him mad: On his second expedition up the Mwtutsi, the explorer had brought, along with the usual

equipment and supplies, 150 passenger pigeons on a barge chris-
tened HMS *Alexander Pope*. Two of these loyal birds eventually
reached the British coastal station at Williamsport with rambling,
incomprehensible dispatches full of giant snakes and midgets and
butterflies big as kites. Carew was never heard from again.

Fifty years later, in 1882, in the market at Bongola, an officer of
the West African Company traded a hunting knife to a Bupu chief
for a leather-bound English edition of the comedies of Goldoni. He
was surprised to find such an incongruous item in the middle of the
jungle and asked the chief where he had gotten the volume. A white
man had given the book to the Iwos in the time of his grandfather,
the chief said; then the white man had jumped into the water of the
lake to live with the fish. On the flyleaf the officer found two words
scrawled in Carew's hand in a dark something that looked like
blood: "Fear Ascendant."

Now, a lavender illumination filled the sky above Lake Tsuwanga,
and the mountain and the waves looked unspeakably lovely against
this sad color, and Wilson thought of the Great Carew's bones
perhaps lying off in the deep water beneath the keel. Washed clean
by cold currents, they kept the company of unnamed mollusks and
strange anemones at the bottom, another Englishman swallowed
whole by Africa.

13

THE *DREAD* DIESELED AT low throttle into a cove at the
western end of the lake. Here a ragged Bupu settlement spread a
half mile along the shore. In the dusky light Wilson saw military
tents and rusty-sided Quonset huts side by side with traditional
cupcake-shaped Bupu haotas—tribal dwellings of tarred reeds built
around a courtyard of green polished dung. At the northern end of

the village, on a mound of earth, was a wooden palisade surrounded by a series of low cages. Instead of a flag, the place was watched over by a dozen severed heads on poles. Clouds of mosquitoes and blood-fed bottle flies drifted out across the water on the wind.

"The Bupus call it M'Gongo epo," Cricket said. "The place of tears. It's their only base in Iwo country."

Wilson was silent.

"There are probably two hundred different Iwo clans, each in a continual state of warfare with the other. I know what you're going to say, that the Iwos are fighting and selling each other into slavery because of us, because they want to get their hands on the flashlights we've got in the hold. Well, the Iwos have been fighting each other since the beginning of the world and will be fighting each other when we're gone."

Cricket plucked at peeling skin on her wrist. Her nose was burnt and red. She'd run out of sunblock two days out of Rigala. She took off her sunglasses, and Wilson saw there were worry lines in the raccoon mask of white around her eyes.

"I don't like it any more than you do," she said after a beat. "But we've got to put up with it for a little while."

"That's what you keep telling me," Wilson said.

"Two years of this life and we're in Paris," she said. "Just try to think about that over the next couple of days."

"Yes," Wilson said. "But how many bones do we have to step over to get to the Champs-Élysées?"

Cricket turned her face away and didn't answer.

The *Dread* shifted to the starboard as Mustapha lowered the motorized dinghy and climbed over the side. The pirate and Schlüber joined him there, and the sound of the seventy-five-horsepower Evinrude disturbed the pristine silence of the lake.

"We're going in," the pirate called over the outboard's steady burp. Then he made an annoyed gesture, and Mustapha turned down the throttle and they slid back to where Wilson and Cricket were standing at the stern rail. The pirate looked up from his seat in the rubber boat, a sour evaluation that passed across the two of them.

"The situation could get a little tricky here, I want your husband to know that," the pirate said, looking at Wilson.

"O.K., Dad," Cricket said.

"No squeamishness, no lapses into fucking middle-class morality, no womanish hysterics. Got that, citizen?"

Wilson turned slowly and stared straight into the pirate's black eyes. "Fuck you, old man," he said after a beat.

The pirate's jaw tightened. "Mustapha," he said, and the African hit the throttle and the rubber boat lifted toward the shore.

Wilson watched them go. Dark figures waited on the stony beach in the diminishing light.

Cricket and Wilson and Ngyuen sat down to a cold dinner in the navigational octagon an hour later. The digital instrumentation on the operational console gave out the cheerful glow of Christmas lights. Wilson ate a cheese and tomato sandwich and leftover potato-leek soup from a Tupperware container. Cricket ate a few rice cakes with honey and a salad. The Vietnamese cook ate cold fava beans from a bowl with a wooden spoon. Perched on top of the taffrail, staring down at them, he looked like a sort of malignant owl. Over the shortwave came raucous static interrupted by an occasional manic burst of Morse code.

"Captain Amundsen could read that stuff like a newspaper," Wilson said absently.

"Don't think about him," Cricket said in a low voice. "Right now our life's all about not looking back."

"Cap Amundsen, he dead," Nguyen said. "Food for sharks."

"I wish it were the other way around," Wilson said. "I wish your ass was food for sharks."

"I wonder how much longer you got, joe," the cook said. "This place not agree with you. I smell bad luck floating in the air. Maybe your luck run out here." Then he began to giggle, an eerie, childish sound in the lake darkness.

"Nguyen!" Cricket stood and pushed her finger at him. "Sick of your shit—" but just then a high-pitched screaming reached them from the shore, followed a moment later by the ominous chanting of many voices.

The three of them turned to look at the village sprawled along the shore, a hazy muddle of firelight and smoke on the edge of a greater darkness.

"They've started," Cricket said quietly, her face hidden in shadow. "I won't listen to that crap all night. Give us some power, Mr. Nguyen. We'll motor back with first light."

The cook hesitated; then he shrugged and went over to the controls. Soon there was the comforting thud of the diesels, and Cricket took them a mile or so out into the center of the lake. She killed the engine and dropped anchor in the dark water, but it would not strike bottom. Lake Tsuwanga is impossibly deep, one of the deepest lakes in the world. The anchor fell through the cold fathoms as through space. The *Dread* listed against the black outline of Mount Mosumbawa.

"So we stay up all night, to keep her off the rocks," Cricket said. "I wasn't planning on going to sleep anyway. You?"

"No," Wilson said.

"I was," the cook said, and disappeared below.

The automatic winch brought the anchor back into the bow casing, and the *Dread* drifted through the black toward morning. There was no light but the inconsequential flickering of the stars and the faint glow of the console.

Cricket unbuttoned her shirt and stepped out of her shorts. In a moment, she stood naked beneath the pale stars, her body glowing with its own phosphoresence.

"Remember this is supposed to be a working honeymoon," she said.

"Yeah," Wilson said.

"So I want you to make love to me," she said, her voice lowering an octave, then she settled back onto the bench and opened her legs.

"We'll say it's five, ten years from now. This is a pleasure cruise. We're in the middle of some tame body of water, Lake Geneva, say. Better, Lake Como. It's a beautiful night in late summer, our children are sleeping below. I am your wife and I love you and you love me—"

"Shut up," Wilson said. He walked over to where she was sitting, legs apart, and dropped to his knees.

14

TWO LONG SKIFFS MOTORED out to the *Dread* across the cool surface of the lake at noon the next day.

Six BPF soldiers, done up in a startling combination of combat fatigues and primitive jewelry, climbed aboard. Wilson saw a necklace of dried fruit that wasn't dried fruit but shriveled human ears, headbands of teeth and finger bones. One of the soldiers gave a few harsh commands in Bupu and gestured toward the shore. The others milled around the deck, bored and dangerous.

"What's going on here?" Wilson said. He couldn't help the tremulous note in his voice.

"Steady," Cricket said. "We're going over to participate in what you might call the, uh, ceremonies closing the deal. Considered a necessary thing. Seals the contract between buyer and seller. I'll warn you, it's pretty disgusting. Don't do anything stupid and try not to vomit."

"You're kidding," Wilson said. The back of his neck felt cold.

"I'm not kidding," Cricket said.

Wilson buckled on his pistol and bayonet, put extra cartridges in his belt, and got into the lead skiff. The smell of blood rose in his nostrils as they landed on the beach of glossy stones and went up through the village. No one spoke. Reddish smoke hung faint as a sigh in the air, and there was the acrid, sweet pungence of roasting meat. A yellow dog gnawed at a long bone in the middle of the street. They came up past the far Quonset hut and turned down a narrow alley lined with small cages of untreated timber. Wilson had to look twice to realize human beings were packed into these cages. Men and women no taller than four feet high stared out as the soldiers passed. A few extended their hands, and the air was filled with a sad, reproachful clicking sound.

When they reached the palisade, Wilson saw it was not made of wood, as he had thought, but constructed from human bones lashed to iron girders anchored in the ground. Across the gate, skulls hung in a clever pattern like an inverted pentagram. Wilson made a quick calculation and guessed that the bones of thousands had gone into this gruesome construction. Horror welled up like an ache in his heart. Inside, the ground of packed earth was red and slippery-looking. A naked Iwo woman sagged at a stake before a wide stone table. At her feet a goat with broken legs foundered around in the red mud.

Captain Page and the others waited beneath an awning made from an old parachute. Schlüber squatted in the dirt, a blank expression on his face. Beneath a larger awning off to the left, a group of BPF officers stood grouped around a naked African seated in an old floral-print La-Z-Boy recliner. The African wore three strands of human molars around his neck and a five-foot-tall headdress of ribs and feathers. His skin was scrawled with tattoos and raised scars, his eyes wide with madness. In his right hand he held an ashtzisi made from carved human bones wrapped in gold foil. Two naked teenage boys stood at attention directly behind his chair. Their uncircum-cised penises were moored to their thighs with braided leather thongs.

"At last your family has arrived, Captain," the African called out in a polite British-accented English. "We have been waiting. Please introduce us."

The pirate took Wilson and Cricket over to the chair. Wilson assumed he was being presented to the devil himself.

"Major Charles Mpongu and staff," the pirate said. "My daughter and son-in-law."

"Yes, very pleased to meet you," the major said, rolling his eyes like somebody in an Oscar Wilde play about to consume the last cucumber sandwich. Wilson hesitated, then stepped over and held out his hand. *How often,* he thought, *do you get to meet the devil?*

"Wilson Lander, sir," he said.

The major looked surprised. The officers made a jumpy move forward; he waved them away and offered a limp handshake. He smiled, but his eyes were on fire.

"That name sounds familiar," he said. "Have we met?"

"I can't think where," Wilson said.

"In London perhaps."

"Never been to London," Wilson said.

"Wonderful city when it's not raining," the major said. "Quite pleasant in the spring."

When Wilson stepped aside, he shook the ashtzisi, and the officers gave an assenting shout and settled on the ground.

"Please sit," the major said politely, and Wilson and Cricket and the pirate squatted at his feet. "There are a few things I would like to discuss with you before the festivities commence."

"This may take awhile," the pirate whispered in Wilson's ear. "We've been listening to the bastard all night. Better have a cigar." He handed over a dark-leafed Cuban that Wilson recognized from Captain Amundsen's private collection. Wilson thought of refusing, then thought better of it and took the cigar in memory of the man. As he lit up, the major rose and began his oration.

"Some years ago the great Sequhue—may we revere his name— bid the nation return to the old ways, the ways of our ancestors. The magnificent Sequhue knew what was inscribed in our hearts. We Bupus are not like the pale, passionless Europeans who honor the sale of men with a handshake, then go off to the bank counting their

money. How immoral—worse, how banal! We Bupus know that
when we sell the blood of our blood into bound servitude, our
bloody God must be propitiated in the old way with sacrifice, with
dancing, with passion.''

He shook the ashtzisi again, and the officers gave out with another
assenting shout.

Wilson blew smoke rings into the blue. A cloud in the shape of
George Washington went by up there, followed by one that looked
like an old Buick.

''I have known life in the West.'' The major continued, his voice
rising to a rant. ''I have been a prisoner of your cities, a passenger in
your buses and taxis. I was once a student at the London School of
Economics, where I studied the ebb and flow of world currency as
today I study the liver of virgins for the will of God. I slept with
many of your women, I ate your bland food, your bangers and mash,
your hamburgers, and I am here to tell you that the world you have
built is a hollow one! Your hearts are hollow; your women are
hollow, passionless creatures who no longer desire to bear children.
You have fallen from the grace of your ancestors, who once built
roads and schools and tamed the land and deciphered the languages
of the earth. You honor nothing; you believe in nothing. Your God
has turned his face from you. . . .''

The major went on in this vein for the next two hours. Half the
time he hopped around on one foot, gesticulating wildly, his voice
falling from a growl to a whisper and rising to a shriek and falling
back again. Wilson fell asleep for a while. The woman at the stake
revived from her stupor and began a shrieking that provided a gruesome counterpart to the major's words. At last he finished what he
had to say, and with a shake of his ashtzisi, the gate opened, the
enclosure filled with soldiers and naked Bupu women, and the dancing began.

The strange glow of Lake Tsuwanga faded with a shudder in the
west, and a thousand dancers danced by torchlight to the headache
rhythm of drum and kalimba gourd and the chanting of a thousand

voices. Wilson could no longer see the dancing after the first three hours. The dancer and the dance merged into one sweat-streaked nightmare of flesh and rattling beads. The thick air smelled like hell itself. The stars flickered up, red in the glow of the torches. A bottle of tejiyaa was passed around, and Wilson swallowed a mouthful and his toes went numb. He felt the power of it and fought to keep himself from being absorbed into their trance. The red moon hung like a question mark over Mount Mosumbawa.

Suddenly Cricket stripped off her shirt and got up and joined the dance, her breasts pale and obscenely animate in the red light of the moon. Wilson shrank back into the shadows. The night was a shroud that hid the shameful works of men. In the middle of everything Major Mpongu let out a meaty fart and threw back his head and laughed, a long, monotonous howl. Then, all at once—silence. The dancers stopped on the beat. Wilson heard the wind rise from the lake, the fast panting of the dancers. Torches flickered against the wall of bones.

A moment later, the skull gate swung open, and a miserable coffle of about a hundred Iwo men and women were led into the enclosure. The plastic flashlights around their necks had long since gone out. A low plaint of sighs and clicks rose in the gloom.

"Seems like such a goddamned waste of horseflesh." Wilson heard the pirate's voice from somewhere. "But it's their culture. Who are we to tell them what to do?"

At this Wilson remembered the pirate's comment about Carthage, and he remembered the rest of the story from old books: how the Romans had been horrified when they came across the Fields of Tanith—acre upon acre of the bodies of children sacrificed by the Carthaginians to an evil god—how it was for this they destroyed that great city and sowed the ground with salt.

Then he heard Cricket's voice low in his ear, and she said, "Feel sorry for them if you want. But last week they sold their neighbors to the same fate."

"What fate?" Wilson whispered, but in the next second the

major hopped up from his floral-print La-Z-Boy and raised the bone ashtzisi to the dark sky. The dancers scattered. A soldier with a machete stepped up to the stake and decapitated the woman with a single stroke. Blood sprayed in a wild arc from her neck; the head toppled, blinking and insensible, into mud. The major let loose a guttural cry. This was the signal. The Iwos were dragged clicking and croaking like sick frogs to the stone table, and the slaughter began. A bloody mist filled the air. Wilson tried not to hear the high-pitched animal screaming, the crack of breaking joints, the slither of viscera—the sound of the butchers at work. From behind the floral-print easy chair, the major's adolescent attendants stared out at the scene in openmouthed ecstasy, their uncircumcised penises straining at the braided thongs.

Wilson shrank back into the blackness. No one saw him slip away, along the edge of the palisade and through the open skull gate. There were no guards at the slave cages. An iron lever released the weights that lifted the cage doors. Wilson took the bayonet from his belt and busied himself with the bonds of the prisoners. The captive Iwos blinked up at him like sleepy children, afraid, not understanding. He carried the first few out into the alley and pushed them along their way. He pointed to the jungle not fifty yards distant.

"Go," he said, "get out of here. Go home," talking as you would to a stray dog.

The Iwos still didn't understand. Gently as possible, Wilson took a plastic flashlight from around the neck of a small old man and clicked it on and swung the frail beam toward the green tangle of vegetation. "Go home," he repeated. "Go and sin no more."

Slowly the Iwos turned and walked into the darkness. It took Wilson about two hours to release all the prisoners. He counted five hundred; then he stopped counting. When it was over and all the cages were empty, he sat down in the dirt against the last cage, exhausted. The sky was still black, but the stars had faded and the red moon had set and dawn was not far.

A moth, its body covered with delicate pink and yellow fur,

fluttered down from somewhere. Wilson slid the Webley-Vickers from his holster. He loaded the chambers with bullets, cocked the hammer, and set it across his knees. Then, without knowing why, he took the Iwo flashlight and put it under his chin and clicked on the beam. Pale light touched his cheeks like a benediction.

PART SIX

BLOCKADE SQUADRON!

1

THE PINK AND YELLOW moth woke him up.

"They're coming," the moth said in a voice like silver in water, and Wilson staggered to his feet as the bloodstained crowd pressed through the skull gate.

Dawnlight above the dark bulk of Mount Mosumbawa showed the color of bruised peaches. The vacant expanse of Lake Tsuwanga gleamed like a burnished spear. Wilson squinted out the sleep junk in his eyes and saw Major Mpongo in the lead, his arm around the pirate's shoulder. Cricket was followed close by Schlüber, who looked dazed and beaten; behind them came the crush of soldiers, exhausted from the night's exertions.

They were about twenty yards from the alley of the cages. This gave Wilson time to scoop the Webley-Vickers out of the dirt where it had fallen. He spun the chamber once and looked over his shoulder for advice, but the moth was gone, flown off to become a caterpillar—or was it vice versa? His head felt muzzy with sleep. The ancient pistol was dead weight in his hand, and he let his arm drop and held it against his leg. The cages stood open at his back like the tomb in the rock. Disbelief and anger spread through the crowd. The pirate's face went white, then red, and he began waving his hands and shouting at Major Mpongo, who alone remained calm.

Wilson seemed to be invisible. No one noticed him standing there in the middle of the alley, gun in hand. He grew impatient, tired of the waiting that was his life. He longed to have an end to the drama, to be delivered up to the fate that had stalked him all the years since his mother was flattened in Commerce Street by a black girder that fell from the sky. He pointed the Webley-Vickers to the sky and squeezed the trigger. The pistol bucked and smoked, and an incredible cracking sound rolled out across the lake. In the ensuing silence Wilson called out, "Hey! Lose something?"

For another second no one moved, then there was a general surge and he was surrounded and Cricket was at his side. Wilson looked into her face; her eyes were dull, without light. Her breasts were covered with a faint layer of grime from the dancing; her legs splotched with dried blood.

"Enjoy yourself last night?" he said.

Cricket didn't seem to understand.

"How does it feel to dance on the bloody innards of a hundred small men and women?" Wilson said.

"Wilson, what's happening?" Cricket said in a raspy voice. "Where are the Iwos?"

"Excuse me, Mr. Lander," it was Major Mpongo, polite as the butler. "But have you seen our slaves? Five hundred and twenty-five Iwos to be exact. They appear to be gone." He smiled, and his smile was perverse because it was lit by madness.

"Yes. I let them go," Wilson said. "All of them."

"You don't mean that," Cricket said, frightened suddenly. "You're kidding."

"I'm not kidding, Cricket," Wilson said. "This is moral lesson number two—slavery is wrong!"

The pirate gave an inarticulate shout and pulled the 9 mm Beretta out of his shorts. Wilson saw the man meant to kill him this time. Without thinking, he brought up the Webley-Vickers, and another loud explosion reverberated across the lake. The pirate fell back dead, a powder-burned hole the size of a golf ball in his forehead a half inch above his eye patch.

"Scheiss!" Wilson heard Schlüber say, "the bastard's gone and killed the captain!"

The first rank of onlookers were spattered with gore. Cricket looked from the end of Wilson's smoking pistol to her father lying dead in the dirt. Red blood pooled at her feet. Her face crumbled from the chin up, and she fell to her knees and began to wail. In the next second, Wilson brought the pistol level with Major Mpongo's eyes and cocked the hammer. The African blinked and stared down at the barrel in mild alarm, as if there were a bee on the end of his nose.

"Nobody move," Wilson said, "this thing's got a hair trigger," though he had no idea what this meant. Major Mpongo's men froze in place. Wilson heard them breathing, not two steps away. He could feel his hand trembling, the pistol growing heavier.

"When stout Cortez entered the Valley of Mexico at the head of two hundred brave Spaniards," Wilson said, talking fast, "do you know what he found?"

Major Mpongo stared, wide-eyed.

"Do you know what he found?" Wilson repeated, and tapped the end of the barrel against the African's forehead.

"No, I do not know, Mr. Lander," he said.

"He found the idols of the Aztec gods drenched with the blood of thousands of human beings," Wilson said. "He found the bodies of men, women, and children lying in great heaps, their hearts cut out with stone knives. He found the Aztec priests wearing the skin of people they had just killed as you or I might wear a three-piece suit. And do you know what Cortez did when he found these things?"

Major Mpongo said nothing. Wilson darted a look to his left. The Bupus were inching closer.

"He smashed their idols," Wilson said in a tight voice. "And he put their priests to the sword." Then he closed his eyes and squeezed the trigger.

The African screamed, high-pitched and womanish. There was an airy bang, like someone slamming a school desk, and a searing heat in Wilson's right hand, and he opened his eyes to see the pistol lying in the ground in the dirt, dark smoke and yellow flames curling from the chambers. His hand was burnt and bloody; a deep gash cut the lifeline in two, and the tip of his thumb hung from one bloody strand of skin.

Major Mpongu looked at Wilson's bloody hand, and he looked down at the gun smoking in the dirt and he began to laugh, a shrill, obnoxious cackle. In a second, he was echoed by his men, and the sound of laughter filled the still morning.

Wilson clenched his fist and jammed it into his pocket. Blood seeped through the fabric of his shorts, began to run down his leg. He felt faint with the pain.

When Major Mpongo had finished laughing, he gave a friendly smile and leaned close. His breath was unspeakably foul.

"You try to kill me, you cannot kill me," the African said in a reasonable tone. "Your gun explodes like a toy. My bloody God protects me. He knocks the sword from your hand. Do you know who my bloody God is, Mr. Lander? I am a Christian, you see. My bloody God is your bloody God! You may wish to kill me in the name of Divine Justice, but who makes justice in this world? Not us poor creatures, but God Himself. Perhaps He has a different end in store for me than the one you had planned. Perhaps you are not His instrument as you think. Perhaps it is I who do His will more perfectly."

Then Major Mpongo stepped back, and his face twisted up into something not recognizably human. The raised scars on his stomach seemed to spell out a familiar phrase: Was it "Fear Ascendant"? Wilson looked down to where Cricket knelt in the dirt, bloody hands pressed against her father's forehead, and he felt bad for what he had done. Their eyes met. She mouthed the words "You're dead."

"Beat him and throw him into the cages," Major Mpongo said.

Wilson almost didn't feel the blows when they came.

2

A GENTLE CLICKING SOUND filtered through the blackness. The pain in Wilson's hand reached all the way up to his shoulder. His face felt on fire. The clicking sound grew more insistent. He opened one eye with some effort and saw the timber bars of the cage as a dark silhouette against the glare. Then he moved his head in the direction of the clicking and made out a squirming, moist sluglike something, suspended half an inch away from his nose. He groaned and pushed himself back, but the little monster followed him and the clicking expanded into croaks and sighs.

"Please, sir, stay still." A voice came from his right. "Your face is the size of a kalimba gourd. He puts the mswimbe to draw the blood away. Mswimbe is ugly, but a good little creature."

Wilson felt hands holding him down, then a cold animal wetness on his cheek and a slight sting. After that they opened his fist, and there was a slithering sensation between his fingers—and he passed again into blackness.

A while later—Wilson couldn't say how long—he woke up feeling better. It was bright outside the cage. He sat up and looked around and found that he shared his prison with two other occupants: The closest, a wizened Iwo man, squatted a few feet away, staring at him with an expression of intense concentration. He was no more than three feet tall, small even by the standards of his people, and he wore three plastic flashlights around his neck on a strand of woven vine and a helmetlike headpiece of dried mud. A rough leather pouch hung from his waist. The other was a normal-size African, slumped in the far corner in a heap of khaki rags that had once been a military uniform. He had a long skinny-horsey face and a crooked nose and bloodshot yellow eyes that showed he had not eaten recently, and he smoked a foul-smelling cigarette in small, greedy puffs. When he saw that Wilson was awake, he made a vague gesture and leaned forward.

"Your face is much better," he said. "And your hand, how does that feel?"

Wilson looked at his hand, wrapped in a bandage of fresh green leaves. He wiggled his fingers; the pain was a bare fraction of what it had been before.

"Not bad, I guess," Wilson said. "Who did this?"

The soldier nodded at the Iwo.

Wilson waved his leafy hand in the little man's direction. "Thanks, mister," he said.

The Iwo did not make a sound, continued to stare.

"I only have a few cigarettes left," the soldier said to Wilson, "but after what you've been through, I am happy to share. Do you want one now or later?"

Wilson shook his head. "That's O.K. I'm not a big smoker. In fact I didn't smoke at all until recently." Then he noticed the gold officer's insignia still attached to the man's tattered collar. "What are you doing in here?" Wilson said, and he waved his bandaged hand at the brightness beyond the cage. "You should be out there with them."

The soldier pulled the collar away from his neck so Wilson could see it better. "This is the staff and crescent moon," he said. "Not the staff and star. I am Colonel Jokannan Saba of the Anda Patriotic Front. These Bupu bastards ambushed my platoon on the far side of Lake Tsuwanga near Imbobo about two months ago. A few of the men got away, I think, but I did not." He gave a sad shrug. "Everyone they could not sell, they killed in the blood ceremonies at Lungwalla. I'm the highest-ranking officer, so they brought me here for special treatment. They're going to boil me alive—privilege of rank, you know. But to tell the truth, I don't really care. I am sick of the war. Been sick of the war for years now. Got to end someplace for me. This place is as good as any."

"I know the feeling," Wilson said, and was about to say more when he was interrupted by a trill of clicks and croaks from the Iwo. The small man duck-waddled forward on his haunches and reached into his pouch and withdrew a handful of leaves. Five leeches, black and shiny, wiggled at the damp center.

"Oh, no!" Wilson said.

"The Iwo says it's time for your medicine again," Colonel Saba said. "Got to put the mswimbe back on your face."

"You can understand his clicking?" Wilson said.

Colonel Saba shrugged. "More or less. I was officer in charge of the Hruke Forest District for three years. There I came into contact with many Iwos. Their language is not that difficult, really. Very primitive. You learn to use your tongue and the back of your throat in ways you never thought possible.''

''Tell him I've had enough of the leeches,'' Wilson said. ''Tell him to forget it.''

The colonel made a few hesitant croaks, and the Iwo trilled back.

''He says he is your physician. And your physician tells you to take the mswimbe right now,'' the colonel said. ''Otherwise your face may fall off. Infection sets in very quickly in this climate.''

Wilson lay back and submitted to the treatment. He shuddered as the slimy creatures slithered around his face and fought down images from his worst nightmares.

The colonel crawled over to take a look. ''You should see the little blighters work,'' he said. ''Very amazing.''

''No, thanks,'' Wilson said.

''Your face was a purple mess of bruises when they brought you in here. Now it's almost normal.''

''Great,'' Wilson said. ''I'll look nice when they boil me alive.''

''I'm afraid that is a fate reserved for officers,'' the colonel said. ''It is not so bad from what I hear. You pass out from the heat before it really starts to burn.''

''What are they going to do to me?'' Wilson said, and the dread took hold of his guts.

''Best not to think about that,'' the colonel said. He settled back into the corner and extracted another cigarette from the crumpled pack concealed in his rags. ''This Iwo, he is a brave man,'' he said as he lit up. ''He's too old for the slave traders; he knows the Bupus will kill him. But about an hour or so after they brought you here, he walked out of the jungle, and he sat down in front of the cage and sang a song in his language until they came and threw him inside.''

''Why the hell did he do that?'' Wilson said.

''I will tell you the name of the song he was singing, and you will understand,'' the colonel said. ''It's called 'The Ghost Man from Far

Away Who Set Free the Forest People on the Night of the Red Stars'; that's a loose translation, of course. This song will be sung by their children and their great-grandchildren. The song is about you, my friend. You are an epic hero now, a great man, like Sequhue or Odysseus. This Iwo was chosen to come and take care of you here before the end. Perhaps if you are lucky, he has a drug in his pouch that will dull the pain of the torture.''

Wilson couldn't think what to say, then the leech slithered over his lips, and he held his breath. When it moved away again, he said, ''Tell him thanks a lot for his help. But tell him I'm not the great man here. He is.''

Colonel Saba delivered this message in halting clicks.

The Iwo smiled suddenly, and it was as beautiful and strange as a smile on the face of a leopard in the heart of the jungle.

3

WILSON HEARD A SAD music on the wind at dusk. He thought he made out the strains of ''Amazing Grace'' played to the calliope lilt of a Tinka band. Then, the sky went bloody beyond the cages and his fellow prisoners grew indistinct and there was the distant boom of cannon out on the lake.

''What do you think that is?'' he said half to himself.

Colonel Saba blew the smoke of his last cigarette into ephemeral freedom through the roughhewn timber of the cage. ''Nothing that will do us any good,'' he said. ''Prepare yourself for the inevitable, as I am prepared.''

Wilson remembered the air thick with blood in the bone palisade and felt despair creep into his heart.

''You're right, we've all got to die,'' he said, but his voice sounded thin and pitiful. "I guess sooner or later doesn't matter. Like the poet says—Accursed! What have I to do with days?"

"Not their way!" Colonel Saba said bitterly. "These Bupus are goddamned savages!" Then he caught himself and sighed. "Though I suppose we Andas are no better. You see, I was present at the soccer stadium in Bandali when we killed sixty thousand of them in one day. This was several years ago, at the beginning of the war. We advertised a free game between Bitumac and the Seme All-Stars— two very popular teams in those days—and we moved through the Bupu neighborhoods handing out free tickets. We had two dozen fifty-caliber machine guns hidden under canvas tarps around the top row of the stadium, and when it was packed with Bupus, we opened fire. There were a lot of families, kids—you know how kids like soccer. When we ran out of bullets, we moved in with sticks and machetes, and when it was done, we burned the bodies in a great stinking bonfire." His voice sank to a guilty whisper. "After something like that, I suppose one shouldn't mind so much being boiled alive."

"Were you behind one of the machine guns?" Wilson said, and he was glad he could not see the man's face in the darkness.

"Worse," Colonel Saba said. "I gave the order to fire."

4

THE SECOND NIGHT WAS calm and quiet. The waters of the lake hushed against the smooth stones of the beach; the jungle was full of the far-off cry of birds and the deep chatter of insects. The Iwo made a few small clicking sounds that Colonel Saba did not care to translate. Wilson tried to keep his mind off the coming ordeal, but this was impossible. How would they do it? He thought he would never sleep again; then he closed his eyes, and when he opened them again, it was almost noon and Cricket stood in the hot sun just beyond the bars of the cage.

"Wake up, Wilson," she said in a hard voice.

Wilson stirred. When he saw it was Cricket, he tried to stand and clunked his head against the low roof. He hobbled over to the bars, rubbing his scalp, and squinted out into the brightness. He could not see her eyes, which were hidden behind Jackie O–type sunglasses with big black lenses, but her mouth was set and her gun hand rested on the butt of her dead father's 9 mm Beretta, stuck in her belt.

"I'm leaving in an hour," she said. "Taking the *Dread* back to Quatre Sables."

"What about me?" Wilson said, half serious.

She ignored him. "The operation here's been a bust. It'll take a whole year to round up those Iwos you set free, you fuck."

"Good," Wilson said, then he didn't know what to say. There followed an awkward beat in which he saw a black-winged shrike flap into the green fringe of jungle. Was it the same one that had followed them up the Mwtutsi in augury of troubles to come?

"Anything else?" he said at last.

"Yeah," Cricket said, and her lip trembled. "We buried Dad last night."

"I'm sorry," Wilson said. "He was your father. But he was also a murderous asshole, and he was going to shoot me."

"You needed shooting after what you did," Cricket said. "I'm sorry I won't be around to see them finish you off."

"So that's it," Wilson said, struggling to keep the panic out of his voice. "You're not going to help me get out of here."

"I couldn't do anything for you if I tried," Cricket said. "You violated a sacred taboo in this part of the world. You cut into their profit margin. And you tried to kill Major Mpongu. That man's a big shit around here. I don't have to say I hope you suffer. You will. If they do it right, you can live up to three days without skin. I've seen it happen, these people are artists. You're not really human anymore, just a quivering pink mass hanging on a pole.''

"I guess you don't love me after all,'' Wilson said.

"You're a bastard,'' Cricket said between her teeth.

"I won you from the Portugee, Cricket. Remember? You needed a good gambler, and you risked my neck because of it. So I'm holding a bad hand right now. Aces and eights, you know? Dead Man's Hand. So you're my wife, we belong to each other now. I need some help here.''

"I don't belong to anyone but myself,'' she said, her voice dull, without expression. "It's been like that from the beginning. There's just myself. The rest of the world is full of stupid assholes.''

"This the sort of thing that happened to old Webster?''

"Fuck you,'' Cricket said. Then she bit her lip and looked away, and Wilson caught a glimpse of her eyes behind the dark glasses and saw the tears on her cheeks.

"I thought we were going to make it work,'' Cricket said, her bottom lip trembling. "I really did. I know you don't believe me, but I really haven't felt as strongly for anyone in my life as I have for you. I guess I've got to stop holding on. I've got to get through my head that it's not going to work out for us. We're just too different—''

"This is ridiculous,'' Wilson said, and he gripped the wooden bars so hard he felt a splinter go into his hand. "We're not breaking up over a cup of espresso at Bazzano's. These bastards are going to skin me alive. You've got to get me out of here.''

Cricket hesitated and looked down. "Impossible,'' she said. "I tried.''

"You did?'' Wilson said. Despite himself, his heart made a flip-flop.

"Oh, Wilson . . .'' Cricket came close and pushed her sunglasses up into her hair and put her hands over his on the bars. Her eyes were a wet, fathomless blue-green this morning, like the color of Lake Tsuwanga in the long hours of dusk. A single blue-green tear fell across his scraped knuckles. "Why couldn't you wait? In two years, in three years, we could have had enough money to live in Paris in high style for the rest of our lives."

"I couldn't wait," Wilson said. "I couldn't swallow the death you wanted to feed me. I couldn't build my happiness on the proceeds of piracy, on the labor of slaves, on a mound of dead bodies!"

Cricket sighed and stepped back. She brought her sunglasses down over her eyes, and her mouth hardened. Wilson saw his battered face reflected in the black lenses.

"You're an idiot," she said. "An asshole like all the other assholes. I shouldn't have come."

"Why did you come?" Wilson said. Squinting out at her, he had the sensation that she was already far away, that he was looking at her through the wrong end of a telescope.

"I shouldn't have come," Cricket repeated, and began to back away.

"Will I be seeing you again?" Wilson said, desperate.

"No," Cricket said.

"Will you miss me?" Wilson said, but Cricket did not answer. She spun around on her heels and headed off into the stark and unforgiving brightness of noon.

5

WILSON PRESSED HIMSELF FLAT against the bars, staring out until long after Cricket had passed out of his line of vision.

When he realized she was not coming back, he collapsed onto the foul dirt floor of the cage as if he had been shot. On his back there in the ashen gloom, as a deeper gloom stole over his heart, his thoughts turned to death. So this is how it would end. What a strange fate! Alone, at the hands of torturers in an obscure corner of

Africa, so far from the life he had known. For the first time in months, he thought of Andrea, no doubt asleep at that moment in her big, clean bed in her fine apartment on the thirty-third floor in the Pond Park Tower. What a fool he had been! He remembered the sound of her tears over the phone the night he left, and he remembered that she had loved him, and self-pity welled up like water in a clogged drain, and tears began to leak out of the corner of his eyes and down the sides of his face to make small dark spots in the dirt.

But the sharp bleat of Colonel Saba's snoring, like somebody snoring in a cartoon, sounded an absurd counterpoint to Wilson's tears. After a few minutes he sat up and dried his eyes on the back of his hand. A hot wind sieved through the bars of the cage. Out there a parched and silent afternoon burned into the African dust. The Bupu guard lay asleep on a reed mat across the way, a bit of canvas propped over his head with a stick. The yellow dog slept in the narrow strip of shade at his side. Wilson imagined the *Dread* gliding away, across the brilliant water of the lake and almost burst into tears again. Then he turned at nothing and saw a pair of bright animal eyes fixed upon him. It was the Iwo, poised like a praying mantis at the back of the cage.

"Hey, you!" Wilson said, annoyed suddenly. "How long have you been watching me?"

The Iwo cocked his head to one side and let out an odd series of low clicks.

"Saba," Wilson called loudly, and the soldier stirred. "What does this midget want?"

Colonel Saba yawned and raised himself on a bony elbow. He yawned again and swallowed dryly and made one or two halfhearted clicks.

The Iwo cocked his head, indicated Wilson with a birdlike gesture, and began an involved clicking and croaking that went on for some time. Wilson watched the bones in the little man's throat orchestrate this symphony and was reminded of the aluminum rods in the throat of the mechanical Abraham Lincoln robot he had seen in Disneyland one summer as a child. The thing had terrified him. A human throat didn't move like that, didn't make those sounds. He had been afraid that Abraham Lincoln was going to eat him alive.

When the Iwo finished, he cocked his head at Wilson and waited for Colonel Saba to speak. The colonel scratched his chin, thought for a moment.

"He says you're very sick," Colonel Saba said. "You've suffered a bad beating, of course, but that's not what he means. He means you are sick inside. Not your body, but your spirit. He says you have a spirit beast inside you that has been gnawing at your guts and making your life miserable for many years."

"Hell," Wilson said.

"The Iwo wants to know if you have a heavy feeling here," the colonel put a large flat hand against his solar plexus. "The feeling that something bad is always about to happen."

Wilson was silent. How did the little man know about his dread? "I've got this anxiety problem," he said at last, feeling ridiculous for explaining. "I've been to psychiatrists back home. A dash of unfocused paranoia mixed in with some unfounded dread. I've gone through some therapy, as far as that goes. Don't worry, I'm on top of the situation."

Colonel Saba translated for the little man.

The Iwo shook his head and duck-walked over to Wilson. He smoothed a space in the dirt with his hand and extracted a stick from his pouch and began to scratch a picture there. He worked on the picture for fifteen minutes, and Wilson saw a frightful animal taking shape: part monkey, part raccoon, part rat—with sharp claws and rows of razor teeth like a shark. When the drawing was done, the Iwo began to croak and chirp. Wilson looked down at it and felt a familiar squeezing in his chest.

"This is a picture of the spirit beast that is now wrestling with your life," Colonel Saba said. "The Iwo says it has wrestled with the lives of people in your family in the spirit world for generations. He says you have been wrestling all alone since you were a child. It is a creature that went to live inside one of your ancestors many years ago in the country beyond the Hruke Forest, which is his way of saying Africa. Have your ancestors been in Africa?''

"I don't know," Wilson said.

"Do you recognize this thing?" Colonel Saba said, poking a bony finger at the picture in the dirt.

"Yes," Wilson said, and he hardly heard his own voice.

"The spirit beast," Colonel Saba said, "enters through a tear in your spirit like a wound, often caused by a tragedy in childhood. Did you undergo such a tragedy?"

"Yes," Wilson said, and his voice was less than a whisper.

The Iwo put his hand on Wilson's arm. His palm felt like the bark of a tree. Wilson turned and looked into his eyes. They were ancient and black, but lit by flashes of color in the depths as if by lightning far off. The little man sighed and pointed to Wilson's nose. He reached into his pouch and pulled out a small tube of lustrous black wood and two small green turdlike pellets.

"Yonowpe," Colonel Saba said, sounding impressed. "A real honor. He wants to give it to you. Yonowpe is a very powerful spirit medicine and very rare. It will help you wrestle against the spirit beast."

Wilson squinted out at the glare of African sunlight. The guard stirred in his sleep. The yellow dog got up and trotted off. Wilson felt a curious malaise running across his body like the flu that was the unease of condemned men everywhere.

He turned back to the Iwo. "What's the goddamned use?" he said. "Today or tomorrow or the next day or the next, I'll be dead. Skinned alive, I'm told. Let's look on the bright side—when I'm dead, the spirit beast will be dead with me."

The Iwo cleared his throat and spit a mouthful of dry greenish phlegm between the bars.

"The Iwo says the opera isn't over until the fat lady sings,"

Colonel Saba said. "The Iwo says in the fight between yourself and life, back life."

Wilson let the Iwo push him back into the dirt. The little man fixed one of the green pellets to one end of the tube and tamped down. He put the tube to his lips and put the other end in Wilson's nostril. Wilson began to have immediate misgivings.

"Hold on a minute," Wilson said, but it was too late. The Iwo filled his lungs and blew. The green turd hit Wilson's nostril with the force of a small explosion. He lurched back, a bitter taste in his mouth. The bony ledge behind his ears seemed to expand. Then he sneezed twice.

He opened his eyes after the second sneeze and found himself at the bottom of Lake Tsuwanga, where the water wasn't water at all, but a gelatin-thick ooze of ice and something else. He waited for a moment there in the ooze and cold, the bones of the Great Carew lying close at hand, until he saw them coming: Strange phosphorous fish compressed to ultimate hardness by the pressure of the water, bringing their own light with them through the darkness like a secret.

6

*W*ILSON MOVED SLOWLY THROUGH *the crowds along the sidewalk up Commerce Avenue. The steady thump of construction came from nearby. He felt the thud of the jackhammers along the cement pavement. The sky above the silver needle of the Rubicon Building showed a peerless blue, free of clouds. A good day in early spring.*

Minutes passed before he noticed the massive old cars waiting at the light of Commerce and Rubicon, then he realized that the street was full of these anachronistic vehicles. They were the finned glossy monsters of another era, huge Cadillacs and De Sotos, Ramblers and Nash wagons and Studebakers, made of chrome and steel and painted in light pastels and upholstered in plaid vinyl, chugging along the clean blacktop at the curb. A moment later, he noticed the pedestrians: businessmen sporting snap-brim hats and skinny ties and shiny three-button suits; secretaries with bright red lipstick and beehive hairdos, or bouffants or flips, wearing stiletto heels and poufy dresses and wrist-length white gloves and carrying big shiny purses of patent leather.

Wilson began to feel a sinking sensation of déjà vu. He was sure he had been here before, this afternoon, this minute, this very second. He looked up and saw the bare frame of the Maas Tower like a skeleton hanging above, and the red crane and the girder swaying out on its cables twenty stories up. Then, he saw one of the cables go loose, and there was a sick snapping sound that no one else seemed to hear, echoing down the glass and steel canyonway.

The woman in the leopard-print coat and the child walked along hand in hand just ahead, the shadow of the falling girder upon them like a long black finger. The child looked up from the tin ray gun in his hand and saw the girder coming down with all the force of destiny. A terrible wonder bloomed in his small face. He wore clumsy black shoes, an oversize tweed coat, and a silly-looking hat with flaps folded over his ears. There wasn't enough time, a few bare seconds that would freeze the child for the rest of his life, pin his wings like a pink and yellow moth stuck to a card.

Wilson lunged forward and caught the woman with his shoulder square in the back. She went sprawling out of the way, and he hit the pavement in the deadly shadow of the beam and twisted up to see the thing just twenty feet above, screaming down, speed increasing geometrically with each falling inch, gravity giving it the weight of a mountain. Then, all at once, the street was quiet. The beam made no sound; the traffic was stilled.

"Look what you've done! You've made me tear my new stockings!" It was his mother's voice.

Wilson stood up, his joints creaking. He suddenly remembered the time he had taken a razor blade from his father's medicine cabinet at age three and for no reason at all carefully slashed all the lampshades in the house. The look on his mother's face now was the look that had been there when she caught him having a go at the last yellow shade in the living room.

"*Come here, Wilson,*" *his mother said.* "*You're making a spectacle of yourself!*"

"*Mom . . .*" *Wilson's voice ascended to a juvenile whine. He pointed at the beam hovering in the air like a giant black bird no more than fifteen feet above his head.*

"*I know all about that,*" *she said, not bothering to look up.* "*You get out from under there. That's not for you.*"

Wilson approached sheepishly. His mother kissed him on the cheek. Then she frowned.

"*Stand up straight,*" *she said.*

Wilson stood up straight, and she removed her wrist-length white glove and licked her thumb and wiped a smudge from Wilson's cheek. Then she took a wet-nap towelette from a small pack in her purse. She tore it open and gave his face a thorough scrubbing. Wilson wrinkled up his nose at the sharp medicinal smell and tried to pull away. He had always hated those things.

"*Don't give me that stuff, mister; you're a mess,*" *his mother said, and Wilson saw that his clothes were little more than torn and bloody rags and that he was covered with dried blood and muck from the slave cage. Then he looked down at his mother and for the first time realized how beautiful and young she had been on the day she died. Her eyes were startlingly blue, her hair black and sheeny as the wing of a crow. In her pillbox hat and leopard-print coat she bore more than a passing resemblance to Jacqueline Kennedy in the days of Camelot. Perhaps all the women of that era resembled Jacqueline Kennedy in some way.*

"*How old are you, Mom?*" *he said suddenly.* "*Twenty-seven, twenty-eight?*"

His mother frowned. "*What kind of question is that for a little boy to ask?*" *she said.*

"*I'm not a little boy anymore,*" *Wilson said.* "*I'll be thirty-four this year.*"

His mother took him by the shoulders again and smiled. "*Yes, I'm glad of that,*" *she said.* "*At least you've grown up good and strong. But*"—*she frowned again*—"*you've made some bad choices, Wilson. You look sad around the eyes. You should go and play outside more often, get some fresh air. I used to tell your father you read too much. Nose always stuck in a book, even when you were two.* Mike Mulligan and His Steam Shovel, *remember that one?"*

"Yes," Wilson said. "And I remember those monkey books—Curious George, the man in the yellow hat. I wanted to be like the man in the yellow hat."

"He seemed nice, certainly very patient," Wilson's mother said. "Always taking care of that troublesome monkey." Then she paused and looked away.

"Mom . . ." Wilson said.

"Yes?"

"I couldn't save you. I was only ten years old. I looked up and saw it coming down, and I froze. I didn't know what to say, didn't know how to tell you to run. Then wham! . . . I'm sorry." Tears ran down Wilson's cheeks.

His mother reached into her patent leather purse, took out a Kleenex, and put it to his nose. "Blow," she said.

Wilson blew.

"There was nothing you could have done, Wilson sweet," she said in a soft, motherly tone, and she put a hand against his wet cheek. "That beam was always falling and always going to fall, and I was always walking under it. My only regret is that you had to be at my side. It seems cruel for a child to witness such things. But think about Nietzsche and his gateway, maybe that will help: two roads leading to infinity in opposite directions, meeting at the gateway of the present moment. What did the man say about that? 'Has not everything that can run already run down this road? Must not everything that happens have already happened?' Of course he is describing a circular universe. If you don't believe in a circular universe, I suppose you have to believe in God. Wilson, I think you believe in God. That's charming, and it suits you."

Wilson was stunned. "You read Nietzsche, Mom?" he said.

His mother put a gloved hand to her red lips and laughed a delicate laugh. "There's a lot of things you don't know about your old mother," she said.

"I guess so," Wilson said.

"This has been nice, but it's time for you to go," she said, impatient now. Then she hugged him and blinked a tear from her eye, and she stepped around and took her place in the shadow of the beam.

"Where am I going?" Wilson said.

"Your father wants to see you for a minute," she said.

"Wait, Mom!" Wilson couldn't keep a tremor from his voice. "Don't you have any advice for me? A nugget of wisdom? Anything?"

"The Nietzsche wasn't enough?"

Wilson shrugged.

"Then my advice is very simple," his mother said. "Stop your mooning around. Live."

In the next second the world rocked into motion, and the sidewalk was full of pedestrians and the big cars rumbled along at the curb and a terrible rushing sound filled the air and the beam hit home with a monstrous roar, shattering the sidewalk and smashing Wilson's mother to a bloody stain. Wilson felt himself borne aloft, then he felt the jerk and shuttle of a train and heard the wheels on the track and saw that he was sitting in a Pullman car beside a man in a gray homburg and a nicely tailored suit of English tweed. The man wore a yellow silk handkerchief in his pocket and yellow socks and tan and white wing tips. An unlit pipe was cradled in his left hand, a copy of the Racing News *lay neatly folded on his lap atop a hardback copy of* The Black Rose *by Thomas B. Costain. He stared out the train window lost in thought, as a red sun set over the Potswahnamee Lagoon and the dark and icy river lay curled like a snake just a few miles ahead.*

"You're lucky there was a seat," the man said. "The express is always crowded," and he turned toward Wilson and smiled in a sad way that was familiar.

"Is that you, Dad?" Wilson said.

His father nodded. "I suppose your mother sent you."

Wilson shrugged. "I'm not sure," he said. "It might be the yonowpe."

"You know what I was thinking?" his father said. "Just now I was thinking that the sunset out there was about the most beautiful thing I've ever seen. Look at the birds rising off the lagoon into the red light. On their

way south, I guess." He put his pipe between his teeth and was silent for a while.

Wilson heard the rustle and cough of other passengers on the train, the dull murmur of conversation. He glanced down at his father's watch, a handsome, gold self-winding Elgin with a red arrow on the second hand. It was a quarter after five.

"Is this the four forty-five express, Dad?" Wilson said.

"You know, I was going to catch the five-thirty, but I got to the station early and just made the four forty-five. Lucky, huh?"

"Dad, we've got to stop this train," Wilson said as calm as he could make it. "It's going to jump the tracks."

"Lower your voice," his father said. "People will hear you."

Wilson stood up and reached for the red emergency handle fixed to the window arch, but before he could pull it down, his father yanked him back into the seat by the belt loops.

"I know all about this train, son," his father said in a low voice. "There's nothing we can do. You know that. I just wanted to sit quietly with you a moment before we go off the tracks. Mind if I put my arm around you?"

Wilson said he didn't mind, and his father put an arm around his shoulder, and the two of them sat quietly and stared out at the beautiful red sunset.

"After I get back from this business trip," Wilson's father said at last, "I should have a little cash on hand. And I promise I'm going to settle down with your mother and you and I won't go away again. I haven't been very good to her when you get right down to it. She is such a beautiful woman, and she could have had anyone, but—God knows why—she married me. Gambling is no life for a family man, remember that, son. Always on the road, always desperate to beat the odds. But I've got a nice piece of change riding on a couple of ponies running at the Fairgrounds down in New Orleans. It's a sure thing, a boat race. After that I'm coming home for good, and you know what I'm going to do then?"

"No," Wilson said.

"I'm going back to law school. I'm going to get my degree and open up a *practice. Boy, will that please your mother! She always thought I'd make such a good lawyer, and you know, I think she's right. Don't tell her, though. It'll be our little secret till I get back, O.K.?''*

"O.K., Dad," Wilson said.

A moment later, they came across the open trellis of the Trohog Bridge, and there was the long shriek of brake like a howl, and a shudder went through the train. Steel-cornered suitcases began to topple out of the racks over the seats.

"This is us," Wilson's father said, and he leaned forward and kissed Wilson on the forehead. Then he sprang up, and as the car tilted out over the river, he grabbed on to the baggage rack and swung the hard heels of his two-tone wing tips against the window. The glass shattered out in a half dozen jagged shards.

"I'm not one for advice, like your mother," Wilson's father said. "I always figured a man's going to do what he's got to do if he's a good man. You've grown up into a good man, Wilson. Find what it is that you've got to do and do it."

"O.K., Dad," Wilson said.

"Now jump," his father said.

Wilson looked down at the river far below, touched with red in the last light of the sun. The train began to skitter off the tracks, and there was the sound of metal tearing and a terrible screaming.

"I don't think I can do this," Wilson said, scared.

"You've got to," his father said. "Go on. Jump."

Wilson held his breath, and in the next second he was falling toward the black water.

7

"FOR GOD'S SAKE, MR. Wilson, give me your hand!"
Wilson heard the voice as he went under for the second time. He fought for the surface and caught a glimpse of green jungle before he

was dragged down again, but this water was brown and warm as blood and far removed from the cold black stillness of the Potswahnamee.

He reached up and felt a strong grip on his wrist, felt himself pulled into the sunlight, where he lay gasping like a fish against a surface of rough wood. When he could breathe, he sat up and rubbed the water out of his eyes. He was aboard a flat-bottomed Bupu dugout on its way with the current down a fast-moving river hemmed in on both sides by jungle.

"If you attempt to jump again, Mr. Wilson, we will bind your feet and your hands for the rest of the journey, and that will not be pleasant as we have a long way yet to go."

It was Tulj seated in the stern, paddle raised, dripping, over the side.

"I will make a note for the *Bupandan Journal of Medicine*," said a second voice. "Half a dosage of yonowpe for a white man is quite sufficient to kill the spirit beast."

Wilson twisted around to see Colonel Saba grinning from the prow. He tried to speak but came out with a half-strangled cough. For a few minutes, he stared mute at the green riot along the banks. He watched the dark places between the trees for the pale beams of the Iwos and saw only shadows. Unknown animals moved in the green dusk there like animals in a dream.

"This isn't the Mwtutsi," Wilson said when his head cleared. He looked up, and at that moment a patch of sunlight touched his brow.

"I think our friend is back with us." Colonel Saba flashed a grin over his shoulder.

"You are right, Mr. Wilson," Tulj said. "This is not the Mwtutsi, this is the Hilenga."

"What happened?" Wilson said. "How did we get here?"

"You remember nothing?" Tulj asked. A green and red dragonfly danced around his head like a halo.

"Last I remember, those sons of bitches were supposed to skin me alive," Wilson said.

"Yes, you are a lucky man," Tulj said.

"Where is the Iwo?" Wilson said.

Tulj waved his paddle at the jungle. "Who knows?" he said. "Back with his own people. Might as well ask where the birds go when they fly into the air."

"And are you a new man?" Colonel Saba said to Wilson. "Did the spirit medicine work?"

"I'm not sure," Wilson said. He still felt a little thick. He watched Saba dip the paddle into the water and draw it out again. "Actually I don't remember a thing. We escaped from M'Gongo epo?"

"Yes," Saba said, splashing him with water. "This river is real; it is not a yonopwe-inspired fantasy."

"How did it happen?" Wilson said.

"In the usual manner," Tulj said. "A little money, a carton or two of cigarettes. A single human life isn't worth much here, I'm afraid."

"But you almost ruined the whole thing, Mr. Wilson," Saba said. "You wouldn't shut up. Last night we had to tie a rag in your mouth to keep you quiet. You were ranting. Out of your head. Who is Curious George?"

"A friend," Wilson said, then he turned to Tulj. "How did you find us?"

"I was waiting for news in Ulundi, as we had arranged," Tulj said. "Then an Iwo brought word of trouble. I started upriver two days ago. That was a stupid thing you did back there, Mr. Wilson. You blew your cover. We cannot use you as an agent after this."

"Couldn't wait any longer," Wilson said quietly. "Not a single second."

"Did you think they wouldn't kill you for what you did?"

"I don't know," Wilson said. "I didn't think at all. I just went out and set them free, every Iwo I could find—" He couldn't go on.

Tulj nodded as if he understood.

An hour or two passed before Wilson felt lucid enough to help with the paddling. He took the position in the prow, and the tired colonel went to sleep. The labor felt good, the muscles in his arms and shoulders working, the sun dappling his back through the trees. But it wasn't until twilight turned the river a deep shade of lavender that Wilson was struck by the singularity of the situation. He stopped paddling and turned around. A dustlike haze sifted through the canopy of leaves. Colonel Saba dozed, mouth open, hand dangling in the water. A soft snoring sound issued from between his lips. Wilson could barely make out Tulj's face in the jungle shadows.

"The two of you . . ." Wilson said.

"Yes," Tulj said, and he smiled.

"He's an Anda, you're a Bupu," Wilson said.

"Yes," Tulj said.

"How come you're not at each other's throat?"

Tulj put aside his paddle and thought for a moment. "Last night, when I came to help you escape, I found an Anda officer and an Iwo in the dirt at your side. And I said to them, 'Are we not all brothers here?' and I took their hands and led them away. Colonel Saba, he is weary of the war and all the killing, as I am weary. He has decided to resign from the APF, and he is joining a new party which I am starting with the support of certain friends of mine. I will call my new party the BUP. The Bupandan Unification party. And one day, when the slave trade is suppressed, we will put an end to this madness. Bupu and Anda will rebuild Bupanda as it was in the great days of Sequhue, when the countryside bloomed with flowers and the streets of Rigala were full of music and singing and there were beautiful women in every doorway."

"Sounds lovely," Wilson said.

When it was almost too dark to see, they paddled over to the bank and hid the dugout among the reeds. As a precaution Tulj did not light a fire. They ate a dark meal of cold pressed meat out of cans in the rustling silence of the jungle; then they made their bed in the reeds. Wilson could not see any stars, just the unfeatured blackness of the leafy canopy, and he stared into this blackness and lay awake and listened to the sound of Colonel Saba snoring and the river hushing along from somewhere to somewhere, and he heard Tulj tossing and scratching himself on the other side of the clump of reeds.

"Tulj, are you awake?" Wilson said.

The man grunted.

"Where the hell are we going?"

"Down the Hilenga," he said. "Go to sleep."

"Where does the Hilenga go?"

There was an empty second or two, and it seemed Tulj would not answer. "To the sea," he said at last. "Sooner or later all rivers go to the sea."

"Tulj . . ." Wilson said.

"We are going to meet friends of mine at a certain spot in the delta in three days' time. They want to talk to us, and they very much want to talk to you. They want to know everything you have learned about the evil men who deal in slaves. Will you tell them?"

"Sure," Wilson said. "Who are your friends? Tell me now so I can know what to expect."

"No. It is not wise for you to have any more information at this point," Tulj said. "What if we are captured? Be patient. Wait and see."

8

THEY PADDLED ALONG FOR three days without setting foot on dry land. The river became the vast swamp of the Hilenga Delta. The sun of noon barely penetrated the dense leafy cover overhead. Mosquitoes hung thick in the thick air; Wilson covered every inch of exposed flesh with a citrus-smelling insect repellent.

Orange monkeys hung lazily from half-submerged trees. Aquatic snakes and muskrats the size of collies swarmed among the monstrous roots of the baobabs. Flocks of azure macaws clouded the uncertain distance.

Once Wilson let his hand fall into the green water and pulled it back covered with leeches. He pried the valuable little creatures off his flesh and repatriated them carefully in the muddy water.

At dawn on the fourth day, Tulj led them to a small island completely obscured by the tangled roots of mangrove trees. In a clearing at the center a lean-to covered with canvas tarp and fronted with mosquito netting sheltered crates of canned food and plastic barrels of freshwater. Wilson washed his face and his neck in the water, put on another layer of insect repellent, and broke open an aluminum package labeled "Yorkshire Pudding," with the expiration date of 10/30/2037. Inside, he found a gelatinous substance covered with viscous liquid, a yellow and brown mess that was surprisingly edible despite its disgusting appearance.

When Wilson finished eating, Tulj took him to the west side of the island and pointed to a break in the trees. "This is a good place from which to watch," he said. "My friends will arrive sometime late today, possible tomorrow."

"What am I watching for exactly?" Wilson said.

Tulj gave a short laugh. "You will know when you see them," he said, then he went off to take a short nap behind the mosquito netting of the lean-to.

Wilson watched the river for the next few hours.

The green light of the jungle didn't seem to change. He had no idea what time it was. His old illuminated digital watch had stopped working way back during the rainy season at Quatre Sables. Just below, the river broke out of the clotted channels into a wider stream. Wilson thought he detected a breath of fresh air on his face, a slight briny tang that made him think of sea. He turned away for a half second at a snapping sound in the trees and, when he turned back, saw that the channel had undergone a remarkable transformation. The sun, now risen directly overhead, shone down in thick, smoky columns of light through breaks in the canopy of leaves. The effect was spiritual, like light shining through stained glass windows. White birds lifted off the water and flew in an upward arc through the smoky light. A few minutes later Wilson saw a vague something on the river in the distance.

Another hour passed before he could make out the approaching craft. It seemed to be coming along very slowly, but distances are deceptive in Africa. The craft grew no larger in perspective for a long while, then Wilson heard the steady burp and splutter of an old inboard, and it was right there, coming through the muck of the channel around the island, and he could hardly believe what he saw: In an odd, wide-bodied turquoise boat stood three naval officers wearing spotless white uniforms straight out of *Madame Butterfly*. They were stiff as statues; the humid breeze did not ruffle their short hair. Behind them, sitting on two rows of padded benches, a half dozen marines in dress tunics of blue and red. From the stern, the white ensign of the British Royal Navy flapped in the breeze.

Wilson watched until this strange vessel came up past his lookout. The flat keel of the thing seemed to be made of glass. Beneath the feet of the officers, monstrous carp swam along, their scales ancient as granite flashing in the green river. In the next minute the boat disappeared into the reed-choked channel.

Tulj and Colonel Saba squatted in the clearing in front of the lean-to, throwing dice across a stained bit of canvas.

"A bad habit I picked up in the army," Tulj said, glancing up as Wilson came out of the trees. "But common to all soldiers, everywhere. Think of the Roman legionaries dicing for Christ's clothes—" Then he saw the look on Wilson's face and stood up. "Well?"

"This is going to sound ridiculous," Wilson said, catching his breath. "On the river, a turquoise boat with a glass bottom full of naval officers in white dress uniforms."

Tulj nodded gravely. "They are a little early," he said.

9

FROM THE DECK OF the big motor launch, Wilson looked back to the place where the brown waters of the Hilenga met the ocean's choppy blue. The last African mud stained the surface red more than three miles out, then fell off as sediment across the continental shelf. The afternoon sky was touched at the horizon with pale, scraggly clouds. Seabirds wheeled overhead. Africa lay in the wake, incomprehensible, vast.

Only now did Wilson allow himself to think of what he was leaving behind. He thought of Cricket, and he thought of the dark interior of the jungle, those sunless glades where no white man would set foot, and he thought of the Iwos living hidden away from the world with their strange language and arcane knowledge—then he set his heart against the past and took a deep breath of salty ocean air and turned to face the great ship riding the waves just ahead.

She was HMS *Gadfly,* a new compact cruiser of the Somerset class. Smaller than a traditional destroyer but larger than a minesweeper, she carried two turrets of 118 mm marine guns, a full complement of Stinger surface-to-air missiles, and a large platform at the stern to which were fixed three Sea Harrier jump jets, their wings folded like sleeping birds. A radar dish turned steadily from the top of the superstructure, and Wilson could almost see invisible signals darting through the atmosphere a million times faster than the Great Carew's carrier pigeons. The white ensign and the captain's pennant—a yellow sea horse on a blue ground—flew at half-mast from the topgallants.

Wilson turned to the nearest officer, a blunt-faced sublieutenant whose nametag identified him as Bunsen.

"Something happen?" Wilson said, pointing to the flags.

"Sir?" the sublieutenant said.

"Half-mast," Wilson said.

"I'm not at liberty to say, sir," he said stiffly.

"Oh, what the hell, Bunsen. He's one of us."

It was another lieutenant whose tag read "Navigating Lieutenant Peavy." This one had straw-colored hair and startling blue eyes like Peter O'Toole in *Lawrence of Arabia*. He came forward, shook hands, and offered Wilson a cigarette.

"No, thanks," Wilson said, then he changed his mind. They were Westminster Navy Cuts, in the gold tin. Lieutenant Peavy held out an old flint and fluid lighter, and Wilson lit up. The cigarette was strong, but with the characteristic flavor of Turkish tobacco. Wilson was becoming a smoker. He blew smoke into the sky over his shoulder. It drifted off over Africa.

"You see, it's our captain," Peavy said, and he lit his own cigarette and unbuttoned the top button of his dress collar. "The poor man died last week, right in the middle of the mission."

"What happened?" Wilson said.

"The same thing that's been happening to Englishmen for centuries in this miserable part of the world," Peavy said. "Some kind of fever. He went ashore at Zanda and caught something. No one knew he was that sick. One morning he didn't show up for breakfast and we went into his cabin and he was dead."

"I'm sorry to hear that," Wilson said.

Peavy shrugged. "Staff Commander Worthington's our acting captain now. He's a good man. You'll be chatting with him soon."

Lieutenant Peavy touched hand to cap and turned aft but Wilson called after him. "I've got to ask you something," Wilson said.

The officer turned back.

Wilson gestured to the turquoise glass-bottomed boat suspended like a dinghy from the hawsers at the stern. "The blue boat, the white uniforms. Do you people usually invade Africa like that?"

Lieutenant Peavy gave a tight smile. "We're not exactly invading," he said. "Sort of reconnaissance. It's acting captain's orders. We're more or less covert here, poking around without authority from the local government. Of course there is no local government, just a parcel of bickering tribes, but if we're captured wearing our uniforms, it will be that much harder to shoot us for spies. As for the boat, it's the Hilenga, you see. We can't go up that damned river with anything of ours—too shallow for the launch and too full of nasty stuff for the rubber boats. We found about a dozen of these glass-bottomed numbers abandoned in a warehouse in Port Luanga last year. Brought over from Disneyland in America in the 1960s for some sort of aquatic safariland scheme, apparently the idea of a millionaire from Texas. Problem is, the Hilenga's too muddy to make out much more than the occasional carp, so the millionaire went bankrupt and flew back to Texas and left his boats behind. We had our engineer fix up a couple of them for our own purposes. Quite stunning little tubs really. Lovely color.''

"Definitely unexpected," Wilson said.

"That's exactly the idea," Lieutenant Peavy said. "If we're taken by the BPF or the APF or any of those chaps we can say, 'Here we are on holiday in our fancy dress uniforms in a blue boat with a glass bottom,' and hope they put us down as eccentric Englishmen and let it go at that. Pretty good plan, don't you think?''

It was not a question that expected a reply. The lieutenant withdrew to the stern, and Wilson went below to check on Tulj and Colonel Saba, resting on cots in the hold. They were ashen-faced and green around the edges, and the tight compartment smelled strongly of bile.

"I am an officer of infantry," Colonel Saba said in a weak voice. "I am not much of a sailor."

Tulj moaned and rolled his eyes. "I agree with Saba," he said. "The navy is not for me."

Wilson went to the first aid station and found the Dramamine. He waved the green bottle of seasickness pills in their direction. "Try a couple of these," Wilson said.

"I prefer organic remedies," Colonel Saba said. "Western medicine is no good for the spirit."

"I became a vegetarian last year," Tulj said. "Do these pills contain any animal fat?"

"Let me put it this way," Wilson said. "This stuff does nothing for your soul. Then again, yonowpe does nothing for your stomach. . . ."

10

BY THE TIME THEY came aboard the cruiser, the Africans were feeling better. But there was no boatswain's whistle, no official greeting. The three of them were hustled past a few curious sailors, through a hatchway and down a metal ladder into a windowless briefing room deep in the superstructure. On one wall was a large map of Africa stuck with pins; on another a recent photograph of the queen looking like someone's grandmother, which in fact she was. Down the center, a long dun-colored table, coffee ring stains marring its surface.

Tulj slumped at the table and put his head down. Wilson studied the map of Africa and the portrait of Elizabeth and paced the room. There wasn't much else to see. The ship's nuclear engines hummed beneath them. Colonel Saba seemed nervous. He sat down, then got up and sat down again. He lit a cigarette and put it out.

"I don't like this at all," he said. "Why are they taking so long?"

Tulj lifted his head. His eyes looked red and tired. "Don't worry, Saba," he said. "These people are working for the unification of Bupanda, as are we."

"Why is that?" Saba said, and his voice sounded strained. "Did you ever ask yourself that, Ra'au? What do they want?"

"They want what they wanted a hundred years ago," Tulj said wearily. "They want a ready market for their manufactured goods. They want our raw materials, tin, diamonds, that sort of thing. And in exchange they want us to stop killing ourselves so we can work happily in their factories for cut-rate wages. Didn't they make you read Karl Marx in the APF?''

"You're thinking of the MPF," Saba said, shaking his finger. "The Anda Popular Front was never Marxist. We were social democrats."

"I don't care what you were," Tulj said. "And I don't care what the British want this time, not really. Call them neo-imperialists, postcolonialists, whatever you like. As long as they can help stop slavery and end the slaughter."

A few minutes later Lieutenant Peavy came in accompanied by a smartly dressed officer with the gold caduceus in his collar.

"This is Acting Staff Commander Tombs, our medical officer," Peavy said. "You will be deloused, and he will examine you. Then you will each be debriefed by Acting Captain Worthington."

Peavy left, and Tombs went to work. "Don't want any nasty tropical diseases brought aboard," Tombs explained, and the three of them were sprayed and showered and poked and prodded and issued new underwear and starched cotton jumpsuits.

As a mark of military deference, they came for Colonel Saba first.

"I do not like this," he said as he was led out the hatch by Lieutenant Peavy. "What if they ask me about the Bandali stadium?"

"Go on." Tulj waved airily. "Just answer their questions politely. These are the British. Afterward, I assure you, there will be tea."

Saba went off, placated.

"He still hears the screams of the women and children at night in his dreams," Tulj said when Saba was gone. "It is time we all forget the screaming in our head and attempt to start over."

"For that I recommend yonowpe," Wilson said.

Tulj grinned.

An hour later, when Lieutenant Peavy returned for Tulj, the African came around the table and took Wilson's hand in both of his own. He started to speak, then his eyes brimmed over with tears, and he enveloped Wilson in a big African bear hug.

"Thanks for saving my skin back there," Wilson said.

"Where will you go after you have spoken to the British?" Tulj said.

"I don't know," Wilson said. It was the first time he'd thought about what he would do with the rest of his life. The idea seemed strange. "I guess I'll go home. . . . Here, let me give you my address. Write and tell me how the war is going."

Wilson took a mechanical pencil and a matchbook cover from Lieutenant Peavy and wrote down the address of his old apartment overlooking the Harvey Channel, now inhabited—for all he knew— by a witch.

"My friend," Tulj said, folding the matchbook cover into the pocket of his starchy overalls, "God has given me the chance to repay you for my life and for my brother's life, and I am grateful. I may not see you again in this world. But I hold out the firm hope that one day I may buy you a fine meal—kif, na-kif, kif-tu, the works—and many bottles of tejiyaa in a Bupanda free from war and suffering."

"I'll look forward to that," Wilson said.

When Tulj was gone, Wilson sat alone in the briefing room staring up at the map of Africa stuck with pins. Then, without thinking, he removed the pins and rearranged them in the shape of a great question mark that spread from the west through the Congo, across the Hilenga Delta, over river and lake and morass and mountain range and savanna and desert—as if the continent itself held the solution to his future.

11

THE CAPTAIN'S STATEROOM WAS large and carpeted, with three brass portholes, an imposing desk of burnished teak, and built-in mesh-fronted bookshelves full of weighty-looking volumes. Age-darkened paintings of naval scenes were bolted to the bulkhead. Wilson saw Nelson dying in Hardy's arms at Trafalgar, the Battle of Jutland, Sir Richard Grenville's *Revenge* fighting a hundred Spanish ships single-handedly off the coast of São Miguel in the Azores.

The acting captain, a gangly young man just a year or two older than Wilson himself, seemed uncomfortable with the position of authority into which fate and virus had pushed him. He was all knots and bones, his uniform didn't fit well, and his hair stuck up like the feathers of a bird. The effect would have been comical except for his eyes, which were large and penetrating and full of a fierce intelligence.

"Mr. Wilson? Worthington here, acting captain, HMS *Gadfly*, Blockade Squadron." He stepped out from behind the desk and shook Wilson's hand.

"The name is Lander, sir. Wilson Lander."

"Ah?" The acting captain seemed momentarily confused. "Lander . . . that name has a very familiar ring. Where can I have heard it before?"

"You're the second person to ask recently," Wilson said. "I don't know. It's fairly unusual."

"Ah, yes?" the acting captain said absently.

"This may sound like an unmilitary request, Captain," Wilson said, "but I've got to do a lot of talking about some pretty difficult stuff. A stiff drink would help."

"Of course. We'll conduct this interview like gentlemen."

The acting captain produced a bottle of scotch, a siphon, and glasses from the desk and mixed two scotch and sodas. Wilson took the drink and sat back in a red leather easy chair tacked with brass studs and began to talk. He talked for two hours straight. He told the acting captain everything he could remember: about the *Compound Interest* and Cricket, about Quatre Sables and the slave trade, about the Bupus and the Andas and the Iwos and the slave station at M'Gongo epo.

Acting Captain Worthington listened in grave silence. He mixed another round of drinks, and when Wilson finished talking, he offered a cigarette out of an engraved silver case, and the two of them sat smoking in contemplative silence. Beyond the portholes the light over Africa went from green to lavender. A storm was coming on. The *Gadfly* shifted nervously beneath them in the waves like a racehorse at the starting gate.

"Tell me once more about the . . . incident at M'Gongo epo," the acting captain said at last. "Try to remember every detail." Wilson gulped the rest of his drink and described again the horrors of that place. The acting captain took out a yellow pad and took a few notes; then he stubbed out his cigarette in an ashtray shaped like a hardtack biscuit, and he walked around the teakwood desk and began pacing back and forth as an angry lavender light filled the stateroom. Beyond the portholes whitecaps were stirring in anticipation of the storm to come.

"This is something of a breach of security, I suppose," he said at last, then he stopped pacing and turned toward Wilson. "Naturally you must hold any information in the strictest confidence."

"O.K.," Wilson said.

"Are you familiar with the activities of the Blockade Squadron?"

"No," Wilson said.

The acting captain took a deep breath. "The original Blockade Squadron was a fleet of British warships in the last century whose job it was to put an end to the slave trade. The squadron stopped suspicious-looking vessels coming out of Africa and searched them for slaves. If slaves were found, they were confiscated and set free in Sierra Leone. The crews were taken into custody and hanged; the slave ships, scuttled. In 1840 thousands of slaves were exported illegally from West Africa to the Americas. By 1860, through the diligent efforts of the Blockade Squadron, this number had been reduced to a mere trickle. By century's end the slave trade had been completely suppressed—we had hoped for all time. You see, the squadron was never officially decommissioned. This is a technicality, but it is important, one of the reasons why we are here now, off the Bupandan coast. The commissioning orders, signed by Queen Victoria herself, were never rescinded and still exist in the vaults of the Admiralty in London. They specify that British warships must stand ready to interfere with any renewed slaving activity and that these warships may be sent out at any time without a direct act of Parliament. In any case, a few years ago British intelligence began hearing strange reports from our agents in Bupanda—men like your friend Tulj Ra'au—"

"Wait a minute," Wilson said. "Tulj is a spy?"

"Spy is an ugly word," the acting captain said. "Mr. Ra'au is not a traitor to his country, if that's what you mean. He passes information through us to MI5 in London. I think you are familiar with his motivations. He wishes to stop the war in Bupanda. You may agree that the best way to stop the war is to stop the slave trade."

"I guess so," Wilson said.

The acting captain opened his mouth to speak. He stopped himself and gazed for a moment out the porthole where the sky had deepened from lavender to lush purple. He turned from this mesmerizing color and came back over to the desk and lit another Navy Cut. When he switched on the lights, a revealing glare filled the stateroom, and Wilson was surprised to see anger and frustration in the man's eyes.

"Modern political reality is a great disappointment to us," the acting captain said. "Regardless of our original commission, the Blockade Squadron has no standing mandate for action. The current interpretation of 'interfere' is rather bloodless, I'm afraid. We just sort of hang about, observing. We can't really do anything. If I so much as fired a pistol without the nod from Whitehall, the Squadron would be recalled immediately, and the officers court-martialed to a man. Believe me, Mr. Lander, I weep when I hear of the atrocities you have witnessed. That sort of thing cheapens the value of human life for everyone, everywhere. But my government regards Bupanda as a sovereign territory. Any sort of military action on Bupandan soil will have to be referred to the United Nations for endless debate in the Security Council. By the time the politicians resolve to act''—he made a hopeless gesture—"the pirates and slavers will have moved on and set up shop elsewhere.''

Acting Captain Worthington swallowed hard. Wilson watched the Adam's apple in his throat move back and forth. In the next moment the man was actually wringing his hands.

"We are practically helpless against this great evil,'' he said, so softly that Wilson barely heard his voice. "I am only the acting captain. Last week I was a lowly staff commander. I don't even have the authority to spit out that porthole. Been at the game for a few years now, but if you ask me, never have been quite suited for the naval life. Studied Shakespeare at Oxford, you know. Didn't want to teach. 'Why not go to sea for a year or two, like your father,' my mum said, 'figure things out?' So I joined the navy, and here I am, right now feeling like a damn helpless fool.''

Wilson was quiet for a minute. He looked up at one-armed, one-eyed Nelson dying on the lantern-lit gundeck of the *Victory*. What would Nelson have done?

"How many ships in the Blockade Squadron?'' Wilson said.

"Two,'' the acting captain said. "The *Gadfly* and the *Hyperion*.''

"How many men between them?''

"Roughly six hundred.''

"Listen to me, sir,'' Wilson said, and he fancied his voice held the quiet strength of his convictions. "Quatre Sables is not sovereign territory. It is not part of Bupanda. Long ago, before there was a Bupanda, the island was given by the Portuguese king to the man who discovered it. That man's descendant is in possession of the place, which he leases as a base for slavery and piracy and other atrocities. Think of Quatre Sables as a rudderless, rotten hulk, full of rats and disease swept by the currents. Would you sink that hulk or let it crash into the nearest beach?''

"Quatre Sables," the acting captain said.

"Yes," Wilson said.

The acting captain began to pace the stateroom again, and when he stopped pacing and turned around, his eyes held the answer.

"Lander," he said lightly. "I believe I know where I've heard that name before. He was the chap who traced the river Niger from its source to the sea, Richard Lander. A bookish, quiet sort from Cornwall who just picked up one day and went off to Africa. He succeeded where dozens of others had failed. Went to Sokoto with Clapperton in 1832. When Clapperton died, he reached the coast on his own. Captain Morris had the man's book somewhere. . . .''

The acting captain went to the shelves and extracted a thick volume with a red leather binding and marbleized flyleaf. Wilson remembered it almost immediately from his childhood, from among the dusty volumes in the library at his great-aunt's house. He took it and opened to the title page: *The Journey of Richard Lander from Kano to the Sea—Along with a Record of Captain Clapperton's Last Expedition to Africa with the Subsequent Adventures of the Author.* The volume felt right in Wilson's hand. He tried to remember something that his great-aunt had told him about an ancestor who had traveled and written a book, but her voice in his head faded out, enveloped by the static of the years. Perhaps Africa had been in his blood all along.

"Would be something if you were related to that chap," Acting Captain Worthington said. "Quite ironic, really—"

There was a flash of white light from the darkness beyond the porthole, and a few seconds later the distant crash of thunder. Thirty-foot waves hit the side of the ship as the storm bloomed out of Africa. But HMS *Gadfly* was sturdy and fast. They weighed anchor and sailed beyond the dirty weather into the open sea.

12

QUATRE SABLES REVEALED ITSELF in morning light as a dark bundle on the horizon. Just before dawn, a faint wind blew from the direction of the island, and Wilson caught the familiar stench of the place, and it was as if a cold hand had grabbed his gut from pubic hair to belly button.

A hundred yards off the port bow, HMS *Hyperion* mirrored the *Gadfly* in dark silhouette. Coded signals flashed back and forth between the two ships; flags snapped in the ocean breeze. The jet engines of the Sea Harriers started with a wheeze, then warmed into a steady scream. Men in camouflage fatigues and combat gear moved purposefully across the deck. Despite the noise and motion, Wilson could hardly keep his eyes open; he had never been a morning person—then, suddenly, he was wide awake and the sea breeze was sharp and fresh in his nostrils, and he was ready for whatever would come.

At 0500 hours, the sky began to brighten in the east. Acting Captain Worthington assembled the crew on the main deck below the superstructure. He wore combat fatigues and camouflage paint on his face but eschewed the heavy armament of his marines and carried only a pistol at his side. He spoke through a small microphone attached to his tunic, and his words were carried electronically to the *Hyperion* riding the waves in the near distance.

"Sailors and marines of the Blockade Squadron," he said, "I will be brief as we have a job ahead of us today. We look around and see a world sliding back into ruin and savagery. Five thousand years of civilization, the intellectuals tell us, are at an end—our beliefs exhausted, our achievements in the past. They tell us we are becoming a footnote, going under with all hands and all engines, sinking into the depths with our God and our laws, our academies of natural and applied sciences, our presidents and kings, our literature and legends, our poets and painters and musicians, our critics and the critics of our critics. Perhaps it is true, perhaps our time has come, and the world is making way for something new, and we may hope something better. That is not for me to say. I am a soldier, that is tomorrow's business, and we are here today. But I will promise you one thing''—he swung around and with a dramatic gesture indicated the white ensign of the Royal Navy flying from the topgallant—''as long as that flag is hoisted every morning to meet the rising wind, chaos will have an enemy!''

He paused to cough into his hand, and a variety of coughs and sniffles echoed from the men below. ''As always, England asks only this of you, that each man do his duty. Good luck.''

The acting captain turned away. But before he crossed the hatch, someone shouted, ''Three cheers for the acting captain!'' and the hurrahs of the men ascended into the brightening sky.

13

AT 0530, THE SEA Harriers lifted off the launch pads and streaked low over the waves toward Quatre Sables. For the next hour they rolled and buzzed above the stronghold of the pirates like angry bees. From the deck of the *Gadfly,* two miles out, the air strikes were silent and beautiful. Plumes of flame shot into the blue; clouds of red and green smoke billowed up like dragons. By 0715 the pirate vessels in the harbor had been sunk beneath half a fathom, the barracoon and wharves were on fire, and a greenish flame burned from the ridge where the fine homes of the Thirty Captains lay in ruins.

The *Gadfly* moved in for a close-range bombardment with its 118 mm guns at 0800, then Wilson went out on the motor launch with the second wave of marines commanded by Lieutenant Peavy. He joked with the men; they seemed in good spirits, eager for a little action after dull months of patrol duty aboard ship. Then, as the launch entered the harbor, Wilson saw something he had hoped he would not see: The *Dread* lay sunk at her mooring near the shipyard. Only the airtight midsection containing the navigational octagon remained afloat, burning quietly, flames reflected in the oily water.

The wharves were a mess of shattered debris. Fires burned everywhere. The bodies of pirates and dockworkers lay bleeding in the rubble, the innocent side by side with the guilty. Wilson joined Lieutenant Peavy's marines as they advanced up the slope. They went at a dogtrot through the shanty city, which had not been touched by the morning's air strikes. He saw the same big-bellied children staring out with hunger-dulled eyes, the same cardboard hovels, the same desiccated corpses lying half buried in garbage in the streets. The stench of this squalid settlement was the stench of a despair that would never go away.

"The poor are always with us," Lieutenant Peavy murmured.

Wilson said nothing.

The gates of the ridge settlement had been blasted off their hinges. Not two of the homes of the Thirty Captains were left standing. Wilson ran down the shell road to Cricket's house, now a smoldering, irregular pile of charred bricks and timber. He clambered over the mess afraid of what he'd find. He found a piece of marble bathtub, smoldering lumps of charred clothing, Cricket's guitar perfectly intact. His old copy of Gibbon's *Decline and Fall of the Roman Empire* lay half burnt beneath a twisted wreck of lawn furniture. It was hopeless. There was no way of telling if Cricket lay beneath the blackened mess. Perhaps it was her tomb.

His knees felt weak. He sat on a bit of foundation and put his head in his hands. Had it been her fault? What could you expect from a girl raised as a pirate? She had been as beautiful and deadly as a shark in the water. And the deadliness had been part of the beauty; it had not been possible to separate the two. The wind blew black smoke over the sun. The wind smelled of jet fuel and burning rubber. The sound of lamentation came from the shanty city below.

"Is this your doing, Lander?"

Wilson turned around and saw Dr. Boursaly stumbling up the pile of rubble. The doctor's medical coat was torn and greasy, his face a dirty smudge. He looked like he had been hiding under a car. In his left hand he held a broken-necked bottle of gin, his lips cut and bleeding from it, the blood dribbling down his chin. Wilson knew the man was a drunk, but he had never seen him drunker.

"Had to do it, Lander," the doctor slurred, and put an accusing finger against Wilson's chest. "Like a good fucking Boy Scout. Brought in the cavalry, you self-righteous bastard!"

Wilson felt like hitting him. An explosion went off below. They held their breath, and a hot wind blew up the slope.

"We had a good thing going here," Dr. Boursaly said when the air cleared of smoke. "Outside the fucking rules of fucking bourgeois society. Where the hell else is a drinking man going to get a job? I told you to do something about the situation, but I didn't mean it; that was just to talk. And you married into the Thirty Captains. You were rich!"

"Slavery," Wilson said. "Remember, Doctor? Piracy and murder. Those things had to be stopped."

"There you go again," the doctor shouted. "Applying your Boy Scout standards to another culture. Boy Scout! Fascist!"

"It's only the fact that I am a Boy Scout that keeps me from punching you in the eye," Wilson said.

The doctor smiled bitterly, took a swig off the broken-necked bottle of gin, and cut his lip again. Blood and gin drooled down the glass. The sight was disgusting. Wilson snatched the bottle away and threw it shattering to the rubble.

Dr. Boursaly gasped. "That was the last bottle of gin on the island," he said in a tragic voice, and for a moment Wilson thought the man would throw himself to his hands and knees to lap up the drops glittering on the shards. Instead he gurgled helplessly, and his eyes rolled up in his head. Wilson stepped out of the way, Dr. Boursaly went facedown in the dirt.

"Need any help up there, Mr. Lander?" It was Lieutenant Peavy with two Royal Marines, just coming over the pile of shattered tiles and masonry that had once been Cricket's patio.

"I've got someone for you," Wilson said. "A doctor. He might be able to help with the wounded."

At Lieutenant Peavy's orders, the marines took Dr. Boursaly by the armpits and hauled him down to the shell road.

"My God," Lieutenant Peavy said, "you say this man's a doctor?"

"Yes," Wilson said. "Sober he's pretty good. Drinks like a maniac, though. Just keep him dry."

Bloody and pale against the crushed shells, Dr. Boursaly looked dead. But when the marines went to lift him onto a stretcher, his head lolled to one side, and his voice issued forth, high-pitched and hollow as a ventriloquist's dummy.

"You think your wife's buried beneath that crap," the doctor said. "Wrong, Boy Scout! Minute she put in, she went straight back to him. She's probably screwing the bastard right now!" Then he laughed and the laugh came out as a bloody bubble that popped on his lips, and he passed out, eyes open, and the marines took him away.

Another explosion from below lit the sky in white flame above the island. Lieutenant Peavy shielded his eyes. The hot wind sucked the oxygen from the air for an excruciating few seconds.

"That's the demolition boys having a go at the oil storage tanks," the lieutenant said. "Looks like they're doing a thorough job."

"Sow the ground with salt," Wilson said, half to himself.

"Not a bad idea from the looks of things," Lieutenant Peavy said. "But what's this about your wife?"

Wilson didn't answer immediately. He frowned down the shell road in the direction of the jungle.

14

WILSON WORKED HIS WAY down the jungled slope into the Portugee's tilled valley. It was hard going, and when he reached the road to the Villa Real, scratched and exhausted, the sun stood at about four in the afternoon. The baroque facade of the villa looked pink as a castle in a fairy tale in this lazy light. Wilson felt a chill as he went up through the empty classical garden, past the long shadows the hedges made on the acre of lawn. When he crossed the bridge over the moat, he glanced down and saw the sheep cowering below, one of them lying dead as two others sniffed stupidly around the bloated carcass.

Wilson's footsteps echoed in the courtyard, scattered with brittle palm fronds. Cricket's Volkswagen Thing was parked next to the big blue Lagonda, beside the dry fountain. The Portugee's glossy vehicle looked seedy, decrepit in this light. It listed to one side on two crumpled tires; rust flecked the chrome of its wire wheels. Wilson went up the stairs and tried the door, which fell open at his touch. The villa was full of the usual oppressive smell of dust, old wax, mildew, and varnish, but there was something different in the air this time, a sharp, sweet odor like burnt perfume.

"Cricket?" Wilson shouted, and the villa echoed with the sound of his voice.

The Goyas and Murillos were gone from the front hall; the salon was empty of furniture. He looked upstairs and down, followed bleached corridors into abandoned rooms. It could easily take a week to find someone in this place, he thought—then he went back downstairs and followed the burnt smell into the library.

The big windows here faced west. Pale afternoon sunlight streamed through the diamond panes of stained glass. The library was lit in a rose and blue gloom like the chapel it had once been. Cricket sat sprawled at the big table, her leg thrown over the arm of the Portugee's easy chair, a silk robe hanging open over her breasts. Besides the robe, she wore a pair of red panties and wet-looking red nail polish on her toes, which were spread apart with cotton balls. On the table, a long-stemmed pipe, still smoking, and the hollowed-out hemisphere of an orange. A jar of opium and a bottle of red nail polish sat open on the collected Byron that Wilson remembered from months before.

Wilson approached the table slowly. Cricket's face wore an over-heated flush, her eyes glassy and red. She was very high on the stuff and didn't seem surprised to see him.

"Hi, Wilson, baby," she said lazily. "Glad to see you've still got your skin."

Wilson came up to the table and stared down at her and put his hands in his pockets. "It's the end, Cricket," he said. "The game is up. A company of British marines will be here soon. Better get some clothes on."

Cricket turned a lazy eye, then she giggled and flexed her toes. "What do you think?" she said. "Jungle Red."

"If you want the truth," Wilson said, "I never liked that color."

"You're a real bastard," Cricket said, then she swung her leg off the chair, and in a split second her mood changed, and she began to sob like a child. She sobbed in great openmouthed gasps till she could not breathe and began to hiccup and gasp for air. Wilson stepped around the table and tried to pull her up. She fell into his arms over the side of the chair and went limp.

"Cut it out," Wilson said.

"No." Cricket sniffed to the floor.

"How long have you been smoking the opium?" he said.

"Days and days, ever since we got back from M'Gongo epo," she said in a quick monotone. "I didn't want to live without you. They were going to skin you alive. I was going to let them. I'm a monster. A freak without a heart. I love you." She started to sob again and Wilson let her go and she slid off the chair and rolled under the library table.

"Get up," Wilson said. "We've really got to get out of here."

"Leave me alone," Cricket said from under the table. "I'm fine right here. Luis is the one to worry about. He sent his beloved paintings and a lot of other art junk in this big crate last week to his family in Paris that hates his guts. This morning, when they started bombing the harbor, he asked to fuck me just one more time and he was so pathetic I let him fuck me, then I let him fuck me again right in that chair and then he smoked some shit with me, even though he gave up smoking shit about ten years ago, and he kissed me good-bye and he went upstairs. Better go check on him."

"Where is he?" Wilson said.

"Try his room," Cricket said. "Second floor, second corridor on the right, second door on the left. I'll wait here."

Wilson went out of the library and up the wide staircase. The Portugee's bedroom was an austere place, the only furniture a free-standing sixteenth-century gilt crucifix and a single bed fit for a monk. The floors of black tile were polished to an amazing sheen. Wilson watched his reflection cross to the bathroom.

Don Luis's body floated faceup in the big marble tub in water that was mostly blood. The water still steamed; it hadn't been long, but it was too late. An old-fashioned straight razor with a handle of polished mother-of-pearl inlaid with silver Hebrew characters lay neatly folded on the marble side of the tub.

"If you're going to do it," Wilson said to the body, "that's the thing to do it with."

The Portugee's eyes were wide open, lifeless. He didn't answer in any way that Wilson could hear. Wilson paused for a moment and said a quiet prayer for the man's soul, then he went out and closed the door behind.

Downstairs in the library Cricket had passed out beneath the table. Wilson checked her pulse—she was fine, just stoned out of her mind—and he hefted her up with some difficulty and got her over his shoulder. He carried her down the corridor to the front door and out into the courtyard, threw her into the backseat of the

Thing, started it up, and drove out over the bridge just in time to meet Lieutenant Peavy and a column of marines coming up the chalk road. Wilson pulled up and got out. Cricket stirred, but she did not wake. Peavy offered Wilson a Navy Cut, and they stood contemplating the Villa Real in the day's last light.

"Looks like bloody Buckingham Palace down there," Peavy said.

"It's not," Wilson said. "How's the action coming?"

"Not bad," Peavy said. "A few pockets of resistance here and there. Got them mopped by noon. Started distributing food to the natives after that. Seemed damn glad to see us."

Wilson thought for a moment. "What will they do when the pirates are all gone?" he said slowly. "I do believe the economy of this place just got shot to hell."

"Not up to us." Peavy shrugged. "Up to the UN, I suppose."

"I wonder," Wilson said. Just then Cricket let out a faint, irritated moan.

"Your wife?" Peavy said.

"That's her."

"She all right?"

"More or less," Wilson said.

The marines creaked in their boots. A long tropical gloom spread over the jungle behind, and dusk came on purple and red as fresh blood. Lieutenant Peavy finished his cigarette and brought his Peter O'Toole blues to bear on Wilson.

"Anyone left in there?"

"No," Wilson said.

"Just out of curiosity, what course of action would you propose?"

Wilson turned again to the Villa Real, brooding in shadow, full of ghosts, and he thought of its four hundred years of stone and mortar and sculptured gardens and tilled fields, all built on slavery and piracy and murder. He thought of the hundred rooms, the halls once hung with paintings of ancestors who were no less slavers and murderers and pirates for wearing high ruff collars and velvet doublets or elegant powdered wigs and three-cornered hats, their fingers resting on a page in an open volume of Voltaire. And he thought of the Portugee up to his neck in blood, floating in the bloody water now like an embryo in formaldehyde, and he shuddered and turned away. Four hundred years isn't so long if you think of the age of the smallest stone. Time to make an end.

"I would call in an air strike," Wilson said quietly.

"Seems a pity," Peavy said.

"No," Wilson said. "It's more like justice. There should be nothing left."

Then he got back into the Thing and put it in gear and bumped down the chalk road toward town. Just before they reached the tree line, the Sea Harriers screamed overhead toward the Villa Real. Wilson flicked on the headlights and did not look back. The explosions reached him as a muffled thudding through the thick leaves and mossy silence of the jungle.

15

THE SMALL ISLAND, BARELY two hundred yards across, would sink to thirty at high tide. There were a few scraps of wood, a couple of rusted tin cans, a battered plastic bottle, not much more. Pocket-size mottled-back crabs scuttled in the surf. A single dune afforded a view of the mainland ten miles to the east, across the Bight of Benin.

They put Cricket ashore with three days' worth of food and water, just in case, and a rubber dinghy for the crossing. She set foot to sand like a cat stepping into the rain.

"This isn't fair," she said. "Marooning me on a desert island."

"Captain's orders, ma'am," said Lieutenant Peavy.

Cricket stared up at the pale blue sky, the circling gulls.

"Give me a few minutes," Wilson said to the lieutenant. "She's still my wife."

Peavy nodded. "You've got fifteen. No more than that. They're waiting for us aboard the *Gadfly*."

Wilson disembarked and helped Cricket drag the rubber raft over the dune to the landward side of the island. There they stood, slightly uncomfortable with each other, staring out at the faint dark rim that was Benin on the horizon.

"It won't be so bad," Wilson said. "Shouldn't take longer than a few hours. If it does, you've got food and a water purifying kit on the raft. Once you hit the coast it's only eight miles inland to Porto-Novo. I checked it out on the map. You've got friends there, right?"

Cricket sat down on the sand and put her head on her knees. Wilson watched her coppery hair stir in the ocean wind, then he crouched beside her.

"It's got to be this way, Cricket," he said in a quiet voice. "They wanted to turn you over to the United Nations for trial with the rest of them. I had to do quite a bit of convincing. . . ." His voice trailed off.

"To hell with that. I want you to come with me," Cricket said. She lifted her head, and her eyes were defiant.

"I can't," Wilson said, but he wouldn't look at her.

"Why not?" Cricket said.

Wilson made an exhausted gesture. "Cricket, this is painful," he said.

"Tell me," she said.

"Think of Webster," Wilson said. "The same thing almost happened to me. Skinned and left out on a pole like a side of beef."

"I'm sorry about that," Cricket said. "But you shot Dad. You killed my father. We both have things to forgive each other for. I didn't know then how much I really needed you—"

Wilson cut her short. "What do I have to do to get a pirate divorce?"

"This *is* a pirate divorce," Cricket said. "You're marooning me on a desert island."

Wilson wanted to get up, go back to men waiting on the beach, but a lingering affection kept him by her side. He felt a final tug at his heart. He took her hard and callused hand and squeezed. He wanted to kiss her.

"You love me," Cricket said, "I can feel it."

Wilson's jaw tightened. He let go of her hand and stared out to sea. "You're right," he said. "I do love you. I love you in the way men love war and drunkenness and everything else that is bad for them."

Cricket said nothing.

Wilson stayed that way for a minute or so, as the sea moved and shuddered like a muscle against the bone of Africa. When he turned back, Cricket had slipped out of her shorts and T-shirt and lay naked and warm-skinned on the sand.

"Have it your own way," she said. "But I want you to make love to me. I want you to remember what you'll be missing."

"No," Wilson said, but she stared at him and her eyes were a pale blue-green in the light reflected off the water and her coppery hair blew in the wind and her breasts were flecked with freckles, and Wilson did what she asked. He unzipped his pants and took her breasts in his hands. It was a bad idea. When it was over, they both felt terrible and wept and held each other.

At last a long, mournful whistle came from the *Gadfly* at anchor, and a moment after that they heard Lieutenant Peavy's voice from the other side of the dune. "We need to shove off, Mr. Lander," he called.

Wilson stood and pulled up his pants and put his sunglasses on and ran a hand through his hair.

"I've got to go," he said.

Cricket blinked up at him. Sand stuck to her naked body.

"I've got to go," he said again.

"Go," Cricket said.

"Take care of yourself."

"Yeah."

Wilson could feel her eyes on him as he turned away for the last time and went up the dune to the waiting sailors.

Later, the last light faded from the sky in the east, and the great steel prow of the HMS *Gadfly* swung north toward England, and Wilson came alone onto the quarterdeck and smoked a Navy Cut and tried to make sense of the things that had happened since he shipped out on the *Compound Interest* so many months before. His recent past presented itself in a series of dramatic images, like a slide show of scenes from the life of someone much more interesting than Wilson Lander. He took them out one by one, held them up to the light of memory and finally came to the last mournful, erotic composition: Cricket stretched out naked on the sand of a vanishing island, a riddle on her lips that he would never be able to answer.

He thought for a while longer, four cigarettes' worth, smoking slowly. The wind blew in his face; his fingers and nose grew cold. The darkness of the sea was a mask covering the earth.

EPILOGUE:

HOME
AGAIN

1

THE CITY LOOKED THE same. The same traffic and the same sky and the same sort of dusty fall afternoon, the same bohemians stumbling from one happy hour to another in the Bend, the same rusty tankers clogging the Harvey Channel, the same blue hills looming in the hazy distance of Warinocco County beyond the interstate.

Wilson went to a cheap hotel called the Rialto at the lower end of Commerce Street, not far from Buptown, and ordered up a bacon cheeseburger platter from room service and ate everything but the coleslaw and fell asleep and slept for fourteen hours. When he awoke in the early morning, it was Saturday. He put on his clothes and went out into the street and wandered among indifferent crowds. At ten-thirty he ate breakfast at a coffee shop he used to frequent where he recognized no one. Then he went into a bookstore and bought a perpetual calendar—a little plastic card with a plastic wheel—and he counted up the months and the days and discovered he had been gone two years, two months, six days, and a handful of hours. After that, he walked aimlessly, feeling lost, like a soldier returned from a war no one cared about. He thought about calling Andrea; then he thought better of the impulse. She was probably married now, with kids, deep in the life they could have shared together. Still, he felt a pang in his heart to think of a future in the city without her.

Sometime after noon he looked up and found himself in the same warehouse district where Cricket's store had been, and his heart quickened. He found the street with no difficulty and found the store there, wedged in between the rubber band warehouse and the French restaurant, which was now a Japanese-Creole restaurant called Sushi New Orleans. The stuffed monkey in the window was gone, and the orange cat was no longer in its place on the pillow near the door, but the same dismal books and love philters and grim packets of herbs and heavy black cauldrons decorated the walls.

A fortyish woman with stringy died black hair and an unpleasant face sat behind the counter. Today there was one customer, an old man in a blue jogging suit, who left quickly as Wilson approached.

"Can I help you with something?" the woman said.

"Are you Nancy?" Wilson said.

"Yes," Nancy said, suspicion like circles beneath her eyes.

"I want my apartment back," Wilson said.

"Who the hell are you?" Nancy said.

Wilson told her, and he told her that Cricket had arranged the sublet two years before.

"Where is Cricket now?" Nancy said.

"In Africa, I think," Wilson said.

"And you expect to get your apartment back just like that, after two years?" Nancy snapped her fingers.

"Happens all the time in this city," Wilson said. "Call it the Return of the Original Tenant."

"A friend of a friend lives there now," Nancy said. "Someone from the coven. Good luck getting her out."

Wilson took the bus to Overlook and walked across the bridge. The neighborhood had the same medicinal-industrial smell, the same melancholy, forgotten feeling. Big trucks rumbled over the rutted streets, big men in plaid shirts and steel-toed boots behind the wheel.

When Wilson got to his building at number 12, he rang the bell and waited. Looking up, he saw unfamiliar faded red curtains hanging in the windows of his apartment. After a few minutes, a pale, skinny girl in her early twenties came to the door barefoot. She wore a long peasant skirt, an unusual green blouse, and big hoop earrings in her ears, as if she had read instructions in a book on how a witch should dress.

"Yeah?" she said. Her eyes, like Nancy's, were ringed with suspicious circles.

"This is going to sound a little surprising, but you're living in my apartment. . . ."

The girl frowned and listened impatiently as Wilson talked. He was the original tenant, he said, the lease was in his name, he'd been gone for a while overseas, and now he was back.

"Don't worry, I'll give you some time to find a new place. Take a month, even two if you need it. But by November I'll definitely want my apartment back." Wilson thought this a generous offer. The girl slammed the door in his face when he was finished. He heard the bolt shooting home on the other side.

"Get the fuck out of here before I call the cops," the girl shouted through the bolted door, and Wilson heard her hard footsteps going upstairs. He rang the doorbell again; she did not answer, then he went across the street and hid behind the Dumpster, where he waited for several hours, squatting in the fetid, rat-infested gloom.

Lights went on behind the faded red curtains about 7:30, and a full moon went up over the Rubicon District. An hour after that, the blond girl came out wearing a black scarf over her head and carrying a black leather backpack. Wilson crossed the street and went into the vestibule. He counted the tile bricks on the floor and found, beneath the third brick from the wall in the third row, his spare set of keys, sealed in a Ziploc bag, exactly where he had left them over two years before.

He unlocked the double locks on the front door and set the bolt behind him, went upstairs and undid the double locks on the apartment door, and went inside. He spent the next hour putting the young witch's belongings onto the sidewalk out front. There wasn't much: A closetful of clothes—long Gypsy dresses and cowled cloaks, strange lace-up bustiers, two S&M-type leather harnesses, one red, one black with a steel ring in the crotch positioned to fit directly over the vagina—the usual obscure CDs, makeup, tarot cards, a poster of Satan, and a seventies-era poster of a kittycat hanging from a bar with the logo "Hang In There, Baby," which Wilson assumed to be ironic. The few sticks of broken-down furniture were Wilson's own, as were the towels and bed and sheets and television set.

The refrigerator was nearly empty, but Wilson found enough there to make himself a quesadilla and salad, and he watched a little television and changed the sheets and went to bed. The next morning, he was awakened by a fearsome banging and the sharp, piercing sound of a woman's voice screaming obscenities. He scratched himself, yawned, and went out to the landing window and took out the screen and stuck his head out. The girl stood on the sidewalk amid the pile of her possessions.

"I gave you a chance," Wilson called down. "Two months was pretty generous, I thought. Now it's tough luck for you."

The girl turned up her face, purple with rage. "You fuck!" she screamed. "You lousy fuck! I'm a witch, did you know that? I'll curse you, I'll cast a spell on you so your fucking little weenie falls off! You better run because when I'm through with you, your luck will be so fucking bad you will wish you had no luck at all!"

Wilson began to laugh so hard he couldn't stop himself. He closed the window and doubled over on the floor with the unrestrained glee of a ten-year-old who has just put a frog in his sister's bed. When he was able to stop laughing, he dried his eyes and went into the kitchen and made some coffee and two slices of cinnamon toast—the kettle and toaster and crockery were all his—and then he washed up and put on jeans and a T-shirt and set about looking for his books and his winter clothes and his pictures, which he eventually found dumped in moldering heaps in the basement. For the rest of the morning he worked on getting the place back together. At three in the afternoon a pickup truck came for the witch's things. Wilson watched out the window in the kitchenette as the witch and a tall young man wearing black leather motorcycle gear loaded the bed of the pickup. When they drove off, the young man stuck his hand out the window and flashed the finger in Wilson's general direction, but then they were gone, and it didn't matter anymore.

Sunday night Wilson stayed in watching television and soaking his mildewed clothes in bleach in the tub. When he woke up Monday morning, he called a locksmith and had all the locks changed. Then he went out to look for a job. He was home.

2

TWO MONTHS LATER, ON a warm Friday night in late September, a nagging nostalgia brought Wilson out on the ferry to Blackpool Island. He wandered along the boardwalk with the Friday night crowds—the young toughs from Spanish Bend and their hard señoritas; the barrel-chested older men in shorts and sandals with socks, reading the sports pages on benches overlooking the sea; the quiet suburban kids from Glizzard and Point Broome lining up for the Tilt-a-Whirl—and around ten o'clock he found himself on the loggia at Bazzano's.

Like everything else in the city, Bazzano's looked pretty much the same. Wilson sat alone at a table beneath the lights and ordered a cappuccino and a shot of whiskey and listened to the wind from the ocean and the sound of the waves against the seawall, and a lump rose in his throat, a longing for something that he could not name. The bohemians with their beautiful lissome women came and went up the pier, and the fragrance of their foreign cigarettes and their laughter and their voices raised in song filled the air as pale stars glided over the dark silhouette of the city across the narrows.

Wilson watched and drank his cappuccino and sipped at his whiskey. He envied their lives, so free from convention and plainness— they were painters or musicians, they didn't have money, but they had talent and beautiful women and friends—then he looked at his watch, and it was midnight, and he asked for the check. He waited for a while and the check did not come and he turned and shot an impatient glance at the busing station. Wilson's waitress, a tall, leggy blonde with a nose ring, lingered there involved in an intense conversation with a shorter dark-haired waitress who stood with her back to his table.

"Something familiar about that back," Wilson mumbled to himself, then the dark-haired waitress turned and approached and sat down across from him.

For a long moment he didn't know what to say.

Andrea looked like a different person from the harried, quarrelsome career woman he had known, more like the fresh-faced ingenue who had come to the city eight years before, straight from grad school in the provinces. She was about thirty-two now and quite attractive in a sad, urban way, and her eyes were big and moist and expressive. Her dark hair was cut in a sexy 1920s-style shag, with strands curled carefully around her ears. There was no uniform for the wait staff at Bazzano's. Andrea wore a tight white blouse open a couple of buttons to show a lacy black bra, a black miniskirt, and black hose. Her lipstick, some undefined effervescent color, shone in the yellow light of the loggia.

"You're back," Andrea said.

Wilson blinked, remembering their life together in quick, bright flashes.

"Aren't you going to say anything?" Andrea said.

"How are you, Andrea?" Wilson said at last.

"Doing well." Andrea nodded solemnly. "How about you?"

"Do you work here?" Wilson said.

Andrea nodded again, her dark eyes fixed on his face.

"What happened to the Tea Exchange?"

"I quit," she said.

"You were vice-president," Wilson said. "Why did you quit?"

Andrea hesitated, glanced at the bohemians at the bar inside. Just then a young man with a ponytail climbed to a table beneath the tin ceiling, saxophone in hand. A second later he began to blow a slow, melancholy tune.

"It wasn't working out," Andrea said in a voice that Wilson had to lean close to hear. "After you left, nothing made sense. I got real sick of the grind and realized I was missing my life. I didn't do anything but work, you remember. Too many twelve-hour days. So I quit and I sold my condo in Pond Park Tower and I bought a little loft apartment in the Bend."

"The Bend? You're kidding." Wilson almost laughed.

"That's right," she said, smiling for the first time. "Actually I love it there. I paint now, and there's plenty of light and space—" Then she stopped and looked away. "I can't really talk. I'm in the middle of my shift. I was wondering if you wanted to get a drink later at some after-hours place. Unless it's a problem for your girl-friend or your wife."

"I don't have a girlfriend or a wife," Wilson said. "There's just me."

Andrea brightened. "Then you don't mind? We can catch up. I'd like to hear what you've been up to."

"Sure," Wilson said.

At 2:15, they caught the ferry to the Bend and went to a smoky little basement bar called the Last Word that had faux shrunken heads hanging from the ceiling and a 4:00 A.M. license. They had a couple of daiquiris there, but it was too loud to hear each other talk, and the shrunken heads made Wilson nervous. Just after 3:30, they found themselves in the street again, the glimmer of false dawn in the sky.

"Not sure where we can go at this hour," Andrea said. "Tony's is closed. The only other five o'clock place is the bar at the Orion Hotel, and that's such a scene."

"Not the Orion," Wilson said.

"I live just a couple of blocks away. Why don't you come over to the apartment for a nightcap?"

Andrea's version of a small loft apartment was the whole top floor of the old Castle Lock Building, redone by an architect she had brought over from Italy. There was a polished hardwood floor the size of a basketball court, exposed brick walls, a million glass blocks, and a whole row of arched windows overlooking the lights of the Bend and the slips of the marina to the south. Half the place had been turned into a studio, and a couple of dozen big canvases lay propped against the walls: heroic nudes in bright colors, urban landscapes, an apple, a snake. Wilson liked what he saw immediately. On the easel now was a half-finished portrait of a woman wearing a long pink skirt, naked from the waist up.

"That's my new friend Pam," Andrea said. "She has perfect breasts. Don't you think she has perfect breasts?"

Wilson studied the painting for a moment and had to agree, then he went around the room, looking at the canvases.

"Damn, you can really paint," he said when he had seen them all. "When did you start to paint?"

Andrea shrugged. "I never told you, but I used to paint in college," she said. "Actually I was going to major in art, but my dad forced me into finance. 'Study finance,' he said, 'paint on the side.' Of course all I ever did was finance after that, and I tried to stop thinking about art because it depressed me that I wasn't doing any."

"Shit, these are great," Wilson said, stopping at the painting of the snake. "I really like this one."

"Some of them are O.K.," Andrea said, and she blushed and went into the kitchen separated from the living room by a wall of glass blocks. She made two screwdrivers and brought them out. "Thought I had some gin and a bottle of tonic," she said. "I don't. I've got vodka and OJ."

"That's fine," Wilson said. He took the drink, and they sat on the leather couch in front of the windows and drank for a minute in silence.

Andrea spoke first. "Where have you been these last couple of years?"

Wilson put his drink on the glass coffee table. "You wouldn't believe me if I told you."

"Try me," she said.

"England, the Azores. But Africa, mostly," he said. "Bupanda. I've even seen Lake Tsuwanga. Been down the Hilenga in a canoe."

"That's something," she said. "I used to have trouble getting you on a plane to Pennsylvania."

"I know."

"So what did you do in Africa? Grow coffee?"

"I was married."

"Oh." Andrea tried to sound disinterested. "And you're not married anymore?"

"No, it was a mistake," Wilson said.

Andrea made a nervous move with her drink, spilled it across the glass-topped coffee table. "Oops!" she said, and went into the kitchen to get some paper towels. She came back with the towels and got on her knees and began to wipe up the orange juice, then she stopped. Orange juice leaked off the table to make a yellow puddle on the hardwood.

"Truth is, I got that job at Bazzano's because in a weird way, it reminded me of you," she said in a small voice. "It was the last place I had heard from you. I've been there for almost a year and a half now, and I still try to imagine what table you were at when you called me. Or were you at the bar?"

"I was at a table on the loggia," Wilson said.

"That's what I figured," she said. "And you were with her, weren't you? Your wife. I could tell by your voice that you had someone waiting."

Wilson was impressed. "Yes," he said. "She was there."

Andrea was quiet, then she leaned back on her heels and looked up at him, and there was a flush to her cheeks.

"I want to tell you something," she said. "You've got to promise not to laugh."

"O.K.," Wilson said.

"I've dated, of course, even lived with this painter for a few months, but there was no one that touched my heart like you. You were a little lost, maybe, but you were kind, gentle. Can I say that? I found out on my own that gentle people are rare in the world. I always thought we were sort of fated to be together. I guess I was wrong.''

Wilson cleared his throat. He started to speak, then shook his head. ''Leaving you the way I did was rotten,'' he managed at last. ''And I want to apologize. I thought about you off and on the whole time I was away. Didn't really realize how much I missed you until I got back to the city a couple of months ago. That's the truth. We used to have a nice, comfortable life together. Took me going half-way around the world to realize how good it was. I'm sorry I wrecked things.''

''I'd like to kiss you,'' Andrea said quietly. ''Is that all right with you?''

Wilson felt his ears burning. She crawled around the glass-topped coffee table on her hands and knees and reached up for him and put her hand on his face. Her fingers smelled like orange juice. He remembered her lips when she kissed him.

3

A YEAR PASSED.

Wilson wanted to forget everything he knew about Cricket and Africa, then suddenly he wanted to remember every detail. This was just about the time news of the British attack on Quatre Sables leaked to the press. Wilson turned on the television one Wednesday evening and saw Acting Captain Worthington on CNN from London: Worthington and a few of the officers of the *Gadfly* had been cashiered out of the navy for their roles in the affair, but the true extent of the slaving operations at Quatre Sables had become known, and there was a public outcry, and the men were recalled to duty. Worthington and Lieutenant Peavy, the newscaster said, had just been awarded the Navy Cross and were going to be reassigned to a Blockade Squadron expanded to six ships of the line.

Wilson turned off the television set after the report, a tingling like electric currents running through his body. He took out a sheet of white paper and a fountain pen and wrote the following sentence: "Many strange stories have come out of the civil war in Bupanda; this is one of them," and he kept writing all night and by morning had sixty-five pages. He stopped doing temporary office work and borrowed money from Andrea and locked himself in his apartment for the next four months and wrote a book about what had happened to him in Africa, as his famous ancestor had done. The book—*To the Dark Continent: An Account of My Experiences with the Pirates and Slavers of the Brotherhood of the Coast, Including Details of a Journey from the Sea to Lake Tsuwanga and Back Again*—made the *New York Times* Best Sellers list and was optioned by TrueSteel Pictures in Hollywood for a small fortune.

Though Wilson was wary of stepping over the broom a second time, his success left him little choice. He married Andrea the following June. With the money from the book and a good piece of Andrea's savings, they bought a restored farmhouse in Warinocco County about fifty miles north of the city, on a rise with a good view of the Potswahnamee's dark waters. The old place had been built in 1790 of sturdy fieldstone, and its six and a half beam-ceilinged bedrooms, Andrea said, promised plenty of room for a big family. Soon, there were horses in the old stables, a few fields planted with winter corn, and the cool leafy evenings of early fall, frost on the grass in the morning. Andrea set up a studio in the converted barn; Wilson was asked to teach a course on Africa at Jerome Martin Community College and afterward accepted the chairmanship of the International Committee for a United Bupanda, or ICUB, which seeks to put an end to the exploitation of that unhappy nation, where—alas!—the war continues.

4

AFTER ABOUT A YEAR of this settled life, one morning in mid-November, Wilson went out to the mailbox on the main road and found an unusual letter included with the usual junk mail and business correspondence. This letter, forwarded to him from his publisher, came in a thin envelope of coarse blue paper, torn at the edges and covered with a half dozen colorful stamps from the Republic of Madagascar, that odd paramecium-shaped island floating in the Indian Ocean off the southeast African coast. There was no return address.

A cold rain fell on the stubble fields as Wilson spread the mail across the kitchen table in the farmhouse, his heart beating. He took the blue letter and turned it over in his hands. The faucet dripped portentously in the sink behind him. The old house creaked in the wind. A pleasant yellow light came from the window of Andrea's studio in the barn. Wilson slit the envelope with a kitchen knife. As his heart had told him, the letter was from Cricket. Also enclosed was a small photo-booth photo of Cricket holding on her lap a young boy, roughly four years old. The child, as was plain to see, had Wilson's nose and mouth, Cricket's green eyes and high cheekbones and mop of coppery hair. The rain picked up on the old slate roof and the attic began to leak as Wilson squinted at Cricket's crabbed, obscure handwriting:

Tananarive, 16 May
Dear Wilson,

I saw your book at Battingly and Sons, the English bookshop in Nairobi, last week. I didn't buy it, I don't want to read the thing. But I made note of the publisher and hope they will forward this letter to you because I have some interesting news. You have a son, who I named Elzevir after my father and my ancestor, the great pirate. He was born on March 3, about nine months from the night we made love aboard the Dread on Lake Tsuwanga. I was pregnant when you marooned me on that miserable sandbar, though I didn't know it at the time.

The boy is wonderful and strong and looks just like you. He has your mannerisms, despite the fact he has never seen you—and I'm also afraid he has your scruples. But he has a lot of years ahead, and we will make a proper little pirate out of him yet. I want you to understand this not to hurt you but to let you know that despite your treachery, our way of life continues. A half dozen of our ships were at sea when the British attacked—six captains and five hundred men. We have founded a new colony somewhere in the vicinity of Madagascar—obviously I'm not going to tell you where—and more join every day to serve under the good old skull and crossbones. You always loved order and the dull charms of middle-class life. I never did. The only way to stand that kind of existence is to swallow so much Prozac you don't feel your own rage and hope. I prefer fire and the sword, so to speak, and always a sail on the horizon.

Still, having said all that, I want you to know that I do miss you and—call me crazy—would like to see you again someday. And I would like you to see your son. Three months out of the year, during the rainy season I am in Paris, usually starting April 1. I bought that gloomy apartment on the Ile St.-Louis, and there is plenty of space for you and your books there. You may contact me through my lawyer anytime: M. Gustave Leconte, 8bis Rue Lamartine, Paris 00017 FRANCE. Think about it.

Love, Cricket

P.S. Remember that mark on your shoulder? According to the Articles of Brotherhood and according to my heart, it means you are mine forever. XOXO—C.

Wilson read Cricket's letter four times, and he studied the photograph obsessively for half an hour. His hands were trembling, his neck was cold with sweat, and suddenly there was a slight briny smell in his nostrils and he closed his eyes and saw the green waves crashing against the side of a ship, the horizon wild with storm, the black flag flying like a curse from the topgallants as a pirate wind rose out of the south. He shook himself away from this vision and went out into the yard and stood there till he was good and soaked and he could smell the wet earth and the horses in the stables and all thoughts of Cricket and the sea had been washed from him by a clean, forgiving rain.

Wilson did not go to Paris that year. He did not go the year after. True, some nights, sleeping next to his wife in bed beneath the beamed ceiling of the farmhouse, he awoke from a dream of Cricket's skin against his own, and it took the entire force of his will to keep him there, to keep him from the midnight roads of Warinocco County, from the airport and the next flight across the Atlantic to Paris, and thence the wilds of Madagascar. Still, he did not go—it is almost certain he will never go—but who can say?

The wheels grind on; the future remains uncertain.

ABOUT THE AUTHOR

ROBERT GIRARDI WAS EDUCATED at Catholic schools in Europe and at the University of Virginia in Charlottesville. He earned an M.F.A. from the University of Iowa Writer's Workshop and is a past recipient of the James Michener Fellowship. *Madeleine's Ghost,* his first novel, was published in 1995. He lives in Washington, D.C.